Cover Designer: Red Fox Creative
Editor and Interior Designer: Jovana Shirley,
Unforeseen Editing, unforeseenediting.com

Paperback ISBN: 979-8-9873236-3-2

For everyone who feels unheard.
Like no one reads your texts in the group chats.
Like the words you speak aren't truly listened to and digested.
Like nobody would really notice if you simply weren't there.

Keep speaking. Keep sharing. Keep typing. Keep telling your story.
There are people you haven't even met yet who will want to listen to every little thing you have to say.

Content Warning

- Profanity
- Sexual scenes and situations
- Underage drinking
- Consumption of illegal substances
- Cheating (mention of, not on page)
- Infertility

THE UNTIMELY REVELATION OF THE GODS is based on the Greek Olympian gods and goddesses. Please be aware that it is not fantasy, fan fiction, or a literal retelling.

This book is intended for mature audiences only. Reader discretion is advised.

Playlist

Everybody Loves Me - OneRepublic

Gold - Imagine Dragons

Wilson (Expensive Mistakes) - Fall Out Boy

Alright - Supergrass

Million Dollar Bills - Lorde

This Is the Life - Two Door Cinema Club

Immortals - Fall Out Boy

Perfect Places - Lorde

Another World - Ruelle, UNSECRET

Eternal Youth - RÜDE

Celestial - Ed Sheeran

Paradise - Bazzi

A World Alone - Lorde

Book One Recap

ZACHARY ALEXANDER HAS GROWN UP having too much of everything—money, attention, lack of rules. He and his girlfriend have been contractually obligated to marry since they were children, and although he isn't remotely faithful, he and Hanna June Pruitt play their roles perfectly as Olympia College's newest *it* couple as they begin their freshman year at the tiny school.

Kai Newport is not only one of Zach's half-brothers, but he must also share a campus with him now. Growing up on the water and being publicly dismissed by his biological father, Kai does what he can to get out of bed most days. Unless Amber Hargrove is there. He's had a crush on her for years, and even when the opportunity presents itself, things always seem to slip out of his grasp.

Amber doesn't care much for her college life in rural South Carolina either, having grown up in the Midwest before moving to Charleston. She takes every opportunity to visit her father and adopted sister, doing whatever she can to wear every hat in her broken little family.

Damon Montclaire fills the slot of Zach's other half-brother, with a handful of years, etiquette lessons, and maturity between Zach and Kai. Glad to leave behind his high-society life in Manhattan with his adopted parents, he attends Olympia to earn his master's degree and will soon begin the path toward his doctorate, alongside his unlikely best friend and walking beam of sunshine, Dawn Sutherland.

Dawn not only brings the good vibes—she *is* the good vibes. An Olympia resident from birth, she's dying to get out of her hometown and forge a path to make the world a better place, and she has a solid plan to do so.

These six Olympians don't have anything in common, until they learn they are all recipients of a scholarship award, headed by Parthenon Studios—an up-and-coming television network based out of Los Angeles. In exchange for showcasing their student lives on a new reality show, *The Olympians*, the network will take care of all their school expenses—pretty cut and dry, right?

Wrong.

With having six people who don't know each other—four of whom don't really want to be on the show and three of them being estranged brothers—one would think that was a strong enough storyline.

But alas, the plot thickens.

During a drunken confession at the group's first attempt to have a "normal" college party Hanna June divulges some information that begins a snowball effect. Upon hearing that Dwayne Kronos, the creator of the show and head of the network, has files on each of them, plus possible new Olympians, Damon makes it his mission to get his hands on them.

While he and Hanna June break into his office, Kai and Dawn play the role of the lookouts, spying on the show's creator and Zach at their weekly Tuesday luncheon. And what they find goes back further than either of them was aware. They collect pictures of everything and meet up with the stakeout team at Amber's apartment, forming a secret group.

As they try to dissect and theorize what's really going on, the world begins to do the same. Everyone is drawn to *the Olympians* and eagerly awaits each week's new episode. As both the season and the semester go on, fans share their own ideas as to who these six college students *really* are—but just for fun.

That is, until Damon makes a connection. He knows it's absurd and completely out there, but he doesn't waste his time on things he thinks aren't worth it. But when he brings up the theory to Hanna June, she immediately dismisses the idea, but she also knows deep down that there has to be a sound reason for him to suggest that the markings on the files they found in Kronos's office align with those of the Greek Olympian gods.

New World Index

Olympians

Zachary Alexander — Zeus, king of the gods, god of the heavens, thunder, and the sky

Hanna June Pruitt — Hera, queen of the gods, goddess of marriage, women, and family

Kai Newport — Poseidon, god of the sea, storms, and earthquakes

Amber Hargrove — Demeter, goddess of agriculture, grain, and fertility

Alexia Chang — Athena, goddess of wisdom and battle strategy

Astrid Radzilowicz — Aphrodite, goddess of love, beauty, and procreation

Gunner McHugh — Ares, god of war and violence

Heath Blackburn-McHugh — Hephaestus, blacksmith to the gods, god of fire, metalworking, and volcanoes

Luca Arturo — Apollo, god of music, healing, prophecy, and the sun

The more she goes down that rabbit hole, the more she discovers. The two of them don't tell the others though—especially not Zach since he regularly shares meals with Kronos in secret.

With the wrapping of the season and graduation for Damon and Dawn with their master's degrees, the fall semester at Olympia College comes to an end. The group doesn't get to see much of each other after that, until they're flown out to a Parthenon-hosted shindig in LA. A few new costars are introduced to them while the suits in the room fawn over them, and the Olympians realize they've got to mentally prepare for not only the spring semester and season two, but also for whatever truths they might uncover, no matter how out of this world they might be.

Camille Arturo — Artemis, goddess of the wilderness, wild animals, archery, and the moon

Max Cruz Oliviera — Hermes, messenger to the gods, god of travelers, athletes, and thieves

Major Gods

Damon Montclaire — Hades, king of the underworld, god of the dead and riches

Dawn Sutherland — Hestia, goddess of the hearth and the home

Fleur Hargrove — Persephone, queen of the underworld, goddess of springtime

Jade Cortez — Hecate, goddess of witchcraft and magic, keeper of keys

Minor Gods

Zoey — Hebe, cupbearer to the gods, goddess of eternal youth

Emma Calhoun — Aglaea, Charite (or Grace) of beauty and glory

Nadine Drake — Euphrosyne, Charite (or Grace) of joy and good cheer

Jack and Jordan — Alexiares and Anicetus, gatekeepers of Olympus

Makena — Iris, attendant to Hera, messenger of the gods, goddess of the rainbow

Traven — Iacchus, attendant to Demeter

Dr. Vladimir Lockett and Dr. Nina Lockett — Paean, physician of the gods

Sonny — Helios, god of the sun, guardian of oaths

Lena – Selene, goddess of the night

Aurora — Eos, goddess of the dawn

Lyle — Hypnos, god of sleep

Titans

Kronos — Cronus, ruler of the universe, leader of the Titans, god of time

Rhianne — Rhea, goddess of fertility

Don — Oceanus, god of the sea and water

Natasha — Tethys, goddess of freshwater

Pierce — Hyperion, god of light and observation

Lucy — Thea, goddess of the sun and light

Phoebe — Phoebe, goddess of prophecy and intellect

Dayo — Mnemosyne, goddess of memory

Grenada — Themis, goddess of law, order, and justice

Muses

Elliana Knight — Clio, muse of history

Valentina — Erato, muse of love poetry

Amara — Melpomene, muse of tragedy

Odette Sottero — Terpsichore, muse of dance

Divya — Urania, muse of astronomy

Heroes

Nolan — Perseus, deified hero, slayer of monsters, king and founder of Mycenae

Oliver Benson — Jason, leader of the Argonauts, rightful kind of Iolcus

Hugo Bettencourt — Odysseus, hero and king of Ithaca

Professor Jeffery Conroy — Chiron, revered centaur, teacher of heroes

Notable Mortals

Cassidy — Cassandra, Princess of Troy with the gift of prophecy, but cursed by Apollo to never be believed

Bailey Pappalardi — Pandora, the first woman, said to be responsible for releasing the evils of humanity into the world

Cash Mulaney — Icarus

Patrick Amato — Patroclus

Mara — Helen of Troy, deified Princess of Troy, Queen of Troy, said to be responsible for the Trojan War

Dear Students,

For those of you who completed lesson one, welcome back! And to those of you who skipped our previous assignment, we can't blame you. We understand introductory lessons can be quite … well, for lack of a better word, boring. Your continued patience with these studies is much appreciated.

We are assuming, if you were paying close attention, you concluded your previous lesson with many questions. We can assure you, by the time you complete this reading, you will have more—and in due time, all will be answered.

Now, onto the subject matter of your next lesson. It's important to recognize a specific god who goes by the name of Kronos. He is the one responsible for resurrecting the Olympians, as we're sure you've pieced together from your first assignment. However, he is *not* the one who should be blamed for the chain of events that happened after. There will be a moment in this upcoming lesson where you may feel as though the premature knowledge of their existence truly *is* due to his carelessness. While that may seem accurate in the moment, do remember, there is always more to a story.

As you are about to learn, while he had an extremely well-thought-out plan as to how to handle the world's recognition of the Olympians, that proposal never did see the light of day. We at the Republic do feel it is imperative to keep in mind that, had everything gone accordingly, it is very likely the world would not be in the state it is in today.

Thank you,

The Republic of the Last City-State

P.S. Oh, and as far as the missing file goes, you will gain access to that as you continue through your lessons. We feel that having this inside knowledge could result in students making untimely and biased conclusions, and … well, doing so could cause severe harm to the people and the world around you. After all, that's how we all ended up like this.

Part I

The Secret Shared Round the World

FEBRUARY 17, 2015, VOLUME 7

An Olympic-Sized Update

by Samara Connors

Last semester was different from anything Olympia College had ever experienced—between camera crews congregating outside lecture halls, to us all putting on our best outfits to head to the dining hall on the chance of being in a background shot, to each of us praying for an assigned group project with any of the six most famous people in the world.

No comment was given from the Admissions office when asked how much the transfer student percentage increased, but given the way apartments suddenly became scarce all over the city—and judging by the way the line to get into Siren's Lounge is four hours long every Friday night—I think it's safe to say it's at least doubled.

While several of the Olympians have opted for online courses where they could get them, most of the ten—yes, you read that right—reality show stars do attend their lecture halls regularly ... though, they're much less talkative this semester. Sad face.

No announcement has been made regarding The Olympians filming schedule for our current semester, but I think I speak for the entire student body—scratch that, the entire globe—when I say that, so far, we are disappointed. Not one camera has been seen on campus during these first five weeks of classes, and with the show being banned from using the Student Center for filming, as they previously did, it seems as though our favorite cast is left without a space to film.

A little lost? Let me fill you in. Two days before classes resumed for the spring session, the Olympians returned to Gold and Olive Country. The rumor is that this was the first meeting with our beloved, established cast *and* the four newest Olympians. You've all seen the glitzy, chaotic photos that have been circulating since the holidays of the wrap party for their debut season in Los Angeles; however, one new cast member was missing from that shindig, so this Olympia-based meetup was a big deal. It'll be in history textbooks someday—mark my words.

What happened at this first meeting that would leave the world's most googled group of mostly twenty-somethings without a home base, you might ask?

The story that's been buzzing across our frost-covered campus is that the group dissolved into an aggressive argument regarding their salaries. Lucky for you, I have come to learn recently that the real reason is actually so much more intriguing than that, in true Olympian fashion.

Through my connections—aka work-study students I was paired with in an Econ class—I was able to uncover the steps leading to the incident that would force Dean Yan to exile the group.

Before Dwayne Kronos—the man we all should thank daily for bringing these people and their show into our lives—even arrived in the famed conference room on the top level of the Student Center, a disagreement had already broken out. I know, I know; you're immediately assuming our golden boy, Zach Alexander, was in the center of this, but you'd be incorrect.

The subjects of this catfight are everyone's favorite head bitch in charge, Hanna June Pruitt, and new

Olympian Astrid Radzilowicz, also known as AskAstrid on YouTube—yes, *the* AskAstrid.

Did Pruitt initiate the fight? That much is uncertain, but what I can—and gladly will—share with you is that she is the reason for the structural damage on the fourth floor. Yes, you read that right, boys, girls, and nonbinary babes. Tiny little Miss Pruitt—as her producer loves to call her—is solely responsible for knocking down the wall between conference rooms, supposedly using Radzilowicz's skull as the driving force.

Eyes boggling out at your palm-sized screen as you read this? You're not the only one. Is it possible that all five foot two of Pruitt was consumed by *that* much hatred and adrenaline that she was able to perform a spontaneous wall demolition using her new costar's head? How much does she bench? Has anyone seen this girl at the Rec Center? Does she even know where the Rec is?

Unfortunately, this is where my knowledge on the matter ends. After asking every Olympian I could find and getting absolutely nowhere, I began buttering up her sorority sisters to try and wiggle some information out. But sadly, they turned out to be just as in the dark as the rest of us—even though Pruitt did move into the Eta house the day before this incident. When was the last time a freshman lived in their frat/srat house? Iconic.

More updates include our new additions to the cast, rounding the group up to ten. As previously mentioned, Astrid has joined The Olympians. She's easily the most well known of them all, even beating out Zach and Damon with their famous political daddy. Although the former UCLA student has been accustomed to the spotlight since a young age—you *do* know who her father is, don't you?—she seems to shy away from any questions about the show when approached. She is, however, always down for a selfie! And while it's been rumored that filming for The Olympians likely won't start until closer to spring break—boo—new episodes of AskAstrid go live on her channel every Wednesday, so at least we have something to hold us over until then.

Not much is known about our other three Olympians—Alexia Chang, Gunner McHugh, and Heath Blackburn-McHugh.

Chang is the same size as Pruitt, but have you seen that girl at the gym? *Dayum*. She's also a walking encyclopedia and definitely smarter than just about everyone else on campus. I approached her to ask why she wasn't at any Ivy and got back, "Because I'm here," before she broke into wind sprints. Like, yes, we know, but why? Help us out here, Lex.

McHugh is a former Army Ranger, having just gotten back from his most recent tour a month ago. It was recently added to his Wikipedia page that he was a military school brat, which checks out. He's definitely more approachable than Chang, but maybe let's make sure we get a few drinks in him first. He and our golden boy did break out into that bar fight last week when the group went out to celebrate Astrid's birthday on Valentine's Day, and it ended with Zach cracking a beer stein over Gun's head, just seconds after our buzz-cut baby slammed Z's face into a cookie cake. It's nearly impossible to miss anything any of these people do, but in case you somehow did, it's literally all over social media—and definitely worth the watch.

Which brings us to our last Olympian, Heath. You might have noticed that he shares a last name with Gunner. Then there's the fact that Heath's sister posted a video over winter break with a woman in the background who looks a lot like Gunner. His profile states that their moms got married nearly ten years ago. Now, Heath's social media accounts have plenty of photos with both of his biological parents, as well as his stepmom, Elaine, whereas Gunner has no photos with any family.

As if we needed another messy brother scenario on this show, am I right? Kidding. We all love it.

What have our original group of Olympians been up to? Well, they've definitely been a lot quieter than last semester—that's for sure. Rumors about the group moving off campus have been circulating for a few weeks now, but, again, no one can get a straight answer out of them.

The most recent thing I heard is that they're hunkering down together to take on this massive snow storm headed our way. With classes canceled for the next week and absolutely nothing to do and nowhere to be, one can only wonder what the Olympians will get into.

Hopefully, it's chaotic as hell—and live-streamed.

Chapter 1

KAI

Somewhere back here …

Dawn said it was right along the river.

"Amber's apartment is literally in the opposite direction!" Alexia shouted.

"Okay, yeah, thanks. I'll see you there later. Safe travels," he yelled over his shoulder, looking around and trying to remember if any of the names of the surrounding streets at this intersection looked familiar from the quick—but not entirely thorough—Google Maps search he had done.

While it was rather amusing to see Alexia's attempts at trudging through the fast-falling snow, which was now well above her ankles, he was still hell-bent on shaking her off his tail despite *her* being hell-bent on following him. For what reason, he had no idea. She'd grumbled something about how if anything happened to him she didn't want to be the last person alive who had seen him.

Glancing up at the dark sky through the fat, wet flakes on his eyelashes, Kai hoped the snow would fall faster and she'd end up barricaded in one spot, right in the middle of the road.

"Why won't you tell me where you're going?" she called.

Ignoring her, he turned down Bellamy Street, hoping maybe a gust of wind would cover him up and she'd lose track of him.

I can't remember what any of the houses around it looked like.

Wait, it had a long, circular driveway on the right side of the house … or maybe it was the left.

Shit, why didn't I bring my phone with me?

Well, the answer to that was obvious—stupid but obvious. What other reason would he have chosen to trek outdoors during a state of emergency—when he was expected to be elsewhere by his fellow castmates and their producer—for someplace that decades' worth of visitors and homeowners had deemed "haunted"?

The answer was simple: Kai was stoned.

Stoned and desperate, to be fair—but mostly stoned. He had the sense of direction of a five-year-old navigating the subway, as Damon liked to say—and that was when he was sober.

But now? Now, he was two well-packed blunts deep, with a stomach full of Waffle House, and on a mission amid a blizzard to find the one place that could keep them all together. That was the most important part of it all—*to keep the Olympians together.*

If he could just find the house and prove that it was livable, then everything would be okay. Hanna June and Astrid would quit with the tension they brought with them everywhere they went—and hopefully, HJ wouldn't put the Californian through a wall again, and Astrid would stop trying to get her back for it. Zach and Gunner would put the bar-fight stupidity in the past and maybe attempt to have a civil, halfway intelligent conversation with each other. And most importantly, Dawn wouldn't leave.

Dawn couldn't leave. Well, she *could*, as she'd reminded them the other day. Two seasons was all that was required of her, and that would be done when classes ended in three months. Then, she'd be gone, on the other side of the country, Kai assumed, saving the world.

And if she was gone, who was Kai going to have his heart-to-hearts with? Who was going to listen to him aimlessly babble about anything and everything and never once judge him on the occasions he might tear up? Amber was his obvious choice, but returning the favor didn't seem to be on her laundry list. To make matters even worse, Dawn's announcement had put the idea of leaving in *her* head because she was only obligated to be on the show for three seasons.

On top of all that, Alexia's presence made him want to argue, or throw hands, or crack all his knuckles at the same time. Every time she opened her mouth, he imagined he was taking on an entire high school debate team. Even being high around her didn't help much—

and he'd spent the majority of the past first month and a half of classes relatively high just to be able to tolerate the Olympians.

To make matters worse, Kronos had not been acting like himself. The cheerful, positive man they'd all seen in Los Angeles just before the holidays was long gone. On that first day back on campus—seconds before HJ grabbed Astrid by the throat and threw her through the conference room wall and into a meeting being held by the Science and Technology faculty—Kai had been behind the head of Parthenon Studios and Damon. The two were arguing in hushed tones, and from the little bit Kai could make out, it sounded like Damon was mad—infuriated really—at Kronos for keeping information from the rest of them.

Their hallway powwow—and Kai's feeble eavesdropping attempt—had been interrupted by the sound of smashing Sheetrock, and their first meeting for the new season never happened that day.

The group of them had been displaced and "uninvited from using the campus facilities," as Dean Yan had worded it. Without anywhere to go, their meetings and interviews had halted, and everything had started to unravel.

Kai had a feeling that during his heated hallway walk, Damon had been referring to the files he and HJ had found the semester before. Something was definitely weird with them. The two of them had been onto something, and then, out of nowhere, they told him, Amber, and Dawn that it wasn't actually anything. None of them believed that they had suddenly dropped whatever theory they'd been working toward. The abrupt stop in their breaking and entering into Kronos's office to continue expanding on the idea had meant that Kai and Dawn's deep talks ended too.

The ten of them needed a space that was all theirs, where they wouldn't be bothered by students or fans, but it had to be big enough to house them all—and any future Olympians, as Kronos had reminded them.

"What about that big house down by the river?" Amber suggested.

"Where?" Dawn asked. Having lived in Olympia her whole life, she was the obvious person to know where anything and everything in the small—but rapidly expanding—town was.

"It's way back behind campus, off of—"

And that was where the memory cut out for Kai. He could remember everything after it—the way Amber had described the massive, boarded-up plantation house, the high fence around it, how the property touched the edge of the Congaree River. But the thing he actually needed to know—the location itself—was where the memory replayed in his head with her mouth moving, but no sound coming out. It was as if someone had muted just those two seconds of a video clip.

The two seconds he so desperately wished he could recall as certain parts of him shrank up from the freezing cold more than they ever should.

Panting and covered in goose bumps, Alexia appeared beside him.

Dammit.

"You're lost."

"No, I'm not."

"You definitely are. Just tell me where you're going so I can help you."

"What do you know about this town? You moved here, like, two months ago," he argued back.

"In case you haven't picked up on it—news flash: I know you haven't—I research everything before I dive into something. I studied maps, history, whatever I could about Olympia, okay? So, just tell me before we freeze to death. You're the last person I want to die with."

He glared at her, knowing he should accept her help but also determined not to give her the satisfaction that she would play a role in finding it. He was supposed to do this himself.

While his inner monologue ran through the possibilities, she asked, "You're trying to find that house, aren't you?"

Well, shit. "Yeah," he begrudgingly admitted.

She took a breath and looked over her shoulder. "I had a feeling. I figured one of you would. I just thought it would be Zach."

"Why him?"

"Seems like he's Kronos's right-hand man," she answered, gazing at the tree line.

"He's too much of a wimp to go try to find a haunted house," Kai explained.

She smirked in agreement and said, "Let's head this way. The tree line disappears over there, so that's probably the river, and Dawn and Amber said the property touched it."

Shit, why didn't I think of that?

As they stomped through the heavy snow in silence, they both scanned their surroundings. The sun was setting, and a bronzy-red glow shone behind them as the land plots on their right got bigger and farther apart. Expansive yards, piled high with snow, stretched out next to them with two- or three-story houses, lit inside, each with smoke puffing out of its chimney.

Kai guessed that several blocks over—on the edge of downtown Olympia and the college campus—the rest of their castmates were gathered in Amber's warm, cozy apartment. It was probably crowded, with eight people crammed into her one-bedroom. Hanna June might sneak outside to take a few drags on a cigarette she knew she shouldn't be having. Dawn would silently monitor Zach from across the room, ready to pull him out of any hairy situation he was bound to get himself into by saying something stupid—and probably offensive. Damon would sip scotch or gin or something expensive and pretentious and do everything he possibly could to not mingle with the others and stay out of the way of the cameras they had installed in Amber's living room. Astrid and Heath would stand next to each other, seemingly going along with the *faux-lationship*—Zach's word they'd all picked up on—that Kronos had arranged for them, even though everyone knew she was going to sneak off with Gunner at some point. And Amber would probably get wine drunk.

That was the part Kai was missing the most.

He went deep into thought, thinking about the way she'd looked in the morning when he woke up next to her a few months back— he replayed that sleepover *a lot* in his head—when two things pulled him back to his freezing cold reality: the ringing in his ear he'd been hearing for the duration of his journey so far suddenly jumped an octave and Alexia's voice.

"That has to be it," she breathed, a cloudy mass puffing out of her mouth.

Her gaze was fixed on a tall black wrought iron fence stretching out next to them. Fat flakes were building up on it and the expansive lawn it encircled. The house on the property was set far back from where they stood on the sidewalk, and the ground rose up into a gradual hill to give it a prominent seat overlooking what Kai assumed was a horribly dark, choppy river view.

The plantation house was huge—much bigger than Dawn had made it seem. It definitely didn't look like it fit in central South Carolina. Kai had gotten glimpses of mansions before, with his mom's clients being those rich enough to own massive yachts that needed regular cleaning, but this was by far the biggest and likely the oldest.

"This way," Alexia directed him, heading down the sidewalk without checking to see if he was following.

"Why?" He pushed on his ear quickly a dozen times or so.

"Do you have to challenge everything I say?"

"You're here because I'm allowing you to be, Chang. I can ask anything I want," Kai answered her.

"And *you're* here because of me, Newport," she responded. "We're going this way because I can see that the driveway is off this side road, which means the gate is over there. Even if it's closed or padlocked or whatever, we'll just scale the gate, but it's worth a try to see if it's open."

"Scale the gate?" Kai asked, a wave of alarm running through his voice.

She threw an incredulous look at him as she whirled around, smacking herself in the face with a curtain of shiny black hair. "What exactly were you expecting? A rolled-out red carpet, bodyguards waiting for you, and a slew of fans and paparazzi lining the drive? I know you might be used to that treatment, but this is an abandoned property in a town full of college kids, deemed haunted and uninhabitable. Use your brain," she reasoned.

Turning down the street and hoping she was incorrect—but knowing it was unlikely—Kai caught sight of the river out ahead of them. The black waves broke up the murky water, rocking and angrily splashing under the dark clouds covering the sky.

The ringing jumped a pitch, but stayed as an undertone, almost like a faded echo.

"Look at that," he breathed as they drew closer to the house.

It was three massive stories with balconies covered in vines, windows that had to be taller than him on every floor, and a front porch big enough to hold the whole cast—times twelve or so.

This was exactly what he had been looking for.

The gate up ahead had chains, doubled or tripled up, from what he could see. *You're gonna have to climb that.*

"See those little buildings?" Alexia asked him, pointing at the row of a half-dozen tiny houses, their roofs caving in and the windows shattered.

"Yeah."

"That's where the students used to stay."

"Students?" The ringing picked up.

She nodded. "The Athanasios family opened what many scholars debate was one of the first boarding schools in the United States. Children were sent from all over the country to learn here, and they'd live in those cottages during the months they stayed with them."

Kai blinked back at her. "You read a lot."

"That's why I know more than you."

He was about to spit something back at her when they found themselves at their destination.

Silence fell upon them as they stared up. The gates had to be at least thirty feet high. He turned to her to ask if she wanted to go first when he saw her pull at her earlobe.

She grimaced as he asked, "You okay?" He didn't care about her well-being; he just wanted to know why her ear was bothering her and if it was the same reason his was pestering him.

"Tinnitus," she answered, still focused on their slick, towering dilemma.

"What's that?"

"Ringing in the ear."

Huh. "Only your left?"

"It's my right …"

"That's what I meant." *How high am I?*

"Yes, it's only in my right ear."

"Me too."

Her gaze snapped to him. "I've had it ever since we started walking."

"I got it as soon as I walked out of my RV."

"Weird," she said, sizing him up and down, before shaking off the expression and slipping a bobby pin out of each side of her hair. She approached the gate and immediately started picking the lock.

"I thought you said we were gonna have to climb it!"

"You're the highest I've ever seen you! You really think I'd have you scale a gate? I just wanted to scare you," she teased him, wiggling her eyebrows at him.

"Wow, okay. Fuck you, Chang," he threw at her.

"Okay, that's fine. I'll just slip in here and leave you out in the cold to rethink all the help I've lent since I jumped off the bus to run after you, ultimately getting you exactly where you wanted to go, so the Olympians would have a home base again." The smirk on her face combined with the knowing tone laced around her words made Kai seriously consider turning around and leaving her here, just to keep from seeing which one of them packed a harder right hook.

"How'd you know that's what I wanted to do?"

"Keep everyone together?" she answered, not looking at him.

He knew he looked pissed, and she seemed completely unbothered by it, which just made him angrier as he watched her work to break open the lock. She was so good at everything—*everything*—while he had to try his hardest, and half the time, that still wasn't good enough. It was one of the reasons he'd never cared for her. Something about her, from the moment they'd met in LA two months ago, had just dug into his soul and whispered, *We don't like her.*

She shrugged. "I could just tell. The more everyone else seemed to fight and talk about leaving, the more anxious you seemed, which would then be followed by bloodshot, zoned-out eyes the next time we saw you. And you hadn't been like that in California, so I just figured that these people had become like a family to you, and seeing it all start to fall apart—while the whole world watched it happen—was crushing you. I figured you'd do whatever you could to keep everyone together. And I overheard you talking to Dawn about her leaving. So, when I saw you walking this way, I assumed it was to find the house." She paused, keeping her eyes trained in front of her. "And," she added, "everyone knows you'd jump at any chance to stare at Amber, but if it all ends, then there is no Amber. So, your priority is keeping everyone together right now, and this house is your only chance."

On her last two words, the lock clicked open. Looking up at him with a satisfied smirk on her face, she added, "Here's your opportunity."

God, I hate her, he thought, as he slipped past the gate and the ringing silenced.

Chapter 2

THE REST OF THE OLYMPIANS are gathered in Amber's apartment, sprawled out among the main living space. Gunner and Astrid aimlessly scroll on their phones, while the other six anxiously pace, jitter their hands, or continuously check the door for any sign of Kai or Alexia, who haven't shown up yet.

Heath: Maybe we should go out and look for them.

Hanna June: Look for them? There's a blizzard outside, Heath! We're in a state of emergency!

Amber: My last text was delivered to Alexia. She just hasn't answered—but that doesn't mean anything! She could just not have service …

Damon: [*peers out the door to the balcony from his stance against the wall by Amber's bedroom*] Phone lines were down at the complex next to mine.

Astrid: [*looks up from her phone and smiles at him*] Which is …

Damon: [*not looking at her*] Still not telling where.

Zach: Let's give them another hour, and if we haven't heard anything, a few of us can go out.

Heath: They didn't say anything about where they were going?

Amber: [*shakes her head and looks at her texts*] Alexia said Kai wouldn't tell her.

Dawn: [*nervously clutches her coffee mug*] Has anyone heard from *him*?

Hanna June: Nope.

Heath: Hasn't answered me.

Astrid: Me neither.

Silence falls among the group. The only sounds are the tapping of fingers on screens, the clock on the wall ticking, and the crackling of the wooded wick candles lit around the room.

Heath: Do you think it's true?

Zach: What?

Heath: That … you know … that we're … *them*.

Gunner: Course it's not true. Don't be a fuckin' idiot.

Dawn: [*grimaces*] That's not necessary.

Heath: [*turns to face Gunner*] Don't call me an idiot.

Gunner: [*drops his phone into his lap*] How would it be real? How? How would *we* be gods? What, did they just float on down and decide to become us? Did—did their souls pick each of us out individually, like Kronos said? Tell me how that would fuckin' work, Blackburn?

Hanna June: Because it just does.

Gunner: [*swings around to face her*] Oh, you believe it, do you, princess?

Hanna June: [*smirks*] Actually, that's queen to you.

Gunner: [*rolls his eyes and mutters*] So fucking stupid. All right, okay, who else believes in this fairy tale Kronos has fed you all?

Zach, Amber, Damon, Astrid, and Heath all raise their hands.

Gunner: Jesus Christ.

Heath: Kai believes it too.

Gunner: Yeah? [*turns to Damon*] And you believe in this—this theory?

Damon: I do.

Gunner: Why?

Damon: [*opens his mouth to answer, but is cut off*]

Amber: I just got a text from Alexia! But … the timestamp on it is seventeen minutes ago. [*looks up at the group*] They went looking for the house …

Dawn: Ohhh no. No, no, no, no.

Hanna June: I don't get what's so bad about it.

Dawn: It's seriously haunted.

Zach: [*an amused smirk on his face*] I've never seen you lose your chill, Dawn.

Dawn: Ghosts and haunted houses and things like that are my one *thing*. [*shivers*] Plus, I've been in that house, before they shut it down.

Hanna June: Wait, how?

Dawn: It used to be a tourist destination. Well … *the* tourist destination Olympia had to offer before … ya know, [*gestures to the group*] all this.

Astrid: What was it like?

Dawn: It's huge. I went on a tour there in the springtime. It was gorgeous. Parts of the grounds are a bit decrepit and falling apart, but the actual house … it's still perfectly intact from how the Athanasios family had it all laid out. It's like how Pompeii is this place that's just preserved in time—almost like the family just upped and moved out yesterday and left everything behind.

Heath: Then what made it so scary?

Dawn: It just … like, you could tell that it didn't want people there.

Gunner: The *house* didn't want people there?

Dawn: [*nods*]

Gunner: [*laughs*] You gotta be kiddin'. You've never made shit up like this before in front of the cameras, Sutherland. Why you startin' now? [*looks at Amber and points at the camera on the wall*] These things don't even have audio, right?

Dawn: I'm not making things up, Gunner. I don't do that. I do tell the truth, and the truth is that *weird* things happened in that house during the forty minutes I was there, and there's a whole bunch of people who had similar experiences. Go ahead—you've got your phone right there. Google *Athanasios Plantation* and just see what shows up.

Gunner: [*shakes his head at her and goes back to his phone, not looking up the house*]

The door to Amber's bedroom flies open, and Fleur stomps into the living area.

Fleur: [*points a finger at her sister*] Okay, if I'm gonna be locked away in your room, I don't want to be able to hear the conversation! That's just a tease.

Amber: Fleur—

Fleur: [*turns to Gunner*] I've been looking up this house since it was mentioned in the livestream and it's definitely too scary for you. Which is fine—you can stay in your little off-campus apartment your daddy pays for and let that be the extent of your relationship with him, and *I'll* take your room in the house. They all like me better than you anyway—

Gunner: [*stands up and steps toward her*] You little bi—

Damon pushes off the wall and immediately steps between Fleur and Gunner.

Damon: I have no problem knockin' you flat on your back, McHugh.

Gunner: Yeah? Thought you wanted to stay out of the spotlight?

Damon: I don't tolerate disrespect, which seems to be the only setting you have. And I'm not the only one who thinks so.

Gunner: [*looks around at the group and smiles*] Fuck you guys.

He gets up, gives the camera in the corner the middle finger, and storms out the front door. Astrid quickly pushes off the couch, stopping to put her boots on.

Astrid: I should go check on him.

She leaves.

Zach: [*stares at Heath, lips pursed, a slightly amused expression on his face*] Well, that's gonna look great on camera.

Heath: What?

Zach: That we're trying to sell this relationship storyline between you and Astrid and she just got up and followed Gunner outside.

Amber: Maybe they'll just edit it out.

Zach: That's a live feed, Grain Brain.

Amber: It's live? [*throws an alarmed look at Fleur*] Please go back to my room now.

Fleur: Why? Gunner's gone, and Kai's probably freezing to death as we speak.

Dawn: [*groans*] Don't say that.

Chapter 3

ALEXIA

A LARGE RECTANGULAR PANEL SAT right in the middle of the wall, not quite touching the weathered crown molding on the floor and reaching up just a few inches short of Kai's height. If it hadn't been for the column carved into the center of it, no bigger than her hand, she might not have even noticed it.

As Alexia stepped closer to it, she could see it had been there, seemingly undisturbed, for a long time—maybe since the last time people had been here. It had a thick coating of dust and small, fluffy cobwebs in the corner. Kai stretched a hand out, running a finger down the center etch of the column, taking a significant thread of dirt with it. However, as he lifted his finger off the emblem upon reaching the bottom, the strangest thing happened—the panel slid upward, disappearing inside itself.

They looked at each other, quickly turning back to the secret they'd now discovered in the kitchen of the old plantation house. Complete darkness hung inside it.

Kai cleared his throat as he peered inside the opening. "I'm … I'm, like, really high right now … so tell me what *you're* seeing."

"I think it's the same thing as you," she answered, looking inside. "Well, shit."

"Wait." Alexia held up a hand, sticking her neck out further into the abyss, listening hard. "Do you hear that?"

There was the faintest squeaking, like a creaky door hinge being opened and closed rapidly, and it was growing louder.

"Are you *seeing* that?" Kai was looking downward, which was something Alexia had been trying to avoid—it made her feel like she was falling, not being able to sense the bottom.

But she did see what he was talking about, and it helped balance the unrooted feeling twisting around in her gut. It looked like a box, light in color and seeming as though it fit perfectly in the vertical tunnel hidden in the wall they now had their heads inside of. It was growing, inching its way toward them, as the high-pitched sound grew louder.

It moved closer and closer, the squealing going hand in hand with its movements, and several long seconds later, it appeared in front of them. Alexia half expected it to shimmy right on past them, but instead, it stopped, right at the edge of the panel. It seemed to shake slightly, as if it were radiating, calling to them.

In the center of the floating platform sat a tiny dish. Dirty silver in color with a funny angular pattern encircling the edge.

Kai reached for where he'd stuffed his phone in his pocket, but Alexia already had her Camera app open and was greeted with an entirely grainy frame.

After cleaning the lens, she tried to take a picture of the scene again and was met with the same picture.

"Is yours, like, pixelly?" Kai asked, his phone now in his hands too.

"Yeah."

"Well, shit. It was fine in the hallway and out in those other rooms," he brought up.

Alexia had just pulled up the pictures she'd taken as they crept through the house … and they were all washed out. Nothing was visible, even though she'd seen the clear images on her screen when she took them.

"Look at this." She tilted her screen toward him to show him.

"Maybe the service here is bad—"

She shook her head. "That wouldn't affect the pictures." *Idiot.*

He let out a huff and shoved his phone away just as the little tray on the platform rattled, a faint jingling sound emitting from it. The two of them froze, too scared to ask if it had done that of its own accord. Alexia noticed that the ropes holding up the platform hadn't swayed.

"I'm way too high to be here," she heard Kai mumble as he reached out to touch the dish. His finger grazed the edge of it, just before he jumped back, like a nervous toddler.

"Dawn didn't mention anything about this, did she?"

"Uh-uh," Kai answered, looking around the room. "I don't see any others on the wall. This must be the only one."

The bowl rattled again. Alexia couldn't shake the feeling that it was somehow communicating with them—which was ridiculous.

But then again, the idea that they were all actually divine beings was entirely ludicrous, and yet Kronos had reassured them time and time again over the last few weeks that it was their new reality.

So—with the foundation that if she did something stupid, at least it was in front of someone whose depth perception was so off that he had walked into the wall twice as they explored the house— she said what she was thinking.

"I think …" She looked at Kai, who was staring intently at the dish. "I think it wants payment," she suggested tentatively.

But apparently, Kai wasn't thinking the same thing as her—no surprise—because his eyebrows knitted together. "What? No, you just—okay, watch," he told her, suddenly pushing her to the side. He hoisted a knee up onto the platform, the pulleys squeaking under his weight.

As the thing had pulled itself toward them in the darkness, Alexia had been tentative to get a closer look at it, much less attempt to mount it.

He must be really high, she thought. From the handful of cumulative hours she'd spent around Sober Kai, she decided that he never would've just jumped on a seemingly floating platform inside a wall of a haunted house.

But as that thought crossed her mind, she had another. One that ran in the background, along with the now-silenced ringing in her ear—that this was here for them.

It was a ridiculous thought, likely adrenaline-fueled … and yet something told her it wasn't completely crazy.

Kai pulled himself into the darkness and on top of the wooden square, but before he could get himself situated, he was tipping to the side, sliding out of the paneled hideaway, and spilling back out onto the tiled kitchen floor.

To someone watching, it would appear as though Alexia were witnessing a gripping tennis match with the way her gaze volleyed to him, lying sprawled out and in shock on the floor, to the platform lowering itself back to its flattened position inside the wall.

Kai had picked his head up to catch the tail end of it returning to its neutral state, then dropped his head back against the freezing floor under him.

"Maybe it wants payment," he suggested aloud, staring up at the ceiling.

Alexia shook her head as she rummaged through the pockets of her coat, searching for her wallet.

"I had been at Amber's. I dropped my things off. She even made me a cup of coffee … and then I realized I forgot my toothbrush. And you know what? She offered me one of hers—a brand-new one, not even out of the packaging yet! I could've just used that, but *noooooo*. No, you see, I have extra-sensitive gums, so I need ultra-soft bristles. So, I *had* to go back to my dorm. After I grabbed it, I got back on the bus, and I was almost back to her place—I was *so close*."

She pulled out a few crumpled-up dollar bills and turned around to face him. "But I saw you. And everyone on that damn bus saw you, too, and because my dad upped and left my mom with shit, I need to be in this program, and therefore, I need to be on TV, and because of that, everyone watches my every move, and I *knew* they all saw me notice you, aimlessly wandering around in the freezing cold in basketball shorts, and I thought, *Well, shit*." She paused, waiting for him to say something—anything.

When he didn't, she let out a dry laugh as she shoved the money into the bowl. "I was so close."

She had barely taken a step back when the platform tilted itself yet again, the bowl along with it, letting her cash slip out and land on the floor.

Kai rolled away from the money as it fluttered down toward him and stood up. "Do you have change or something? I don't think it'll take a card—"

"It probably wants its own kind of money," she stated, knowing that even if he hadn't smoked, he would still have no idea what she was talking about. "We'll have to come back." And she turned and began walking back toward the doorway.

"We haven't looked at the rest of the house yet! There are two more floors," Kai whined.

She let out a sigh but agreed to explore the rest of the plantation. As they left the kitchen, she caught a glimpse of the little door on the wall. It was sliding back down into place, the Greek column on the front looking slightly less dusty now. She thought she heard a faint squeaking, rolling down and away from her, as she exited the room.

When they found the first library, she planned to pull up her Notes app to write down some of the book titles, but her screen just glitched repeatedly, so much so that she couldn't use it.

The idea of simply taking the books crossed her mind, but from the horror stories she'd read online from people who had toured the property, she wasn't sure how the house would react.

Which is a crazy thing to think. I'm worried about a building retaliating against me for taking a book out on a loan.

And I'm thinking about how to get into a dumbwaiter that moves on its own.

This can't be my life. I'm supposed to be reading a Criminal Law textbook right now, not mentally listing where I can get ancient Greek currency.

This can't be my life.

Chapter 4

HEATH

HEATH'S ENGINEERING CLASSES HAD GOTTEN him used to planning on plotter paper. Vellum was a fine alternative, too, but he always found himself concentrating extra hard when he was tasked with using that—he had to make mental notes to relax his shoulders and jaw after. Even regular sketch paper worked just fine, which was what he usually mapped out early ideas on.

What he hadn't ever used before tonight was a white cotton tablecloth.

When Alexia and Kai had pounded on Amber's door an hour ago—well after the sun went down and the temperature dropped into the teens—both of them too amped up on adrenaline to register the frost dusting Kai's eyebrows and Alexia's chattering teeth, the thought had never crossed his mind that this would be his task for tonight.

They took turns finishing each other's sentences and spoke over each other, correcting the other on how the house—the one Dawn had specifically told everyone *not* to go out and find—was laid out. Alexia had asked Heath if he could draw out everything they'd seen—as, somehow, all the pictures they'd taken on the property were grainy and pixelated.

"We didn't even go up to the top floor, but that second one had, like, twelve huge bedrooms."

"There were eight," Alexia told the group. "But there's a total of sixteen, not including the individual cottages."

"Oh shoot! We didn't even look at those!"

"There's a greenhouse there, right? And I heard the gardens were huge," Amber jumped in.

"Is this box supposed to be a ballroom? Zach, baby, there's a *ballroom.*"

"Describe the thing in the kitchen again." Heath tried to tune everyone else out and focus on this duct in the wall they'd described, where a magical object had seemingly floated up from the abyss and communicated with them …

Which definitely sounded like something they had both imagined after nearly freezing to death in the freak blizzard that had taken over much of the southeast. Because the only other possibility was that the two of them had worked together to devise some joke to play on the others, and even though they were past the point of tolerating the other one's presence, it wasn't that far past it. Anyone could tell that Kai and Alexia still did not care for each other.

Nevertheless, Heath sketched out what one might be able to call a blueprint of their description of the house interior.

With a few nods, Dawn would shrug her shoulders and say, "Yeah, I remember it looking like that."

And extremely carefully, he drew out exactly what lived inside the kitchen wall, according to Kai and Alexia.

The door pushed open, and along with a blast of frigid air, in came Gunner and Astrid. Heath knew it was well below freezing outside, but combining their flushed cheeks, their exuberant smiles, disheveled jackets, and Astrid's wild blonde hair, he was led to believe they weren't feeling the cold as much as two people who hadn't just fucked in the breezeway outside would be.

"What'd we miss?" Astrid asked, grinning at the group as she took off her jacket.

Alexia took a step back as Kai jumped at the chance to stand close to the other new female Olympian. As he explained how he'd fearlessly chosen to seek out the house—"Not the word *I'd* use," Alexia muttered—Heath got up from his seat and stepped into the living room, noticing that Amber was ushering Fleur back to her room now that Gunner was back.

"Please don't argue with me," she pleaded with her, sounding more like a mother than a big sister.

Which was fitting because Fleur was acting more like a child than a teenager as she stomped her foot at her. "This is so unfair! I don't want to go sit in your room by myself anymore!"

Heath took a step forward before he really registered what he was doing. "I can keep you company—if that's all right with you, Amber." He shoved his hands in his pockets. "I'm pretty sure my job is done, and I don't really wanna be out here anymore," he added, sparing a glance at the crowded dining room table.

Damon took a step up. Heath was a pretty big guy, but, damn, Damon made him feel small. Heath watched as he peered down at Fleur.

"I'm going with you," Damon said, the tone laced around his words coming out like a reminder.

From somewhere behind him, he heard Gunner scoff as Kai filled him in on his and Alexia's discovery.

Heath tried not to think about his stepbrother and his fake girlfriend together. He didn't want any part in this twisted little dating game Kronos had come up with, all with the hopes of upping his popularity level with fans.

Amber nodded, and he left the crowd with Fleur and Damon in tow.

The rest of the Olympians were starting to get a little too rowdy for his comfort—probably caused by the cabin fever and the higher-than-normal alcohol consumption. Add in the general discomfort Heath always had around Gunner and Astrid, and he felt like Amber's little apartment had become somewhat claustrophobic. And of course, now the group was riding high on the adventurous tale Alexia and Kai had shared.

Heath was glad to excuse himself.

With the door to Amber's room closed, the music was muffled, and the leftover traces of incense burning calmed his brain.

"It was all right with me, by the way," he heard Fleur say, as he peered out the window.

"What?"

"It was fine with me for you to come back," she explained, raising her eyebrows at him in a way that made him feel a little guilty for not thinking to ask her.

Which is ridiculous. She's, like, twelve.

"You didn't need to get my sister's permission."

"I just—ya know, she's had Damon playing bodyguard for you ever since the first time we were all here. I just didn't wanna step on any toes," he explained, knowing he didn't need to, but also feeling obligated to.

Her tone reminded him of his stepmom, reprimanding him when he was younger and did something wrong. It was sensible and steady, without being condescending—a harsh contrast to the way she'd crossed her arms and pouted when arguing with Amber just minutes earlier.

Damon leaned against the wall, arms crossed and his gaze fixated on the snow falling outside. "That's more so for … the other *gentlemen Olympians*," he input. His words came out in a dry yet mocking way.

It was no secret Damon had not wanted to be on the show, and when Dawn told them all she was considering leaving, Heath had wondered if Damon would be right behind her.

"And you're still not gonna tell anyone what happened between you and Kai?" The words had been sitting on the tip of his tongue, begging to be answered for months now.

Damon would tell everyone who asked—whether it was to a fan on campus, or even to any of the Olympians—that it was between the two of them, but Heath was hoping that, in a different space, he might be more willing to share.

He just hadn't really planned on actually asking it because … well, Damon kind of scared him.

He cocked his head at Heath, his gaze pulling from staring out the window to his face now. His lips pursed in thought for a moment, and Heath could see Fleur eagerly waiting for his response.

"Kai said something he shouldn't have."

Out of the corner of his eye, he could see Fleur's face wrinkle at the vagueness of his answer. "What does that even mean?"

Damon's attention pivoted to her. "It means he insulted you, and now—"

"He was probably stoned when he said it; he probably didn't mean it, if he even remembers it at all!" Fleur interrupted him, practically yelling back at him. *Well, she's not scared of him at all.*

With his upper body leaning away from the wall and toward where she sat cross-legged on Amber's bed, the two of them launched into disagreement. Their words weren't mean to each other, and their tones never turned condescending. They reminded

Heath of his mom and dad arguing. They hadn't been together in years, but they still very much cared about and respected each other.

It was just bizarre to see this obnoxiously tall man in his mid-twenties debating with a highschooler about human decency and morals, intertwined with alcohol and cannabis consumption. He wondered if Damon and Dawn ever argued and if it looked like this.

Their bickering stopped, and Damon's dark eyes took hold of Heath's again before he said, "It's better for everyone's sake if Fleur just stays away from the other guys now, and Amber agrees."

An annoyed huff spilled out of Fleur's mouth as she crossed her arms over her chest and turned away from him.

Fleur muttered, "Nobody asked me what I wanted," under her breath, yet it was loud enough for them both to clearly hear.

"How long had it been since you and McHugh saw each other before the show?" Damon asked Heath, apparently choosing to ignore Fleur.

"Several years," Heath answered, trying to track back to their last encounter. "Maybe eight?"

Fleur snorted. "Amber wouldn't let us go more than a month without seeing each other."

"Gunner went to military school in New York for, like, the entire time we knew each other as kids, so aside from once or twice a year on holidays, we didn't really see much of each other."

"So, that article in Columns was right?" she asked.

Heath shrugged. "Part of it at least."

Damon made a sound next to him as if he was digesting the information before asking, "Why'd he leave the service?"

Out of a newly formed habit, Heath peered around the room. "There're no cameras in here," Fleur said, as if picking up on his subconscious need for privacy.

"Medical discharge," he answered.

At the same time Damon's eyes narrowed in thought, Fleur's widened. "Did he get shot?"

"No, he didn't." *Has he ever been shot?*

"Damon, don't shake your head at me! That's a valid question!"

For a moment, the two of them dissolved into an almost argument, with Damon seemingly knowledgeable about bullet wounds—no one asked how—while Heath waited patiently, planning out his words carefully for when Fleur inevitably asked what he had been discharged for.

I don't even know if Gunner knows I know … I wouldn't want anyone to know. It's embarrassing. I mean, my shit's gonna come out at some point, but that should only happen if I share it. I probably should. But his situation— whether he wants to acknowledge it or not—is gonna happen. It'll all come to light—a big, bright spotlight.

But that moment where Fleur's question might arise didn't come because Hanna June burst through the door.

Heath hadn't decided if he liked her or not yet. He had decided he didn't care for Zach, and she was his counterpart, so how good could her judgment be?

She first did a double take in Fleur's direction, then hung on to Damon's expression. After wrapping up their telepathic conversation, she turned to Heath. "Kronos texted—well, Rhianne texted for him. He wants to know why you and Astrid aren't together."

Before Heath could finish rolling his eyes, Fleur spoke up again. "Yeah, what's up with that? Because I don't believe it, and neither does, like, anyone else." The challenge in her tone wasn't subtle, and the pointed look she was giving him told Heath that she was expecting an explanation.

"Rude," Hanna June shot back at her. "What do you mean, nobody believes it?"

"Like, on socials." Fleur shrugged back, glancing at her. "The blogs and accounts I follow just say it doesn't make any sense."

Scoffing one last time and muttering something that was masked by her thick accent, Hanna June grabbed Heath and pulled him from the room.

But she didn't drag him back to the party yet. Instead, she pulled him farther down the hall, and there, in front of the bathroom door, she lowered her voice and gave him a look he'd seen his mom give him before. Before she even spoke, Heath knew what she was about to say.

"Nobody believes it 'cause you're not sellin' it! C'mon, Heath! I know you hate it—we all do. But Kronos and Zach only came up with the idea to—"

Knowing it was rude, he cut her off. He didn't need to hear the spiel again. "I don't care about that," he reminded her, though it didn't matter. He had never wanted to go along with the plan anyway, and he'd made that very clear to them all. "I can just be that quiet one in the background who's there but everyone forgets about him. I'm okay with playing that role."

Hanna June shook her head before he finished though. "No can do. Damon's already got that role locked down. And you have a followin'. I know you don't really *do* social media, but I see all the girls in your comments! It's workin'. But we need you to go along with it—at least for now—just until filmin' starts. Please, Heath."

Disbelief coursed through the entirety of his body. After all the shit he dealt with—he was *learning* to deal with—adding this to the mess was the last thing he wanted.

"She literally just fucked my stepbrother twenty minutes ago, Hanna June."

He could see from the look on her face that she was digesting this, unsure of what to say. Because what *did* you even say to that? Instead, after a few moments of contemplation, her expression twisted as she looked up at him.

"Have *you* fucked her?"

"Wha—no!"

"Well then, maybe you should," she suggested. "She has needs, and if her fake boyfriend won't fulfill them, then she's gonna go look elsewhere."

That same feeling of disbelief somehow multiplied as he stared back at her. "Why are you defending her? You threw her through a wall a month ago!"

She whispered back through a hiss, "I didn't try to do that! It just happened!"

Now it was his turn to scoff. "Oh, yeah, you didn't *try* to. Just like how the wall actually opened for Kai and Alexia. Crazy things are happening round here!" He tossed his hands up and shook them over his head for a second at her, hoping to mimic how completely fucking ridiculous it all was.

From the show, to the stupid shit that went on behind the cameras, to a magical house with hidden tunnels in the walls, Heath wanted nothing to do with it.

With whatever meager following he could gain from the fake dating game he had been forced to play, he would invest his money wisely, finish up classes quietly over the next year and a half—maybe stay for the summer semester to get ahead, if he didn't have another multiple sclerosis flare-up like last year—and be done with it all.

If the show even lasted that long. Because with the way they were all falling apart, it wasn't likely they'd make it past the second season alive.

Chapter 5

Amber: [*grips her mug as she stares out the window*] Do you think we'll get in trouble if we go outside?

Gunner: They can't control us.

Hanna June: [*scoffs*] They absolutely can.

Damon and Fleur walk out of Amber's room, observing the conversation in the overpopulated living room.

Dawn: We probably shouldn't go out though.

Kai: The snow stopped; I think it'll be okay.

Dawn: That's not a good idea. The city's still in a state of emergency.

Fleur: Who's going where?

Dawn: No one's going anywhere.

Fleur: Ugh, I need to get out of here! I'm going crazy.

Astrid: Yeah, we've been stuck in here for four days. We should all get outside.

Hanna June: [*grimaces in her direction*] I don't think so.

Dawn: We can all take turns out on the balcony!

Gunner: Why are you so adamant about us not going outside?

Dawn: Why are you all so adamant to *go* outside?

Kai: She doesn't want us to go to the Anthastasios house.

Alexia: *Athanasios*.

Kai: That's what I said.

Everyone turns to look between him and Dawn, heads volleying like they're watching a tennis match.

Dawn: Yes! Okay? Fine, I don't want you to go to the haunted house down the road that you've somehow convinced everyone— even Kronos—to go live in!

Zach: [*a smile creeps up the side of his face*] I've never seen you freaked out about something like this, Sutherland.

Dawn: [*turns to him*] You haven't been there, okay?

Kai: I have.

Gunner: You were stoned until yesterday.

Alexia: I was there.

Kai: [*jumps up*] Yeah! Yeah, Lex was there!

Alexia: Alexia …

Dawn: And when she got back here, she was shaken by what she'd witnessed!

Heath: Or because it was ten degrees outside …

Dawn: She was terrified, but just putting on a brave face because she was the sober one in the situation.

Alexia: I *was* scared, but I was also very, very much intrigued. I'd really like to try a few different ideas I've been tossing around, but I can't do them yet because—

Dawn: Okay, see? So, no one should go outside. It's settled.

Everyone stares at her. Fleur looks up at Damon, who glances down at her and then back to his friend. He slips from Fleur's side and into the common area, and he approaches Dawn.

Damon: What happened while you were there, Dawn?

Dawn: [*glances up at him, her eyes wide with resentment, and the look on her face tells him she does not want to share*] That house is, like … alive.

Gunner: [*rolls his eyes*]

Damon: In what way?

Dawn: [*takes a minute to gather her words*] Nearly everyone who went on the same tour as us got hurt … by the house.

A shuffle goes around the room at her words—people adjust their stances, rub their arms, cock their heads at her. Dawn registers that everyone is looking at her, waiting for her story, and even though she does not like the spotlight, she swallows the lump in her throat and keeps going.

Dawn: Doors would slam in people's faces when we walked into rooms, the rugs would slide out from under their feet, [*turns her attention to Alexia and Kai*] and one man on my tour fell halfway down that big staircase. He swore that some of the steps on that main staircase had gone flat, just sloped down on an angle—kind of like how you said the thing inside the kitchen wall did.

Astrid: What happened to you?

Heath: Yeah, did you get hurt?

Dawn: [*shakes her head*] No, I was fine. Along with another boy, who was with his parents too.

Hanna June: That's so weird.

Amber: I wonder why nothing happened to you two.

Zach: What happened to your parents?

Dawn: [*looks up at him and swallows*] My mom got locked in a hall closet for a minute or two, and my dad got hit in the head as he walked past a candlestick that was mounted on the wall in one of the bedrooms.

Fleur: Whoa.

Heath: Jeez.

Dawn: The tours were shut down a week or two later. They'd only operated for about a month. I think some law office tried to move in there at one point, but it didn't end up happening. The place has been boarded up for years.

Damon: [*turns to Kai and Alexia*] And you guys were fine?

Kai: Define *fine* because—

Alexia: Aside from the platform rejecting Kai and making him spin out onto the kitchen floor, yes, we were fine.

Damon: And you believe that happened because it wanted something else?

Alexia: [*gives him one curt nod*] Correct.

Damon: [*nods, lost in thought, then turns back to Dawn*] And you and that other boy were the only two left unharmed?

Dawn: Yeah.

Hanna June: Do you know who he was?

Dawn: [*shakes her head*] No. Most people on the tour were locals or from not far outside of town, but I never saw him again.

Hanna June: Hmm …

Dawn: It's weird—don't get me wrong—that you guys were fine, along with the other kid and me, but please, please, *please* believe me when I say that house does not want humans in it.

Kai: Yeah, but we're not humans.

Gunner: Oh my God, this shit again.

Fleur: [*turns to face him*] It's real!

Gunner: Prove it!

Fleur: HJ put Astrid through a fucking wall!

Amber: Fleur! Language!

Fleur: [*rolls her eyes but otherwise ignores Amber*] Explain that. Explain how any normal human being can pick up another one and put them through Sheetrock?! And Astrid was fine!

Astrid: I had a headache!

Heath: Yeah, but you should've had a cracked skull and brain damage or something.

Fleur: Exactly. Explain that!

Gunner: Adrenaline.

Zach: [*in a much louder voice than any of the others were yelling in*] Wrong.

Everyone turns to look at him, but he is on his feet, facing Gunner.

Zach: Who says that? Who just tells a group of college kids— ones he corralled together for a multitude of reasons, who otherwise have virtually nothing in common—that they're gods?

Gunner opens his mouth to speak, but Zach keeps talking.

Zach: Even though he asked us not to, he knows we could all very easily go online and tell everyone. It wouldn't take long before it made international headlines. With all the rumors and shit going around about why we were chosen, it would all make sense. Most people wouldn't even bat an eye. So—I'll rephrase it for you—why would Dwayne Kronos make that up?

A heavy silence floats around the room, and a very uncomfortable seven seconds pass before Gunner speaks up.

Gunner: Okay. Okay, let's entertain this idea for a second then, if you're so adamant about it being real. How would we be gods?

Zach: What do you mean?

Gunner: [*contemplates this for a second, then looks around the room*] I mean, what makes a god different from a human?

Astrid: They're immortal.

Gunner: Bingo, they're immortal! Now, I, for one, don't particularly want to test this idea, but I'm pretty sure that if one of us were to get shot right now, we'd bleed out and die.

Damon: I agree with the idea of not testing that theory; however, Hanna June *did* throw Astrid through a wall, and she's still here.

Astrid: [*throws up a peace sign and says in a monotone voice*] Thirty, flirty, and thriving.

Amber: You just turned twenty-one.

Gunner: Like I said, adrenaline.

Damon: [*shakes his head*] Adrenaline wouldn't stop brain bleeds or any injury as detrimental as that. She either wouldn't be here, or we'd be able to tell that something wasn't right with her. She seems fine to me.

Astrid: [*perks up*] But if you're offering a physical exam, I'm open to it.

Gunner shoots her a look that she doesn't care to acknowledge, and Heath shakes his head slightly from where he's seated next to her.

Gunner: I just don't get how all y'all can put blind faith into a guy who gives you life-changing information and then tells you that you can't ask questions about it. *And* he forbids you to talk about it with each other. Like, how do you just trust someone who tells you your whole life is a lie, but—oh, don't worry!—if you just keep quiet with this secret for another month, he'll give you the full story, right before he props you in front of a camera?

Zach: He's asked that we trust him before, so that's what I intend to do.

Gunner: Why, because he made you an instant celebrity?

Zach opens his mouth to speak, but as Hanna June puts a hand on his biceps, Alexia opens her mouth and the attention turns to her.

Alexia: Wait. Hanna June, how *did* you pick up Astrid?

Hanna June: [*her words come out in a menacing tone*] By 'er neck.

Alexia: No, I mean, *how* did you pick her up? You shouldn't be able to hold more than twenty pounds by the looks of it, and you had her completely off the ground.

Hanna June: [*stares at Alexia, then Astrid, a blank expression on her face*] I don't know.

Kai: [*widens his eyes and slowly sits up*] Wait. [*turns to Alexia*] Are you—are you suggesting … no … oh my God, you are!

Fleur: What?

Kai: Superpowers.

Gunner: [*laughs in spite of himself because he cannot believe this is actually a real conversation he's witnessing*] Holy fuck.

Heath: How would that be a thing?

Gunner: You believe it?! Holy sh—no. No, no way. Do you people even hear yourselves?

Zach: Well then, how do you think she did it?

Gunner: I don't fuckin' know!

Amber: I think … [*her voice comes out soft, and everyone turns to look at her*] I think we should do the only thing we can do. Go to the source we know of that might have the answers.

Kai: [*nods*] The house.

Dawn's head jerks toward him, eyes wide and glazed over with a fresh coat of alarm.

Amber: What? No. We ask Kronos.

Chapter 6

ASTRID

HEATH'S HAND WAS SO SWEATY, which was remarkable really because it was twelve degrees outside.

"How far is it to the library?" she asked no one in general.

Alexia turned around, a look of genuine horror on her face. "Have you never been to the city library?"

Astrid gave her a shrug. "What would I need there?"

Her jaw dropped. "Books! Research material! Quiet time! Fast internet! Coffee!"

"Sometimes, if I'm nearby and I have to pee, I just go in there. Nicest bathrooms within a five-mile radius," Amber joined in.

"Really?" Astrid asked her, scenes already forming in her head.

As if through some sort of telepathic connection, Gunner must've picked up on it. Their gazes locked in on each other and she wiggled her eyebrows at him.

As he smirked before refocusing on the walk ahead of him, out of the corner of her eye, Astrid caught Heath's redirection as well.

He saw.

Oh well.

Dawn's hair bounced gently up ahead as she added to the conversation. "It's a lot quieter than Aarden."

A strand of her hair flew in front of her face as she cocked her head. "What's Aarden?"

If it hadn't been for the blizzard forcing just about everyone inside, except those who absolutely needed to be out, a picture of the Olympian pile-up on the sidewalk at the intersection of Carolina and Court would've been headlining news.

"What's Aarden?! Aarden Library? On campus?" Alexia's voice rang out over the sheet of stillness that had settled on the city.

Pushing his way through his stumbling costars with Fleur in tow, Damon gripped Alexia by the forearm. "Keep your voice down," he hissed to her, pulling Fleur along by her elbow.

God, I wish he'd grab me like that.

Five minutes later, the eleven of them seated themselves in what was a significantly smaller room than the Student Center, though much roomier than Amber's. Kronos surveyed the group, taking several silent, uncomfortable seconds to assess each of them before circling back to the tagalong, situated between Dawn and Amber.

"What are you doing here?"

A smug grin painted Fleur's face. "I need supervising," she said.

Lucky little girl. She loves the attention. It's so obvious.

Wait ... she wants to be on the show. So, what if she devised a plan to somehow make it so she has to be included in everything we do? What if—

"Miss Radzilowicz?" Kronos's sharp, deep tone cut through her inner monologue.

She could feel how high up her eyebrows jumped when she was pulled from her thoughts. Fixing her face first, she asked, "Yes?"

"Did you hear me? I was asking how you're handling Mr. Blackburn's newfound stardom as his partner?" The producer looked back at her, seemingly expecting a genuine answer.

What is he talking about?

Around the table, nearly everyone else was watching her.

No, seriously ... what's happening?

"I'm sorry." Her voice came out tied to a nervous laugh. "What exactly are you referring to?"

His narrowing eyebrows and the turning down of the corners of his mouth couldn't be a good sign. "Are you saying you haven't been on social media in the last ten hours?"

"Of course I have. But, um, what—"

"Did you miss the light Mr. Blackburn shed on his illness? Making it known, worldwide, that he has a chronic disease he battles?"

Astrid's mouth hinged open, but no sound came out. Seeing as she had nothing to contribute to the conversation, Kronos continued on.

"Mr. Blackburn, I, for one, applaud you. What you did took immense bravery. Fans have been pouring out their hearts, giving condolences, showing their admiration for you, and—"

Across the table, Astrid could hear her fake boyfriend's rebuttal. "I didn't do it for the pity vote …"

"Your popularity on the show has skyrocketed!" Kronos closed his praise, a proud grin stretching across his face.

He definitely has a tan. Where the hell was he while we were stuck in a snowstorm?

Rhianne stood behind his chair, looking out the little window on the door multiple times a minute. She didn't seem quite as relaxed as their producer. Both of them had been rather uptight and stressed since January, up until they left Olympia, days before the blizzard hit, only telling the ten of them that they had important business to attend to and to all hunker down, preferably together.

If Astrid hadn't been situated just so, she probably wouldn't have noticed Rhianne's anxious behavior or terrible posture. She likely would've just assumed they'd gone on a tropical vacation somewhere warm and left all their unacknowledged troubles behind.

But Astrid *could* see Rhianne, and it was very clear to her that whatever worries the two of them had been hanging on to were not actually gone.

"Now"—a clap of Kronos's hands pulled her from her thoughts as he changed the subject—"what exactly did you all wish to speak to me about?" His gaze was eager, excited, as he looked around the room.

Gunner spoke up, to everyone's surprise. "What you told us in January."

Maybe it was all for show, maybe he was trying to distract them all, but his face twisted, and he appeared to be confused. "There were many things discussed at that meeting. What exactly are you referring to, Mr. McHugh?"

"The part where you told us we're not humans."

The puzzled look on his face changed so drastically that it could've been slapped off. But what replaced it was simply a blank stare back at Gunner. Several beats passed without anyone saying anything, just the two of them holding empty eye contact, before Amber spoke up.

"We know we're not supposed to ask you about it," she started off, an audible shake in her voice. "And we know we're not even supposed to be talking about it among ourselves. But if we could just have some sort of … reassurance that it *is* real—since some of us don't fully believe it—then we'll leave it alone until you're ready to tell us more."

Kronos answered without tearing his gaze away from Gunner, almost as if he knew, somehow, that Gunner needed the truth more than any of the rest of them. That he was the nonbeliever in this force-fed fairy tale they'd all been told they lived in now. "It's true."

The next sentence was almost to be expected. "Prove it," Gunner challenged him.

Their muted, non-blinking contest continued on as their leader took in a huge breath, blew it out, and then gently shut his eyes.

Nobody moved, waiting on Kronos to do something. What, exactly, they weren't sure. A stillness fell over them as they watched him. Astrid saw Rhianne glance once at him and then turn her focus back toward the door, dropping her shoulders in a silent show of relief. Astrid could've sworn she saw a faint smile dance across her face as she peered out the window.

"Dear," Kronos suddenly said, his eyes open now, trained on Gunner, "would you look at the time?"

In the quickest two seconds, Astrid watched as Gunner glared back at him, and then his gaze suddenly shifted over Kronos's bald, gleaming head and onto the massive grandfather clock that sat at the back of the room. Everyone seemed to pick up on his new focal point as his expression morphed from defiance to bewilderment to astonishment.

The hands on the grandfather clock were moving backward while each of the twelve numbers on its face spun around in circles at their stations. Bells and chimes sounded from it, all off-key and out of tune.

In front of her, Alexia turned around, promptly letting out a gasp and pointing at the clock that hung on the opposite wall. "Look!"

Heads turned to where she indicated to find another unexplainable scene. The numbers on this clock floated all over its face, dancing up and down and traipsing across. The seven was where twelve should've been, and the one and ten were mashed together in four's spot. One hand wound itself forward while the other reeled counterclockwise at double the speed.

"Wait," Astrid heard someone mumble across the table.

Heath had pulled out his phone and was staring at the screen. Noting Hanna June leaning across the table to try and get a glimpse of what he was looking at, he placed the phone atop the long table. Nothing was happening. The numbers weren't moving or spinning around. He unlocked the phone and pulled up the analog clock app, but still, nothing.

As he pushed his weight off from the table, the clocks all seemed to slow down, and the numbers returned to their normal spots. The grandfather clock stopped singing, and the hands caught up to the current time. They all ping-ponged their gazes back and forth between the two as the chaos returned to its normal state, as if the last two minutes simply hadn't happened, and a wave of disbelief painted across their faces. Zach looked mildly impressed while Fleur had the faintest trace of a smile as she clutched the sleeve of Amber's sweater.

"I have no effect on your new kind of technology, Mr. Blackburn—good observation. My powers do indeed have a limit. But"—he paused to assess his audience—"it's likely that yours will not."

"YES!" Kai was out of his seat and climbing up onto it in nanoseconds. "I told you! I fuckin' told you! We have powers. *Super-fucking-powers!*"

He danced and whooped and ran around the room, and Zach and Heath even joined in. Rhianne peered over at them, shaking her head and laughing at their excitement.

"You don't have any powers yet, Mr. Newport. Please, settle down. There are civilians in this library—we don't need anyone hearing this conversation."

On the opposite side of the room and nowhere near his chair, Kai had somehow morphed into a five-year-old. "Wait. We don't have powers *yet*? How do we get them? You said they wouldn't be limited, like yours. Why don't we want anyone to know? I literally only see positive outcomes with this new development."

And he's totally sober.

"Mr. Newport, please take your seat," Kronos directed him, his voice getting harder.

As Kai dropped his head and crossed the room to his assigned rolling chair, Hanna June, Amber, and Dawn had their heads huddled together. Astrid couldn't make out any of what they were saying, but wanted so badly to be involved. She could see Dawn's curls bouncing as her head shook when she spoke. Thick strands of Hanna June's not-so-blonde hair were tossed over her shoulder as she agreed with Dawn. None of them had noticed that Fleur, who had been excluded from their gossip circle, had bolted around the table and was deep in conversation with Damon.

"Everyone, please," Kronos said, his voice loud and clear, and the buzzing died down.

Rhianne had sidestepped Fleur, indicating her to stand up at the front of the room, and made her way around to relocate her now-vacated seat and put it at the head of the table, right next to Kronos.

"I will gladly discuss the topic of your powers further with you, but at the next meeting. As stated, it is imperative that you do not share this information with anyone—not your significant others, your parents, your friends, no one. I wish for you to not even discuss it among yourselves. Not everyone views the supernatural as enthusiastically as, say, Mr. Newport, and we don't want to scare anyone unnecessarily. Understood?"

They agreed with him—because what other choice did they have?

Kronos continued, "I do hope my demonstration was enough to make you all understand that the information I'd shared with you last month was factual. It is indeed far-fetched, absurd-sounding, and possibly even intimidating to come to terms with. But I think you'll find that, upon acceptance and with the proper knowledge and training, these beings—these gods—are who you're meant to be.

"I want you all to write down any questions you have for me regarding this topic—as I'm sure you have plenty—and we will answer them all at our next meeting. Again, this is something that should not be discussed anywhere, *even* with one another. It has come to my attention that there are internet forums dedicated to ideas such as this one, and while you will all have the opportunity to confirm your fans' suspicions, now is not the time.

"I do, however, want to introduce you to someone who I think you will find to be of a great deal of importance to you." Kronos turned to Rhianne, who opened the door.

In walked a tall, beautiful woman, her arms open wide, as if she longed to pull one of them in for a hug. Her kimono floated behind her—all bright pinks, yellows, and oranges—and a dazzling white smile hung on her face.

"Ah," she sighed, taking in the view of them. She brought her hands around and clasped them together, drinking in the sight of them.

It reminded Astrid of the first time her grandma had seen her in ten years, the way she almost seemed mesmerized at her existence, wanting to know everything about her life. Enamored with her. With a father who paid no attention to her unless she did something of worth to provide him with either praise or a financial benefit and a mother who pretended she hadn't borne her, it had been a drug to little Astrid.

"Look at you all," the woman said. "Yes, yes, wonderful job, Kronos. Wonderful." She nodded at them all.

"Olympians," Kronos said, "this is Grenada Solomon. She's going to be with us from here on out. We'll discuss in further detail at the next meeting. I don't typically give you homework—yes, Mr. Newport, you'll be getting assignments, and they *will* be mandatory—but seeing as you'll be resuming your studies soon, I would like you all to research the Greek goddess Themis."

Chapter 7

Kai: HOMEWORK???

Alexia: Mandatory homework*.

Gunner: This is such bullshit

Zach: guys, it's all connected, it has to be. Whatever he wants us to look up is only gonna help us

Kai: And what's with the whole no superpowers yet thing???

HJ: Maybe we have to go through the schooling in order to get them?

Heath: Maybe we have to do something to earn them

Damon: Has there been any mention of Grenada before, to anyone?

HJ: Never last semester

Heath: I've never heard that name or seen that woman before

Zach: so maybe she's like one of them, not one of us

Astrid: What do you mean?

Zach: like how we're the Olympians. Kronos and Rhianne belong to the group that came before them, so maybe she's in with them?

Heath: Does anyone know, off the bat, who Themis is?

Alexia: Themis was the Greek goddess of law, order, and justice. She created the divine laws, which can even suspend the authority of the gods themselves.

Gunner: Like the 1st justice system?

Alexia: Exactly.

Zach: so not even the gods are above some of the laws? huh that kinda sucks

Alexia: She was also the second wife of Zeus.

Zach: oh…

Kai: Ha Z was married to a narc in another life

HJ: Funny.

Astrid: Wait…wasn't Themis a Titan?

HJ: How do you know that?

Alexia: Yes, she was. One of the 12 Titan gods.

Damon: Themis was a Titan, as was Kronos.

Heath: There's a Titan named Kronos?

Alexia: Kronos or Cronus- the spelling varies. But yes. He was the youngest of his siblings, and the strongest. He briefly ruled the world through the Golden Age.

Kai: Pls stop talking like a textbook

Heath: The Golden Age? Like everything was perfect?

Alexia: The vices hadn't been invented yet. Pandora's box hadn't been opened yet. Which, funny story, wasn't really a box. It was more of a chest. But that doesn't sound quite as good. Pandora's chest. See, it just doesn't flow.

Kai: Omg

Zach: ok, so the gods do their weird marrying their siblings thing- who was Kronos married to?

Alexia: Rhea, the Titan goddess of Fertility.

Astrid: Rhianne!

HJ: Thanks captain obvious

Astrid: You are SO welcome queen bitch

HJ: God I should've thrown you through that wall harder

Zach: ok, so 3 out of 12 Titans. do we focus on finding the other 9?

Gunner: Y? Wut's the point?

Damon: I don't think that's something we need to focus on. Nothing to worry about with them.

Amber: I feel like we'll get introduced to the rest of them over time

Gunner: R efforts should be focused on the house 4 now. Hopefully in the near future we'll be able to also consider the superpowers thing, along with the immortality thing

Zach: oh so you believe it now?

Gunner: He made the clocks go all weird. Gotta believe in something.

Gunner: & I'm not sayin this stupid greek god thing is it, but there's definitely sumthing goin on, and that's the only lead we have, so I say we follow it until sumthing more plausible comes up

Damon: Wow, plausible. That's a big word for you.

Gunner: Bite me montclaire

Chapter 8

HANNA JUNE

"GOTTA LOVE THESE STARBUCKS LOVERS," she hummed to herself as she reached down to tug her laptop out of her backpack. As she sat upright again, she was met with an amused, green-eyed smile from Amber.

"I don't think those are the words," her friend said to her.

"Course they are," she replied as she plugged in the charger. The last thing she needed was for her computer to crap out on her in the middle of their meeting—again. "What else would they be?"

Amber shrugged and took a sip of her tea. "I don't know, but I don't think it's that."

The rest of their little group slipped into the room quietly as Damon propped open a third cocktail table to fit them all. They were hiding out in what was basically a storage closet at the back of Washboards. It was roomier than the two-person study rooms in the library, but much more cramped than any of their other usual meeting places. The problem was that they couldn't continue to utilize the same hideouts routinely, as they weren't supposed to be meeting.

Especially without all the Olympians.

"Okay." Hanna June wiggled the projector just a tad to get it centered on the wall, knowing that if she didn't, Alexia would request it. "Is everyone ready? No bathroom breaks this time."

A nod went around the group and she started up her presentation.

"Oh my God," Kai droned. "You made a PowerPoint?" He sounded both annoyed and repulsed.

"*Yes*, Kai, I did."

Alexia leaned forward. "I love this already," she told HJ.

Giving her a grateful smile, she moved on. "Based on what we found in the files and what Kronos has told us, we can confirm that this *is* a thing. It's real. I don't know how … but it is."

Clicking her laser pointer on, she directed it at the first chart she'd made. "These blogs and accounts I've listed here were the first to post about the whole Greek god theory last October. It started off with most of 'em just discussin' how certain behaviors and things about us lined up with the gods. One account suggested that we were sent down from Mount Olympus to eventually establish rule over the humans, and a few of 'em said that we're here to save humanity."

"Oh God," Amber mumbled against her mug, her eyes wide.

"No pressure, right?" Heath chuckled, looking equally as overwhelmed.

HJ continued, "All we know is that Parthenon sought us all out—"

"*Sought?* You don't say that—" Damon interrupted, but she kept talking.

"And never considered anyone else to take our places in the program. It was always meant for us. But … why? Why put us on TV if we're gods?"

Wheels seemed to be turning in everyone's mind as they pondered her question.

"Maybe … maybe it's to get us acquainted with, like, being famous? You know, having people admire and appreciate and eventually … *worship* us—like it's all preparation?" Alexia suggested.

"Definitely a possibility," Heath agreed.

"Well," Amber started, "you can't just make an announcement that somebody is a god, ya know?"

Everyone turned to look at her.

She pushed on, her gaze staying locked on the plastic folding table in front of her, deep in thought. "Imagine that. Imagine if suddenly, someone—*a reality show producer*—just told everyone that some college kids were actually immortal beings who controlled everything on the planet? Think about the riots and the chaos and the divide it would cause. We aren't immortal, and we don't have powers. We have no way to prove we are anything, except … what? High Instagram follower counts? And what does that actually amount to? What makes us different from any other celebrity? Nothing. Kronos doesn't want us to say we have powers or we are gods or whatever because there's no way to prove it yet, and that would scare people and piss them off."

She looked up slowly, and everyone was nodding along.

She's right.

"I mean, we're hidin' in a closet above a Laundromat right now," Hanna June said, gaining a laugh from the others. "Not exactly godlike behavior."

"Well, that's because we don't have anywhere else to hide out," Heath contributed.

"If Damon would just offer to let us use his apartment—" Hanna June started, giving him a hopeful smile.

He didn't even look at her as he replied, "No."

I'll try again tomorrow.

Reining the conversation back in after Amber's monologue, she wiggled her laser on the wall opposite them. Flipping through the next series of charts, she reviewed how the first six of them had come into the program and how the new four had ended up with them.

"I firmly believe Astrid just wants more attention, even though she has one of the most visited vlog channels. And as for Gunner"— she glanced around at the group—"has anyone gotten anything out of him?"

Her gaze landed on Heath. He had told them all time and time again that they were basically strangers, but she wasn't ready to accept that. She still was hopeful that he could get something—some reason as to why he'd leave the Army to be on a reality show—out of him.

But Heath just shook his head, so she moved on. They'd find out sooner or later. Even if it involved another breaking-and-entering scheme.

Squinting at the next slide, Damon spoke. "Do you spend this much time on your schoolwork?"

She felt her face screw up and quickly softened her features. "What? No. This is way more interestin'."

As she turned back to her presentation, she caught a quick glimpse of Alexia. She was nodding gently, enamored with the display, a satisfied smirk on her face. HJ felt something warm grow inside her, like one of those videos of peonies blooming that were sped up so it happened in a matter of seconds.

"There are twelve Olympians," she began again, on what she deemed the most important part of her slideshow. "And there are already ten of us. But, like Kronos said last month, we're missin' four."

Kai and Heath both cocked their heads in the same direction, at the same time, right next to each other.

"Hades—Damon's counterpart—was never an Olympian. And Hestia—Dawn—is kind of up in the air. Some scholars consider her an Olympian; others don't. But what I found to be the most-agreed-upon status was that she *was* an Olympian—the first, actually—but gave up her throne when Zeus made Dionysus one of the Olympians. No one wanted thirteen 'cause that was unlucky, so she kinda switched with him."

A collective, "Huh," went around the room, although everyone's face looked just as confused as she had felt since making this discovery.

"Now, Dawn agreed to be on the show under the pretense that—"

"Did you get a thesaurus?" Damon interrupted her again.

"She only had to appear in two seasons, and then was free to leave. So, that kinda lines up with Hestia being there for the beginnin' and then leavin'. But Damon wasn't given any sort of circumstance like that, and Hades wasn't ever part of the group. So … why?"

She allowed the silence to sit for a moment before bringing up the second part of her biggest roadblock. "And to make the whole thing even more confusin', Amber—who's the new Demeter—only has to be on for three seasons. Except Demeter is one of the original Olympians and stays as one. So, again—"

"Why?" Alexia finished for her, but provided nothing else to the topic.

Which didn't make Hanna June feel very good. If Alexia couldn't come up with something, it was unlikely that any of the rest of them could.

"So, that's one major thing we should try to figure out. Along with who the last four counterparts of the Olympians are," she informed the group.

Dawn's hand rose into the air slowly. "Actually, I think I found two of them."

Chapter 9

DAWN

HANNA JUNE'S EYES LIT UP. "Really?"

"I think so," Dawn answered. She was fairly certain, but there were hundreds, maybe even thousands, of Greek gods, so it was possible she was incorrect.

And then, of course, there's the possibility that we're all just normal people. That this was all made up for the show or to get ratings. Or even that we're all just much too in tune to our devices that we're clinging on to one crazy idea and holding hands as we spin down the rabbit hole.

Maybe Gunner was right.

Damon leaned forward toward her. "Who?"

She took a breath. "Artemis and Apollo."

"You found the twins?" Hanna June's voice climbed an octave or two out of excitement, and Amber motioned for her to lower it.

The establishment they were hiding out in was usually busier later in the day. With the Laundromat portion of the business on the first floor, and the board-game café above, it wasn't exactly busy on a Tuesday afternoon. Still, Damon had paid the man he knew at the counter to keep their presence in the broom closet silenced and said he trusted him. Dawn had felt that was out of character for her best friend.

"I *think* so," she repeated.

Everyone shifted to face her. The sides of their faces were illuminated by the projector light as they watched her eagerly.

"I mean, Kronos had the files on them, but remember how theirs only had one or two pictures and nothing more than basic information?"

"No location listed for 'em. It was just places they'd been seen randomly, like on vacations or somethin'," Hanna June addressed Alexia and Heath.

"Right," Dawn agreed, appreciating the quick background she'd given.

They had caught up the two newest members of their self-formed secret group once they were deemed trustworthy and filled them in as much as they could in the short moments they all managed to congregate. Alexia shared with them all her own suspicions before Kronos confirmed the whole—unbelievable—Greek mythology parallel. The original Olympians then agreed that having the embodiment of Athena on their side was a necessity if they were going to get to the bottom of what was really happening in Olympia. However, Alexia had only agreed to come if she could bring Heath, but seeing as how quickly he and Kai had connected and the little bit of information he had on Gunner, it had made sense to include him too.

"Well, they live here, in Olympia. I've actually been tutoring them for a few weeks now and—"

"Wait, wait, wait," Kai interrupted. "They live here?! Well, why the hell are we sitting in a broom closet? We should go find them and—"

Now, Damon interrupted him. "And what? Ask them if they possess any superhuman abilities? If they'd like to sign their privacy away to be on TV? Not to mention, Kronos would lose his mind. No, we don't do anything." He shook his head, turning back to Dawn. "Continue."

Giving him a tiny nod, she resumed. "They're still in high school. They'll graduate in two years, and seeing as Kronos wouldn't allow Alexia on the show until she was eighteen, I doubt he'll make an exception for them.

"I *did* mention them to Kronos the other day. But after he and Rhianne nearly jumped out of their seats when I told them that they were just on the other side of the city, they asked me to leave," she added, her shoulders dropping at the end.

The idea of abandoning her friends, especially with all *this* going on, made her nauseous. She would've at least felt a little better if she could have given them more information to work with about the next group of incoming Olympians.

"He still didn't mention the files? Did ya see any when you were there?" Hanna June asked, apparently indifferent to her lack of good news.

But Dawn shook her head as Amber suggested the same thought that flashed through her mind. "I doubt he'll ever mention the files to us. Maybe if someone hadn't broken in and taken everything, he might've." She shrugged her shoulders at the thought. "But imagine if we had no idea about them and then he told us that not only did extensive documentation on us—which dated back *years*—exist, but also that was *gone* now, and impossible to figure out who had taken it," she said, her green eyes rimmed with disgust.

Heath spoke up. "Well … that's exactly what happened. Except that we *do* know they were stolen … and we're the only ones who know."

"And it needs to stay that way," Damon added, grimacing.

Dawn knew he was making use of the connections his family had to locate them. But she also knew that if they hadn't turned up by now, it was likely they never would.

The truth about their situation seemed to hover over them like a haze as they all zoned out in the small broom closet and mulled over the idea, over the things that had been told to them in the last six weeks, over the ways their lives had supposedly changed forever. In some ways, they already had.

Kai interrupted their quiet time with, "Okay, so back to the superpowers thing."

"No." Damon shook his head, but didn't suggest what topic to focus on next.

"The Titans?" Alexia asked, but he shook his head again after considering the subject.

"I don't think that would be the most productive piece of this puzzle for us to focus on," was all he said. "There are two more Olympians and two other files we found with the rest—Hermes and Dionysus."

Hanna June smirked at him. "It's pronounced *air-maze*," she informed him.

A giggle started to shadow over Dawn's mouth, but she suppressed it as Hanna June and Damon began the disagreement.

"It's *her-me-ez*, Hanna June."

"I have four bags from 'em. I think I know how to say it!"

"We literally don't have time for this."

Alexia intercepted and very quickly explained the confusion.

She suggested their efforts should stay focused on the other files. Two young men, Nolan and Oliver, but there was next to no information about them. As a result, the seven of them didn't make it very far in a conversation.

Feeling as though they'd hit another wall, the group recoiled back into silence.

Until, that was, Alexia's voice broke it. "Fun fact: Hades wasn't made an Olympian due to the fact that he didn't reside on Mount Olympus. As king of the underworld, he lived *there*. However, Poseidon didn't reside on Mount Olympus either, and yet *he* was an Olympian. You see, he actually had a palace at the bottom of the sea, where—"

"God, stop, stop, STOP!" Kai interjected her mythological history lesson, as he always did when she tried to teach them a little something.

Dawn loved hearing her little tidbits of information, but it was a widely known fact that Kai did not.

"Stop talking! We don't care!"

"I do," Dawn corrected him, causing him to immediately shrink back against his chair.

Instead, Hanna June pointed at them. "You two need to stop jumpin' down each other's throats. I know it's, like, ingrained in you, 'cause Athena and Poseidon hate each other, but get over it. I can't take the arguin'."

Heath laughed. Everyone turned to him.

Dawn saw Hanna June's eyebrows shoot up her forehead. "Somethin' funny?"

"You're one to talk. You and Astrid do the exact same thing," he shot back.

She pointed a finger at him now. "That's different."

"It's really not."

Dawn did not like the vibe. The tiny room was getting heavy and hostile, and the idea of working together to decipher this puzzle was long gone. Her hands lifted slightly, the way a conductor did at the symphony.

"I think," she began, "we all need to take a moment. Back into the silence. Just for a second." She saw Hanna June slump against the back of her chair as Amber's eyes closed gently. "Let's all remember why we're here. We want to figure this out. There are answers here, somewhere, to all of our questions. Turning on each other, focusing on our differences, will only drive us apart. We need to work together to conclude what this all means," she said to them.

The group stayed in their peaceful doze for a minute, until Dawn raised her hands gently and then placed them in her lap. At that same moment, it was as if she'd lifted them from a trance.

Rubbing the sleep from his eyes, Kai murmured, "I don't know how you do that, Dawn. Every single time, without fail, you just calm everyone down when ... you ... *oh shit*."

Heads turned to him at the harsh change in his tone, and somehow, Dawn suddenly knew what he was about to say.

No. It can't be. It doesn't make any sense.

Does it?

If it's true ... which would be insane ... what do I do? What does this mean? How do I control it? Was I born like this?

Why do I feel scared? Shouldn't I be excited?

No. No, no, there's no way. It's not possible. I am Dawn Avery Sutherland, and I definitely don't have—

"Superpowers."

Chapter 10

GUNNER

For the seventh time in the last ten minutes, his mom's name lit up his phone as it buzzed on the floor.

He shouldn't even be looking at that though—Astrid's ass was pounding against his hips, over and over, so why did he even care?

God, she feels so good.

Running his fingernails down her back and watching her arch even more, he instructed her, "Faster."

And she did just that.

And then his phone started buzzing again, this time vibrating right up against his belt buckle. The noise was heavier and more demanding, and seeing as he couldn't pull his thoughts from it, he told her to get louder to drown it all out.

It worked.

For a minute.

Then he noticed Keala's name.

Why is his *mom calling me now?*

He could feel his buildup fading quickly.

Fuck.

It was just like them to cockblock him.

He grabbed her around the waist and threw her onto her back and finished, keeping his eyes glued shut.

A minute later, he pulled out, leaned down to scoop up his phone, and walked into the bathroom.

Shutting the door with his foot and leaning against the cool subway tile, he assessed the damage—thirty-seven missed calls between his mom and stepmom and a string of texts from the both of them and Heath.

He wrinkled his nose at the sight of Heath's name among his notifications.

Knew I shouldn't have saved his number.

All the texts shared a common theme—urgency.

Keala: Please pick up the phone.

Mom: I really need to talk to you.

Heath: Just want to make sure you're okay.

Keala: I can't imagine what you're going through. I'm here if you want to talk.

Mom: I wish you'd just check in, honey. I know you're scared, but it's going to be okay. You can do this, you'll be so great at it.

What the hell?

He began typing out a text to his mom, then backspaced it all. He wasn't going to say anything until he knew what they were talking about, and he definitely wasn't going to ask them to explain. Maybe he'd ask Heath on Friday, when they all went out. When he was drunk enough to not give a shit about anything.

Yeah, that's a good plan.

Moseying back into his room, he paused for a minute to stare at Astrid. She was lying belly down on his bed, her naked butt out for all to see. Well, for him to see, which was what he wanted.

He crawled over her and gave one cheek a squeeze, causing her to giggle and turn over underneath him.

"Um, excuse me, *Captain*," she teased him, poking at the bottom of his rib cage. "But I never heard the water turn on."

"That's 'cause I didn't turn it on," he informed her, gently pinning her hands on either side of her head while he lowered his body weight on top of her. He ignored the nickname she'd given him weeks ago when they first got naked together. Though it was nice to hear again, even if he no longer had the title.

Her face wrinkled as she giggled. "Then what did you do in there?"

He shrugged and murmured into her neck, "I was stretching."

"Stretching?"

"Mmhmm. I thought of this thing we're gonna try," he joked, pulling her knee up to her ear.

She laughed more. It sounded like the bells he could remember hearing in church at Christmastime, the few times his mom had taken him as a kid.

Their naked flirting subsided and she let out a breath. "No, seriously," she prompted.

Gunner hesitated at this. They talked, more than he ever had with another girl.

Well, aside from Katie.

But still, they never got too in depth with anything. She never brought up her family, even though everyone on the planet knew her dad was famous and her mom neglected her existence. He never mentioned his parents or their significant others. Just the idea of saying Heath's name in the same sentence as his mom made him want to punch something. Would it cross a line if he talked to her about his family? Especially since she was faking a relationship with his stepbrother?

On the other hand, he hadn't wanted to talk to someone the way he craved to have conversations with Astrid in a long time. Okay, fine—in a few months. But that was a big deal because, for a while there, he'd genuinely believed that he would never come across someone who made him want to exist in the same time and space as them.

It felt like a boulder was sitting on his chest as he opened his mouth to speak. "My mom was trying to call me. I was just checking her texts." His brain seemed to act in slow motion, as if watching the scene unfold.

She paused in answering him back. "Do you need to call her back?" Her words came out serious, and maybe ... concerned?

"No, it's fine." Sitting up next to her, he reached into his nightstand and pulled out a chocolate bar. It was a routine they'd fallen into easily after the first time they hung out.

Breaking off a piece and handing it to her, he let out a breath and added, "My stepmom called me too."

She didn't look at him, but chewed her piece in silence before asking, "Heath's mom?"

He nodded.

"Do you like her?"

Gunner shrugged. He'd been asked questions like this many times over the years, but never had a real answer. The truth was, he never gave it much thought because he simply did not want to.

The facts were that his parents had never loved each other, had him by accident, not even attempted to make things work between them. As a result, Scott stayed deployed for as long as he could, and Elaine went and found someone who *did* love her.

It just so happened that person was Keala Blackburn. After, of course, amicably splitting from Heath's dad, Keala met Gunner's mom while she was "finding" herself.

Elaine's solo trip to Honolulu had changed her life, and even though she tried to butter him up with presents and trips to the beach and the promise of stepsiblings, Gunner was no idiot. He knew what was going on. He wasn't good enough to make her stay with her real family, so she'd left to find a better one. And—*good news for him*—he would get to visit them sometimes. Yippee.

Astrid didn't press him during the silence that followed, and instead, she did something she hadn't done before, just as he had. "My mom pretends she never had me."

He knew this. It had been headlining news when her addition to *The Olympians* cast had been announced.

Love Child of '80s Heartthrob Monty Radz and Choreographer to the Stars and Former Ballerina Annette Silvestri to Star in Worldwide Phenomenon, The Olympians*!*

It was on every magazine in the grocery store checkout aisle, every interstate billboard, and plastered in the center of Times Square for a while. Everyone knew who she was and how messed up her family situation was. But she never talked about it—not on the show, not on her channel, not to anyone.

Except that she just had. To him.

And not only that, but she had done it naked, in his bed. Talk about being vulnerable.

She looked over and silently held out her hand for another piece of chocolate.

He broke it off and placed it in her palm as he replied, "Yeah, I heard something about that."

She turned away from him after a minute, and still chewing, she opened her palm again for a third piece.

They didn't talk about much else after that, but instead finished the jumbo-sized Hershey's bar, naked.

Chapter 11

Kai: I can't wait until Tuesday. We need to talk to him NOW

HJ: You need to calm down

Alexia: We promised him we wouldn't bring it up again.

Kai: Water. I definitely control water

Kai: Can I make waves? Can I make it rain?

Kai: Ayyeeee make it rain

Damon: God, please shut up.

Kai: WAIT

Kai: Is the rain the weather though???

Kai: WHOS IN CHARGE OF THAT

Alexia: Zeus.

Amber: I still don't really get Dawn's powers...

Dawn: They're not powers. I just have a calming aura.

HJ: Idk dawnie…

Kai: I beg to differ, almighty goddess of chill vibes

Alexia: Hestia was the goddess of the hearth, along with the home and family. I'm guessing that her ability to calm the behaviors of people is an extension of both the warmth we physically feel from the hearth and the warmth we emotionally feel from being in a familiar place with our loved ones.

Heath: Can she maybe manipulate heat?

Kai: Oh shit look at blackburn brainstormin up shit

Alexia: I think that's definitely a possibility, if we have multiple powers.

Amber: Kronos said "powers," like plural

Alexia: All of the books I checked out from the campus library mention the gods using their powers… but they don't actually clarify what the powers are…

Heath: Maybe we can ask Grenada at the next meeting?

Kai: And then maybe we can casually bring up what our powers might be! Great idea blackburn

Dawn: I don't think that's a good idea. If we ask her, she'll definitely tell Kronos.

Kai: Ughhh I don't wanna wait 3 weeks

Kai: Maybe I'll just ask him myself, without any of u guys around

HJ: You will absolutely not. We just discussed this, Kai

Kai: You're just mad bc you can't think of any powers you might have

HJ: stfu

Chapter 12

ZACH

WELL, THIS HAS GONE TO shit, he thought as he turned yet another corner and tried to lose the growing crowd a few hundred feet behind him.

He'd never run from a photo op—never. He'd been trained since his preschool picture day that if a camera was ever in the vicinity to keep a smile on his face and another one in his pocket. As he'd gotten older, his politician father had changed the quip to being more relatable: *Smiles are like condoms—you never want to be caught without one.*

This, however, was not a desirable situation to be in.

Anyone who had any knowledge of the city of Olympia would take one look at any of the pictures these people were taking and be able to tell he was on the back streets behind campus, headed toward the water. If any of his costars saw it—or worse, Kronos—he was gonna end up in some sort of trouble. They'd all be able to quickly piece together that he was headed toward the house.

Kronos had intently listened to Kai and Alexia discuss how the house had called to them and had enough space for everyone. He then gave Dawn several minutes to debate her side of things, holding strong to her stance that no living creature should ever set foot near it again. After hearing that, although the house had seemingly tried its hardest to take several people out—Dawn had brought newspaper articles she'd found at the city library as evidence—it hadn't attempted to harm any of the three from the show who had the opportunity to go inside.

I should've gone there. It should've been me. I'll go there and claim that it didn't hurt me, too, and that my phone worked so I have pictures and I got inside the wall tunnel, and everything's good because I stepped up. Different versions of these thoughts ran through his head as he stomped along the muddy, melted slush from the snow and headed toward Front Street, tuning out the desperate calls to get him to turn around and smile.

After losing precious time due to ducking into someone's driveway and hiding behind their garbage cans in an effort to lose his entourage, Zach waited for another few minutes before dipping back onto the sidewalk and continuing his walk.

He was almost there—he could feel it. Well, actually, he could hear it. Alexia had explained how both she and Kai had heard a ringing in their right ear on their trek to the house and how it stopped for both of them the second they made it past the front gates of the property. Amber said something about having a ringing in her ear when she was in Olympia, but not when she went back home, and Heath threw something in there about getting the ringing in his ear every time he was on campus too. Several theories surrounding the annoying little medical condition that all the Olympians seemed to have had been shared until Dawn reeled them back in.

But Zach hadn't forgotten it—he knew what it meant. He knew the house was calling them. Everything that had happened over the last few weeks solidified the idea—this crazy, extraordinary situation he'd been lucky enough to land right in the middle of.

Except that he wasn't right in the middle of it. This whole season of the show had gotten yanked out from under his feet, and it hadn't even started yet. He only had a few weeks left before filming began, and right now, Heath was the main point of topic—and the worst part was, he didn't even want the headlines.

Up ahead of him, the house came into sight. A sprawling plantation home, set up against the river. The thing was huge, and despite being hundreds of years old, its exterior condition wasn't terrible. According to Alexia and Kai, the inside needed a good dusting, but aside from that, it was immaculate.

I'm going to walk right up, through the gates, push open the front door, and it'll be fine. The house won't hurt me because it wants me there. I'm going to take videos and show everyone that it's totally livable, and Kronos won't even be mad because I'll be the reason everything gets back on track—he'll thank me. And then he'll buy it and bring in a team of high-end interior designers from LA or New York or somewhere, and they'll redo it, and we'll all live here. It'll all be fine, and it'll all be thanks to me. I got this.

An uneasy feeling rocked through him as he stared back at the gate, seeing the wrought iron had indeed been pulled shut. He specifically remembered Alexia letting out a groan as she recalled forgetting to close the gates behind them. They'd only just brought the house up to Kronos two days earlier, so was it possible that he'd been out here? Or sent people out here? Were they in the house now? Did they see him coming? Was he going to get in trouble for coming here? Would he lose his brand deals?

Stepping up against a bush to hide from any passersby on the street and from any possible visitors inside the house, he peered through the high fence around the property line. Minutes passed by without any movement, both in the house and on the street. He climbed out of the bush, hoping no one was watching from the stretch of dilapidated homes on the opposite side of Front Street.

Sidestepping in front of the gate, he pushed it open gently, the bottom scraping the slush that had built up around it, and slipped inside, making sure to pull it shut behind him. The structure made a locking sound, which made Zach jump since there was no lock on it.

Must be hearing things.

Mounds of dirty snow sat in piles along the drive and in front of the cottages Alexia had talked about. There were no prints that he could see—whether made by a person or a vehicle. He took that as a sign that he was alone.

Taking pictures of the property outdoors wasn't part of his mental checklist for his exploration around the Athanasios Plantation, seeing as Alexia and Kai had managed to capture a few pictures of the grounds. It was true; the lighting in theirs sucked, and most of Kai's were blurry, but they still had them. Zach took a few of his own though, just in case anyone wanted a clearer, daytime image to refer to.

He circled around the property, even venturing to go up the massive staircase to the second-story balcony, overlooking what once had been a pool, but after the concrete edges crumbled away on the third step, he jumped back down and told himself that if he got hurt weeks before he knew he was scheduled to be in front of a camera *and* when he was supposed to be going to Fiji, he'd be in for it—from both Kronos and his dad.

Finally, he ascended the steps on the right staircase. Zach had been in his fair share of massive houses. His own was one of the largest mansions in Washington, DC, but this took the cake easily.

Leaning against the railing of the front porch, he looked out over the river—wishing the water weren't quite as brown because it really was ruining it—feeling like a king.

No, feeling like a god.

Chapter 13

HJ: Astrid knows somethin

Damon: What?

HJ: She knows something

HJ: About the GM thing

Damon: GM?

HJ: Greek mythology. It's too long to keep writing out

Damon: Understandable. What do you mean she knows something?

HJ: Did you see her at the meeting with the clocks and Grenada? She was so far away, like mentally.

HJ: I've been thinkin about this for a while, but I'm sure of it

Damon: And that means that she knows something?

HJ: AND she was saying stuff in the group chat. The one with everyone. Like she knew Themis was a titan and stuff

Damon: And that couldn't mean that maybe she just knows some things about Greek mythology?

HJ: No

Damon: Hanna June, there are things you just KNOW because you care about them, you're interested in learning about them. I'm the same way—everyone is. That's normal. It's not sneaky behavior or whatever this is that you're trying to pin on Astrid.

HJ: You don't believe me

Damon: I believe you and this girl have not liked each other from the start. And maybe that has something to do with your "GM" parallels not particularly getting along, maybe it doesn't. I also believe, whether you'll admit it or not, you feel at least a little bit threatened by her presence on what's been deemed as "your" show. And, whether you've had the conscious train of thought to do this or not, I think that you just might be looking for ways to get her thrown off the show.

HJ: Wtf are you kidding me

HJ: Of course I'm looking for ways to get her thrown off the show

HJ: But threatened by her? HAHAHAH NO

HJ: She knows something, something we don't, and I can prove it. I was reaching out to ask you for help in figuring out exactly what that is so that there's not more information about us in someone else's hands. But since you don't want to help me, I'll just do it myself. Thanks for nothing.

Chapter 14

HANNA JUNE

Dropping her phone on the table was a ballsy move when it didn't have a case on it, but she was frustrated. *Why doesn't he believe me? It's got to be obvious to anyone … well, anyone who's been payin' attention.*

Maybe that's the problem—maybe I'm payin' too much attention to Astrid. Like when Cady became obsessed with Regina and would have word-vomit attacks.

No, no, this is different.

"What's wrong?" Amber's skeptical tone from the swivel chair next to hers pulled Hanna June from the Mean Girls clips that had started playing in her head.

She let out an obvious sigh and said nothing, but Amber stared back at her.

She spoke slowly, worried that Amber—who she definitely considered more of her friend than Damon despite having spent more time with him—also might not back her theory. "I think Astrid knows somethin' that we don't."

Kai and Heath both lifted their heads from their coursework to stare at her, while Amber's features softened.

"I've been thinking that too."

HJ felt her eyebrows slide up an inch in shock. "Really?"

"Yeah." Amber nodded back. "Ever since the first meeting actually. Well, not the *first* one." She stumbled over her words, turning a faint shade of red.

HJ assured her that she did not care if she brought up the first meeting. Yes, it was her fault—hers and Astrid's—that they'd lost their meeting place, but she definitely wasn't embarrassed about it. That bitch had had it coming.

Amber forced a small smile and said, "Ever since Kronos told us … you know … she's just seemed … distant."

Heath closed his notebook after dog-earing the page he had been scrawling an essay outline on. "Distant? What do you mean?"

"Well, notice how she never brings it up and only says something about it when, like, it's a fact? Like, it's never her thoughts about it? And when Kronos does talk about it, she … well, just try to sneak a look at her face the next time. She almost looks like she's reading a book she doesn't quite understand. Or like she's watching a movie she used to know every line of, but now she's looking at a remake and it's not the same way she remembered it."

"Like it's familiar, but she can't pinpoint how she knows it?" Heath suggested, nodding gently as if he knew the feeling.

"Yeah, exactly." Amber turned back to HJ, who was lost in her own thoughts.

"But what would she know? No—*how* would she know anything? She shouldn't have any inside information; we've all been here longer. Not sayin' anythin' against you, Heath—"

"No, I agree. But … the six of you have all been with the show equally as long … so why did your boyfriend get special treatment last semester?"

His question was valid, completely, and maybe if Zach hadn't been *her* boyfriend, she would've asked it too. But the truth was that it sank heavily in her stomach, and it didn't taste good. She didn't want to entertain it, not for a second.

Kai joined in on the conversation, diverting any attention from Hanna June now—*thank goodness.*

"Well, we know she didn't really need any bribing or anything to come on to the show; she wanted to do it. So, he wouldn't have given her any intel to get her to say yes," he began, the group silently agreeing. "And, Am, you said Kronos first visited you guys years ago, when you were in high school. He didn't necessarily give you and your family any information, but what if he did with other families?"

Hanna June hated to shoot down his idea, especially since it was clear to everyone that he'd been making more of an effort to be mentally present since finding the house. "Astrid said that she didn't meet Kronos until the party in LA and then didn't see him again until that first meeting."

Amber's attention went back to her. "When did she say that?"

"In one of her vlogs."

Amber's expression grew in suspicion, and before she could think of some better way to dress it up, Hanna June had her own episode of word vomit.

"She did a Q and A about the show, and I thought it was weird since we don't film till after spring break, so I watched it to see what she was tellin' people, just to be aware!"

Immediately pulling the video up on his laptop, Kai clicked on his bookmark for her channel—too busy to see the disapproving look HJ threw him—and played the video. Much to their dismay, nothing seemed questionable or out of place, and they were left to circle back to their question without any direction.

"God, we only have a few weeks left until we're back juggling all *this*, plus interview sessions." Amber grimaced at the Environmental Law textbook in front of her.

Heath nodded. "I already know I'm gonna have to cut back my hours at the shop. Isn't it weird?"

"Which part? Wait, never mind—yeah, it's all weird," Kai cut in. "The delayed reaction time you have to give, talking about stuff that happened, like, the day before that you're not even mad about anymore, but you have to act like you are. The cameras that just drift in and out of your classes to catch the 'studious' shots, as they call them—"

"Actually, they're not doing those anymore," Amber corrected him.

"Really?"

"Yeah, it was part of Dean Yan's addendum to letting them film on campus. She added it after the incident."

"Thank God."

The four of them fell into a series of conversations they flowed easily between, and Hanna June found herself looking at them—at her friends—with a full heart. The school year wasn't over, but so far, it had been … well, she couldn't come up with a word for everything they'd gone through. Extraordinary? Surreal? Insane? It seemed to be something new every week, and sometimes, they could figure out how it all fit together and how to navigate the unpredictable waters. Other moments felt like they'd all been left to fend for themselves. It was true that they'd all been—quite literally, in some cases—at each other's throats, but it was also true that she couldn't imagine having her whole world change with anyone else next to her. Most of her sorority sisters definitely couldn't handle it, and minus one or two friends from high school, she knew most of them couldn't even begin to comprehend the way every single aspect of their lives had been completely flipped upside down.

Sometimes, *she* couldn't even comprehend it despite being the most gung-ho Olympian about the group's secret. She knew most of them were still at least somewhat on the fence about it. Having spent as much time debating and researching and digesting the idea as she had, she was also painfully aware that if her mindset wavered, even just a little bit, they would all pick up on it, like the insecure bloodhounds they were, and latch on to it. And Hanna June was not going to let that happen.

Even if she questioned the legitimacy of it all sometimes too.

Maybe she'd wake up tomorrow, in her bed, back in Bethesda. Maybe her mom would be downstairs, making cinnamon praline pancakes. Maybe she'd be days away from starting her first semester at an SEC school, just like she'd always wanted. Maybe this would all have been a dream.

But the next day came, and she woke up with the sun, on the second floor of the Eta house, facing a cluster of dead trees that stood between the School of Communications and Myrtle Residence Hall.

She met Amber and Dawn at Ground Floor before they walked in the brisk March breeze to the Olympia City Library—the show's new but temporary headquarters—with her bodyguard trailing behind them.

It had appeared to them that the city was still asleep—until the library steeple came into view, that was. Everything happened in a blur after that—the dozen or so security guards running toward the girls to stay ahead of the crowd, the yelling and chanting from the several hundred people who had swarmed the front of the building, the frantic looks they got from Kai and Heath, who'd gotten there a minute before the three of them, as they were pushed into the building.

Colors blended together, and no sound around her was audibly defined as she gripped Amber's hand in one of hers and her latte in the other. She could feel her guard whisking them along, huddled in the middle of the rest of them, and Dawn's hand on her bag strap over her shoulder.

Suddenly, there were steps under her feet, and then the shade overtook them at the same moment a layer of coldness blanketed them. They were pulled inside the building, and the doors slammed shut behind them.

Everyone else was there—Kronos and Rhianne with Grenada standing next to her. Behind them, several other people shifted uncomfortably, watching all the rest of the Olympians. Some of them looked angry; others were clearly nervous, maybe even scared. Kronos was absolutely livid, but said nothing. No librarians were anywhere to be seen, and nobody moved from their places near the entrance way.

As Hanna June lifted her coffee to her mouth, looking for some form of comfort after the storm of chaos she'd been pushed through, Kronos began talking.

"I'm going to ask this once, and I *demand* an answer," he began. Then, without warning, his voice changed, and when words came out again, they were bellowed. The whole building seemed to shake. Maybe it really did. HJ's coffee spilled all over the floor as he yelled at them, "WHO TOLD THEM?!"

Chapter 15

AMBER

The panic settled in quickly over Amber, cloaking her in the way her mom used to wrap her up in a blanket after helping her remove her snowsuit to warm her up. Except not like that at all because that was comforting, loving, even silly sometimes.

This was not that. This was riddled with anxiety—for everyone. This was the highest level of stress she'd ever seen their show's producer exhibit. Sure, he'd been uptight and on edge for the majority of this semester. In the few moments he managed to crack a smile during their sporadic meetings, it never seemed genuine. At least, not the way it had back in the fall. The break-in had not only made him angry—which only their small, secret group knew about, thanks to Damon—but it was obvious to any of the ten of them that he was scared and with good reason. After Hanna June had plucked up Astrid like she was a Barbie doll and chucked her across the room and through layers of Sheetrock, he'd been livid. But this … oh, this was far worse.

And now they had an audience. Staring back at them all were seven new faces, who looked equally distressed. With the way Grenada stood comfortably among them, Amber ventured a guess that they were other Titans. Not that she dared say anything out loud.

Kronos started up again, pacing in front of the Olympians. "I'm expected to give a press conference later to discuss 'what this means for the world,' " he angrily told them, aggressively using air quotes in the right manner for the first time ever.

After a beat of silence, Damon's voice spoke out, strong and clear. "What *does* it mean?"

Kronos halted in his movements, immediately locking eyes with the grad student. Neither said a word, and Amber got the feeling they were exchanging words in a silent debate, with their stony expressions fixated on one another, before he finally pulled away and addressed the rest of them.

"It means there will be a lot of questions. From you, from the mortals—we ultimately don't know how people are going to react. There was a plan—a well-thought-out plan! We'd get the entire world to love you, to trust you. That was going to take *years*—we were aware of that. We planned for that. The transition of you all into seats of ultimate power would've been a seamless one." He paused for a moment before another eruption—and another violent dance from the crystal chandelier that hung above them—unleashed, solidifying them all where they stood, too scared to move fully out of the foyer.

"But now we have no chance at that! Now we have to deal with the skepticism and the outrage and the *chaos*!" His words ricocheted off the walls around them, echoing around the high ceiling.

The transition of you all into seats of ultimate power would've been a seamless one. His words bounced around in her mind.

Did that mean—

Kronos's voice rang out again, harsh and unrelenting. "Do you know what's happening around the world right now? Any of you? Huh? Riots have broken out all over Europe, the Middle East, and they're making their way to the States, as humans here are waking up to find headlines that some kids—who are barely adults—actually rule the entire planet. People are questioning their faith. Their entire belief systems have gone up in flames overnight because someone had to share that we're"—he gestured to every single one of them around the room—"in control of it all."

She could see some of her costars out of the corner of her eye— Kai, Astrid, Heath. They all looked terrified. She imagined her own expression matched.

They were gods. Okay. Weird, but okay. They had known this. He had told them all. But most of them were still fantasizing about it, not completely sold on the idea, even after the clock scenario. How had that proven that *they* were special? That these celestial beings had somehow inhabited the ten of them? And more importantly, *why* had they?

The idea that they were somehow expected to ... what? Take over the world? That was just absurd.

Amber had woken up this morning, unexpectedly gotten her period, and slipped in the shower while she was shaving, and in a state of distracted frustration, she had poured hot water meant for tea into her bamboo plant. That kind of shit didn't happen to gods.

No. No, this isn't real. It can't be.

Gunner's voice cracked through the silence now, not quite as unyielding as Damon's, but nevertheless, he spoke. "So, now what?"

Kronos rubbed his temple.

Do gods get headaches?

"Well, I don't know what, Mr. McHugh. Several countries have mentioned immediate exile. Most just demand some sort of proof. Peaceful proof, to be specific. A display, something to prove you are who the world now believes you all to be. Except ..." He let out a shaky laugh.

Amber could tell that whatever he was about to say wasn't funny though.

"You all have nothing to prove! No, you see, another reason we needed to wait was because we needed to scour this godforsaken planet to find your coffers. Yes, your powers are locked away somewhere—could be anywhere! I've no idea. We've located one of them, but a whole lot of good that'll do when the humans are expecting a public exhibition of the twelve Olympians and the powers they possess in a matter of hours—*OH!* And we're still missing Olympians! God, that'll be a fun one to decipher—mortal after mortal claiming to be inhabited by the divine soul of Dionysus!"

He laughed some more, somewhat maniacally, until the sound morphed into a strangled yell. The echo reverberated off the walls as the sweat trickled down his forehead. One last frantic look was thrown at them before he turned and stalked away toward the back of the library.

Not a beat passed before three of the probable Titans ran off after him. In the same motion, Rhianne stepped up, facing them all.

"You're not going to like what I'm about to tell you, but please, I beg of you, do as I say." She looked directly at Dawn, and somehow, Amber knew what she was about to ask of them all. "You're going to be taken to the house—yes, Dawn. Please, you all must stay there—at least for now. It was meant for you—I can't explain how right now; there's not enough time—but that's why it won't hurt you. It's been waiting for you all, I promise. These are Kronos's orders, not mine. There are cars waiting out back to take you there now. Stay on the property. No mortals are able to get past the gates. Should you encounter any … fans … on the way, do not engage with them. We are going to handle this, and it will be okay. I promise."

Amber was always taken aback at how soft she spoke, how much it reminded her of her mother's. And something in her voice told Amber that, despite the chaos of their situation and whatever was sure to follow, everything would eventually be okay.

Chapter 16

DAMON

SNEAKING OUT OF THE LIBRARY wasn't an easy feat.

The Olympians were ushered down a long hallway, cluttered with broken book carts and computers that easily could've been older than most of them, until they reached a doorway.

Pierce—one of their new guests Rhianne had addressed previously—had run ahead of the group and was waiting for the first half of the Olympians. Sectioning them off, he directed Zach, Hanna June, Dawn, Alexia, and Gunner to exit the building and get into the town car waiting to take them to the Athanasios Plantation.

Damon could hear the screams erupt as they left the library, the swarm of people spotting them around the back of the building and running for them. He could see bodyguards jump in from every angle as they were escorted toward the car, just before Pierce slammed the door shut. It was hard to tell if the over enthusiastic yells were in excitement or anger, and before leaving the library, Damon argued with Rhianne over going at all. Feeling the skeptical stares from Kai and Amber, he dropped it, telling himself that the fans wouldn't get close enough … he hoped.

Twenty minutes went by before he was led out to the second car behind the rest of the group. No hands managed to grab him, but Damon didn't like how close they got. Stretching and reaching toward him like he was an animal in a zoo.

The car ride to the property wasn't long, and Kai, Amber, and Heath talked the whole time, scrolling through social media outlets and naming theories and accounts that had somehow had it right all along.

Damon knew that one of them—easily one of the most popular accounts—was run by Fleur. He'd been so impressed when she figured it out. She had a lot more confidence than he'd had at her age—that was for sure. For months now, she'd been growing an audience across several social media platforms, calculating the likelihood of several of the more probable secrets behind the show, but never attaching herself to any one theory.

But Damon also knew she wasn't the rat. Honestly, he didn't think it was any of the fans behind the social media accounts. Without any real proof connecting the two incidents, he hypothesized that it was whoever had stolen the files back in December. Which wasn't a very comforting thought to have, as he still had no leads on who that could have possibly been.

He knew he'd get recruited to track down the culprit as soon as Rhianne told him about the theft just after Christmas, which he was thankful for, as it shirked him of his family business—despite Ernesto's vicious rebuttal—and it ensured getting the Olympians back on track. His uncle hadn't sent him a job since the night Kronos had chuckled darkly as he pulled his knife from his bloodless chest before casually handing it back to Ernesto. But as for the other advantage of tracking down the thief … he was still coming up empty. No evidence, no fingerprints, absolutely nothing to go off of. Damon had interviewed the rest of the Titans, even though they were all supposed to be working together, but they were all just as lost as he was. Several of them suggested their two other Titan brothers, who remained missing, but no leads for them had shown up either. Damon was left without any way to help the Olympians, and that bothered him more than any other thought.

Who else knew the secret? Who else knew of Kronos's plan?

The car pulled up just outside the gates, and Astrid climbed out first. A small crowd was already gathering along the sidewalk as they were ushered inside the property lines, and barriers were being moved into place by dirty machinery as a few security guards held the fans back.

Damon hadn't had a chance to visit the property yet—he had thought he'd have more time before Kronos inspected it and could get everyone on board with living there after Dawn terrified them all.

He could tell it was beautiful back in its day, but now it just looked tired. The sprawling mansion on the river was covered in vines, and several of the windows were boarded up. Damon could see some steps on the outdoor staircase cracked and crumbling toward the bottom, and most of the cottages were without a roof. The greenhouse had clearly been neglected the most, and he hoped Amber hadn't seen it yet.

Just before they entered the house, their phones were collected by another security guard.

"They won't work in there anyway."

"What if I need it?" Kai asked, his voice raising. "I really need to call my mom before she calls me."

Grenada, who'd been standing off to the side and chatting with Pierce and Keaton—another Titan brother they'd all just met not an hour ago—turned around and addressed them. "Don't worry about your families; we're taking care of them."

The group was pushed forward into the house, just as a shrill scream from fans plundering down the sidewalk rang out. Kai's gaze swung around and met Damon's, the panic in his eyes palpable.

"She didn't mean it like that," he told his half-brother, knowing what he was thinking.

The other five were waiting for them in the foyer, arms crossed and alarm sketched on their faces.

"You did this," Gunner spit at him at the same time Hanna June opened her mouth to speak.

"Who told—" was what she'd started to ask him before cutting herself off and volleying back and forth between the two of them.

"It wasn't me," Damon answered, annoyed at Gunner for even suggesting it. He could somewhat understand his reasoning behind the accusation, but nevertheless, he did not appreciate it. He knew parts of Kronos's plan and how vital it was that the news didn't come out until a certain time, which was why he hadn't told anyone. And yet it'd happened anyway.

"I'm certain that whoever did this is someone we haven't met yet," he told them. *Hopefully the same person who stole the files—that would be easiest. Two birds with one stone.*

"Yeah, but that could be anybody," Zach chimed in, unhelpfully. Which was consistent with Zach's behavior.

Astrid spoke from where she stood, leaning against a windowsill and staring outside. "Do you think it was any of them?" She was watching Kronos's "new colleagues." Damon knew who they were, of course, but the others didn't. Though their detective skills were getting sharper—for the most part—and he figured at least a handful of them had put the pieces together.

Rhianne's going to tell them anyway, he reasoned with himself before shelling out the basics.

"No, it wasn't any of them. Those are the Titans"—he heard someone inhale a small gasp—"and I'm fairly certain they were in on Kronos's plan to keep this all a secret until they had a better understanding of things."

A rebuttal was anticipated, but none of them questioned him, not even Gunner. The only query came from Alexia, who stepped up alongside him and Astrid, trying to name who was who, but without much knowledge of them, they didn't get very far.

The ten of them began to wander through the drafty house as a group, stepping in and out of empty rooms and trying to remember how Heath's drawing had compared to the blueprint copies he got his hands on from city hall days later. They made their way upstairs, which Kai and Alexia hadn't gotten a good look at between the uneasiness from the dumbwaiter and the sun setting. Massive bedroom after massive bedroom lined the hallway, and the girls took turns arguing over who was getting which. Dawn stayed close to Damon. Every once in a while, when a step creaked or a floorboard shifted under their weight, she'd reflexively grab his forearm.

"Kronos said they have to find our … what did he say?" Kai looked between the group.

Alexia answered before he could. "Coffers. They're small boxes that hold valuables, like a chest or a safe."

"And … our … *powers* are inside them?" Gunner questioned.

He still doesn't believe this is happening. God, I wish we could watch the press conference somehow.

"That's what Kronos said," Astrid answered.

She looks tired. Confused maybe. Definitely lost in thought. I wonder if … ah shit. She knows something. Hanna June was right.

Before Damon could begin to form an idea of what to say to her, the words were coming out of his mouth, and everyone was looking at him, Hanna June the most intently. "Astrid, what are you thinking?"

She looked up at him, blinking more than necessary, her expression not entirely readable. Was she scared? Or just exhausted? He wasn't sure.

"Nothing," was all she said. Her gaze stayed glued to him, but he could tell that she was aware of the other eight Olympians watching her.

"If you know something, we really need to hear it. We need to all be on the same page."

Several beats passed before Astrid opened her mouth. "Let's go sit," she suggested and took off for a room down the hall they'd passed through earlier, which was significantly warmer than the others.

They sat on the floor in a circle, the muffled noises from the crowd outside barely audible now. Several times, a tree branch scratched the window from the spring breeze, and finally, Astrid began to talk.

"I grew up on sets. I didn't really go to school until I was, like, eight, and I had a few nannies who took care of me."

Damon had never heard this, but knowing her father had been a major celebrity heartthrob in the '80s and her mother hadn't been in the picture, he thought it made a lot of sense.

"There were three women who would sort of watch me in rotations. They used to tell me stories. Stories I never heard of anywhere else. You know, I could never find them in a fairy-tale book. Once I started school, everyone seemed to know all the same legends and fantasies, and the ones I'd been taught weren't even close to the ones my classmates knew. I guess I just forgot about them eventually because I stopped hearing them and never shared them with anyone else since no one ever knew what I was talking about. But lately ... I don't know ... I guess I've just been remembering them."

Dawn shifted closer to Damon as Amber leaned forward, propping her elbows on the floor and resting her chin on her palm. "I want to hear the stories."

"Me too," Alexia agreed.

As some of the others nodded, Astrid took a breath. "So, they told me a long time ago, the planet used to be ruled by gods and goddesses. They had distinct domains and parts of life they were in control of, and the humans on the earth worshipped them. Different religions would come into the world, and as the primary faith shifted and morphed over time, the gods who took the seats of power changed. Usually, the gods who had previously been there still had followers, but they no longer had sole control over the planet since a new theology was what most humans believed in. Then, when Christianity stepped onto the scene, all the gods belonging to polytheistic religions were no longer paid much attention to. But they were gods—they couldn't die, and they literally didn't have anywhere else to go. So, they just stayed up in the heavens and hung out.

"My nannies would each go off into varying details and tell slightly different versions of that, but what always stayed the same was how the Greek gods realized the Roman gods were becoming the new religion that the mortals honored and they knew they'd be losing their places of power. So, what they did was …" Astrid took a breath and glanced around the room, as if to make sure no one else was listening. As if the house didn't make some sort of sound every time any of them took a breath.

"They promised the mortals that they would never try to overthrow them because they knew that the whole reason they had gotten to establish themselves as the greatest rulers of their time was because of the mortals believing in them and worshipping them. So, they took … a rather significant part—from what Miss Bernadette used to say—of their powers and conjured up small boxes. Each was made out of thin air, right in front of the humans, and each was designed to match the god it belonged to. Then, they gave the boxes—coffers—to a group of humans who praised them, like a cult of theirs, and told them to hide them. They used to tell me that the earth was littered with the powers of the gods, and someday, if the gods ever returned, should they each open their own coffer, their powers would be instantly reinstated, and their divine beings would restored. They said that if all twelve of the gods could manage to do that, their powers would come back tenfold, and they'd be able to rule for as long as they wished."

Chapter 17

ALEXIA

A MIGRAINE WAS SETTLING IN. *Trixie was right. Well, she was a little bit off, but she was close. Closer than I was.*

Rubbing her temple and knowing it wasn't going to do anything helpful, Alexia pinched her eyes shut. As if not seeing it—the house, the Olympians, the blatant truth sitting right in front of her—would make it easier to digest.

"So, wait, let me get this straight. We—*the* reincarnated Greek gods and goddesses, specifically the Olympians—are expected to take over and rule the world once we scavenge the entirety of the planet, to find these tiny little boxes that might or might not still exist so we can restore our superpowers … is that right?"

Gunner grunted.

"They told me they still existed—that they'd last through any and all disasters and couldn't be destroyed. They were supposed to be indestructible," Astrid said, some sense of calm returning to her voice. *Well, that makes one of us.*

Kai had jumped up from his spot at Astrid's first mention of the word *coffer* and had been pacing the room since. Dawn had recently joined him and was nibbling at her fingernails. Zach was leaning back, his gaze at the ceiling, with his lips moving, as if talking to himself, but Alexia, who sat next to him, couldn't hear anything coming out. Amber hadn't blinked in an alarmingly long time, and

Gunner was shaking his head in disbelief and refused to make eye contact with anyone. Hanna June and Damon were in a staring contest, apparently. That had seemed to be happening a lot lately, and she did not care for it.

Heath was gone. She hadn't even seen him leave the room, and no sounds came echoing down the hall so as to give away his whereabouts.

Without any warning, a yell grew from outside. Screams and shouts erupted as the group ran over to the windows in time to see a car pull up, slowly making its way through the fans—which now had to have amassed several thousand people—and stopping in front of the gates. Rhianne climbed out and was pulled inside by two large security guards. The property was covered in them now.

Not quite running down the front walk, she clutched her clipboard and made her way to the front of the house as the Olympians flew down the stairs.

Heath was at the door before the rest of them, and she let them all get out their questions, one on top of another, before simply raising her hands.

"Let's go sit," she said calmly despite the sweat outlining her hairline.

Wall mounts, which had been empty during their exploration of the house, now each held a candlestick, lighting aflame as Rhianne strode down the hallway past them. Double doors toward the south end of the house gently swung open as they neared, and what appeared inside now was not how it had been when the ten of them ventured in earlier.

The sitting room had been completely empty not an hour ago. But now … well, now, it looked like a display in a furniture store. Upholstered sofas and squishy armchairs lined the room with small tables and plants scattered around. More candles were lit in the holders, and a fire crackled in the fireplace that had just been sooty and abandoned. Pastel-colored paintings hung on the walls, and the windows were framed with neutral-toned curtains.

Nobody sat. The Olympians all spun around, glancing at the walls and gaping open-mouthed at the furnishings, evidently thinking the same thing.

Rhianne didn't seem to notice as she took a seat in the highest-backed chair and watched them all.

Shuffling footsteps sounded from down the hall before a small girl appeared. She smiled politely at them all, giving Alexia the feeling that she knew her from somewhere.

"Should I bring the—"

"No, Zoey, just tea will be fine," Rhianne answered her.

Hanna June put herself into their conversation, thankfully asking the question Alexia was about to bring up. "Can I actually get coffee?"

"Me too, please," she said, and the girl took everyone's orders.

Shifting into a comfier position, sinking in the cushions, Alexia wrapped herself in a blanket and asked Rhianne in a gentle voice what was going on.

She smiled apologetically at them all as she spoke. "This was not meant to happen like this for you all. The plan was to get the world to fall in love with you, which has so far proven to be extremely easy. Humans love you, which we figured might happen, but it's been incredibly reassuring to have it confirmed. After we identified all twelve of you and hopefully had at least some leads on your coffers, we aimed to let you in on the real plan. You were never supposed to be blindsided like this, and for that, I apologize."

"Okay, but how? How are we them? When Kronos told us this, that was it—he didn't give us much reason to believe it, even though we did. He didn't let us ask any questions 'cause he said he'd explain everything. Except now all this has happened and we still know nothin'!" Hanna June rapid-fired at her.

All valid, but a little aggressive with the tone. Which, actually, is also valid.

"There was a war. A long time ago, the gods belonging to Greek mythology were evicted from the heavens. They battled against forces they couldn't identify and fought hard, but ultimately, when you don't know who your enemy is, it can be hard to take them down," she explained, giving another sad smile. "Deities from many other religions fought alongside them, sacrificing themselves, but in the end, they were ambushed and could not defeat the being that had forced them out of Mount Olympus.

"With no suitable place to reside and unable to conjure a human form without the full strength of their powers—as they reside in your individual coffers—the souls of the gods wandered around the closest space to them, some for longer than others. When the time came that a new body was available that would appropriately suit them, the soul inhabited the body … in each of you."

It was only about four seconds of uneasy silence that passed before Gunner's voice broke through. "We've had the souls of gods living inside us the whole time we've been alive?"

Rhianne nodded. "Except for perhaps the very first few seconds, yes, Gunner, you have."

The girl Rhianne had addressed as Zoey returned carrying a massive tray covered in mugs, passing a drink to each of them. Alexia watched as Astrid glanced inside her cup, sniffed it, took a small sip, and raised her eyebrows in satisfaction. She raised it again and gulped at her drink.

Whatever blend was in Alexia's was fantastic. She downed half of it, feeling it spread through her body and warm her up the same way alcohol did, but this just made her feel *good*. Alert and happy with her senses dramatically heightened. The colors in the room were suddenly brighter, the flowers in the vases littered around the room gave off light scents, and the couch felt softer underneath her.

"So," Zach began, still inspecting the drink Zoey had handed to him, "what about the whole *ten of us, twelve of them* thing?"

"Dawn and Damon were never meant to stay since Hestia and Hades weren't Olympians. We had the idea that we could use them as placeholders until we found the rest of you, but it's unlikely that will happen. Phoebe, who you will all meet shortly, claims it won't. And, as the Titan goddess of prophecy and intellect, she's always right."

Amber's voice piped up—soothed over from how scratchy it had been earlier, thanks to her tea or whatever was in her cup. "What happens when I leave?"

Another somber closed-mouthed smile came from Rhianne as she answered her, "You aren't leaving, sweetheart."

Auburn locks cascaded over her shoulder as she cocked her head. "Yes, I am. It's in my contract," she argued back as politely as she could, though the anxiety was rising in her voice. Hanna June scooted closer to her.

Rhianne grimaced before answering her, "There's a clause toward the end, stating you're signed onto the show as long as it exists, just like everyone else's. I'm so sorry, Amb—"

"No!" Her voice came out loud and shaky, bouncing off the walls of the room and echoing down the empty hallways. "No, no, okay? You're lying. You have to be. My father had his lawyers review that contract multiple times. There's no way they would've missed that, and the second you people give me my phone back, I'm going to call him and prove that you're wrong!"

Rhianne's lips pinched together, and Alexia swore her eyes glistened for a moment. "It was your father's idea to put it in there. He knew you'd never agree to stay on past your graduation date, and we anticipated it going on much longer than that."

Amber's eyes really were a very pretty shade of green—it was just a shame that they were only as massive as they were because she was utterly horror-struck. They all were. She gripped Hanna June's hand at the same time her blonde cohort erupted.

"You tricked her? What the hell? You can't do that! She's a fuckin' adult!"

"Kronos approached her father about the best way to get her to agree to the show, and seeing as he knows her best, we went with his suggestion," she gently explained.

Alexia chimed in now, anger bubbling up inside her for Amber. She'd always been so nice to her, to everyone. She didn't deserve this—to be crying on a chaise that had somehow been conjured out of thin air, her handsshaking profusely as she clung to Hanna June's manicured one. "But you led her to believe that she *would be* leaving in a few months—by the end of the year! What if she'd made plans? What if she'd applied to jobs or internships? You can't mess with someone's timeline, with their life plan, like that!"

"You know what it is? It's unethical. What's in the rest of our contracts, huh? Other clauses an' shit we don't know about? You said we'd be doin' this for years? I'm fine with that, but Lord knows most of the rest of 'em aren't!" Hanna June gestured to the other Olympians in the room.

Dawn was doing her best to calm Amber down while Damon, Kai, and Gunner had all resorted to pacing the length of the room. Zach had scooted to the edge of his chair and was taking a sip of his drink every two seconds while Astrid twirled her hair around her fingers—it was bright blue and pin straight today. Heath had moved himself closer to Rhianne and was trying to barter Amber's exit from the show in a polite manner. Alexia knew it wouldn't work.

Hanna June's voice was the one that stuck out over the rest of the noise in the room. "How can you just take time away from her like that? From all of us? This is gon' be years we can't get back!"

A half second of silence presented itself, and Rhianne did not hesitate in grabbing it. "You'll have all the time you could ask for," she said. Ten heads turned to her, confusion on their faces. "Gods are immortal. Well, that is, once we make you immortal," she added like it was an afterthought.

As if on cue, a small gasp sounded through the chaos from the front of the room. Eleven heads turned to catch small little Zoey, her eyes just as wide as Amber's had been before they began pouring out tears.

"Zoey?" Rhianne asked, eyeing her skeptically.

"I—no, no … no. I, um …"

Her gaze ping-ponged frantically between the empty tray in her hands and the collection of oversize teacups she'd just passed out. With the exception of the mugs she'd handed to the eldest two Olympians, the rest had taken at least a sip from theirs. Astrid's and Zach's appeared empty from where Alexia was sitting, and hers wasn't far behind.

"Zoey?" Rhianne asked a second time, alarm running through her tone.

"I, um …" She swallowed down hard before picking up her head. "It was a mistake, Your Majesty! I didn't mean to! I—well, you see, I had prepared it beforehand! I must have forgotten—"

"What is going on?" Damon interjected her panicked ramblings.

Ignoring him, Rhianne pressed Zoey. Alexia couldn't help but think that she didn't look old enough to even be in high school. "Please, Zoey, please tell me you didn't—"

"I did, Your Majesty. It was an accident though! I never would have—"

Damon erupted, depicting a brash resemblance to Kronos that morning. "WHAT THE HELL IS GOING ON?!"

A sigh left Rhianne's mouth as Zoey dropped her head and turned to leave. Alexia thought she heard her sniffling.

"She accidentally made you all immortal."

Part II

Unexpected Isolation

This Is Not a Joke: Olympian Edition

by Samara Connors

Make sure you're sitting down, boys, girls, and however else you may identify.

I'm sure you've seen the news. If you're a person on this planet, I can guarantee you have.

But, of course, I have an inside scoop.

Let's start with what we know. Hundreds of fan theories surrounding the Olympians came out, tracking back as early as mid-November. Most of them suggested that the "scholarship" they all attended Olympia College on—aka OC—had actually been designed specifically for them.

Many of these suggestions also centered around the idea that our six new favorite people were all "something else"—whether it was time travelers, extraterrestrials, or divine beings. I think it's safe to say that we all had our suspicions, even if it was just for shits and giggles.

But then, earlier this year, four new members joined, and certain theses clicked into place just *that* much more—which, yes, got more fun to think about and fantasize over … but also made things a lot weirder.

Less than a week ago, those silly Tumblr ideas were confirmed, and because of that, the world as we know it has forever changed.

In a now-deleted video, the show's creator and producer, Dwayne Kronos, could be seen speaking with one of his supposed Parthenon colleagues, who we've only been able to identify simply as Phoebe. (I assume Phoebe is another god, and I guess they don't need last names.)

Although any and all traces of the video have been scrubbed from the World Wide Web, I managed to transcribe it before it disappeared, and it reads as follows:

Kronos: They still don't believe.

Phoebe: Of course they don't. You upended the lives they'd lived up until now and told them the world they'd always known wasn't actually how it should be.

Kronos: What should I do?

Phoebe: Keep treating them the way you have. Train then, educate them, prepare them. They need to be ready for when the world finds out because they'll need to show they are who we've said they are—in a peaceful way.

Kronos: I know, I know.

Phoebe: The humans suspect it anyway. They're smarter than we give them credit for.

Kronos: What if they're not ready when the time comes?

Phoebe: Once they're fully awake, everything will make sense. It'll come to them. If they choose to accept their true beings, they won't fail.

Kronos: I just don't understand why some of them are making it this difficult. What human wouldn't want to be a god?

As it comes from the man in charge himself, there's no denying it.

If you were crowded around the Olympia City Library approximately seven hours before the video made its way onto just about every single social media outlet, like I was, you might've heard the thunderous roar from the man—and OC alum—we all have to thank for *The Olympians*, demanding his stars divulge who had leaked the news that ten college students were actually gods.

Joke's on you, Kronos. Happy April Fools' Day.

MAY 3, 2015, VOLUME 10

Fact: Life as We Know It Is Over

By Samara Connors

I grew up in a Christian household. We went to church most Sundays, we prayed before meals—even in restaurants, thanks to my dad—and never missed an Easter sunrise service.

As I got older, I began to dive more deeply into my faith and spirituality. I think that's part of growing up that a lot of people go through. Some rip away from everything they were once taught, much to their parents' dismay. Others become more in touch with the religion they've always known. And lots of people end up somewhere in the middle: wanting—nay, *needing*—to believe in something because the idea that nobody is out there listening is just too daunting and leaves you feeling helpless, but also not wanting to put too much faith in something you can't see or prove is on the receiving end of your prayers and wishes and hopes and dreams.

Well, lucky for literally everyone on the planet, we no longer have to tread out in unknown waters. No, now we have ten gods ... in the form of college students. Well, technically, most of them are dropouts, according to recent student records I stumbled upon, but still.

It's terrifying, and no part of it seems real, so let's just dive right on in.

The cast of the insta-worldwide phenomenon *The Olympians*, are actually gods. The Greek gods, to be specific. The Greek Olympian gods, to be even more specific. Like ... *duh*.

Immediately, the questions posed are things like: Do they control the world? Should we be praying to them? How do we *know* they're gods? Basically, everything we thought we knew is different. But is it? That last question is my favorite and one I ask myself daily. Because how do we know? How did they know? Why are some people so quick to believe this group of people we've been obsessing over on our screens for the last several months actually are divine beings while others simply refuse to accept it?

My parents called me up as soon as they heard the news. They're nonbelievers, which is okay. On the other end of the spectrum, all my friends at Olympia latched right on to the idea.

Now, hours after the news broke, the man responsible for making The Olympians known to the world, Dwayne Kronos, held a press conference, which was ultimately ... well, chaotic. Which tracks for the vibe of his show.

The point he must've reiterated fifteen times was that he wanted everyone to carry on with their lives as they had before and that nothing was changing at the moment. He did not directly answer questions as to *if* there'd be changes in the future, but I think it's safe to say that if we have actual gods who can control the weather and homelessness and poverty, things are going to change.

I'd like to say a big, personal thank you to the guy who asked if they had any special powers or abilities. Kronos laughed it off, saying that they didn't, but I think that's a lie—as do plenty of other people intently waiting for one of them to breathe fire or lift a piano over their head.

The most popular thing brought up during the conference was the announcement of Olympia Con! A full weekend in Los Angeles with the Olympians sitting on panels and attending meet and greets, and while he didn't promise anything, Kronos mentioned the possibility of some sort of demonstration—hmm, wonder what that might be.

As far as how they actually ended up here, it is still very much a mystery, one we'll hopefully uncover at Olympia Con in three weeks. I have VIP passes, so I'll be taking in every sound bite I can get, just to spit them back out at you, OC.

Every single person has unanswered questions right now, and it's looking like we won't be getting any information until the event at the end of the month—maybe not even then. No one has heard from the Olympians ever since the day the news broke and they were whisked away to that massive plantation house behind campus, off of Front Street and Water Street. It's said it has ties to ancient Greece, and there's an exhibit about it in the Olympia County History Museum that's been getting quite a lot of traction over the last few weeks.

We're told the event will be aired, so for those million or so of you who weren't able to snag a ticket, you'll still get to see what happens in those chaotic-as-hell seventy-two hours. Which is much deserved since we haven't had any new *Olympians* content this year.

All I know is, Olympia Con will be epic. Hopefully, we'll gain some insight as to what's really going on because I, for one, feel like, after being told that gods walk among us, we kind of deserve it.

Chapter 18

ALEXIA, HEATH, AND DAMON SHARE an annoyed glance as a bass line thumps louder and louder from outside. *The rest of the Olympians are sprawled out across the patio, very drunk off of an ambrosia-wine mixture Zach convinced Zoey to secretly make for them while the Titans are away.*

Alexia: [*appears on the terrace, clearly pissed off*] Can you guys please keep it down? We're trying to study!

Gunner: [*yells over his shoulder to her*] Not our fault y'all stayed in school.

Kai: [*very drunk*] Fuck yeah, college-dropout life!

Hanna June: Why don't y'all use the other study? That way, you can't hear us.

Alexia: Because that one's closer to the kitchen, and you can just hear that stupid dumbwaiter moving *all the time*.

Amber: I wish we could get in.

Alexia: Well, until someone figures out where to get coins from the ancient world that are no longer made, we have no chance of that. [*goes back inside*]

Heath: What did they say?

Alexia: They're all different kinds of intoxicated, so nothing helpful. I wish they could've put up some sort of soundproof barrier …

Heath: Still can't believe they're as wasted as they are. That wine had to be from the last time people lived here.

Alexia: Well, the alcohol content of wine doesn't change past the fermentation process, so they're as drunk now as they would've been had they had it, say, twenty years ago.

Heath: [*watches her*] You know so many things.

Alexia: [*shrugs*] I read a lot. It's likely that it tasted like vinegar, but I doubt they noticed since—

Heath: Everything tastes weird now.

The group watches Amber very seriously scold a lemon tree for not releasing enough oxygen and then collapsing in a fit of giggles, telling the plant she was only joking.

Damon: Maybe we *should* move into the other room …

Alexia: [*slams a hand down on the books she's holding*] No! No, I can't listen to it. My room is right above it and I hear it all night long— the tapping against the door and the walls, the pulleys we can't even see squeaking as it moves. Why is it moving? Why? We're not there because we can't get there! So why is it moving?

Heath: [*steps toward her and gently places his hands on her shoulders*] Okay, okay, deep breaths. No more coffee for you today—maybe the rest of the week.

Alexia: [*pushes his hands off and slumps down into her chair, letting out a sigh*] Thanks, but you're not Dawn.

Damon: [*grunts*]

Heath: [*to Damon*] We all miss her.

Alexia: She's off saving the world, and really, can you blame her? She's doing more than the rest of us to build up the humans' trust.

Damon: Well, that's because Kronos won't let us do anything.

Alexia: True. Which is why it's important that we support her, even if we have to do it silently instead of grumbling that she got to leave when none of the rest of us did.

Damon: [*shakes his head*] I can't believe I didn't think to have that addendum in my contract.

Heath: We all would've liked to have something like that in ours.

Alexia: Except the blonde twins out there. [*gestures to Zach and Hanna June, who are laughing hysterically and drunkenly leg wrestling in the grass*]

Heath: At least she's in a good mood.

Damon: For now.

Heath: Hopefully, it'll last longer than two days this time.

Damon: Doubtful.

Alexia: Well, aside from them, none of us want this to go on any longer than it has to.

Heath: And Astrid.

Alexia: [*faces him, confused*] I thought you didn't like her? You were so glad when Rhianne said they would announce that your—and I hate this word—*faux-lationship* ended.

Heath: No, I *am* glad it's over! God, the whole thing was so stupid anyway. I'm just … ugh, I don't know. I guess I'm just mad I had to waste time on the whole thing. Plus, like, how does that make me look?

Damon: Why are you so worried about it?

Heath: [*snaps his head to face him*] No one. I mean, nothing. Nothing. No reason.

Damon: What's her name?

Heath: [*gives him an annoyed look*] Emma.

Alexia: [*a huge smile spreads across her face*] Really? That's so exciting!

Heath: Well, yeah, I guess. But she's hesitant to, like, even go out with me because she thinks I'm not her type. Because that [*gestures to Astrid, who's prancing around the lawn in her bikini, trying to find the best lighting for a selfie*] is all she's seen me with.

Damon: If you like her, just keep trying. You'll be fine.

Alexia: Speaking of, uh, significant others [*subtly nods in Gunner's direction*]—is he gonna be okay?

Heath: [*lets out a big sigh and walks away from the French doors*] No idea. He's still in denial.

Damon: Well then, he's in for a brutal awakening in a few weeks.

Alexia: A few weeks? I didn't know it was that soon!

Damon: I think she's due, like, right after we get back from Olympia Con.

Alexia: [*lets out a horrible noise*] Aghhhh, I don't want to go to that. We're all going to look so stupid, getting up there and having no proof that we're *them*, and they're going to riot, and then someone's going to do something—I don't know what, but something dangerous—and it'll ricochet off of us, and they'll all freak out because, suddenly, we should be dead, but we're not, and that'll just terrify them all *more* because they don't know we're immortal because we're not supposed to be, and—

Heath: [*crouches in front of her and lightly grabs her wrists to stop her arms from their flailing motion*] No. More. Coffee.

Chapter 19

AMBER

"Just tell me."

"No."

"Fleur, come on."

"Fine, but you have to tell me who's making *you* smile all stupid at your phone, then too. And you have to go first." Her little sister smiled at her, knowing she had backed her into a corner.

Amber's mouth mashed together in a tight line. *Dammit.* "Okay, fine. I'll leave you alone." Fleur shrugged proudly and did a little dance as she backed away from Amber. "But I'll find out who it is! Whether you tell me or not."

"Oh, I don't doubt it," Fleur agreed, coming over to press a kiss into her hair.

After Fleur unpacked her bags, the girls left the guest cottage and made their way past the greenhouse and onto the terrace. The doors on the second-story balcony were left wide open to let the early May breeze blow through the house, leaving the curtains fluttering in the wind. It was no secret Amber missed her childhood home the most, but the Athanasios Plantation was much homier than her family's Charleston house had ever been—at least to her. She missed having her apartment, a space just for herself—not that she was alone much, but the waterfront mansion made the most sense. And when she wanted alone time, she could just go out to the greenhouse or downstairs to the conservatory. After all, she was really the only one who visited them. Amber liked to think that Dawn would've accompanied her occasionally, if she were here. They all missed her, even Gunner, though he'd never admit it.

Fleur was going through Amber's closet when the girls heard the noises. First the footsteps thundering across the patio, followed by soft, heavy sobs. They grew louder and louder, floating up the stairs toward the balcony. With Amber's room being at the end—mainly so she could just peek out her window and have a view of her "domain," as Rhianne had put it—she was able to peer out and see the source. Alarm flooded through her as she tore away from the window seat and booked it to her doorway. If Amber grabbed her in time, she could prevent the hallway camera from recording her meltdown.

Pounding footsteps broke out into a run just as Amber reached the doorframe and pulled at Hanna June's wrist, yanking her inside. Her face was covered in tear streaks, her hair matted to her face. It was the kind of cry that had snot coming out of her little nose. Her chest heaved, and she gasped for air as Amber sat her down on the edge of the bed.

Her sobs came out harder and louder, and Amber feared the other Olympians would hear her. Amber didn't want that, and she felt as though Hanna June wouldn't either.

Before she could ask herself, *What would Dawn do?* Fleur was gently leading HJ into the closet. She waved for Amber to join them, indicating to her older sister to shut the door behind her and to turn off the light as she guided the embodiment of Hera to sit down on the floor.

There, in the darkness, she continued to cry, but only for another minute or so. Her wails seemed to fade away into the abyss as they sat cross-legged on the warped hardwood, and soon, there was nothing coming out, aside from the occasional sniffle. Amber thought she inhaled the faintest scent of lavender, but before she could ask Fleur if she'd placed a few sprigs from the garden in her closet—because that made sense—Hanna June's voice came through the darkness.

It was raspy and defeated as she said, "He cheated on me."
Oh.
Oh.
Oh dear.

What do I say? We all know he cheats on her. I've told her to leave him a dozen and a half times, and she just says that she can't. Which … is true. She really can't. Who signs their child into an arranged marriage anyway?

But, seriously, what do I say? Does she mean she caught him? Oh God …

Why? Why did this have to happen now? Everything had been going so right. She'd been a wreck at first, but the last few weeks were so good, for all of us, but especially for her.

Of course he had to ruin it.

"I went to go ask Fleur 'bout somethin', and I thought she was in the cottage next to Damon's, but apparently not 'cause *he* was in there with some girl."

A groan sounded from Fleur, who was just a faint head near Amber. Her eyes were starting to adjust, and she could see Hanna June had pulled her knees up to her chest and propped her chin right on top. She looked exhausted and so, so broken—the exact opposite of the queen of the heavens.

"I don't think he even knew I was there. I saw them through the window as I walked up. And I watched! I just froze, and I stood there and watched 'em!" Her words came out as a barking laugh, quickly turning into another strangled sob, and Amber and Fleur let her cry.

Notes of lavender became present for a second time, and once HJ calmed down again, she whispered, "I can't leave. I had my contracts—both of 'em"—she let out another sad laugh—"reviewed by four different lawyers to see if there were any kind of loopholes, just outta curiosity after Dawn, and nothin'. Absolutely nothin' I can do about anythin'."

"What if you tell Kronos?" Fleur's voice squeaked out hesitantly, like she knew it was a stupid suggestion, but couldn't think of anything else to say.

And judging by HJ's laugh, she thought the same thing. "You know what he'll tell me? He'll say it's in his nature. That Zeus cheated on Hera *all the time*. That it's just the way he is or somethin' like that."

Amber saw her close her eyes and gently shake her head as a tear rolled down her cheek.

The girls stayed on the floor in Amber's closet in the dark and let the calming scent fill the space for the rest of the afternoon. None of them had any idea how much time had passed when they heard a knock on the bedroom door. Amber excused herself, and very quietly, so as not to draw any attention, she stepped out into her bedroom and silently shut the closet door behind her.

Zoey was standing at the door. "Miss Amber," she greeted her, presenting her with the contents of the tray.

"Thanks, Zoey," she said, removing the plate.

"Are you aware of Miss Hanna June's whereabouts? I can't seem to find her anywhere," Zoey asked her, peering out onto the balcony.

"I'll find her. Is this one hers?"

Amber took Hanna June's ration, and Zoey left, skipping down the hall.

With both platters, as quietly as she could, she retreated back toward the hideout they'd established. Fleur edged the door open, taking HJ's ornate little plate and teacup and passing it to her.

The Olympian girls took a bite of their ambrosia and sipped at their nectar-filled mugs as Fleur gazed longingly at them.

"I wish I could have some."

"Kronos said no," Amber reminded her, not caring how annoyed she sounded.

Fleur whined about not being allowed to consume the celestial treats of the gods every single time she saw Amber have hers. Now that they were down to a once-a-week regimen, it was definitely less often. The timing had been unfortunate when the Olympians first started taking it two months ago.

After the secret came out, Zoey had taken it upon herself to prematurely fill their drinks with nectar before Rhianne told her not to. Amid the chaos and confusion, she had forgotten to remove it and accidentally begun their immortalization process. Kronos had been furious initially, but had given the go-ahead for them to continue consuming it.

This way, if things got really far out of hand with the mortals and they tried to take down one of the Olympians, they'd remain unharmed. However, this meant they were sipping nectar and chewing away at ambrosia clusters three times a day, every seven days now. They could have mortal food, but nothing tasted right to them anymore. Kronos had told them this would likely change over the course of several months, but Amber really just wanted carbs.

As her dad was traveling for work, he hadn't taken Fleur's living place into consideration when he sold the Charleston house. Amber had promptly moved her into one of the guest cottages on the plantation, but with Fleur still needing to be glued to Damon's side, she would enviously witness "feeding time," as they all called it, begging Kronos, Rhianne, Zoey—really anyone—to give her some. They never obliged.

She let out a scoff and crossed her arms. "You guys are so lucky you get to be immortal."

Daggers shot out of Hanna June's eyes. "Yeah, we're so lucky we get to live forever, and nobody trusts us, and we don't have any powers, and we have to have our meals delivered to us like we're animals in a zoo."

Chapter 20

GUNNER

STANDING IN FRONT OF THE mirror, he stared back at his reflection. His new shoulder tattoo looked good. No one had even noticed he'd snuck out to Ink Injector or that he had been gone for four hours.

Well, except Astrid. But he'd made it up to her.

He'd slipped into her room across the hall the second he was back in the house. She was taking a bath with her headphones on and never even heard him sneak into her room. He started stripping down before she sensed the presence of another person and was just taking his pants off from where they'd dropped around his ankles when she saw him. After wordlessly scooping her up, he pinned her against the glass door on the shower, balanced her on top of his thighs, and slid right in—no foreplay, no warm-up. He had texted her when he was on the way back from downtown and told her to be ready for him. Maybe she had thought he was kidding—he was not.

A knock sounded from the entrance of his room and he was begrudgingly pulled from his memory of her.

It was Heath.

No, thank you.

"Hey, I've, uh—I've been looking for you," he managed to get out, making broken eye contact in the process.

They never talked. They hadn't before this all blew up and their seemingly never-ending quarantine began, and Gunner didn't feel the need for that to change. Even if Heath seemed adamant to do just that.

"Why?"

Now he looked up, locked right on to Gunner's gaze. "You know why."

Not inviting him in still, he replied, "You're wasting your time."

"Wasting my—you're wasting your own time!" Heath pushed off the doorframe, but still did not step inside. "This is happening, whether you want to accept it or not. And the thing is, if you *don't*, you're gonna hate yourself for it, *and* literally everyone in the world will see you as a shitty father. Because that's how your life is now. Maybe a few months ago, you could've pretended this wasn't happening, that it wasn't your life, but it is. They're gonna interview her as soon as they can, and if you're not there, you will have made yourself the world's shittiest dad. Even if there are other guys who are worse, it'll always be you because of who you are. You'll be the forever poster child of being an absent, ignorant parent."

The deodorant he'd been holding left his hand and flew across the room, smashing into the wall display he hadn't even wanted. Apparently, with enough force and anger behind it, a small plastic container could shatter a mirror. Who knew?

"Don't fuckin' talk to me like that! Who the fuck do you think you are? My own father doesn't even talk to me that way!"

"Which is why someone needs to," Heath spit back at him before turning on his heel and storming out, leaving Gunner both pissed off and guilty with glass shards littered all over the floor.

He stalked over to it and looked down at the few dozen splintered versions of himself staring back up at him, knowing that, even if he gripped the little weapons hard enough, no blood would come out of his body. Not anymore.

Chapter 21

AFTER A DAY OF RESEARCHING, reading, and learning in one of the libraries, Astrid walks in. Letting out an overexaggerated sigh and sinking onto one of the leather couches, she waits for Alexia to ask her what's wrong. However, Alexia doesn't. So, Astrid sighs again. This pattern continues four times before Alexia slams her hand down on her book and erupts, her uber-productive day coming to an early close.

Alexia: What do you need, Astrid?

Astrid: Someone to talk to.

Alexia: And that person has to be me? I'm a little busy.

Astrid: [*peers up at the stack of books Alexia has amassed on the desk*] With what? Aren't finals almost over?

Alexia: I still have two more, and *this* is actually research for everything you told us.

Astrid: That was, like, two months ago. Aren't you done reading books by now?

Alexia: There are three libraries here, Astrid. I haven't even gone up to the one on the third floor yet. And putting together everything you and Rhianne shared that day—there's a lot of information to piece together. Like, *a lot*.

Astrid: About the boxes?

Alexia: They're coffers, but also everything about the battle and displacement of the gods. I'm trying to map out possible locations where the coffers might be, based on where other ancient Greek artifacts have been found and other notable places from the time period. It's the only thing I can really work off of since the war doesn't seem to be documented anywhere. Which isn't surprising, but it *is* incredibly frustrating since—

Astrid: Listen, do you wanna have a spa day?

Alexia: [*sighs as she goes back to her book*] No, Astrid, I don't want to have a spa day.

Astrid: Please! We've never hung out! [*pouts*]

Alexia: [*looks up at her slowly, considers the offer for a moment, then slides a bookmark into* The Isles of Ancient Greece, *and closes the book*] You know what? Sure. Let's have a spa day.

In Astrid's bathroom, Alexia finds herself given a foot mask, a manicure, and, somehow, highlights. As Astrid gives herself a pedicure, Alexia applies a face mask carefully, making sure to not disturb any of the foil in her hair.

Alexia: You know, we all thought you were just dyeing your hair, like, every other day.

Astrid: [*smirks*] And if we hadn't all been forced to move in together and Amber hadn't walked in on me arranging my wig wall, you all still would!

Alexia: You have so many ... [*peers out of the bathroom and into her bedroom to stare at the display*]

Astrid: Thirty-seven.

Alexia: Oh my gosh. [*points at the walls in Astrid's bathroom*] What's with all the magazines on the walls?

Astrid: They're all different Playboy covers.

Alexia: And the giant blank spot in the middle?

Astrid: That's where my cover's gonna go one day—if we ever get out of this house.

Alexia: We have Olympia Con soon.

Astrid: [*scoffs*] Psh, yeah. We're gonna be trailed around by security; they'll be at every doorway, outside our suites, and we'll still be on lockdown.

Alexia: It's just until things settle down.

Astrid: The others think that most of them who don't believe just hate us. But I don't think that. I think they're scared of us, which makes sense if you think about it. They think we're frauds—that's the problem. We need to show them that we're exactly who we say we are.

Alexia: [*recognizes her opportunity and seizes it*] So ... I've been thinking a lot about that. The easiest way to do that is to demonstrate our powers, right? Good powers, obviously. But we can't because we don't have them.

Astrid: Well, if Dawn had just opened her coffer when Kronos asked her to, we wouldn't be in this situation.

Alexia: Okay, but Dawn wants nothing to do with this show, and she had every *legal* right to walk away from it. Plus, Hestia isn't a permanent Olympian, so who knows if it actually would've worked? The humans probably would've seen through that.

Astrid: [*stares back at her, mulling over the idea*]

Alexia: Astrid, please, I need you to think really, *really* hard. Did your nannies ever say anything about where they might be?

Astrid: [*slowly shakes her head*] I don't remember them ever—

Alexia: Or, maybe, do you know where *they* might be now? If I could talk to them—

Astrid: I doubt they're even alive anymore, Lex.

Alexia: [*upset and annoyed*] It's Alexia.

Astrid: You never go by Lex?

Alexia: Never.

Astrid: What about, like, your best friends? Or your family? You have a little sister, right? What does she call you?

Alexia: Alexia.

Astrid: That's it?

Alexia: [*rolls her eyes*] Well, when we get our phones once a week, there are always texts from her, where she calls me Your Majesty just to annoy me. She called me Athena once, and I told her to never do that again.

Astrid: What? Why? I love when I get referred to as Aphrodite!

Alexia: I don't know … it's weird! I'm Alexia Ruth Chang, valedictorian, honors student, future Supreme Court judge … not Athena, Greek goddess of wisdom and battle strategy.

Astrid: [*chuckles as she gets up and begins to take the foil out of Alexia's hair*] You're gonna have to find a way to be both, babe.

Chapter 22

HANNA JUNE

A SOFT KNOCK ON HER door awoke her.

Thank God. She'd been having the same recurring nightmare for the last four days—Zach with someone else. Anyone. It didn't matter who. Sometimes, they didn't even have a face. All that really mattered was that it wasn't her.

"Hanna June? Sweetheart?" Rhianne's voice came from the other side of the massive door.

Sometimes, she pretended it was her mom calling her that way, and it usually made her feel better. But not now. Her mom was the only person she'd wanted to talk to for days, but the Olympians hadn't been allowed to have their phones yet this week.

"You can come in," she mumbled into her pillow, and the door opened gently.

No footsteps sounded as she crossed over to her bed, and HJ was glad she had adopted Amber's habit of throwing rugs down. She couldn't stand hearing Zach and Kai moving in their rooms across the hall.

Zach.

Zachary fucking Alexander.

How she hated him. And loved him. And hated that she loved him.

"Are you able to come with me for a bit?" Rhianne asked gently, lightly running her fingers over her hair.

If Hanna June couldn't see her mom, Rhianne was the next closest thing she had to a mother. Well, Amber was also a good stand-in, but she was only two years older than her, so it was a little weird. And Rhea was Hera's mother, so it made more sense anyway

"I don't want to see anyone," she answered, still not lifting her head.

"You'd just be speaking with me, Phoebe, Natasha, and of course Kronos," she told her, causing Hanna June to lift her head.

"He's back?"

"He is."

"Did he find anythin'?" she asked, hopeful he had returned with a coffer.

It didn't necessarily have to be hers, but of course she was hoping she'd get her powers first. This was primarily due to the worry—before the Zach incident—that she didn't have any special powers. It was a given that Alexia would have the ability to just *know* things, and that Kai had control over bodies of water, and Heath of volcanoes … but as she was the goddess of marriage, women, and family … what powers would that entail? She got to bless marriages? Protect women during childbirth? How was she supposed to defend herself, if she needed to, with abilities like that?

Her hopefulness faded away as the corners of Rhianne's mouth turned down.

"He did not. He's going back out searching after the convention is over though, so don't give up hope."

Too late.

HJ pushed herself up out of bed, grabbed her slippers out from under her bed, and followed Rhianne out her door. The massive staircase was directly next to her door, and she was about to begin her descent when the door across the hall flew open and a head poked out.

"HJ?"

She looked up at Zach, but ignored him and kept following Rhianne down.

He stepped out into the hallway and leaned over the balcony, still adamantly speaking to her. "Hanna June? Is everything okay?"

Rhianne stopped in front of her and looked back over her shoulder at her. Her expression had traces of concern and protection on it, and Hanna June was about to answer him when she did it for her.

"She's coming with me for a meeting."

"When will you be back? Can I talk to you later?" he asked, ignoring Rhianne.

"We're not quite sure when the meeting will be over," she answered him.

Looking up at him, she added in a slightly threatening voice, "We're gonna talk later," and then pushed past Rhianne and flew down the stairs.

The office that had been constructed on the far end of the house wasn't quite finished, but Kronos sat at the desk in the center like he was in the Oval Office, proud and distinguished, despite the unfinished walls and lighting fixtures piled up in an armchair in one corner.

The others were waiting in the room too, standing off to the sides or sitting uncomfortably in the mismatched chairs that had been brought in.

He'd had all his things from his office at Olympia College that hadn't been stolen set up—the oversize, vintage globe; the picture of the original six Olympians on the steps of the library they'd taken last semester; his diploma from Olympia, which the ten of them had suspicions wasn't real. There were a handful of other trinkets she'd never seen before around the room. Namely, a large wooden armoire, similar to a wardrobe but twice the size and with tarnished gold engravings around the edges, and a dark cabinet propped up against the wall, patiently waiting to be displayed.

"Miss Pruitt, take a seat." He gestured to the displaced patio chair across from him.

It bothered HJ how they each called the Olympians by a different version of their name. With Kronos, she'd gotten used to being Miss Pruitt, and even Rhianne had picked up on it. But when the other Titans joined the group, sometimes, it was the same way Kronos called them. Other times, they would be formally called by their first name, and every once in a while, they'd get called by their god names. HJ hadn't quite gotten used to being referred to as Hera, and she doubted she would anytime soon.

Sinking onto the wicker, she looked at Kronos. He didn't seem quite as defeated as she looked, but just as tired. She was about to ask where he'd been when he spoke.

"We know about Mr. Alexander's … mistake."

She lifted her head slowly to meet his gaze. He looked … sad? No, that couldn't be right. He was Kronos or Cronus or whatever. Unrelenting Titan god who had overthrown his own father and later eaten his children. He would never feel sad for her or anyone else. The cheery man she'd met months ago was long gone, though HJ felt as though that version of him might return at the presence of a camera. He'd been angry since the secret had gotten out, and it was likely he'd remain that way.

And yet his eyes softened around the edges as his hand stretched out across the desk toward her, and he said, "I know you want to leave."

Heavy tears immediately barreled out of her eyes and poured down her cheeks. Hanna June gripped his hand as hard as she could and resumed sobbing—like she hadn't just been bawling an hour ago—and became vaguely aware of Rhianne stroking her hair again.

They let her cry for a short time before a tapping sound pulled Hanna June from her hole of sadness. Phoebe was in front of her, leaning on her cane for support as she bent down to meet HJ's eye level.

"It will all be all right. I promise you."

As she lifted her head slowly to meet the woman's gaze, she could feel her own burning. Knowing she sounded like an adolescent in her response, she asked in a raspy, hopeless, and tired voice, "How do you know?"

The woman smiled back at her and said, "Because I know everything." It wasn't a brag as much as it was a reassurance. Then, she started to push herself up, and Natasha stepped in to steady her and guide her back to the folding camp chair behind Kronos's desk.

Hanna June turned back to Kronos. Despite desperately wanting to fall asleep, she also wanted to hash things out with someone, and if this man and his colleagues or siblings or whatever they were knew more about her life, then he might be the best one to do that with.

"I *do* want to leave, but I can't."

Pursing his lips, he nodded slowly. "That's true. But there might be something else you can do."

Scrunching up her features in confusion made her eyes burn, but she did it anyway. "What do you mean?"

"I'd like you to talk to someone," he said, folding his hands and leaning forward.

"Like a therapist?"

"Not quite."

Natasha spoke from the back corner. "Come over here." She gestured to the far wall, where the unusable cabinet stood.

After both Rhianne and Phoebe assured her it was okay to follow her, HJ got up and passed across the room, sitting cross-legged on the floor next to Natasha.

They had been twelve days into lockdown when their lives, which had all but stopped when they were forced into the house, finally restarted—but moving in a direction they'd never gone in before. Although they'd been informed they were no longer required to attend Olympia College, it was proposed to them that the schooling they'd anticipated going through would still be happening. Beginning sometime after Olympia Con, an unnamed cohort would instruct them all on the bare necessities they needed to know.

Alexia, of course, had taken it upon herself to get a head start on the materials outlined by Phoebe on that first day of their quarantine, and occasionally, Hanna June and some of the others would join her. It was kind of fun to learn about who she had been in a past life she couldn't remember; how the Titans and the Olympians had fought against each other once before, but Kronos and the other Titans were determined to make sure that didn't happen again; the Golden Age the earth had once existed in because of them ... until, that was, she remembered it was actually her life— that Hera wasn't just a goddess, but that Hanna June *was* Hera. Despite not having any abilities or a way to prove the soul of the queen goddess was alive inside her, she *was* a god.

Learning about her had been interesting and, when the family tree got involved, disgustingly complicated. Although Rhea was her birth mother, she had been raised by another Titan goddess— Tethys, whose soul now inhabited Natasha.

The two of them had spent little time together, what with Titans scouring the globe for any traces of their coffers, minus Rhianne. So, as HJ sat on the floor next to Natasha, staring at an empty antique curio cabinet, she felt slightly uncomfortable.

Even more so when Natasha turned to Hanna June and pulled a dagger out from her sleeve. As the sunlight poured in from the windows, glistening off of the weapon, she said, "Hold out your hand."

Chapter 23

[REDACTED]

This file is property of The Republic of the Last City-State. To gain access, all students are required to have completed the mandated prerequisites.

Please continue reading.

Chapter 24

A FAST WHOOSHING SOUND IS heard on the other side of the oversize armoire. Both doors fly open, and Keaton practically falls out of it, out of breath, slamming the doors shut behind him. His chest heaves as he holds up a small box.

Hanna June: Wha—wait, is that—

Kronos: Whose?

Keaton: He—Heph—it's—

Hanna June: Heath's?

Keaton: [*nods*]

Kronos: [*turns to Rhianne*] Fetch him.

Rhianne swiftly exits the room as Phoebe approaches Kronos.

Phoebe: They're children, dear. You don't fetch children.

Kronos: She knew what I meant.

Hanna June: Where did he come from?

Kronos: It's, the, um—you really shouldn't—

Phoebe: You will learn, but not right now. Promise. [*gives HJ a small smile and gently taps her cane against her foot*]

Hanna June: [*eagerly asks*] Am I allowed to stay? For Heath?

Kronos: Umm … yes, I suppose that's all right.

Natasha beckons HJ over to the basin on the counter opposite them. She walks over and hesitantly looks down at the water.

Hanna June: Wasn't that empty when I got here?

Natasha: It was. Just splash some onto your face, dear.

Hanna June: Why? What is it?

Natasha: It'll clean you up a bit. I doubt you want to explain to Heath the reasoning behind the tear streaks when he gets here.

Hanna June: [*unsure about it, but slowly leans forward over it*]

Natasha splashd up a small bit of water. It hits HJ in the face, and she stands there, shocked, as the water runs down to her chin. Instead of dripping down further, it disappears at her jawline, and her face is left smooth, dry, and glowing.
Hanna June touchs her face lightly, amazed and very, very confused, before running over to the window to look at her reflection.

Hanna June: How—how'd you do that?

Natasha: I'm the goddess of fresh water.

Hanna June: That's … *wow.* I mean, you just splashed it and—wait, where was that from?

Natasha: [*gestures toward the window*] The river, of course.

Hanna June is about to recoil in disgust when Rhianne and Heath arrive, both slightly out of breath.

Heath: Is it my box—uh, coffer? Is it mine? Did you find it?

Kronos: [*nods with a mildly amused look on his face from Hanna June and Natasha's interaction*] Keaton found it.

Heath: Where was it?

Kronos: [*tilts his head, intrigued, and turns his attention to Keaton*]

Keaton: At the base of Methana. Just like you suspected.

Kronos: Excellent. Go on, bring it forward. [*turns to Heath*] Ready, son?

Heath: [*staring wide-eyed at the coffer*] What's gonna happen?

Kronos: You'll have your powers restored, maybe establish some new ones to better fit the—

Heath: No, I mean, what's gonna happen to *me*?

Kronos: Oh. It's really not that terrible—a slight jolt, running from your fingertips up to the center of your chest. Should be over in a few seconds.

Heath: You mean, like, an electrocution? To my heart? [*looks quickly between him and HJ*] Can't I die from that?

Kronos: [*smirks at him*] Are you forgetting, Mr. Blackburn? You can't die.

Heath blinks rapidly at his words, digesting them as his gaze drops to the floor. Several long seconds tick by as his eyes search the hardwood, until he takes a step toward Keaton with his arms outstretched.

Hanna June: Wait, how do you know it's his?

Keaton: [*gently holding it out for her to see*] Do you see the inscriptions on the top? The etchings? Those were all associated with Hephaestus. I am entirely certain I've unearthed his box, to now be turned over to Heath.

Taking the box from Keaton in shaky hands, Heath stares down at it. After readjusting to hold it in one hand, he hovers his other hand over the lid. Without taking his eyes off the coffer, he opens his mouth again.

Heath: Remind me what happens if this isn't mine.

Rhianne: Absolutely nothing. Since you are a god, opening another's coffer will not affect *you* in any way, meaning you won't receive their powers or negate your chances of reestablishing your own. You won't get powers that do not rightfully belong to you, and that god who should have them won't suddenly obtain them by the wrong owner opening their coffer.

Heath: And what happens if I'm not really him? If I'm not the reincarnation of Hephaestus, god of volcanoes and metalworking and fire?

Rhianne: Nothing. Mortals cannot claim otherworldly abilities, especially not those left by an Olympian, a divine ruler of the universe.

Heath: It won't backfire on me and kill me?

Rhianne: Of course not.

Kronos: You can't die. If your soul was not truly inhabited by a god, you would never have been able to consume any amount of nectar or ambrosia. You likely wouldn't have even been able to be in the same room as the substances. But seeing as you have been consuming it for several weeks now, you've not only reignited your immortality, but you've also proven you *are* the new Hephaestus. Especially because, if you weren't, that box likely would have burned your hands off your wrists by now.

Heath: [*slowly looks up at him*]

Kronos: You are him, son. Open the coffer and remind yourself.

Heath looks back at the box, his hands still hovering over the top, and slowly lifts it.

Chapter 25

GUNNER

GUNNER STARED DOWN AT THE hole in the wall. He was going to make it. None of the others had tried brute force, which was why they were all still whining about the dumbwaiter calling to them, yet not letting them in.

Well, none of them were here to tell him no, like they'd done the twenty-something other times he'd brought it up. He'd get in; he could break through whatever magical barrier this had around it.

His knees sank slightly as he dipped into a lunge, keeping his eyes on the target. He'd removed his shoes and socks because he swore the thing could hear people coming, and he couldn't have that. This needed to be a complete sneak attack.

On a door. More specifically a door leading to a platform that floats and moves on its own, yet the movement of a pulley is nearly always audible. A magic door that opens to reveal a magic dumbwaiter that might lead you to a magic … something. If you could get on it. Because, despite calling us all, it won't actually let us climb on.

What the hell has my life come to?

I was doing actual work this time last year. Things these kids couldn't even imagine. I was a fucking sniper. I was a Ranger. And now I'm planning to … what? Sneak up on a door?

Shaking his head at some sort of feeble attempt to shove those thoughts away before they fully invaded, he deepened his lunge and took off running.

Less than halfway across the kitchen, he saw it, and a mini second after that was when he registered his target closing itself up. His attempt at stopping before he smacked into the now-solid, wall was in vain, and he crashed into it. The momentum he'd built up and harnessed in his upper body—with the intent of needing to throw himself into the air to be able to slip inside the open panel—couldn't be stopped in time. His chest and shoulders hit first, but once his feet caught up, he was thrown onto his back.

White spots clouded his vision, and the solitary light on the ceiling multiplied itself a dozen times over. Gunner stayed there, on the kitchen floor, much longer than he should have. If someone walked in, he was prepared to say that he'd tried to get in again. He'd leave out the details of what had happened, and they'd all buy it since the damn thing had taken turns spitting them all out of the human-sized duct in the wall.

He guessed three minutes had gone by when he heard soft footsteps heading in his direction and let his eyelids shut. He was aware when they stopped in the doorway, knowing that whoever it was, was surveying him.

He hoped it was Astrid, but he also knew he wasn't that lucky.

"Would you like some help getting up?"

He knew that voice … hadn't heard it in a month or so. "No."

"Okay," he heard her respond.

No sign of her leaving followed though, and after a moment, he opened his eyes and turned to look at her.

"Do you need something?"

She shrugged. "I came to see Kronos, but he's in a meeting."

"I'm sure any of the others would be happy to keep you company until then."

"Probably. But I would like to talk to you first."

His eyes snapped open. "Dawn, no offense, but I really don't want to talk to you." Truthfully, he didn't care if she took offense to it or not, but for whatever reason, he'd felt obligated to add it in.

She gave a small nod and leaned against the molding. "I know that. But I think you need to talk to *someone*. I also think that, seeing as I don't live here and I'm not going to be on the show when it resumes, I'm the best person for you to talk to. I won't be around to share anything we discuss, but even if I were, you know I can keep a secret better than any of your housemates."

Gunner rolled his head over to look at her. "What do you think I need to talk about?"

He knew what she was going to say. It was all anyone wanted to talk about. Most of the others complained about not having constant internet access, but he was glad for it. The ten of them were all anyone was talking about, but the spotlight on him was a bit brighter than on the others.

Her curls bounced as she tilted her head at him and answered, "Your ex-girlfriend, Katie."

Gunner pushed himself up to a seated position, then turned to look at her. "I don't want to talk about her."

"That's fine," she replied. "But I'm going *to* talk to you about her."

Beginning to collect his things, he made notes of everything around him in an effort to ignore her as she began talking.

Divot in the floor molding under the cabinet to the left of the sink, one inch long.

Chip in the tile in front of the fridge, half an inch wide.

Paint peeling on the windowsill on the—

"And I think you'll end up hating yourself if you aren't there for her. Just because your mother and father couldn't do the co-parent thing in a more functional way doesn't mean you're destined for the same fate. Talk to her. I know you want to—everyone does. And if you're thinking that, in the future, this will all blow over and you'll be old news at some point, think again. This is forever. *You* are forever."

It's the same shit Heath spewed at me. Nobody had anything new to say.

Every curse word Gunner could think of came to mind; they jumped right up to the tip of his tongue and begged to be let out. But he couldn't.

"I don't have to listen to you," was the best argument he could come up with, but he had to stick with it, knowing that if he backtracked to try and deflect from himself sounding like a six-year-old, he'd only dig himself further into the hole.

"That's true." She nodded back, still speaking calmly to him, which he hated. "Those are just my thoughts. But parts of what I said are facts."

He shot a glare at her across the spacious, outdated kitchen. "I didn't ask to hear your thoughts."

"I know," she agreed. "I'm sharing them anyway. And I'm sure you gathered this much from what I just said, but I don't agree with how you're handling things."

"Yeah, well, for the record, I don't agree with how you're handling things either," he spit back at her.

As if recoiling from hearing shocking news, she dropped her jaw open and narrowed her dark eyes in confusion. "What do you mean?"

"Not wanting your powers," he told her, gripping the counter behind him. *So fucking stupid.*

Her expression softened, followed by a small shrug. "I have no use for them."

"You don't even know what they are! Kai could be right—you could be able to, like, spread your kumbaya shit for miles! You could establish world peace, Sutherland! Isn't that exactly what you want?"

That got her attention—he could tell by the way she cocked her head and her eyes suddenly looked far away. She was picturing it, imagining it, even contemplating it. He almost had her convinced.

"Look, none of us know what we're gonna get. Like that Forrest quote, right?"

She looked up at him and shared a soft smile.

"But you *could* get something super fuckin' cool. Something that could actually help you with your whole plan to organize world happiness or whatever it is."

She mulled that idea over. "No, that's basically it—world happiness, world peace," she agreed.

"I can't imagine you'd get anything destructive or whatever. And, fuck it, if you did, you wouldn't *have* to use your powers," he suggested, hoping to seal the deal with the idea that it was all in her hands. It was true after all.

After a minute of her sitting with his words, she finally took a step toward him and proposed a new plan to him. He accepted, although he wasn't sure if he'd hold up his side of the bargain—but she didn't need to know that.

"I don't want to make a big deal out of this though," she added.

"Doesn't have to be. They didn't call us when Heath opened his. I think most of 'em were kinda pissed 'cause, ya know, it was the first one and only HJ got to see. But she said nothing really happened, so …"

She nodded a few times, still lost in thought, when he had an idea. He didn't know *why* he was thinking of ways to make her feel more comfortable, but he didn't look too far into it.

"You could just open the box on your own time."

Her expression went from slightly anxious to confused again.

"You could, like, steal the box—it's yours anyway—and open it when you're in your own safe space, without an audience and any pressure," he explained.

An amused chuckle came out as she raised her eyebrow. "As much as I appreciate that, I don't want to steal anything, even if it is rightfully mine. Plus, I can't just grab it and leave, not without seeing everyone. Amber and Zach already saw me, and I would never do that to Damon. Kronos would know if I took it anyway—it's sitting in his office. He's been trying to get me to open it since March."

With that, a slamming noise sounded from down the hall, and they both heard several voices call out, "Dawn?!"

"Kitchen!" she directed them, giving Gunner a real smile. "Thank you," she added, but only so he could hear, before turning and exiting.

"Open it!" he yelled after her, knowing she likely hadn't heard him, as an obnoxious squealing sound of glee filled the entirety of the house, and Gunner was left in the kitchen, feeling much calmer than he had minutes earlier. He'd forgotten all about the maddening wall a few feet from him and found himself thinking about Katie and the way both of their lives were going to change in a few weeks.

Chapter 26

Kai: FIRE BREATH?!

Dawn: [*shrugs*] I guess so.

Zach: You're like a dragon.

Heath: Okay, okay, back to your sparking abilities 'cause I swear I just saw it. So, just focus—really focus—on channeling your energy here, right in the center of your palm.

Amber: Do you have to hold your hand out when you do it?

Heath: Kronos said that with more practice, we won't, but I've been practicing since I got them, and I still have to.

Hanna June: He said it could take close to a year, if we aren't havin' effective trainin' sessions.

Kai: They're gonna add our power strength training to those god lessons we have to start after Olympia Con, right?

Hanna June: [*shrugs*] I think that was the plan, if more of us had powers. I don't really know now.

Damon: It could still be helpful if we sat in on Heath's lessons.

Astrid: Kronos hasn't slipped up and said who'd be teaching us?

Amber: Nope.

Zach: Alexia, was there, like, a teacher or something for the gods?

Alexia: Not for the gods, but a lot of the heroes in the epics were trained by Chiron.

Kai: The goat man?

Alexia: He's a centaur—half man, half horse.

Kai: Where's he gonna fit? We can't just have him out here! Not with people chanting death threats at us, day and night!

Amber: We don't know what they're chanting.

Heath: [*projects his voice*] Okay, focus, Dawn, just tune them out.

Everyone else gets the hint and quiets down. They watch Heath and Dawn silently as he urges her to channel her powers, eventually suggesting she should tune into her calming aura ability, offering up the idea that she should combine the two while keeping her focus on the manic fire jumping around in the hearth.
Dawn drops her shoulders, lifts her chin, and takes a breath in, and while she makes the almost-insignificant motion of pushing her palm downward, the blaze calms down. The flames drop almost a foot in height and fade from an angry orange red to a cloudy blue, hovering over the logs and embers.

Zach: Holy shit!

Astrid: Oh my God …

Heath: You did it. You freaking did it! I *knew* you could control fire! Ha-ha-ha! [*throws his arms around her*]

Everyone starts crowding around the two of them, congratulating Dawn on her achievement.

Alexia: Pyrokinesis powers—very helpful. [*writes in the notebook she's been holding*]

Damon: Logging?

Alexia: [*nods*] I'm interested to see if any of our powers might overlap and how they exhibit themselves. I'd really like to know what abilities stay the same and which ones are new additions, but it's unlikely I'll ever get an answer on that front.

Astrid: Any ideas on what the rest of us might end up having?

Hanna June: Probably herpes for you.

Astrid: Listen, bitch—

They step toward each other but are immediately restrained—Hanna June by Damon and Astrid by Gunner.

Damon: Months. You have gone months ignoring each other, but now that we all live under the same roof, you want to start it up again? And not to mention, we're all going to be crammed into airplanes and hotel rooms for seventy-two hours soon. Seriously?

Astrid: She started it.

Hanna June: No, you started it in LA, and you fuckin' know it!

Dawn: [*steps toward them, putting a hand on each of their shoulders*] Both of you could use some fresh air. Let's go for a walk.

Hanna June and Astrid don't take their eyes off each other as they hesitantly agree, and the three of them leave.

Kai: [*turns to Heath*] What happens if you focus your energy on yourself?

Heath: [*hesitates*] I don't know.

Kai: Well, like, you can burn things, right?

Heath: Yeah …

Kai: What if you channel that energy on yourself?

Heath: You … you want me to burn myself?

Amber: Uh—

Kai: Yeah! I mean, what's the worst that could happen?

Heath: Well, seeing as I'm still learning to control all this, I could not be able to stop it and end up with third-degree burns—or worse.

Kai: *We can't die.*

Zach: No, that's true.

The two of them stare at each other—Heath in deep contemplation between the dozen questions his suggestion raised and Kai hoping his friend will try to burn himself.

Damon: If I can interject for a moment?

Heath: [*grateful for a potential voice of reason*] Please.

Damon: [*to Kai*] I think he's worried about accidentally covering his body in burns before we have to see a couple thousand people this weekend.

Zach: There's aloe inside.

Damon throws him a glare, but Zach just shrugs.

Gunner: [*to Heath*] Did you say the Titans have that bowl in Kronos's office? It can, like, cure and heal things?

Heath: [*glares at him*] Yeah.

Gunner: So, you'll be fine then. There's a magical first aid kit right inside for ya.

Alexia: I don't—

Kai: See? You'll be fine.

Glances are exchanged between the group, but ultimately, Heath agrees to try, but only outside. The remaining seven exit the house and make their way toward the back of the property, away from where Dawn is trying to get HJ and Astrid to hold hands and apologize—it's not going well.

Amber: Do we have to walk all the way back here? I can barely see anything.

Gunner: Well, since Dawn wants to play mediator, we're just gonna have to be without a light source.

Heath: Okay, [*takes a breath*] can you guys just back up? I don't want to hurt anyone.

Kai: Dude, we hear it fifteen times a day—we *cannot* die!

Alexia: That isn't a good mentality to have …

Damon: Back up.

They all listen to him, although Gunner takes a step forward after his three back.

Heath: Okay …

His efforts can be seen, although nothing immediately happens. He pinches his eyes closed and begins to make a straining face while Zach, Kai, Amber, Damon, Alexia, and Gunner watch. Without any warning, Heath's body is ripped to pieces and blown apart every which way in the darkness, accompanied by a loud boom.

A massive jolt instantly ripples through the trees, and everyone is knocked on their backs, including the three girls on the far side of the property. The patio furniture is flipped around midair, Alexia and Gunner are both thrown on top of the manicured hedges, and Amber somehow lands on the chaise lounge on the second-story balcony. The pool water rises up into a towering wave and crashes down threateningly on the lawn. The murky river water can be heard colliding against itself, as if thrown off course from the ricochet. A Top 20 pop song with an aggressive bass line keeps playing, undisturbed, from the ballroom through the wide-open French doors.

There is no sign of Heath anywhere.

The Olympians all begin to gather themselves and stand up, moving over to where he was standing seconds ago. Their horror-struck realization settles on many of their faces, and Amber lets out a wail from above them all.

Amber: HEATH!

Hanna June: Did … did he—

Kai: Oh my God, I killed him!

Zach: No. No, you didn't. [*nervous laughter*] I mean, we can't die. He eats it and drinks the nectar, so, like, he can't. He's not—he—he can't be.

Damon, Alexia, and Gunner begin to inspect the ground where he just was, noting the grassy space that was previously under his feet is now reduced to a plot of dirt. Behind them, HJ starts to cry, and both Astrid and Dawn hold her. Amber's sobs get heavier, drowning out the choppy river, until a whoosh sweeps in around them.

The group simultaneously looks up at the sky, the source of the sound, though they can't see anything. It gets louder on all sides of them. In the dark, Damon pulls back Alexia and Gunner, and not a second later, blurs of color and space whip past them, landing on the dirt spot. The group watches—again horrified, though much less anxious—as Heath is built back together from all sides of the nighttime around them.

As his left ear flies into place, he seems to come to and jolts, staggering a bit, but catching his balance as he looks up at them.

Kai: [*runs up to him and throws his arms around him*]

Astrid: What the hell was that?

Heath: I … I don't …

Zach: Did you just blow yourself up?!

Heath: [*looks down at his hand in awe*] I … think … yeah, I did.

Alexia: [*scrambling to find her notebook and mumbling to herself*] Heath, did it hurt?

Heath: Uh, only for, like, a second.

Alexia: [*scribbles*] Mmhmm, and what happened after the pain? Was that when you started to get put back together?

Gunner: How—*how* is that even a real sentence?

Heath: [*ignores him*] No, it hurt for a second, felt like I was … I don't know … being pulled? And then it just felt like I was floating … for a while. It felt like a long time, but [*looks around at everyone still making their way toward him*] I don't think it was long at all.

Alexia: Okay … and what happened after the floating?

Kai: [*to himself*] This feels like therapy. I think—I wouldn't actually know.

Heath: Then it was … really fast. Kinda like if I was hanging out of a car window going a hundred miles per hour.

Alexia: And now?

Heath: Now, I … I think I'm getting a headache.

Zach: Huh.

Heath: What just happened to me?

Alexia: You successfully self-detonated. And then reassembled yourself. Well done.

Chapter 27

DAMON

THE CONTENTS OF DAMON'S SUITCASE were undoubtedly too dark for a weekend in sunny Los Angeles—even for him. Everyone was packing nice outfits for the panels and dinners and the parties they'd be going to after, but he wanted no part in that. Two meet and greets were all he was expected to show up for. He felt bad for the others who didn't want to be going, knowing they had no way out of the weekend's events.

Alexia had been begging Kronos to get her out of it since the announcement of Olympia Con had been dropped, knowing she didn't have an excuse. Knowing that not only was she expected to be the Olympian with all the answers, but also that she needed to appear cool, calm, and collected—three things she hadn't been since they'd all been hidden away in the house. The charts she'd drawn, focusing on what Astrid knew and what Rhianne had told them that first day, along with the never-ending trail of information she'd pulled out of the books in all three of the house libraries she was slowly making her way through—it was enough to drive any normal person insane. Aside from him, she and Heath were the only Olympians who had chosen to continue her classes at the college— with Zoey playing messenger, delivering her assignments to and from her professors, of course. None of them had seen a lecture hall in weeks, and Damon knew she was missing it.

Hanna June was losing it too. She had come back from their holiday break, completely sold on his idea that this somehow all traced back to Greek mythology—a harsh contrast to how she'd initially taken his theory. After Alexia became suspicious of the authenticity of the network—once she realized that she never actually submitted the scholarship essay and yet was *still* awarded it—she reached out to Hanna June, questioning the idea of any ulterior motives. Hanna June took time to text Damon about it, informing him that she was going to let her in on their smaller, secret group—it hadn't been a question of whether or not Alexia should be included. Which he was fine with. He was just happy to see her applying herself to something for a change.

Once Kronos confirmed their suspicions, she acted surprised, just like the others who had already had developed an entire hypothesis around the idea, but immediately organized secret meetings around the others' schedules.

But after they were all thrown in quarantine in the Athanasios Plantation when the news came out … well, Damon still hadn't quite figured out where her sharp change of heart had come from. He assumed it was just the confirmation of it all despite her having fantasized about it for months at that point.

After Zoey's slipup, Rhianne had insisted they continue with the soul-changing process, and Kronos concurred—they informed them it would be "most painful to stop once it started." Damon had too much to do to lose time, writhing in agony. Most of them were hesitant, understandably so, but ultimately felt like they didn't have a choice.

Hanna June, on the other hand, bolted. The house was still surrounded by beefy security guards, and it remained that way for the following week, so she was confined to the gated-in property lines. Kronos recruited the Titans to find her. She'd hidden in the darkness to keep from slowly becoming immortal. It took several hours, but they trapped her in the greenhouse, with thousands of people just on the other side of the gates, entirely unaware of what was happening inside the confines of the wrought iron. Kronos urged them to use their powers to capture her—specifically Lucy's X-ray vision and Pierce's lighthouse floodlight ability—but seeing as they had a rather abundant audience—and he had *just* stated in his press conference that none of them had powers—Rhianne quickly vetoed the idea.

Keaton, the Titan of oracles and wisdom, calmly spoke to her, explaining that this was meant to happen—he was sure of it—as Pierce carried her over his shoulder back to the house. Once back inside the downstairs study, she had to be held down as the nectar was carefully poured down her throat. It was awful to watch, which they were all required to do.

Damon was never one for torture—get it over quickly, in whichever way the victim so deserved. Hanna June didn't deserve this.

She stayed rather quiet after that and refrained from hanging out with the rest of the Olympians, aside from occasionally joining Alexia in one of the libraries. Then, last week, everything changed. It was an act—he was sure of it. There'd been a few days where she resorted to being miserable again, but ever since Heath got his powers, she'd been almost back to normal.

But Damon knew better.

A knock sounded on the door of his cottage, and he called to the visitor to enter. Knowing it was either a Titan or an Olympian didn't matter much to him; he didn't want to see anyone.

Amber peered her head in. "Hey," she said, closing the door behind her.

"Hey," he greeted her, folding the towel and returning it to the oven handlebar. "What's going on?"

A frustrated sigh came out as she heaved her shoulders. "This is gonna be so weird … but can I talk to you about Fleur?"

Shit. "What about her?"

"She's been acting funny," Amber began to explain, her hands moving as the words tumbled out. "She's singing and painting, and she hasn't seemed at all upset about having to live here for the last few weeks."

No idea where she's going with this. "That all sounds good, right?"

Another sigh. "I guess." A long pause went by, and Damon was about to ask what was really bothering her when Amber added, "She seems *happy.*"

"Do you not want her to be happy?" He stared back at her.

Amber dropped onto the small love seat Rhianne had insisted on putting in his cottage to make it "homey" and propped her elbows on her knees and dropped her chin into her hand. "I think she's talking to a boy."

Damon's internal monologue snickered back. *Yeah, right.* He couldn't say that to Amber though—she would ask questions, and Damon didn't think Fleur was ready to talk to anyone about it. Confused silence was decidedly the best option.

"You spend a lot of time with her, and I know you don't want to be doing it, so please know that I'm so grateful for it. I know it's inconvenient for you, but it really does make me feel better, especially since we're all stuck here," Amber babbled out, her head bobbing up and down as her chin stayed resting on her palm.

Nodding back, he told her he really didn't mind keeping an eye on her little sister.

"I hate to ask you, but, like, has she mentioned anything to you?"

"No, she hasn't," he responded.

The small room plunged into silence again as they both dived into their own thoughts on the matter.

Amber isn't stupid … but she hasn't brought up anything about a Hades and Persephone parallel. Maybe it makes her want to rip off her skin, too.

"Okay, well."—Amber spoke again— "have you noticed her … ya know, doing anything … different?"

There was that night I had to play babysitter, before all this, when you all went out and she told me exactly what she was planning. When she swore me to secrecy and gave me a detailed outline of how she envisioned her future, and that she was determined to make it her reality, whether she's a goddess or not.

"Nope."

"Nothing … special?"

Now he narrowed his eyes. *Special?* "I need you to be more specific, Amber."

"I think—this is going to sound ridiculous." Amber laughed nervously as she pulled her fingers through her hair. "I think she might have powers too."

The surprised look that fell over Damon's face was deserved; he had not seen this coming at all. "Huh."

"I know, I know—it's crazy!" She bounced up and nervously began pacing. "I heard her talking one night and figured she was on the phone with *him*, whoever he is. And, yes, I know we don't have service here, and none of us have our phones for more than a few hours a week! Anyway, she was on the balcony one night—I saw her through the window. But … she wasn't talking to anyone. She was, uh … she was talking to a plant."

Oh no. "A plant?"

Amber nodded. "It was a Carolina jessamine, sitting right in her lap. The vines were just trailing out, and I *know* how crazy that sounds, but I *watched* them. I watched them just triple in length. I watched petals all over it blossom in half a second, Damon!"

He hadn't even considered this—how stupid of him. Was it possible? Kronos hadn't mentioned it, but that could simply mean that even *he* hadn't thought about the likelihood of it.

"I don't want to bring it up to her because if I do, she'll know I was spying on her, and she'll think I don't trust her," Amber continued.

Damon stared back. None of this conversation was happening the way he had thought it would. "It *does* sound like you don't trust her."

Another exasperated noise spilled from the redhead's mouth as she dropped her head back and groaned at the ceiling. "I don't want to ask you to keep tabs on her any more than you already do or to try and get information out of her, but, maybe, ya know, while you're back in bodyguard mode at Olympia Con, you can hang out with her? I really don't want her wandering around, and I'd feel a lot better if someone kept an eye on her—especially you. You won't have much to do aside from the three hours you're expected to be with the rest of us, and she probably doesn't want to sit and watch the weekend go by from the wings. You'll have plenty of time with her— that is, of course, if you're okay with it!"

Damon nodded back at Amber. "Yeah," he said, "I'm okay with that."

Chapter 28

ASTRID

AS ALWAYS, HER SHOTS CAME out perfect. It was the other two kids who casting had chosen to fill the smaller roles. All they have to do is react, and yet both girls seem to be having trouble playing excited seven-year-olds.

"Let's try it again. Girls, remember, you're the first people to ever play with the Holiday Dream Mansion! Ever! In the whole world! You're excited, you're eager, you're ecstatic! Roll it!" the director yelled from across the set as cameras started gliding around their targets.

"Now, Astrid," Miss Yvonne redirected her attention, "do you remember where we left off?"

She nodded eagerly, excited to get back to the fairy tale. "Yes, ma'am. You were sayin' how Demeter, who controlled all the plants and vegetables all over the world, gave her box—uh, her coffee—"

Her nanny chuckled at her. "Coffer, dear."

"Yeah, she gave her coffer to the people who worshipped her and her daughter and lived in Greece for a very long time, but they never actually hid her coffer there. Why not?"

"Well, you see, the followers of Demeter hoped that she'd return quickly. When the Roman gods moved into the thrones, they would still pray to Demeter, but they also worshipped Ceres. Now, she had just about all the same jobs and magical powers as Demeter. But as her coffer was passed down from generation to generation and the tale of the Greek Olympians, harnessing most of their powers to be entrusted to humankind, was reiterated to anyone who would listen,

it was kept safe. Now, when Christianity took the driver's seat"—she paused to give Astrid a knowing glance—*"they all took that as a sign that she might simply never return. They moved inland, far north from where they'd come, safe on the other side of the Alps. There was a small yet beautiful island set just off the mainland, in Lake Constance. There, they decided it was best to hide her encased abilities away for safekeeping. That is where, one day, it can be found and reopened by the new Demeter. But it will be up to you to help them find it— you can do that, right?"*

Astrid nodded again, feeling the pressure of this task she hadn't asked to take on, yet from Miss Yvonne's tone, it sounded like she was the only one who knew of its whereabouts. And if she didn't remember it when the time came to find it again, who would help the new Demeter regain her powers so she could grow the best fruits and veggies in the world?

"Yes, ma'am," she reassured her nanny, "I can do it."

Miss Yvonne beamed down at her. "I know you can."

Astrid's eyes flew open. *Holy shit.*

The back of her head was still pinned to her pillow when she yelled out, "I REMEMBER!"

Gunner jumped awake and rolled over in shock. His upper body flew over the side of the bed, but his legs got tangled up in the sheet. With half his weight being held up inside the linens, he just sort of hung there in a state of surprise for a moment as his head slowly lowered to touch the hardwood.

"I remember!" Astrid yelled out again, in awe of herself. She really hadn't thought she'd be able to recall anything her nannies had told her.

As she bent down to begin helping Gunner up, he grabbed her around the waist so she was sitting at the very top of his chest.

"Gun—" she started.

"No, just stay right there, and I can just—" he said as he lifted the hem of the Kings hockey shirt she had slept in and slid his fingers down her thigh.

Letting out a sigh, she gave in. "Okay, but we have to be quick because I just—" she began to say, slowly dropping her weight down onto him, watching his fingertips get closer—

And then her bedroom door flew open. *Of course.*

"Agh!" Amber exclaimed as she pulled Fleur away from the scene, Heath and Alexia recoiling at their heels.

"Wait—" Kai started, knowing he was missing something.

Hanna June leaned against Astrid's door. "You aren't confused, are ya?" she asked Kai, a disgusted smirk on her face. "You don't yell out 'I remember' when you're horny?"

"Uh—"

Now her attention turned to Astrid and Gunner, who'd ungracefully pulled themselves up. "See, we all came runnin' to see what you were yellin' about. We thought maybe you remembered somethin' important!" She was in the room now, leaning into Astrid's space.

Astrid leaned right back. "I did."

Leaning back, Hanna June blinked at her twice, then lifted her chin. "Oh."

"Wait, wait, what was it? Was it the coffers? Whose?" Kai stepped in closer to them now, and Zach leaned in from the doorway.

"Amber's," Astrid replied.

Not thirty minutes later, the eight of them stood in the temporary office space as Kronos darted into the room. He didn't stay in the house with the rest of them, and although they'd asked him why, he never gave them an answer.

He didn't look at any of the others as he asked Astrid what she'd remembered. She repeated the information from her dream. But *had* it been a dream? Weren't dreams things that hadn't really happened? Or versions of true events but slightly different than how they'd actually played out? This wasn't that. This was a memory. One that, until it had reappeared in her subconscious hours earlier, she had completely forgotten about. But now that it had been dug up, Astrid could recall everything about it: the Lakers shirt she'd worn to set that day from their championship earlier that year, being reprimanded by one of the producers that she couldn't be stomping her light up sneakers on set, and—the most vivid recollection—the way Miss Yvonne always smelled like traces of honey and freshly baked bread.

From somewhere behind her, Astrid heard words she didn't recognize being whispered. When she turned around, Alexia stood there, wearing a plaid skirt and loafers. Two months ago, Astrid would've said that she didn't have even the slightest sense of style, but ever since they had been moved into the house, they had all changed. Rhianne had told them that the more they embraced who they actually were, the more they'd feel comfortable in their own skin in ways they never had before. Astrid had always felt like that though, and she wasn't sure how much more herself she could be.

"What was that, Miss Chang?" Kronos peered around Astrid. His tone suggested he was annoyed with her intrusion, but allowed it because … well, who in their right mind would tell Athena to shut up?

"Insel Mainau," she repeated. "It's a garden island in Switzerland, in the exact location Yvonne told Astrid Demeter's coffer was relocated to."

Off to Astrid's left, she heard a soft, "Um …" that no one else seemed to acknowledge.

Kronos turned to the Titans. "Have we searched there?"

They all glanced at each other and mumbled, shaking their heads.

"No, sir," Lucy answered.

"Excuse me," was heard over the movement and chatter, and some of the others turned their attention to the speaker.

"Let's get on that. Now." Kronos ignored the voice.

There was a moment of chaotic coordination, where they all seemed to be talking at once, prioritizing and delegating, before Amber yelled over them all, "HEY!"

Everyone, Olympian and Titans both, turned in shock to look at her.

"I said I want to go!"

Rhianne stepped toward her, reaching out to place a gentle hand on her shoulder. "Darling, that might not be the best idea."

Stepping back, Amber insisted, "But it's mine!" Her unfazed concentration passed between the beings who, in another life, had been her parents.

"Miss Hargrove, this expedition could take days, maybe weeks. You are expected to be on the other side of the country tomorrow afternoon. If you are not walking the olive carpet tomorrow night, that will raise even more questions, which will defeat the purpose of this whole weekend."

Kai jumped in, but was ignored by the man when he asked, "Wait, did you say *olive* carpet?"

Amber maintained her argument with him, but ultimately conceded when Zoey walked in, tray in hand, telling her that she'd been on and off the hunt around Methana Volcano for four months before Heath's tiny chest was unearthed. Without changing the unsatisfied look on her face, Amber accepted defeat and agreed to allow the Titans to search the Swiss island without her, and Zoey promptly handed her a small plate with a tiny cluster of ambrosia. She walked around the room and passed everyone theirs and then saw herself out.

As Kronos and Rhianne approached Astrid to thank her for her help, she gave their praises half-hearted responses. She was more focused on what was happening in the back corner of the room.

Zach had taken HJ's tray from Zoey after she refused to accept it—again. Now he stood as close to her as he could get, gently urging her to eat it. She, however, kept up the toddler-like behavior—arms crossed, shaking her head, lips sealed. Astrid watched them, not understanding in the slightest as she bit into the sticky, sweet honeycomb shape. *Why would anyone not want to be immortal?*

Chapter 29

A PARTIAL GROUP OF THE Olympians files into the second-story study. Kai meanders to the other end of the house, Amber remains in Kronos's office, and Fleur—noting her sister's absence—promptly decides to include herself in with the rest of them. Damon, however, is not present.

Gunner: How many rooms does this place need?

Heath: [*dryly*] It used to be a school, so they needed them all.

Alexia walks over to an old chalkboard, which is separated into columns and charts with scribbles everywhere.

Gunner: Jesus.

Hanna June: That's not necessary.

Alexia: Gunner, Astrid, you're new to this room, so welcome. And, Zach, you haven't been up here in a while—I've changed things a bit since then.

Everyone settles into chairs or on giant pillows on the floor.

Alexia: Over here, I've listed all the accounts that proposed a theory similar to what's actually happening.

Gunner: What about the accounts that had different ideas?

Alexia: You mean, like, suggesting we're aliens? I didn't include those.

Astrid: [*mumbles*] I'd love to be an alien.

Alexia: Over here is what Rhianne told us about the war, and I had plans to list all information I found while going through the library books that went along with that, but …

Heath: There's nothing there.

Alexia: [*gives him an uncomfortable look*] I haven't found anything.

Zach: How many of the books have you gone through?

Alexia: About half of the downstairs library—the big one! Not the little one near Kronos's office. And I haven't even really looked at the one upstairs.

Gunner: [*mumbles*] I forgot about that one.

Zach: [*hopeful*] So, maybe they'll be something in one of those!

Alexia: Yeah … okay, so [*clears throat*] here is what Astrid told us. [*directs her attention to her*] As you remember more, I'll fill more in. And on this side, I started to list the magical *things* we've come across— like, Hanna June, you mentioned that basin in Kronos's office? I put that in here, and we'll add any others we find—I'm sure there will be more.

Astrid: And we have to tell you to add it?

Alexia: No, [*shakes her head*] Anyone can come in here and add whatever they want. Just please don't get rid of anything, even if it seems ridiculous. It might be something we learn about later.

Astrid: But still no aliens?

Alexia: [*ignores her and flips the board over*] And on *this* side, I've separated it into two sections—one for the dumbwaiter, which, yes, *I know* is empty, and the other for our abilities.

Zach: You've got stuff written down for almost all of us … but we don't have coffers yet?

Alexia: They're just ideas, things I remember learning about or that I've read. Most of this has come from *The Powerful Pantheon, A Dozen Hosts for Infinite Potential,* and … what was the other—oh, *Understanding the Unlimited Power of the Gods.*

Fleur: Wow …

Astrid: Impressive.

Gunner: I'd like to add a topic. Did Kronos really "let it slip" that … we're the, ya know, Greek gods?

Hanna June: I think so.

Zach: Yeah, me too.

Astrid: [*goes deep into thought, but doesn't say anything*]

Gunner: [*shrugs, an unconvinced smile on his face*] Just somethin' to think about.

Fleur: [*gestures to the board*] Oh, 'cause there isn't enough of that.

Gunner: You shouldn't even be here!

Fleur: And yet here I am.

Alexia: Okay! So, the main thing we want to focus on here is the dumbwaiter. Everyone agree?

Astrid: Eh.

Hanna June: Definitely.

Alexia: So, you're all dismissed … unless anyone wants reading suggestions?

Gunner and Astrid leave immediately. Zach and HJ talk together as Heath approaches Alexia and asks which book has the most information on how to control their powers. She sifts through her stack of completed reads and hands him the last one she mentioned to the group.

Alexia: The authors—Margot and Katerina Federova—are sisters. There's a bunch of books by them here, but most of them are in the library near Kronos's office. I'm going straight for those as soon as I'm finished in the other room.

Zach joins Heath as he exits, and both Fleur and HJ approach Alexia.

Hanna June: [*to Fleur*] Not to, like, cut you off or anything, but [*turns to Alexia*] I need to tell you somethin' … you know that big closet-type thing in Kronos's office?

Alexia: Yeah, I've seen it.

Hanna June: There's somethin' *inside* it. It's not a closet.

Alexia: [*confused*] What do you mean?

Hanna June: I was in his office when Keaton came out of it with Heath's coffer. He came *out of it*, Alexia. And they found his coffer "at the base of Methana," he said.

Alexia: [*wheels turning*] Methana Volcano is in Greece, which, as this all does, makes sense.

Hanna June: And you could tell by the way he practic'lly fell out the doors that he'd just gotten ahold of it. *In Greece!*

Alexia quickly steps over to the board, and underneath where she scrawled out Basin, *she adds a new section—*Wardrobe.

Fleur: It's like Narnia.

Hanna June: I just didn't wanna say anythin' in front of the others, but, ya know, we've all seen it. I just wanted you to be the first to know about it.

Alexia: [*nods*] No, no, I get it. I haven't read about anything like this, but I'll see if I can find anything.

Hanna June: I asked what it was, but Kronos didn't wanna tell me, and Phoebe just said that we'd find out at some point … but that's not helpful.

Fleur: I wonder if some of these *things* they have now are new to them. Like, they didn't have them the last time.

Alexia: I've been thinking that. My theory is that they had different versions of them—objects and tools that fit in the world back then and now they've morphed to fit the world as we know it.

Fleur: Yeah Kronos has said a few times about how his powers don't affect *our* technology, and it's really weird that our electronics don't work on the property …

Hanna June: Yeah, um … um, listen, I'm gonna go. I'm not feelin' great. I just wanted to mention that.

Alexia: Yeah, thank you! And just let me know if you come across anything else that we can add.

Hanna June: [*hesitates, but drops her head and leaves*]

Alexia: [*suspiciously watches her for a second, then turns to Fleur*] And what do *you* have to tell me?

Fleur: [*takes a breath*] It's about HJ.

Chapter 30

KAI

AMBER SHOULD'VE BEEN ALLOWED TO go. If this stupid thing wasn't happening, none of them would have had any excuse, and I bet they still wouldn't have let her tag along. Such bullshit.

God, I hope nothing happens to her box. Imagine …

Wait … I can't say that anymore—God. I mean, I guess I can, but it doesn't really mean anything now. Does it?

Oh … shit. That has to be it—that has to be what Ma was so upset about the other day.

Wonder how HJ is taking that … losing your whole faith backbone. God. Agh.

A flash of fiery auburn hair pulled him from his thoughts as he watched it streak across the patio. Some loose pieces of grass that had been lying around the stones swept up around her dress as she stormed off toward the greenhouse.

Before all this had happened—before the powers and the house and the secret got out—Kai would've stood where he was and just watched. But now—now that he'd begun to embrace who he really was and who he'd been all along, as Rhianne had suggested they do—Kai was proud to admit he was the most confident he'd ever been in his life. Even Ma had said, in the few times they'd spoken on the phone since their quarantine, she could hear the change in his voice. That he sounded happier, surer of himself. And he was.

So, now that Kai had allowed his inner god to take over, he followed her.

A group had started forming around the gates a day or two ago. Now that OC classes had finished, it seemed like most of the people who stayed in the town had nothing else to do.

"It's Kai! Kai! Poseidon!"

"Are you excited for Olympia Con?!"

"Can you breathe underwater like a fish? Kronos said no, but I don't believe him!"

"I'm going on a cruise next week. Will the waters in the Gulf be rough? I get seasick!"

The second he closed the door though, every sound drowned out. Amber was directly across from him, on the opposite end of the greenhouse—of *her* greenhouse—kneeling down to fill a watering can. She attempted five times or so to tuck a loose strand of hair behind her ear, but it kept falling forward into her face. He could hear bits of her agitated mumbles.

"Freaking Olympia Con … expected to be there. Well, guess what. I don't want to be there. No one asked us … rather go to Switzerland. It's mine anyway … open it right away …"

"Hey," Kai said softly.

Her head lifted, and their eyes locked. He could see the earthy shade of green from where he stood. Well, maybe he couldn't actually see it, but he'd memorized it by now. Just like he could clearly see the freckles dotted across her cheeks and the flecks of golds traced through her hair.

"Saw you come in here," he explained, taking a step closer to her.

She shut off the water and stood up.

"I'm really sorry you can't go with them to get your box."

Amber shrugged. "It's fine."

"It's really not," Kai disagreed. "This whole Olympia Con thing is gonna be so lame anyway. No one's gonna wanna see us. And if they do, it'll just be to throw tomatoes or some shit at us."

She chuckled at that. "Yeah, I think it's gonna suck too. I really don't want to go."

Carefully leaning on a table with colorful, spiky-looking plants, he added, "Finding your powers should totally be a freebie."

"A freebie?"

"A *get out of jail free card*," he explained.

She laughed again. It sounded like a chorus of angels to Kai, which, of course, he'd never heard. But seeing as, this time last year, he had been a depressed college student and now he was a god and would someday have magical powers, he didn't doubt he'd ever come across a group of them. When that moment happened, he'd ask them to all sing together for just a moment, and then he'd be able to confirm that they indeed sounded like Amber Hargrove's genuine laughter.

"Yeah, that would've been nice," she sighed, then asked, "Where do you think yours is?"

Kai had thought a lot about this, but ultimately hadn't been able to come up with anything. "No idea. I mean, yours and Heath's were both in Europe, which makes sense. Maybe mine is there somewhere? Like … I don't know … in an alcove in the Mediterranean or somewhere at the bottom of Lake Como or washed up in Portugal …" He imagined.

"Where did they say Dawn's was?"

He racked his brain, but couldn't recall that part of the conversation. "I … I don't think they did."

"Me neither," she agreed, sounding deep in thought too. "I don't think it ever came up."

"Probably not, with all the arguing."

"I've never seen her so mad."

"Good thing she couldn't breathe fire yet at that point," he threw in as an afterthought, and she laughed again.

She was standing right in front of him now. They were so close that he could see thin strands of her hair resting along her shoulders.

Kai pointed up at one of the planters hanging above them with leaves trailing over the edge. "What's this one?"

She glanced up. "Eucalyptus."

"And that one?"

She took a step closer to him.

She smells like flowers, Kai thought.

"A philodendron."

He made a circle motion. "What about the purple one around the whole thing?"

"You mean the one outside?"

"Yeah."

"Wisteria."

"Hmm …" Kai hummed, pretending to be contemplating something.

He saw her tilt her head in his peripheral vision.

"What are you thinking?"

"No, I was just hoping one of these was mistletoe," he replied, then promptly looked down at her.

Her mouth was slightly ajar, likely in surprise, but the look on her face said otherwise. He'd shot his shot with her multiple times—too many, some would say. But that had been before all this. Before they each knew who they really were. Before they began to embrace their true selves and everything in their world started to change. And, of course, Kai had taken it upon himself to immediately research if Poseidon and Demeter had ended up together—spoiler alert: they had not.

They all knew that outside the property lines of the Athanasios Plantation, out in the real world, things were changing. Riots about religion had broken out, and attacks on the remains of the Parthenon and the Acropolis had almost been executed. Many countries had ceased international trade with the entire country of Greece and even a few of its neighboring countries, and several had threatened to do so with the United States. Other countries were in an uproar as to why their ancient deities hadn't been reincarnated, and many did not even believe the claim.

But what Kai did know—the thing he'd been sure about since he had first spotted her at orientation—was how he felt about Amber. And if they all got on that plane tomorrow and the whole thing went to hell and they were ridiculed and targeted and it all went away, he needed her to know that he still cared about her. Shit, maybe he even loved her.

Can you love someone you've never had a relationship with? Never had sex with? Can the way you feel about someone really just be that chemical and that strong and that blatantly obvious that you just can't help but love them?

"Well," Amber said, her voice softer than it had been seconds ago, "mistletoe actually has little white flowers on it. It doesn't—" She cleared her throat. "It doesn't look like what you're probably picturing in your head."

Kai gently shook his head. "I've never seen mistletoe. No idea what it looks like."

Again, she tilted her head, and if Kai hadn't been trying his hardest to make sure this all went perfectly, he would've just kissed her right there.

"Really?" she asked.

"Really."

"Hmm … okay, can I get a redo?" she proposed, and now it was his turn to cock his head.

"What do you mean?"

She took a breath. "Like, let's back up. Tell me again that you were hoping one of these was mistletoe."

Oh shit, she's gonna play along.

Kai looked up again and, at her request, replayed the scene. "I was just hoping one of these was mistletoe."

Amber stepped closer to him and pointed to the small flowers above their heads. It was coming; it was really going to happen—he could feel it. He was so, so sure of it.

"That one is."

She'd barely gotten the last word out when he grabbed her face and pulled her into him. Their lips crashed into each other's over and over as his fingers tangled in her hair. He let her tongue explore every inch of the inside of his mouth as his fingers slid up her neck and cradled the back of her head. The moan she let out as he pushed his way into her mouth was orgasmic—there was no other word for it—and his hands slipped to her waist, although there was no reason, as she'd already pressed herself up against him.

Which wasn't terribly smart because Kai tumbled backward and the two of them fell over.

But they didn't care. There, on the soil-strewn floor of the greenhouse, Kai held her against him and refused to stop kissing her.

Amber's hands pushed up the hem of his shirt as her lips moved to his neck.

"God," he breathed out, "I've dreamed of this."

In between planting kisses along his collarbone, she asked, "What? Of making out on the greenhouse floor?"

"Of you," he told her. "Anywhere. Everywhere."

She kissed him back harder, and in their frantic squirming, one of them must have kicked the nozzle for the sprinkler system. Within seconds, there was a mist raining down on them, and that little bit of moisture made the dirt and loose leaves and flowers stick to their skin, as their bodies intertwined and they lost track of time.

Chapter 31

ALEXIA

"I DON'T THINK I'M SUPPOSED to share this, so *do not* mention anything to anyone."

"Of course." Alexia nodded.

Glancing around the room first, even though everyone else had left, Fleur looked her in the eye and said, "Zach cheated on Hanna June."

Oh.

She'd heard about this. During her viewing of the show, her little sister had demanded to join in—Trixie had stated that she'd already watched all of it, and seeing as she followed pages and accounts and forums dedicated to the cast and their lives both before and during filming, she could provide much-needed background information. One of the first things she'd told her big sister was that Zach didn't always seem the most faithful to his significant other, and after watching just one episode, Alexia unfortunately concurred. She'd been around them all long enough to pick up on the vibe the two of them had. It had almost seemed like Hanna June knew about it, but never confronted him—at least not in front of an audience.

However, Fleur said a few more words that caused Alexia's mouth to clap shut. "She caught him."

OH.

"Oh no ..."

Fleur was nodding, still glancing around the empty study. "The other week."

"The oth—*when?*"

The sixteen-year-old's gaze drifted off as she tried to recall the timeline. "A few days before Heath got his coffer."

Alexia nodded, feeling horrified for her friend. Well, her friend who hadn't been her friend at first, truthfully. She'd been rather rude to her when they first met, but now that—

"That's not all I have to tell you—listen!" Fleur hissed at her, waving a hand to grab her attention. "She caught him with a girl on the property."

Staring back, Alexia waited … and waited for something to click. But whatever it was, it wasn't clicking. Sensing that she was simply on information overload, Fleur repeated herself, this time including the necessary emphasis, "She caught him with a girl *on the property.*"

The change in her facial features was so drastic that she could feel her glasses shifting on her face. "Oh. Okay, okay … Hanna June doesn't know who she was?"

"Doubt it." Fleur shrugged as she followed her over to the board, where Alexia picked up a sticky note on the ledge and began scribbling notes to herself.

She couldn't risk writing this on the board and having someone see it.

"And no one else has mentioned anything about another person—mortal or otherwise—on the property?"

"I haven't heard anything."

"M'kay …" *What was Zach thinking, bringing someone else inside the gates? Does he know something we don't? Aside from what we already* do *know? Does Kronos know?*

"I didn't even think about it at first. I doubt HJ realized it with how miserable she's been. And I'm pretty sure Amber didn't pick up on it. I feel like she would've mentioned it to you if she had."

She shook her head. "This is the first I'm hearing about this. I can't believe we don't have cameras here."

"Who needs those when you constantly have seven security guards around the property lines at all times?" Fleur joked, but it gave Alexia the idea to ask them.

She knew it wasn't likely she'd get any information from them, but it was worth a shot.

Chapter 32

ALEXIA LOOKS AROUND SEVERAL TIMES before she mounts the trellis on the balcony and begins climbing. As she reaches the top, she pulls herself up and crawls across the roof to meet the group.

Kai: Why did you crawl?

Alexia: So I wouldn't fall …

Kai: And what? Die? [*scoffs*]

Alexia: I could probably still break something, which I don't feel like doing. Especially since we're all expected to be on a plane in a few hours.

Amber: You think we can still break bones?

Alexia: I'm not sure. From everything I've read so far, it's only our blood that's been replaced. I'll add it to my list of questions when we start lessons though.

Kai: God, I don't want to go back to school again. I don't think I can.

Amber: You'll like this kind of school. I think we all will.

Alexia: Heath, how are you feeling?

Heath: Honestly … I feel great. Better than I have in a while.

Alexia: I wonder if that's just the ambrosia-nectar combo or if it has to do with the ability awakening …

Kai: It's definitely the powers.

Amber: I think so too. Like, I feel good … but not great.

Hanna June: I feel like shit.

Everyone turns to look at her, recognizing that they're all aware she hasn't been acting like herself since they moved into the house, but this is the first time she's talking about it.

Amber: [*scooches a bit closer to her*] Do you wanna talk about it?

Hanna June: [*slowly looks up at her*]

Amber: [*regretfully*] I know I don't have Dawn's aura thing. But I wish I did.

Hanna June: [*lets out a breath*] It didn't hit me till we all got locked away in here.

Amber: What didn't?

Hanna June: All of this. I was havin' so much fun, like, learnin' and … imaginin', and I *was* on board with the whole thing 'cause it was really still just a fantasy. Even when Kronos confirmed it all back in January, nothin' changed. We were all still us; we still had cameras and contracts and little fan gatherin's at the dinin' hall. But this … *this* … I don't know … this just made it all real.

Alexia: What part of it makes you wish it weren't real?

Hanna June: The part where my life is over—all of ours! Before we've even lived it! And we had no choice—they just took it away from us.

Amber: We're still alive—

Hanna June: [*throws her a look*] Hardly.

Heath: You mean, like … this is how we're stuck … forever, right?

Hanna June: Yeah.

Heath: Like, you weren't ready to be frozen in time while still living?

Hanna June: [*nods sadly*] Exactly.

Kai: What happens if we stop taking it? Do we become mortal again?

Alexia: Well, according to the tale of Persephone's kidnapping, while Demeter was scouring the earth, looking for her, she not only ignored the crops on the planet, thus creating winter, but she was also so focused on finding her daughter that she didn't consume any of the divine fruits and lost her immortality.

Amber: Uh—

Alexia: Until she replenished herself, of course. Then her immortality was restored.

Kai: So yeah, what I said.

Alexia rolls her eyes as Heath turns back to HJ.

Heath: So maybe just stop taking it for a little while. No one will know. We won't tell. And, ya know, just don't get hurt or anything.

Amber: [*cringing*] Umm, I don't know, HJ. Maybe wait until we start seeing those doctors next week.

Damon: What doctors?

The group turns to see him strolling across the roof toward them.

Hanna June: Been wond'rin' when you were gonna show up. What took so long?

Damon: Lost track of time while I was studying.

Hanna June narrows her eyes at him, not believing his excuse, but also not calling him out on it.

Damon: What doctors are you talking about, Amber?

Amber: Kronos mentioned something about a pair of doctors coming in. Supposedly, they're like us, so they know how to treat us. Guess we can't go to regular people anymore. Wonder if I should have my records transferred …

Alexia: [*ignoring Amber mumbling to herself and turning to Damon*] Yes, I found it quite interesting when he said it earlier—he mentioned a husband-and-wife duo, as opposed to just a singular Paean counterpart. Isn't that weird? I doubt any of the rest of us have multiple counterparts.

Damon: Hmm.

Hanna June: [*changes the subject*] All right, Montclaire, since we're all finally here, what's goin' on?

Damon: [*confused*] I don't know.

Hanna June: [*rolls her eyes*] C'mon.

Damon: I didn't call us here. I got a note too. Look—

As he reaches into his pocket to pull out the sticky note, his expression quickly changes. His gaze shifts down to his pants pocket, where he pulls out a small stone. The rock glows a faint gold color as he holds it in front of him for the group to see, balanced in the center of his palm.

Kai: Whoa, whoa, whoa. What is that?

Alexia and Heath quickly reach into their own pocket to pull out the memo they found in their rooms, summoning them all together. Their square, pale yellow papers morphed into glowing stones, identical to the one Damon has. Hanna June, Amber, and Kai produce theirs, and the group stares down at them all, unsure of what to do.

Alexia: [*holds hers up right in front of her face*] Whoa.

The face of the stone appears as though it fogs up, the same way a mirror would. Using the sleeve of her cardigan, Alexia wipes it clean to reveal a message: This is a lexi-stone.

Alexia: Holy shit … look.

Hanna June: Oh My lanta …

Kai: Wait, wait—

Damon: How did you do that?

Amber: A lexi—what does it say? I can't read it upside down.

Heath: Lexi-stone.

Kai: Is it like a tablet?

Damon lifts his to his face and breathes on it, the same way Alexia did while examining hers. A copy of the message also appears under the fog on his stone. The others follows his lead, producing the same memo—except Hanna June's lexi-stone.

Hanna June: [*embarrassed*] Why isn't mine workin'?

Alexia: I'm not sure.

Heath: Is something wrong with yours? It's not glowing as bright as ours.

Kai: That's so weird.

Hanna June: And that's *so* not helpful, Kai.

Kai: Oh my God, sorry, jeez!

Hanna June: Ugh, whatever.

Knowing that no one has any information that can help her and being beyond frustrated with the situation, she throws the stone across the roof. The others all gasp as it soars through the air, expecting it to shatter upon its landing. It clatters against the shingles, still in one piece and still faintly glowing, leaving everyone confused.

*Damon walks over to it, picks it up, breathes on it, and watches the message—*This is a lexi-stone—*appear on it.*

Alexia: [*to Damon*] It worked?

Damon: [*nods as he hands the stone to Hanna June*]

Hanna June: [*begrudgingly takes it from him and mumbles*] Thanks.

Alexia: It's as if it unlocks when we breathe on it … but they're not designated to each of us, individually. It must sense who we are. Okay, my working theory—

Kai: That you just came up with right now?

Alexia: Is that it can trace the ambrosia on our breath. And since Hanna June doesn't consume quite as much as the rest of us, that's why it wouldn't unlock for her.

Heath: Yeah, I can buy that.

Damon: That makes sense.

Kai: [*whines*] No, no, this feels like school. Make it stop.

Alexia holds her stone up again and fogs up the face of it, revealing a new message.

Alexia: Everyone, do it again!

The others follow her instructions, and Amber breathes on Hanna June's.

Heath: *Use this to communicate among yourselves when you can't all gather.* Wait … who's writing this?

Damon: Someone who knows the six of us meet in secret.

Kai: No shit.

Amber: Who else is there though? We haven't told anyone else.

Heath: Maybe someone found out.

Hanna June: I feel like it's one of the Titans.

Damon: My money's on Kronos.

Alexia: Really? You think he knows?

Damon: I think he's *known*.

A murmur goes around the group as they debated the possibilities while Alexia surveys the lexi-stones. After a minute, she silently gets up and collects Hanna June's and Amber's stones. As she resumes her cross-legged position, she begins to assemble the three stones together, angling them until they seemingly click into place.

Alexia: Heath? [*holds out a hand, waiting for him to offer his stone to her, keeping her eyes glued on the Pangaea-like puzzle in front of her*]

Once she assembles all the lexi-stones, they fit perfectly in a jagged circle with just the center piece missing.

Alexia: [*points at the absent shape*] That. That's the shape we're looking for. If it's Kronos who's messaging us, he either won't let it out of his sight or off his person, unless it's with Rhianne.

Hanna June: What if it's another Titan?

Damon: We'll have to wait until they get back.

Heath: And … what if it's someone we haven't met yet?

Everyone turns to look at him.

Heath: Well, there are two Titans missing. And even if we take those two out of the equation, think about how many gods there are in Greek mythology. And then think about how many we know of. There are a couple hundred more out there—good, bad, or more or less powerful than the Olympians or even the Titans. We have no idea who's seeing these messages too.

Damon: No, no, you definitely have a point.

Kai hastily grabs his piece from the jagged ring Alexia formed the lexi-stones into, breathes on it to reveal a blank space, and uses his fingers to write out, Who are you?

Hanna June: What are you doin'?

Kai: Figuring out who this is. And how to work this thing. God, it's smaller than my phone.

Seconds later, the stone glows a brighter gold color.

Kai: *We've met before.* Well, great. That could be any of the other four Olympians, the ten Titans, the little ambrosia delivery girl. [*turns to Amber*] Oh shit, it could be Fleur!

Amber: [*gives him an annoyed look*]

Damon: Or it could be a lie.

Amber: I'm sure whoever this is wouldn't lie to us.

Hanna June: [*gives her a pitiful look*] Ehh …

Everyone's attention is pulled to their glowing lexi-stones once more when they each light up brighter for a split second. Kai reads aloud the new incoming message they all received.

Kai: *Kronos does not know I have left these with you all. Do not tell him.* Well, shit.

Hanna June: It's Rhianne.

Amber: Really? You think she'd keep a secret from him?

Hanna June: [*shrugs*]

Just then, the group can hear a faint call for Hanna June coming from below them.

Hanna June: Shit, Zach's lookin' for me. And I still haven't packed—

Alexia: We leave in [*checks watch*] three hours!

Hanna June: I know, I know! Look, hold on to these and do *not* let any of the others see you usin' 'em. And don't lose 'em—Kai, I'm talkin' to you.

Kai: Yeah, yeah, I know.

Hanna June: Okay … we shouldn't all leave at once. I'm goin' first.

As the group makes their way back over to the trellis, they complain in whispers about the convention.

Amber: Everyone's going to hate us.

Kai: If anyone even comes.

Damon: It's sold out.

Amber: It is?!

Alexia: I, for one, agree. I am not looking forward to this.

Heath: [*to Alexia*] We haven't even filmed anything, and yet everyone knows who we are. It's just so weird.

Hanna June: Hey, it's a weekend away from this place, and I'm countin' that as a win.

Kai: And taking a private jet out there doesn't sound too bad.

Alexia: Amber, my sister is so jealous Fleur is going. She wants to come so badly.

Amber: Fleur is only going because my daddy is in Tulsa all month, and I can't leave her with Meemaw that long.

Hanna June: Fleur doesn't seem to mind livin' here.

Amber: [*shrugs*] She'd rather be here than anywhere else.

Heath: She really wants to be … on the show? Or one of us? Something like that—I'm not really sure.

Amber: [*sighs*] She wants it all.

Alexia: It's highly likely she'll end up living a lifestyle similar to us. My theory is that, once she turns eighteen, Kronos will formally introduce her to the world. It wouldn't surprise me if he previewed it this weekend—

Amber: [*comes to a halt*] What are you talking about?

Alexia: Fleur … how she's the reincarnated Persephone.

Amber: [*gets defensive*] There's nothing to prove that.

Heath: [*snorts*] Uh, yeah, expect everything.

Amber: Like what?

Heath: Like how Persephone was raised by her mother, Demeter—who, in case you forgot, is *you*. And you basically raised her. How Demeter is super overprotective of her, which is also you—no offense. How she's the goddess of springtime, and that girl is always looking at or drawing or painting flowers. She practically lives in the greenhouse.

Amber: That doesn't mean she's one of us.

Heath: Okay, well, how about how you put her in Damon's care and he does it so willingly? And it's funny because he doesn't really like people—I'm not even sure he really likes most of us—but he's always in a slightly better mood after he's been around her.

Amber looks between the group, but doesn't linger on Damon too long, aghast. After a minute of her shocked, sputtering sounds, he swings himself down the trellis and into the darkness.

Chapter 33

GUNNER

"OH, *FUCK* YES," HE BREATHED into her hair for the fifth time that minute.

"Harder," Astrid whimpered as her head bounced against the mirror behind her.

Gunner shifted his weight under one hand behind where her ass was perched on the sink counter, and gave her hair a gentle tug with the other. She tilted her head back, knowing his signal. He'd much prefer to actually pull her hair, but he also knew her well enough to know she changed wigs constantly—not that he'd stopped mid-fuck when he accidentally pulled one off before, but he knew a repeat scenario wasn't necessary.

"Fuck, it's been so long," he moaned against the shell of her ear.

She shivered underneath him as she hummed back, "We fucked yesterday."

"Mmhmm, and that's way too long," he replied before pulling out, grabbing her hips to pull her down from the counter and spinning her around.

A full-length mirror would've complemented the scene nicely, but airplane restrooms didn't exactly allow room for that.

Pushing his cock against her ass cheeks, he ran a finger down her spine, making her knees give just enough. "Ready?"

Her head bobbed as she nodded, and he ground against her one more time, deliciously watching her relish in the sensation before sliding back inside.

He grabbed a tit and, using it as leverage, leaned her back against his chest. They watched their reflection in the small, spotless mirror as he fucked her aggressively while she begged for more, until they both finished.

With no shame—because why should they have any?—they exited the bathroom together and returned to their leather seats next to one another.

"You guys are really fucking loud," Kai greeted them, not bothering to open his eyes or pull his hoodie down.

"I doubt your headphones are turned up all the way," Astrid argued back sweetly. "Did you even try to tune us out?"

From the row in front of him, a grumble was heard. "We all tried," Heath assured them.

Gunner knew he should be at least a little bit sorry ... but he wasn't. His stepbrother and Astrid had never been in a real relationship, and the two of them weren't in one now either, so it didn't *really* matter. And it wasn't like he and Heath actually got along well enough for him to feel bad for fucking his "ex."

As he sank down into his leather chair, he pulled his phone from his pocket. Nine new texts, all from his mom.

Elaine: Any day now, sweetheart. I'd ask you if you're ready, but nobody's ever really ready for this. I remember how nervous your father and I both were right before you were born. I think the stress level was what made you a week late.

Slipping from his hands, his phone plunged into his lap. Out of the corner of his eye, he could see Astrid leaning around to the seat in front of her.

She's talking to Alexia. She didn't see, he told himself as he pushed his earbuds in, desperate to drown out everything around him—his mom's words rattling around in his head, the horrendous whir of the jet engine, Amber giggling across the row from where he sat, all of it.

But he couldn't.

Upon getting his phone back this morning, Gunner had opened his web browser immediately to search for a new pair of sneakers he'd seen on one of his secret treks out of the mansion, only to find his name trending.

Gunner McHugh and Katie O'Hara to Welcome First Child.

How Is New Olympian Gunner McHugh Preparing to Be a First-Time Parent?

Will the Birth of Former Army Ranger Gunner McHugh's Child Cut Olympia Con Short?

Those were just some of the titles he'd seen before tapping his thumbs as fast as HJ normally did to get out of his home page.

Kronos had assured him that the baby wouldn't be a demigod, without him even asking … so that was one good thing.

The articles had made it seem like he would be right there with his ex-girlfriend, metaphorically holding her hand through it all, when the reality of it was that he was going to be in Los Angeles all weekend and probably wouldn't even know when she went into labor.

Unless I go. I could go.

No. No, that's crazy. I haven't answered her in months. I can't just show up at the hospital while she's pushing out a kid. My kid. Our kid.

Yeah, no. No, I can't go.

But I should. Fuck, I know I should.

But if I leave in the middle of the convention, everyone will know what's up.

Well … everyone's gonna know anyway.

Maybe the baby won't come till after … and then maybe I can get out of these god lessons. Take parental leave or FMLA or something.

How Is New Olympian Gunner McHugh Preparing to Be a First-Time Parent?

How do you prepare for that? Mom said no one's ever really ready for this … which doesn't make me feel any fuckin' better.

I'm gonna have to go. Fuck.

Chapter 34

Kai: K but why would we need the lexi-stones if we have our phones?

Heath: Well, aside from this weekend, we don't have them in the house.

Alexia: Whoever set this up probably knows we get our phones once a week for a few hours, and even then they barely work.

HJ: Yeah, that's what I was thinkin

Kai: U know wut I mean

Heath: Maybe because phones can be easily hacked?

HJ: Huh …

Damon: Heath has a point.

Alexia: Did we all bring our stones?

Heath: I brought mine.

Damon: I have mine.

Amber: Got mine

Kai: Same

HJ: Yeah I have mine and I can actually use it

Amber: You ate this morning?

HJ: Yeah

Kai: Do you think we need to charge these things?

Alexia: You let me know where you find the spot to plug it in.

Kai: I was just asking jeez

Alexia: Well, it was a stupid question.

Amber: My daddy says there's no such thing as a stupid question- just stupid people who ask questions.

Amber: Oh wait

HJ: Lolol

Damon: Ha.

Heath: Haha

Kai: Thanks babe

Heath: Wait

Alexia: Uhhh ...

HJ: BABE???

Damon: Ha.

HJ: DID YOU CALL AM BABE???

Kai: Typo

HJ: NOOOOOO

Kai: YESSSSS

Amber: Oh God

Kai: That's what she said

Kai: She being u obvi

HJ: OMG

Alexia: Well this went from cute to ick really fast.

Heath: Omg what is happening

Amber: Kai!!!

Kai: Eh they know now, might as well go along with it

Amber: They know bc you told them!!!

Kai: In a typo

HJ: I FEEL MORE ALIVE THAN I HAVE IN WEEKS TY GUYS

Kai: See, there cool with it

Alexia: They're*

Kai: DONT RUIN IT LEX

Alexia: DON'T RUIN GRAMMAR, KAI.

Heath: There's so much going on rn

Amber: Omg I cannot believe you outed us

Kai: Then why are you smiling?

Amber: I'm not

Kai: I'm sitting next to you

Heath: Yeah, I can see your reflection in my window

Damon: We can all see you, Amber.

HJ: YOU LOOK SO HAPPY

Amber: Ughhh

Chapter 35

ZACH

"WELL, THAT WAS FUN," HE started, holding the door open for his girlfriend. "We've never celebrated your birthday in Los Angeles."

"Yeah," she murmured, floating past him into the room, the fanfare drifting down the hallway toward them.

"Did you have a good time?" She'd been present at dinner, but the second they all got into the limo to head back to their hotel, she'd shut down again. Zach knew she was in there somewhere though.

"Yeah."

"Food tastes so weird now."

"Mmhmm," Hanna June murmured as she took off her bracelets.

"Like, it's pretty good, but not as good as I remember. And that lobster was cooked to perfection—like, I know it wasn't the food, ya know?"

"Mmm."

"Wonder when we're gonna get a delivery. Zoey didn't go with them, did she?"

"Mmm."

"HJ? Baby?"

She quit mindlessly fussing with her necklace clasp and looked up at him, her eyes wide. "Huh?"

"You're not listening."

"Oh … sorry."

Zach pulled at his cuff link as he strode over to her. "What are you thinkin' about?"

Shaking her head gently so the soft curls grazed the edges of her face, she replied, "Nothing. Just a long day."

"Jet-lagged?"

"A little."

At least she's talking to me, Zach thought as he watched her take out her earrings. "Did you have a fun time tonight?"

"Mmhmm. Lots more people than I thought."

"Yeah," he agreed. "Kinda thought the place was gonna be packed with people hating on us."

Her gaze zeroed in on him, reflecting off the mirror. "Me too." She gave a soft smile. "Was not expectin' that group of kids who started prayin' to us." She laughed.

Zach chuckled back. "Yeah, I'm glad security stopped them. Not sure what we were supposed to do in that situation."

At his words, her smile dropped, and her vision glazed over as she was halfway through running a brush through her hair.

"I lost you," he murmured, watching for some sign from her.

This had kept happening, ever since they'd all been forced into the house. Random things would make her just completely disassociate, and nobody ever seemed to be able to break her from the depression-led trance she would sink into.

He'd seen her on the plane, mostly zoned out, even asleep for some of it. There was a short period when he went to talk to Kronos and had a perfect view of her. She was looking at something and had the biggest smile hiding under one hand. He assumed she was just rewatching a show she'd seen a million times, in an attempt to cheer herself up.

What had bothered him was that that was the only point in their six-hour plane ride where she looked genuinely happy, and he hadn't been next to her.

Pushing up from where he had been stretched across her bed, he walked over to where she had frozen and placed a hand gently on her hip. She'd worn a glittery gold dress for their red carpet—scratch that, *olive* carpet—entrance tonight. Everyone looked sensational, and Amber's ensemble definitely garnered the most attention, but Zach couldn't take his eyes off his girlfriend. He hadn't seen her completely put together up until the moment when she stepped out behind him. It had been like something out of a movie—the hundreds of camera flashes going off, the thunderous applause as little sparkles of light reflected off her, and the half second where their gazes met and the most genuine smiles graced their faces.

She was still wearing the dress, and, God, he wanted to take it off of her so badly, but this wasn't the time. Maybe he could get it to go there, but not yet.

A mumble slipped out of her lips as he traced the thin straps down to the middle of her back. "What if I don't have powers?"

Okay, maybe this isn't going to go there. His forehead wrinkled together so aggressively; he could feel the pressure. "What?"

"What if I don't have any powers?" she repeated, this time turning to face him.

As she lifted her chin to look him in the eye, he could visibly see the hopelessness in her dark brown irises.

"That's not possible," he convinced her as he took her hands in his. "Kronos and the Titans have reassured us that we'll all have, ya know, enhanced speed, memory, and senses, and stuff."

"I'm talkin' about the special powers. The ones the Titans are searchin' around a Swiss island to, ya know, reinstate for Amber as we speak."

Zach had thought about this. After learning they were all getting actual abilities designated for who they had been in the Greek mythology world, he'd done some of his own research and listed out a few possibilities regarding who got what. He'd come up empty-handed for Hanna June.

What powers did the goddess of marriage get? Was blessing a marriage still considered a special thing, if people could get ordained online in five minutes nowadays?

He'd never dare to say that to her though. "I'm sure that won't happen."

"How do you know that?" she fired out. "What can Hera do that makes her special? Makes *me* special?" The hopelessness was gone and had been replaced with a feverish need, a craving for answers, for sincere consolation.

His mouth fell open again, but this time in a different sense of astonishment.

She continued. "What if you all get powers and nothin' happens for me? What if I open my coffer and nothin' changes? What if I don't even have one? Where would it be anyway?"

His hands gripped hers tighter. "We're going to find them all—yours included."

"What if I'm not really one of 'em? What if somethin' went wrong when her soul went into me and it—I don't know—didn't stick or somethin'? What if I'm only half of a goddess? What if I'm not special?"

"You *are* special, Hanna June."

"What would I say to all those people? How would I explain that I wasn't the divine goddess *queen* they were callin' me tonight?"

His hands flew up and grabbed at the sides of her face. "Baby, baby, you're spiraling. Look at me. That is not going to happen. Okay? I won't let it. I'll tell Kronos first thing tomorrow morning that locating your coffer needs to be the main priority, okay? You're exactly who the world thinks you are—I know it. And you do too—I know you do. And I know that's really hard to believe when there's not really anything to go off of, to prove that, but we're going to show everyone that you can do amazing things—even without superpowers, okay?"

She didn't nod in agreement, and as far as Zach could tell, she hadn't even heard him. The only thing he could sense in her eyes was fear.

It took twenty minutes, but he was finally able to get her changed into pajamas and have her wipe her makeup off. She told him she could brush her teeth on her own.

As soon as the bathroom door shut behind her, he grabbed his phone. Not having it constantly accessible for the last several months had been both refreshing and nauseating. The compulsive need to know what was going on at all moments of the day and *not* being able to find out on a whim had been a battle they all went through together, but now that he had it back in his possession, that desire hadn't returned full force with it.

Zach: Rhianne, I need to talk to Kronos ASAP

Rhianne: Is everything okay?

Zach: HJ's losing it. She thinks Hera didn't leave her any powers and she's afraid of how people are going to react to a god… ya know, not being able to act like a god.

Rhianne: Darling, I can assure you Hera left Hanna June powers to be restored. Remember, I was there.

Zach: Ok yeahhh… can you talk to her maybe? It would probably help if she knew what she was getting

Rhianne: I will schedule a time to meet with her once we return to the Athanasios Plantation.

Zach: Thank u so much

Chapter 36

HEATH

> **Emma: Hey, good morning. I know I won't get to talk to you much today, so I just wanted to say that I hope your panel isn't terrible (you're silly for worrying, bc you're gonna do great), and that your breakfast with the new recruits goes well!**

HEATH WAS STILL GROGGY WITH sleep as he smiled at his phone through blurry eyes.

He had been so worried that not having any way to communicate with her during their quarantine would ruin the progress they'd made since last semester. That, combined with the whole fake-relationship thing earlier this year, was a huge setback. Especially since his flare-up in the fall had put him in the hospital for a few days and left Heath feeling as though she'd forgotten he even existed.

He knew his presence on the show had likely played a role in him becoming a more regular fixture in her life, but she never brought it up. He assumed everyone in the world watched it, but Emma never once mentioned it.

As he began to type out a response to her, something clicked.

And that your breakfast with the new recruits goes well.

Wait, what?

Heath: Not to skip over most of your text, but what breakfast?

Emma: The contest thing.

Heath: What contest?

Emma: You know, the thing Kronos announced like a week after he announced Olympia Con. The essay contest.

Heath: Em, what are you talking about?

Emma: It was actually kind of silly, if you ask me. But it was like if you thought you might be a god or goddess, Parthenon wanted you to write a paper supporting your theory. The one that seemed most probable would win a private breakfast with the Olympians this weekend.

Heath: What the fuck? He never told us this.

Emma: Oh wow, never heard you curse before.. not that I actually heard you, but you know what I mean.

Heath: Listen, thank you so much for telling me this, but I have to go. I'll call you later? Is 6 still okay?

Heath didn't wait for her response to come through—he'd check it later. He pulled on a pair of shorts and bolted out of his room, pulling his shirt over his head in the hallway.

Kronos's room was just down the hallway from theirs, but before he made it to the producer's room, Damon and Fleur stepped out of another doorway.

Doubling back, Heath gestured to Damon frantically. They leaned close together, with Fleur taking it upon herself to make the conversation for three people. "Are you aware of this breakfast thing?"

Damon's eyes narrowed. "What are you talking about?"

"Well," Heath started, "you're probably excluded from it—lucky—but apparently, Parthenon organized some sort of essay contest. People who thought they were like us could write in and explain why they felt that way and who they thought they were. The winner is having breakfast with us this morning!"

As his eyebrows slowly rose, Fleur piped up. "Yeah, I tried to write in but Kronos said I was *necessarily exempt*," she told them, shaking her head.

"You knew about this?" Damon asked her.

"Yeah," she said. "I thought you all did …"

Her gaze bounced between the two of them, and Heath could see the realization cloud over her face that they, in fact, had not known anything about it.

Damon took a deep breath and pinched the bridge of his nose. "Moving forward, assume we know nothing. Always tell me when you hear about something like this. Please."

Fleur began to slowly nod, considering this, before she looked up at him. "Does this mean we can't go down for breakfast now? I'm starving and I don't want room service again. I can't have a waffle iron brought in—I already asked."

Agreeing that Damon and Fleur likely wouldn't be required at this last-minute agenda addition, the two of them left, and Heath stepped down to Kronos's door, pounding a fist on it.

The door swung open immediately. "Good morning, Heath," Rhianne greeted him.

"I need to talk to Kronos," he replied back, feeling bad for passing by her without being invited in, but also too frustrated to care.

At the window, Kronos pulled back the curtains, and the sunlight poured into the suite as he turned around. "Good morning, Mr. Blackburn. How can I help you?"

"We have a breakfast this morning that you never told us about?" he blurted out.

The light bounced off his head as he nodded, knotting his fingers together. "You do. I had plans to tell you all last night, but some other news distracted me, and I apologize for that."

Despite his tone being sincere, Heath didn't feel any better.

"And why didn't you tell us at any point in the last three months? You had *plenty* of time," he demanded.

Another angry-sounding knock came from the door. Rhianne opened it, greeting Gunner and Astrid just as serenely as she'd greeted Heath.

Not the people I want to see.

"Exactly what the hell are we doing?" Gunner pushed past her in a way that made Heath's uninvited entrance look welcome.

Rhianne excused herself, announcing she was going to alert the other Olympians of their change in itinerary.

"I didn't pack for a breakfast event!" Astrid chimed in, and Heath looked away so she wouldn't see him roll his eyes.

Kronos assured the three of them that he only hadn't told the group because of the focus on their coffers while simultaneously putting out fires around the globe that had risen due to the news of their existence getting leaked earlier than anticipated. However, Heath didn't care much to hear the same excuse for the hundredth time.

With the truth out, Heath left the room. He didn't want to be around his stepbrother and his fake ex any longer than necessary. And recognizing that he still had some time before he was expected downstairs, he retreated to his room to call Emma, much earlier than planned.

It makes sense that the table has to be this big, but I can't hear anyone on the opposite end, Heath thought as he pulled in his chair.

On one side of him, Alexia was on her third cup of coffee, according to her, and looked like she hadn't slept. Knowing she had never gone to bed after their roof gathering with the lexi-stones, combined with the fact that he'd never seen her fall asleep in the seat next to him on the plane to Los Angeles, he knew she'd crash at some point.

On his other side sat Kai, with Amber right next to him. They both had the faintest traces of weed floating around them and goofy smiles on their faces, and Heath only realized he was watching them when HJ cleared her throat. He looked up at her, expecting her to glare at him and maybe mouth something about staring being rude, but she just smiled back at him. He knew she was happy for them also.

Kronos's voice broke through the early morning chatter as he graced the group with two young women on either side of him.

"Olympians! What a treat! This morning, before the rest of the world gets their eyes on you, we have not only one fellow goddess joining you all, but *two*! And not just any two goddesses, but two who belong to different groups, both key identities in our past, present, and future."

Groups ... Alexia mentioned something about ... the Fates? Was that one of the groups of gods? Yeah, no, that sounds right.

The girls glanced at the group and then at each other, very unsure of what the show's creator was saying.

"So ... they're gods, but not Olympians?" Kai asked as he stared at his water glass, likely trying to make its contents move.

"That's correct, Mr. Newport," Kronos told him as he guided one of the girls to the reserved spot in between Astrid and Alexia. "Miss Knight here, is one of our New World Muses! Anyone wish to venture a guess as to which one? Miss Chang, I know you know this," he coaxed Alexia to lead the table in a lesson.

And, being the goddess of wisdom, she did know exactly what Kronos was talking about. "There were nine goddesses who inspired literature and the arts and sciences, known together as the Muses. In some earlier accounts, there weren't actually that many, but most philosophers count nine, and they're most commonly identified as the daughters of Zeus and Mnemosyne."

Astrid cocked her head as she added, "So ... Zach and ... Dayo?"

"The Titan goddess of memory?" Heath asked, trying to mask the disgusted tone that came out with his words at the idea.

"Oh, she's too nice for you, dude," Kai added in, chuckling at his own joke. Most of the Olympians emitted a disturbed sound at the thought.

Kronos shook his head. "In another life, yes, the Olympian god of the skies and the Titan goddess of memory were their parents. In *this* life, you know them as Mr. Alexander and the lovely Dayo."

"Weird."

Alexia spoke over Astrid, focused on the new girl seated next to her. "What's your name?"

"Elliana," the girl answered.

"And, Kronos, don't tell me—I'm going to figure this out."

"I know you will."

Their servers interrupted briefly to take their orders as Alexia asked Elliana questions in an effort to get to know her better. Heath kept up with everything the girl said, but with his knowledge of the more minor Greek gods being nowhere near as extensive as the New World Athena, he couldn't keep up.

She must have a mental catalog she just flips through.

Halfway through her fourth cup, Alexia nodded once before looking at Kronos. "She's Clio, the muse of history."

"Very good, Miss Chang. Would you like to attempt decoding our other guest's New World persona?"

Nadine Drake, the other winner, took much longer for Alexia to figure out. Hanna June and Heath both interjected with their own ideas at one point, only to have Kronos shake his head while thanking them for their effort.

"She reminds me of Dawn," Heath said, more to himself than to the group, but it caught everyone's attention.

"I was thinking that too actually," Amber agreed, poking another banana pancake onto her fork. "But there can't be two Hestias, can there?"

"There are two of Paeans or however you say it," Kai joined in. His eyes were still red.

Kronos leaned on the back of Zach's chair. "Yes, we're all still intrigued by that as well. However, Miss Drake is not a double."

Alexia turned back to Nadine. "Yes, you do give off a very Dawn-like vibe," she pondered.

It was on the last bite of her eggs Benedict when her lead lifted. "Oh—*duh*. How did I not put it together sooner? Kronos, she's a Grace, right?"

He began an unnecessary thunderous applause. "Well done, Miss Chang! Yes, Miss Drake is one of the Graces, but do you know which one?"

Alexia's short hair swung across her face as she turned to analyze the girl again. "She's Euphrosyne."

"Bless you," Hanna June said without looking up from her phone.

"Euphrosyne was one of the three Graces—or Charites. She's the goddess of happiness, basically. Good cheer, joy—that's why she reminds us of Dawn," she told the table.

Gunner leaned forward. "Who were the Graces parents?"

Heath saw him flash a look in Zach's direction.

As she sliced open a biscuit and began covering it in jam, Alexia answered, "That changes a lot. Well, a lot of things in Greek mythology have more than one possible answer. Usually though, it's Zeus and Eurynome."

A knife seemingly slipped from HJ's hand and clattered to her plate loudly as Alexia ran through the list of other possible mothers they'd had.

Heath spoke up as soon as Alexia finished. "Kronos, I was told that this contest would only have one winner. Why did you invite two?"

It had been bothering him since the Olympians had arrived for breakfast an hour earlier. After being hurriedly filled in by Rhianne on their change of plans as they got ready for their day, they'd gone down to breakfast, just to be introduced to the *two* winners of the contest. Emma had specifically said there was only going to be one.

A smile stretched across his face. "I'm glad you asked, Mr. Blackburn. You see, there were millions of submissions. Most of them weren't worth much; however, about two dozen actually seemed to provide substantial evidence that the writers *could* be someone. We didn't have enough time to evaluate everyone to conclude if they were like you all or not, but Miss Knight and Miss Drake here seem to have passed every test—well … *almost* every one."

Elliana turned around. "What else is there?"

"Consumption," Kronos told her plainly.

The second Heath caught sight of Zoey entering the room with a massive silver platter in one hand and a galvanized pitcher in the other, he realized what was about to happen.

As Zoey began dropping gooey ambrosia clusters in front of each of them, Kronos kept his eyes glued on Elliana and Nadine.

"Oh, thank God," Zach muttered as he took a huge bite, oblivious to what was really about to happen.

Heath was glad to have the food his body really wanted in front of him too, but the emotion taking center stage inside him right now was complete fear. He felt petrified.

What if these girls aren't really gods? Rhianne told us that humans couldn't eat the same thing we do—they'd die. Actually, "burn from the inside out" was the exact phrase she used. And Kronos is just willing to see if that might happen? There has to be something else, some other way to prove it—

Before Heath could manage to get a sensible sentence out in objection, he felt Alexia's death grip on his knee cap under the table. Everyone watched in silence as Nadine picked up the ambrosia pod and took a bite. She chewed … and chewed … and chewed … and swallowed.

She was fine.

Elliana, who'd watched the whole thing, tentatively looked down at hers. *She said she's a history major at Chicago, so she has to be somewhat of a history buff. She probably knows what's going on, knows what could happen if she isn't who she thinks she is. If she really is …*

Picking up the treat, she broke off a small piece and, as she pulled it apart, produced a long strand of what resembled honey connecting the two pieces. Using one finger, she swiped it up and licked it off and waited. After ten seconds, she bit off a tiny bite from the small piece in her hand and chewed slowly.

"It's sweeter than I thought," she mumbled.

Nothing happened. She was okay. Alexia's grip released, but Heath could feel the marks her nails had left.

More than anything, he wanted to lean over and assure her that Kronos never would have risked a mortal dying … in front of them … but Heath wasn't really all that sure.

Chapter 37

THAT NIGHT AT OLYMPIA CON, the New World Greek Olympian gods are the guests of honor at a gala. Tickets for this portion of the event were very limited and overly expensive. The event is televised, so the few million fans who unfortunately cannot be present at the event can still witness the first public affair the Olympians are appearing at since their true selves were shared with the world.

During the event, dinner is served, drinks are endless, and the attention stays on the nine gods in attendance despite several of them attempting to vanish into the shadows. Many behind-the-scenes moments are shown throughout the night, and Dwayne Kronos himself even makes a toast to his stars, where he also expresses his hopes that Dawn will succeed on her personal venture, adding in that he and the rest of the Olympians miss her dearly and hope she's watching wherever she is. As he brings his speech to a close, he thanks them for trusting him to take them on the adventure of a lifetime—a never-ending lifetime.

Kronos: And now I'd like to invite two of our youngest Olympians up to the stage now. For those of you who have read a history textbook, or perhaps an encyclopedia—[*chuckles, and the room laughs*]—you might know them now as the king and queen of the gods, Zeus and Hera. However, I'll always know them as Mr. Alexander and Miss Pruitt. Whichever way you may address them, please understand that they are without a doubt two of the strongest, most resilient beings I know, [*applause*] and I really mean that. I do! Please help me welcome to the stage Mr. Zachary Alexander and Miss Hanna June Pruitt!

The two can be seen at the front of the table closest to the stage as applause fills the room. Zach stands up proudly, fixes his bow tie, and holds out his hand for his significant other.

Hanna June jerks her head around, shoots an anxious glance at Amber, who simply shrugs back, before she mouthes to her boyfriend, What's going on?

He urges her to take his hand and go with him, and after hesitating, she obliges.

As cameras pan around, getting shots from every angle of the two, Zach leads them up to the stage while Hanna June glances around nervously. The rest of the Olympians remain at their tables with dazed looks on their faces, not knowing what is about to happen.

Zach: Good evening. Thank you all for joining us. I just wanted to say a few words before we carry on with our evening. First of all, the biggest possible thank-you to Dwayne Kronos for changing our lives. This man sought us out, driven to ensure we'd fulfill this destiny we had all been given, but not actually known about. And I know a *lot* of things have happened in the past year between the show, [*gestures to where the Olympians are seated*] the group of us growing to what it is now and what it will be in the future, and to now having a new kind of spotlight shining on us. And—I'm gonna be honest with you all—we are still figuring most of this out as we go.

Zach: The second thank-you I want to extend is to you all. We know that we're only here—*I'm* only here, up here, right now—because of you all. Whether you're in this room, piled into Times Square and watching there; or at home, whether that's in LA or Olympia County; or across the world, this is possible because of you. Because you all believed in me and HJ and everyone else at those tables right there. And we know you'll believe in the last four of us once we find them—that isn't lost on any of us. We want to do the best thing, no matter what that might be, for the people, whether you watch the show or you believe we're the Olympians, or you don't.

Zach: And the last person I want to thank [*turns to HJ*] is standing right next to me. Hanna June … God, I love you. I love you so much. And I know, sometimes, I don't always show that in the best way, but I'm going to do everything I can to change that, I swear. You're my best friend, and you're the love of my life. I am going to love you every day of forever because that's how long I get to have you now. [*nervously laughs*] Isn't that crazy—that we'll never have to live a moment without each other?

Hanna June: [*smirks back*] Yeah, it is.

Zach: And I'm saying this in front of all these people and the world and literal gods so that the whole world knows how serious I am about loving you. You are the best thing that has ever happened to me. I know we had our story planned out for us … which, if you think about it, even if it hadn't been, we were always destined to end up together. I just … [*lets out a shaky breath*] I … [*drops down onto one knee, and a collaborative gasp rockets around the room*] Hanna June, will you marry me?

Cameramen climb up the stairs on the side of the stage and zoom overhead.
As people excitedly whisper all around the room, Amber can be heard over the crowd exclaiming, "Oh no," right before Kai turns to her, frozen in surprise.
Hanna June stares back at him, mouth agape. Her eyes pan quickly to the ring in his hand, her hands shaking. Maybe the timing is simply coincidental, but in the second after Amber's remark, she closes her mouth and swallows hard before slowly letting out a breath.
Hanna June: Yes.

Chapter 38

ALEXIA

"YOU DON'T GET IT—SHE *had* to say yes!"

"I don't think so, Trix. We don't have to do everything they did. At least, I don't think so. I'm still trying to figure it all out ..." Her thoughts faded out as she took a mental survey of what she'd packed into her suitcase.

"Even if their parents hadn't made it a whole legal thing, she still would have had to! Think about it—Zeus and Hera were, like, the original *it* couple!"

Alexia sighed as she jammed her phone in between her ear and shoulder. "Zeus had to take animal form *frequently* to seduce women, and when Hera tried to overthrow him, he chained her in the sky," she explained to her little sister, who she knew wasn't listening to a word.

"They're meant to be together."

Yeah, not listening at all.

"Am I going to get to go to the wedding?"

Oh God, there's going to be a wedding. "Um, I don't really know what their plans are, Trixie."

"Well, find out if Damon has a date," she suggested.

"He is eleven years older than you, Beatrix!" Alexia's voice jumped an octave as she dropped her socks into her luggage.

"So? I'm not much younger than Fleur," she pointed out, making Alexia grip her phone.

"Well," she reasoned with her, hopefully speaking her language, "if you're sticking with the idea of soulmates, they're another *it* couple of Greek mythology, so ..."

Trixie went quiet at that, likely contemplating the validity behind it.

The conversation turned to when the girls would be able to talk again since the Olympians were returning back to the plantation tonight, which meant their access to the outside world would go back to being extremely limited.

"Well, the convention was a huge success, according to Kronos. He keeps saying how wildly impressed he is with the mortals and their support, even if a chunk of the world population is still on the fence about us."

"Well," Trixie started, and Alexia could practically see her sister rolling her eyes, "if that demonstration he talked about had actually happened, then maybe they would believe in you all."

"Like he explained, Heath is the only one with established powers at the moment, and ... he's having a hard time controlling the ... non-emotionally scarring ones," she reiterated, trying to stick to the way Kronos had outlined the situation to eager fans.

There's no good way to explain, Well, he's really good at blowing himself up, but we don't exactly want the whole world to witness that as the first superhuman capability a so-called god has ...

A knock sounded at her suite door. "Trix, I gotta go. I'll talk to you later though. Okay? As soon as I can, promise."

"You'd better," Trixie replied.

Heath was waiting at the door for her. "Ready?"

"Yes, please," she said. "I've had enough human interaction this past weekend. I think a few weeks of silence is much needed."

"Oh ... you didn't hear." Heath hesitated, suddenly refusing to look at her.

Pulling up her suitcase in the doorway, still half in her room, she stared back at him. "Hear what?"

Heath's lips pursed as he glanced at her. "Kronos announced at his solo panel this morning that ... well, even though we're going back to the house, things are gonna be different than last time ..."

"Heath ..." she groaned.

"They're going back to filming. They're going to have the cameras in the house with us."

Chapter 39

GUNNER

AS THE SUV PULLED AWAY from the nicest hotel he'd ever been in, Gunner's stomach twisted. It was the kind of feeling that made you feel like you should chug a bottle of Pepto *right away*. The closer they got to Los Angeles International, the more aggressive the discomfort got.

A few more minutes, just a few more minutes.

But this was Los Angeles, so a few more minutes wasn't really a thing.

Finally, Gunner dug out his phone. He hadn't touched it since he'd left the hotel, but now he needed a distraction.

Seven missed calls and forty-one texts. Most were from his family, but there were a few from Katie.

> **Katie: Hi. I don't know if you still hate me or what, but I'm letting you know that my water broke. I'm going to the hospital now.**

Oh.
OH.
Oh shit.

Hovering over his screen, his fingers did nothing but shake. He knew he wasn't going to be able to talk on the phone, and even if he did call her, what was he supposed to say?

But he had to go. He knew he did.

Clearing his throat, he spoke up. "Uh, Kronos?"

His voice rang out clear from the front of the car. "Mr. McHugh?"

"I, uh … I'm gonna need to get to the hospital when we get back to South Carolina."

Now, he turned around to face Gunner. "Is everything all right? We're going to have Doctors Lockett take care of you all, and I know you haven't met them yet, but they—"

"My ex just went into labor."

Every single person in the limousine turned their attention to him, eyes just as wide as when Zach had gotten to his knee the night before. Gunner kept his eyes trained on Kronos though, in an attempt to not go tunnel-visioned.

But, "Oh … oh my," was all he could say.

His stomachache had faded, thankfully, but now his hands wouldn't stop shaking. Out of the corner of his eye, he noticed Astrid scoot closer to the window, away from him.

Kronos and Rhianne began whispering in a huddle while the Olympians shifted uncomfortably in their seats, giving him sideways glances. Except Heath—in his peripheral vision, Gunner could see he was watching him.

"You know exactly where you need to go, son?" Kronos asked him.

Gunner replied before their whispering resumed. It was only when the private hangar came into view did the New World Cronus and Rhea break apart.

"All right. What's going to happen is, you're going to come with me. We'll get you there as fast as we can. The rest of you will stay in Rhianne's care for your trip back to Olympia."

"Do you have another jet?" Hanna June asked him, making Gunner roll his eyes. *Of course she has to pipe up and be a part of the conversation, when it has nothing to do with her.*

"We do not, Miss Pruitt. But not to worry—we'll get Mr. McHugh where he needs to be in plenty of time."

Gunner wasn't the biggest guy, but he felt rather small, standing next to Kronos in a massive jet hangar, watching the rest of the Olympians climb aboard the plane.

He hadn't asked how they were getting to his destination, but that was because Gunner kept feeling like he was on the verge of throwing up. His upset stomach hadn't come back, but he truly felt like he could be sick at any second.

As the plane started taxiing, Kronos leaned his head down slightly. "Come with me."

They made their way toward the back of the building in silence, the one small duffel bag Gunner had opted to bring bouncing off his leg as they walked.

It was in the same moment that Gunner noticed there was absolutely no one else around, but he heard a heavy clopping noise. The two men rounded a corner, and what Gunner saw caused him to take two steps back.

It was a horse—a huge white stallion—just standing there. Well, maybe it wasn't necessarily huge, but he'd never seen a horse, so he wasn't sure exactly how big they were supposed to be, but he felt like it was bigger than necessary.

As Kronos approached it, he held out a gentle hand, leveled right with its nose, and the horse took a deep bow.

What am I watching? What's happening? Gunner was positive he was going to hurl.

As the creature stood up to its full height again, Kronos turned to Gunner. "This is a Pegasus. We're going to be taking it to the hospital. Much faster than the jet."

But Gunner wasn't looking at him. He was watching the massive horse that stood proudly in between two shiny Boeings.

"We're … we're taking a horse there," he said because it simply did not sound like an actual sentence. It couldn't be a real thing. It just couldn't.

"That's correct," Kronos answered, contradicting Gunner's inner monologue.

Silent seconds ticked by, and Gunner held his gaze with the oversize farm animal before he asked, "How?"

Before Kronos could answer, out from the sides of the Pegasus spread two fantastic, feathery wings. They were bright white, just like the rest of it, but the ends seemed to be tinged in gold. Gunner swore they sparkled as they swayed slightly, settling from their abrupt display.

The creature held its wings out proudly, staring Gunner back in the face, and he somehow knew it was daring him to question its ability.

Kronos took a step toward Gunner. "We're going to fly."

Being a former Ranger meant Gunner had been in a handful of situations he had never been in before: hostile simulations, drug raids and victim rescues, water survival training—and that was before deployment. Some of the things he had seen overseas he could never unsee.

He had been recruited to join the Olympians shortly after being medically discharged, thinking it would be a calmer, less emotionally strenuous route for him to take. Which he wanted at the time—he thought a sense of normalcy would be good for him, especially given the reason for the behavior he'd exhibited that caused his discharge.

But joining the show had been anything but normal. Before this weekend, he had been in front of a camera exactly once. He'd been arrested due to a bar fight he had initiated with Zach—*but that little prick deserved it.* He had the best sex he'd ever had every single time he was with Astrid. He had been forced to be around his stepbrother, and although they barely spoke, a therapist would probably say it was a step in the right direction, even if it was against his will.

And he'd found out he was a god. Not just *a* god—he was Ares, god of war and bloodlust.

And that just didn't make any fucking sense.

How was he a god? How was anyone a god? Even after Kronos had explained how it had happened—in a shortened version of what Rhianne had told them on their first day of lockdown—Gunner still wasn't buying it.

Months had gone by since they'd been exiled to the Athanasios Plantation. Even though weird things happened in that house and

Alexia was constantly learning facts and events and sharing with them all about who they really were, he never admitted it to any of them, but too many things were starting to make sense. And that damn dumbwaiter … he hated that thing. He probably wouldn't hate it as much if they could get in, but until then he hated it. And he couldn't even destroy it—he'd tried.

However, when it came to his list of things he never thought he'd do, there were certain items that he'd never considered making the cut, simply because they weren't possible. And yet here he was, sitting atop an enormous winged horse, holding Dwayne Kronos—Titan god of time and, at one point, ruler of the universe—around the waist, getting ready to take off down the runway at LAX to fly to the other side of the country so he could meet his child.

"Ready?" Kronos yelled back to him.

"No," Gunner said.

But Kronos didn't question his hesitation. He bent down and said something to the horse, and not five seconds later, it scuffed a hoof on the tarmac.

Gunner tightened his grip around the massive man and swore he felt him chuckle.

Then they were moving—fast. The Pegasus was galloping, picking up speed at an alarming rate, making its way toward the exact same spot it seemed a passenger jet was about to touch down on.

The roar from the plane's engine was deafening as the two neared each other, and he felt the wind whip through his hair.

Kronos leaned forward slightly, and Gunner went with him.

They were headed right for the other plane, and he could see the window shades lifting open as they got closer and closer. It took everything in him to not hurl when he could make out the passengers' faces, etched in terror and confusion, as the entirety of the plane peered out the window to watch a huge flying horse, with a wingspan as wide as a football field, and two grown men inch nearer and nearer to them.

Not being able to hear anything and filled with more dread than he'd ever felt, Gunner ducked his head down, forcing his eyes shut, not wanting to see the outcome.

And then something weird happened.

His stomach seemed to jump inside his abdomen, the same way it did when you went over that first big drop on a roller coaster. He had stopped bouncing, which meant the Pegasus had stopped galloping, which meant …

Gunner opened one eye.

He was holding on to Kronos's waist as they climbed upward at a steep angle, and LA and the Pacific Ocean got farther and farther away underneath them.

They were flying.

He was on a flying horse.

A horse that soared effortlessly up through the clouds and well out of sight of the mortals below. It took a sweeping turn and pointed them in the direction of the East Coast.

Chapter 40

THE SECOND THE SEAT BELT sign clicks off, Amber unbuckles and drops herself into the vacant seat next to Astrid, who's been silent and staring out the window since Gunner left with Kronos.

Amber: Hey.

Astrid: [*without looking away from the window*] Hey.

Amber: You okay?

Astrid: Yeah.

Amber: [*hesitates*] You know, lying is frowned upon.

Astrid: I said, I'm fine.

Amber: And I'm saying that I don't believe you.

Astrid turns to face Amber, whose mouth parts slightly when she does. Astrid's eyes are puffy and red-rimmed, and the tear streaks down her face are too well defined to ignore.

Amber: Astr—

Astrid: I'm fine.

Amber: [*pauses again, considering her next words carefully*] I know I don't have Dawn's aura-extending thing … but if I did, I wouldn't think twice about pushing it your way.

Astrid: [*stares back at her*] Why?

Amber: Because you're my friend.

Astrid: [*scoffs*] Am I?

Amber: Well … maybe not before this moment, but you are now.

Astrid: [*rolls her eyes and turns back to the view of the clouds passing by*]

Amber: You don't want to be friends?

Astrid: [*snaps back to face her, annoyed now*] You have been in a bubble all weekend.

Amber: [*speaks softly*] And you've been in a bubble since we moved into the house.

Astrid: [*taken aback*]

Amber: You have! And now … well, now I think you're worried that your bubble just popped. So … I think you need a friend.

Astrid: [*considers this for a moment, then narrows her eyes*] Did you run this by Hanna June?

Amber: No.

Astrid: Maybe you should.

Amber: Why?

Astrid: 'Cause you guys are, like, best friends and because she hates me, in case you forgot.

Amber: [*shakes her head gently*] She doesn't hate you. She hates that you slept with her boyfriend. Uh, fiancé.

Both girls grimace at the word, immediately morphing into a small smile at their identical reactions.

Amber: The mortals think she's supposed to end up being, like, the queen of the universe or something. But she's not in charge of me. I can be friends with whoever I want, and I want to be your friend.

Astrid: [*watches her, trying to determine her ulterior motive*] I still don't understand why.

Amber: That's okay. You don't have to.

Astrid stares back at her as Amber relaxes in the seat, kicking her sandals off before curling up and turning to face her.

Amber: So, seriously, are you okay?

A long moment passes by, and the girls sit in silence, staring at each other. Amber can see Astrid willing herself to not cry, but ultimately, big, fat tears roll down her cheeks. Amber immediately holds her hand out, palm open and facing up. Astrid looks at it, then back at Amber before taking it, and as her fingers squeeze down and Amber can see silent sobs rack her body, she turns to stare back out the window. The girls sit like this for the rest of the ride back to Olympia.

Chapter 41

Damon: I'm going to tell you something, but you have to remain calm.

Fleur: ok...

Damon: As in you're going to be surprised, but don't look at me.

Fleur: I'm sitting next to u...

Damon: You cannot attract attention to this conversation, Fleur.

Fleur: ugh omg ok fineee

Damon: You got caught.

Fleur: Wut r u talking bout?

Damon: Your plant-focused abilities.

Fleur: WUT

Fleur: HOW????

Damon: Stop looking at me. Relax your shoulders.

Fleur: Ughhh wtf

Damon: Any of them can look over. Not to mention there're cameras on the plane.

Fleur: WUT

Damon: Fleur, please.

Fleur: Omg ok ok how did I get caught???

Damon: Before I explain, this conversation stays right here, between you and me, understand?

Fleur: Duh obvi

Damon: Amber saw you doing it through a window.

Fleur: A window?

Fleur: Oh nooooooo

Fleur: Ughhh it must've been the other nite, wen I was playing w/ivy

Damon: And ivy is...

Fleur: A fern duh

Damon: That you named Ivy?

Fleur: Yah, that's wut I said

Damon: I don't know why I asked.

Fleur: I told u I have flash cards for u so u can learn there names

Damon: Their*

Fleur: Whatevs

Fleur: Ok wait back to my problem pls

Fleur: Wut am I gonna do???

Damon: She's very certain she saw you making it grow. And even if she wasn't, I don't particularly like the idea of gaslighting. I say, if she asks you, point-blank, you tell her exactly what you first told me—that it's something you can just do. You don't know how or why. You've just always assumed you had a very green thumb.

Fleur: 2 green hands is more like it

Damon: My point is, don't deny it, but don't feed into it. Especially since you're already lying to the mortals about not knowing anything that goes on with us, abilities included. We don't need to tangle a more complicated web.

Fleur: Hey Kronos asked me to tell them that!

Fleur: They bombard me w/questions all the time about you guys, so I kinda had to

Damon: I completely understand that, and I do agree that, at least for right now, it's the best option. I just think if she finds out you blatantly lied to her, it's going to make everything more tense, and we don't need that.

Fleur: Ugh ur rite

Fleur: Wait a sec

Damon: What?

Fleur: How do I have powers?

Damon: What do you mean?

Fleur: Like I'm not an olymp, so I shouldn't have any, rite?

Damon: I'm honestly not sure.

Fleur: What if I got them from something different?

Damon: Unlikely.

Fleur: How do u know?

Damon: Because I just do, Fleur.

Fleur: Ughhh don't say my name

Damon: You didn't get them from something different because there isn't anything different to get them from.

Fleur: But how do u KNOW? If someone had told u 2 yrs ago that the greek gods were actually alive inside college kids and they had superpowers, u would've laughed at them. But now oh look ur one of them. So I ask u again damon montclaire, HOW DO U KNOW

Damon: Because I do, Fleur Hargrove. You need to believe me on this, and stop pressing the matter. And as far as the question of you possessing powers but not being an Olympian, I wouldn't look too far into that either.

Fleur: Y not?

Damon: Because I'm not technically an Olympian either and I have them.

Part III

Dumbwaiting (Finally)

POV: You're Still Running off the Olympia Con Weekend High

By Samara Connors

Introducing a highly anticipated, week-late article, but it's oh-so worth it, I promise.

The world is still buzzing after all the excitement from last weekend, and whether you were physically—and lucky enough to be—in Los Angeles or not, you know what happened.

But just for fun, let's recap in superlative fashion, shall we?

Most Anticipated:

Season two is coming! That's right; the man in charge confirmed it just before leaving on Sunday afternoon. Our favorite celebrities are getting back in front of a camera—finally. He did emphasize that this new season will be different from the last one and is set to take place primarily where the Olympians have been isolated since their life-changing bombshell was dropped back in March—a bombshell that was dropped by Dwayne Kronos himself, just to remind you. Curious as to what specific riverfront South Carolina property I'm talking about? Stay tuned for a special edition of Columns, where I do a deep dive into the plantation home that now houses our favorite global superstars.

Most Disappointing:

While it's true we were never promised anything, the show maker did allude to the possibility of some sort of a *demonstration* … which never happened. What's even more upsetting is that we were all thinking it was supposed to be about one specific thing—superpowers.

I know, I know; Kronos denied the Olympians having any "at this moment in time," but if you're thinking that isn't code for *they'll get them at some point,* just you wait.

We'll be revisiting this topic—mark my words.

Most Unexpected:

Don't even lie; *no one* saw the proposal of the century coming. I mean, since the day our gossip-bingeing brains first heard the names Zach Alexander and HJ Pruitt, we knew they were meant to be—legally contracted or not.

The ring is even bigger in person—take my word for it. Our New World Hera definitely gives off vibes that she's been planning this day her whole life, but I'm predicting a late spring wedding with a pastel color scheme and a ball gown fit for a queen.

Also, did anyone hear our favorite redhead's comment? I bet anything that she'll be muted, if they even show her, when the episode showcasing Olympia Con airs. Perhaps not though—everyone loves a good *speak now* moment.

Most Frustrating:

Yes, the weekend was saturated with the stars, but if you looked closely, there was a little non-Olympian lurking in the shadows at every event. If you're part of the vast majority of the population who has accepted the Olympians as the reincarnated Greek gods, then you probably already placed Amber's adopted, younger sister, Fleur. Most fans firmly believe she is the New World Persephone—myself included. Personally, I think she should've been allowed to sit on at least one panel.

Kronos was asked about the possibility of her appearing on the show, and unfortunately, he said there were currently no plans to feature her.

If you ask me, I think all the siblings should guest star at least once—especially Trixie Chang. If you don't follow her on socials, you're doing yourself a disservice. The girl is hilarious and highly intelligent, and even though she's an avid fangirl of her big sister's show, she's the first to call any and all of them out on their shit.

Most Life-Changing:

Had the cameras been rolling since the beginning of the semester, like they were supposed to, we would have already formally met the four newest Olympians. The panel featuring just them was the perfect opportunity to show off Alexia, Astrid, Gunner, and Heath; however, it also gave us the chance to find out that this is much bigger than just the twelve Olympians.

In case you missed it, the winners of the essay contest Parthenon hosted was announced at Olympia Con, and let's just say, none of us was expecting it. All the theories, polls, and logical reasoning pointed to one of the last four Olympians being presented

However, *two* girls were also graced with the same extraordinary stroke of luck as our Olympians and recently found out they were goddesses. Elliana Knight, junior at the University of Chicago, is one of the nine Muses. She's a history major, so it only makes sense that she is our New World Clio. The other winner, Nadine Drake, is what I'm told is a Charite, or a Grace, specifically Euphrosyne. She just wrapped up her first year at Ohio State, but shared during her brief time on the panel that she was planning to transfer to Olympia.

Okay, let's digest all that. Elliana is one of nine Muses, and Nadine is one of three Graces—not to mention the hundreds of other gods, heroes, and demigods this chaotic and expansive mythology offers us. Anyone could be any of them. The person sitting next to you could be the New World Achilles or Medusa—pro tip: don't look her in the eyes. Any one of us could have a stagnant divine soul living inside us; we just need to wake it up.

And remember, the Olympians still lack four gods. If you're confused about Dawn Sutherland and Damon Montclaire's presence—or rather, lack thereof—please refer to the Olympia Con prep video on my socials, where I break down the who's who.

Well, that's all I have for now. Which, let's be honest, is plenty. We'll be mulling over all of this for the next few millennia.

Chapter 42

ZACH

"SEE, THAT WASN'T SO TERRIBLE, was it?" Kai asked Amber, tucking a loose strand of auburn hair behind her ear.

She answered him through gritted teeth and unmoving lips as they all reconvened outside Kronos's office after their first group interview, "He'd better not be serious about another tour. I don't want to do the convention again."

"I thought you were excited for it?"

"I felt like a monkey in a zoo the whole weekend."

"But we're going to *Tokyo*, Am. Think about how sick that's gonna be." Kai attempted to change her mind.

Turning his back to them, Zach faced Hanna June. "What about you?"

"I can't wait!" Her smile beamed up at him, but he could see his reflection in her dark brown eyes. There was no excitement.

Leaning in so his lips brushed the shell of her ear, he wrapped his arms around her tightly as he whispered, "Don't lie to me, HJ. It's okay. You can talk to me."

He felt her shoulders droop against his chest in defeat. "I'll tell you later. I think there's one in the corner."

He gave her one small nod, and as he let her go and turned around, he glanced up to where she had just been looking. She was right. There was a camera up in the corner, aimed right down on them.

They had been popping up around the house in common areas ever since they had gotten back from Los Angeles. Of course they'd approached Kronos about it, but he had only assured them that while they were installed, they weren't actually on and to continue their daily lives as normal. None of them really believed that though.

"All right, all right." Their ringmaster redirected their attention as he approached them, exiting his office. He clapped his hands together too loudly, and a smile sprang onto his face. "I have a surprise for you all."

"Oh, please, no," Heath groaned. "No more surprises, please. I still wake up thinking I'm a normal person sometimes and then it hits me all over again."

"No, no, Mr. Blackburn." He laughed. "I believe this is one you will all enjoy. This way."

And he led the way out of the atrium that had mysteriously appeared off of his office when they returned from Olympia Con. Where there had once been a wall with several large-paned windows looking out at the murky Congaree River, there was now a massive set of wooden double doors. Inside, the ceiling stretched higher than the house itself, and the tiling on the floor was so intricate and detailed that Zach couldn't stare at it for too long without getting dizzy.

Opposite from where they'd all followed Rhianne in through earlier stood two equally large doors—one they had all been ushered into that led to a series of individual recording rooms where they'd now be able to have their own private time in front of a camera without scheduling or having a crew around. Past those were large, open stages for group interviews and photo shoots.

The other door was a mystery. They had asked the Titans where it led to the other day, but to no one's surprise, none of them offered an answer. Zach had looked around for Zoey just before they went through the other new door for their interview, knowing there was a chance she might let it slip if he could trick her into it, but she was nowhere to be seen.

Despite the eight of them being constantly monitored since they'd returned, there had been a minute where no one was watching them, in which Gunner tried to open the door. When it didn't budge—not a turn of the handle or any give against the lock—Zach and Kai stepped in to help, followed by Heath coming to assist them. Nothing happened, and before Alexia and Astrid could add to the driving force, they heard Rhianne's heel clicks coming in their direction.

He figured they'd find out sooner or later, just like the squeaky dumbwaiter inside the kitchen wall that hadn't been mentioned in weeks. Zach assumed the others had forgotten about it, but he hadn't.

Kronos peered at them all over his shoulder as his hands hesitated on the door handle. "*Best* behavior."

Gunner recoiled. "Why are you looking at me?"

"Wait, I thought he was looking at me," Kai said.

"He means everyone," Rhianne redirected. Zach was about to speak up next—he could've sworn the man had really meant it for him.

The second the front doors opened, they were met with deafening accolades from the crowd at the gates. Ever since they'd moved in, a steady gathering had taken up residence on Front Street.

At first, the crowd had been a mixture of fans supporting them and "understanding why they were forced to hide their identities," as the tabloids and news channels had phrased it, and people who chanted loudly that they were some sort of unholy guild who had sold their souls for ultimate power. Which most of them found kind of funny actually. Laughing about the ridiculous rumors they'd heard about themselves had proven to be the sort of bonding experience they needed at the time—well, maybe *bonding* was too strong of a word. But at least HJ and Astrid hadn't tried to attack each other again, and Zach and Gunner studied each other well enough from a distance to know when they shouldn't get closer.

But ever since Olympia Con, the crowds were constant.

Not even a year ago, Zach had recognized that being a celebrity came with a severe and sudden loss of privacy. However, the last two months had canceled that out completely. Fans had done their best to map out the layout of the house inside, and if one of them had a high-quality camera and a hardcore zoom, they could see right inside. Last week, there had been an article that showed Zach walking through the house to meet with Kronos with thousands upon thousands of questions about what they might be discussing. It had been the first thing to show up when they got their phones back for their allotted screen time, as if it was a trending topic.

It's a complete invasion of human rights.

But I'm not a human anymore.

At least the drones fall right out of the sky when they get past the gates.

And now, although the sounds of cheers and yells erupted from way down the drive, it was the two people making their way up the steps of the Athanasios Plantation house toward them that caught his eye.

He heard Hanna June suck in a breath and whisper, "Oh my God," as her fingers tightened around his. She knew who these people were.

He didn't. *Should I? I don't think—no, wait, maybe ... no. No idea who they are.*

They beamed up at the Olympians as Rhianne ushered them inside, the doors slamming behind them. The echo bounced off the walls around them as the excitement from the sidewalk abruptly halted, leaving them all staring at each other.

Kronos rounded the group with a smirk on his face. "Olympians, say hello to your newest brother and sister."

"I hate it when you say shit like that," Kai said back, shaking his head.

"Are they—" Hanna June started to ask, but was cut off by Astrid.

"You're the twins—the new Artemis and Apollo, right?"

As she jolted her head—likely to glare at Astrid and her lack of manners—HJ's hair swiped angrily across Zach's chest. Even though he couldn't see her face, he knew that she was hoping for some Matilda-like powers that would make the vase in the corner fly across the room and whack the New World Aphrodite in the face.

The boy spoke up, tilting his head in Kronos's direction. "That's what the big guy says, yeah. Name's actually Luca though," he told them. As he stepped forward, holding out his hand for Zach to shake, Astrid jumped in front.

"I know you! Yeah, you're that kid on YouTube!"

"Yeah, and you're AskAstrid!" And that was how the other people in the room became temporarily invisible.

Hanna June pushed herself forward. She stepped right in front of the girl, introduced herself, and asked her what her name was.

"Camille." The girl lit up.

"I love your skirt. I have one just like that," Hanna June complimented her, and Zach could tell that, unlike her reply about her feelings toward another convention tour, she was being genuine.

Amber stepped in to join their conversation, and within minutes, Zach watched as a group of Olympians crowded around Camille. Astrid and Luca finally realized they had isolated themselves and joined the rest of them. A sly smile drifted across Hanna June's face as she took in Astrid trying to get caught up in the conversation she'd missed out on.

He'd also taken notice of how Kronos and Rhianne had quite literally stepped back from the group and stood near the bottom of the stairs, just watching. Every once in a while, they'd mumble something to one another, but for the most part, they simply observed their behavior together.

They were watching their Olympians come together.

And now we need two more.

Chapter 43

HANNA JUNE

HANNA JUNE CAUGHT THE TAIL end of Rhianne's head tilt and knew she was pursing her lips in complete annoyance.

"Blessin' marriages isn't a special power, and you both know I'm right—anyone can get ordained online in minutes. One of my sorority sisters did it at our holiday party right after a keg stand," she said, not caring how snippy she sounded. "You don't have to be special to marry people."

Natasha let out a sigh as she circled around to the back of the couch and leaned against it, peering down at HJ. "Dear, we told you everything we remember. I can assure you—*again*—that in time, we will all remember more and the full extent of the abilities you have awaiting you will shock everyone."

The sound that came out of HJ's mouth was anything but ladylike, but she didn't care. She had met with Rhianne and Natasha four times now about her powers, hoping to unearth some memory as to what mythical skills she could look forward to upon the opening of her coffer … if it was ever found. Natasha made sure to remind her at each meeting that she'd had to, once again, leave the rest of the Titans on the hunt for Amber's coffer just to speak with her.

I've looked it up. It's a tiny island. What is taking them so long?

Rhianne leaned back against the bookshelf, her fingers gripping the ledge. "Hera—Hanna June, the way in which a celestial being can do things does not even begin to compare to what mortals can do. I know that doesn't hold much value to you at this moment, but please trust me. Hera's way of blessing marriages is not equivalent to that of your sorority sister."

Mmhmm, yeah, sure. How am I supposed to trust anyone?

Speaking of …

She hated the part of her that urged her to say *her* name, to give her any space in what was supposed to be a reassuring time, but she also knew that, if she was going to get any sort of answer, she had to at least ask.

"What about Astrid?"

Both women's expressions morphed. "What about her?" Rhianne asked.

"Maybe she remembers somethin'."

Natasha passed a look to Rhianne, who raised an eyebrow back. "They're all going to find out," Natasha said.

"But he hasn't even spoken to Aphr—to Astrid about it yet."

Natasha's tone hardened. "Well, after this, we'll tell him that now he has to!" Then she turned to Hanna June. "Kronos has plans for Astrid to learn how to … dive into her past and, ultimately, how to pull those memories out at will."

HJ pushed herself up, coming face-to-face with the woman who had raised her in another life. "That's great! Let's get her goin' with that right now," she babbled excitedly, ready to run out the door, up the massive staircase, and bolt to the end of the hallway to knock on her door and drag her back down to Kronos's office.

But Natasha held out a too-thin hand. "It's not that simple, dear. You see, the goddess who needs to first teach Astrid exactly *how* to retrieve her own memories is … well, she's missing."

"Missin'? You're missin' a *goddess*?"

"She's *somewhere*," Rhianne reassured her. "Initially, Kronos and Rhianne were set on locating the Olympians, and the handful of other gods who had been located were focused on regaining your coffers. Until …" She drifted off, locking eyes with Natasha, who gave her a small smile.

"She's quite smart, Rhea. I suggest you tell her everything, so she doesn't have to uncover the truth herself."

Rhianne cleared her throat and continued, seemingly unhappy to do so, "Until Kronos's office was broken into and everything was stolen. Then the quest for your powers was halted while we all tried to track down who had done it."

Surprised. You're surprised. They don't know you know. "Broken into? When?"

"Shortly after the gathering in Los Angeles back in December."

"December?!" she sputtered, immediately telling herself to dial it back. She didn't need to be *quite* this dramatic. *Reel it in.* "What did they take?"

"Everything. Many of Kronos's … artifacts are missing."

"And you have no idea who did it?"

"Correct. There is still a team out searching, but the Titans' primary efforts have been pivoted back to the coffer quest."

Natasha added in, "The goddess we're having trouble finding goes by the name of Jade. She ventured out alone, trying to track down the thieves, but that was several months ago, and nobody has seen or heard from her since."

Jade … do we know a Jade? I don't remember seeing that name anywhere … I wonder who—

Hanna June abruptly interrupted her own thoughts. "But she isn't dead, right?"

Rhianne shook her head. "She was fully immortal."

"Fully?"

If HJ hadn't been staring right at the woman, she would've missed the millimeter her eyes widened when she repeated that one very specific word.

"As in she's consumed enough of the divine sustenance to not have any mortal functioning traits," Natasha answered quickly.

Rhianne added, "Just like all of us."

Although her gaze was still trained on the reincarnated Rhea, Hanna June could see Natasha's reaction. Combining the sudden slight nod of her head with the tension between the two Titan goddesses, Hanna June somehow knew that Rhianne was signaling to Natasha that she'd shared enough.

Chapter 44

AMBER

"Is it even worth exchangin' money? I don't wanna go all the way there and cause a ruckus if it's gon' be for nothin'," HJ whined from the middle of Amber's bed. She'd practically sunken into it, nearly smothered by all the pillows.

"That's not even a possibility. It's a currency that isn't used anywhere anymore," Alexia explained as she continued her pacing.

"But then how can we get it?" the blonde mumbled into a pillow.

Amber stopped biting her fingernails to ask, "And, HJ, you're *sure* that's what you heard the Titans say?"

Just her tiny head lifted from the mattress. "I'm positive!"

Alexia's head shook. "No, it makes sense. I've considered it many times, although it doesn't make the task of obtaining them easier … I suppose there might be some on display in a museum somewhere."

Now HJ sat upright, aggressively crossing her legs. "We don't have time to go to a museum! We need to get up there, like, *now!* Plus, we can't be seen doin' any of this! How would that paparazzi moment go?

"Oh, hey, what are you guys doin' with these old coins?

"Oh, see, we actually need 'em to get into this panel inside our kitchen wall, where there's a floatin' platform waitin' to take us to …

"*You* finish that sentence and tell me it doesn't make a perfect tabloid cover."

"Is it something we can make?" It was a silly question, but Amber had to be sure they weren't racking their brains for no reason.

"No, it'll be a minted coin, thousands of years old." Alexia shook her head sadly.

I could use a joint right about now. "Could we ask Kronos for one?"

"NO!" both girls answered together.

"I don't think it would be a smart idea for him to know we're actively trying to get up there. It's one thing if we simply know about it and ask questions periodically, but I'm afraid of what he might do if he knows what we're up to," Alexia explained.

"Exactly."

Amber looked between them both. The three of them had been anxiously brainstorming in her room for hours and had gotten nowhere. "So ... what do we do?"

Alexia sighed. "I'll grab a few more books from the libraries. I haven't looked much into the one upstairs. There has to be something about obtaining drachma in a book somewhere. This house was left for us—Kronos and Rhianne have both said it, and we all know it. The answer is here somewhere. We just have to find it."

And they did find it. Well, to be honest, Fleur found it, completely by accident. Amber saw it happen, too, although she wasn't sure of it right away.

Fleur had been acting differently ever since Olympia Con. Her behavior had changed prior to that, but ever since they had gotten back from California, she'd been ... strange.

So, naturally, when she saw her little sister wander onto the grounds one morning, she watched her, simply to see if she was trying to get cell service somewhere—*good luck with that*—or was going to find somewhere to cry or mindlessly pick off daisy petals off ... and then regrow them possibly. Amber still firmly believed she had powers, but couldn't come up with a crafty way to go about asking her, and Damon hadn't returned any helpful information to her, so Amber decided she would just have to find out on her own.

She watched her meander around the property, visiting the rose garden and the in-progress topiaries. She stopped to look up at each of the few willow trees on the far side, closest to the river, and the massive oak tree that had several limbs hanging over the fence, shadowing the sidewalk, where small crowds had gathered early to watch her. Occasionally, she would give them a wave, but otherwise, she ignored them.

At the back of the property stood a miniature version of the Acropolis—because *that* wasn't an obvious nod. The Olympians had been informed that the structure was intended to be used for photo shoots and, at some point, a tourist spot. But for now, it stood in disarray. Several columns had crumbled over the years, and others had chunks missing out of them. Tiles were cracked, and just like several of the guest cottages, the ceiling was caving in. The poor thing was also a slight shade of yellow, tinged with age, and in desperate need of a paint job.

Amber watched Fleur closely as she approached it. Upon their arrival at the property, most of them had stayed inside for the better part of the first two weeks. If they ventured outside to explore the grounds, they did it under moonlight, when the throngs of people on the sidewalks were greatly thinned. None of them had paid much attention to the structure, especially after Kronos had told them it wouldn't be utilized for a while. Even with the weather nice now, it was really just an eyesore.

But apparently not to Fleur. She inspected every inch of it, gazing up and down the chipped columns and tile shards under her bare feet. Amber cringed every time she could hear the ceramic scraping and gripped her windowsill too hard while restraining herself from running out there and forcing her little sister to put on shoes.

An ungodly amount of time passed before Fleur reached down and shifted one of the tiles. As Amber hoped she wouldn't slice her foot open, she watched Fleur slide it over and slowly reach down. She picked up something small in her hand and inspected it. Turning it over time and time again, she stared at the thing before she hastily reached down and grabbed a few more, replaced the tile, and stood up. Her walk back to the house was calm but purposeful, and Amber watched every step she took as she approached the cottage she had taken residence in and slammed the door behind her.

It had most definitely been strange behavior, and Amber debated the entire thing with herself, until there was a knock on the door. She didn't even have a chance to open it before Fleur pushed her way through. She closed it suddenly but silently and simply stared at Amber.

"Are you okay?" Her foot didn't appear to be bleeding.

"I found something," was all she said.

"Found what?"

And there, in Fleur's open palm, lay five, dirty but silvery half-dollar-sized coins. In the center was an owl, glistening up at Amber through the sunlight that snuck across the room, and Amber didn't need to ask any more questions. She knew exactly what they were.

Chapter 45

Amber: I have drachma

HJ: I'm sorry what

Damon: You better be serious.

Heath: Whoa whoa what

Amber: I have drachma. Fleur found it.

Alexia: Are you serious??

HJ: Oh man, double q marks, that means she's super excited

Kai: WAIT I've been with you for the last two hours and you didn't tell me this!

Amber: You took a nap

Kai: Bc I was tired. I would've been wide awake if you had told me that!

Amber: Sorry

Alexia: Do NOT blame Amber for you falling asleep. You're just upset that you're not the first one to know about it.

Kai: Shut up lex

HJ: Omg Alexia I love this side of you

Heath: Amber, where'd she find them?

Amber: In that thing out back. Some of the tiles were broken and she saw something shiny down there

Alexia: Are there more? Or did she grab whatever was there?

Amber: She said she took them all, but I haven't gone out to check. There's so many ppl out there today

Heath: Maybe we can check tonight

Kai: No... we have to go up tonight

Damon: I can't go tonight.

Kai: Are you kidding me montclaire

HJ: Wait

Kai: Why???

HJ: Did you guys hear that?

Heath: Oh good, I thought I was the only one

Alexia: I heard it.

Kai: I didn't hear anything

Heath: I think it's Rhianne. I think she's calling Amber

Amber: Me??

Alexia: You're Amber...

Amber: What do you think she wants?

Heath: No idea

HJ: She's coming up the stairs, I hear her

Kai: I'm going to hide in the bathroom

HJ: Just see what she wants, we'll wait

Amber: Ok

Amber: Omw to K

Amber: She said smthng bout my box

Amber: Frkng out

HJ: I'm sure it's fine

Alexia: Maybe they just haven't found it yet and want to give you an update.

Heath: Maybe they want you to go with them to help find it

HJ: Just go see what he has to say, we won't go without you

Amber: Promise?

HJ: Promise

Chapter 46

ASTRID

ASTRID HOLDS HER SMILE, AWARE of the camera trained on her, as she waits for Kronos's next question during her solo interview—finally.

Kronos: Some fans seem to think you've always had some sort of idea you were a goddess.

Astrid: [*shrugs*] Maybe on some level.

Kronos: And you lived a rather high-profile lifestyle prior to coming to the East Coast and being on the show. How has your life changed since not only becoming an Olympian, but also learning you're the New World Aphrodite?

Astrid: [*ponders this for a moment*] I don't think it's changed much. Well, aside from the social interaction [*smiles sarcastically*]—or rather, lack thereof. It's hard to be a public figure if you don't venture out into the public, wouldn't you agree?

Kronos: [*smiles back*] And yet you're excelling at doing just that within the safety of the property lines.

Astrid: [*inaudible noise*]

Kronos: There's been much discussion about what types of abilities you might have once your powers are established.

Astrid: [*perks up*] I've been thinking a lot about that too! Dawn and Heath both seem to—oh wait. [*looks around*] Can I start that again? I don't think Dawn wanted us to mention anything about her powers.

Kronos: Of course, Miss Radzilowicz. [*motions to the camera crew*] Whenever you're ready.

Astrid: I've been thinking about that a lot! It's really been bothering me—how my nannies gave me hints as to where they might be, but not *what* they could be. I think it would—

Kronos: [*cuts her off and waves his hands to the camera crew*] Cut, cut! Miss Radzilowicz, it would—

Astrid: [*cuts* him *off right back*] You do know it's quicker to just say my name, right?

Kronos: [*lets out a frustrated sigh as he pushes himself out of his chair and goes over to her*] Miss Radzilowicz, it would be in your best interest to, perhaps, *not* mention the fact that you, um, let's say … have inside information.

Astrid: But … it's not inside information. I told all of you about it.

Kronos: Yes, yes, you have, and we're immensely grateful for that. It's been quite helpful, and I'm sure your memories will help us more in the future, but, you see, we don't plan to let the mortals know all that.

Astrid: Why not?

Kronos: Well, you've seen how the world has reacted to the news about you all. Several countries have closed their borders to travelers, and a handful of nations have chosen to stop selling goods with the United States because they don't trust you all.

Astrid: That's a really small amount of the world though. Most people love us!

Kronos: But the goal is to get everyone to love you—and if they don't love you, we need them to at least *trust* you, remember? That's all we're aiming for here—trust.

Astrid: [*stares back at him*] They're going to find out eventually. They'll be mad that we didn't tell them right away, and then you'll have made your relationship with the mortals even more strained.

Kronos: [*considers her words*] I'm curious, Miss Radzilowicz—given the state of the world currently and the shaky ground the ten of you stand on, with no way to control the mortals, should you need to … what would you do if you were in my position?

Astrid: [*shrugs like it's a no-brainer*] I would tell them. I would be up front about the entire situation, about everything.

Kronos: You would risk the possibility of sending the world into an even more severe state of panic?

Astrid: *You* would risk losing the trust you're working so hard to build?

Kronos: [*narrows his eyes at her*] I will not be responsible, nor tied to, the reason this dying planet continues to destroy itself! You're all supposed to save it—that's the only reason we're doing any of this!

Astrid: [*challenges him*] What if I just keep talking about it?

Kronos: We'll edit it out. Just because we film in a different area code doesn't mean this show—this facade we give to the humans—isn't exactly what they do in Hollywood. You should know how show business works, Miss Radzilowicz.

Chapter 47

AMBER

AMBER POKED HER HEAD INTO the hallway and cringed as the wall sconces silently shone to life when four other bedroom doors hinged open. Kronos and Rhianne had both left with the Titans after she met with them all hours earlier, but there was still the possibility that the plan the five of them were executing could be ruined if any of the Olympians not involved heard them. The hope of getting up the dumbwaiter was the only thing she'd been looking forward to since she'd told their secret group she'd secured the mysterious, necessary drachma.

"Ready?" Hanna June whispered through the darkness.

A faint movement came from down the hall, past the steps, and Amber hoped both Alexia and Heath were still on board. She was not in the mood to deal with any cold feet tonight; she needed a win.

As the five of them met at the top of the grand staircase, Alexia looked between them all.

"And you're sure Damon can't join us?"

"Positive." Amber nodded her head. "He said he's got a lot of work to catch up on."

The others vaguely nodded and began their descent, but Hanna June gave her a funny look—almost like she didn't quite believe her.

Hanging back behind the others, she leaned in toward her friend. "He's watching Fleur," Amber hissed out. "I think she's been sneaking out at night."

"Huh … and you think having Damon watch her is the best way to keep her from … gettin' into trouble?" HJ spoke slowly.

"Yeah, I mean, he keeps an eye on her all the time, and—"

She stopped on the stairs now, frozen in space, as the others continued tiptoeing down the carpeted steps. "Am, you're not dumb. You know how their stories … like *who* they are … you know how all that goes, right?"

Amber stared back at her. This wasn't a conversation they had time for. And even if they *did* have time, Amber was well aware she needed to have a long conversation with Fleur first … but even before that, she needed to have one with herself.

"I know, I know," she sighed. "Hades steals Persephone and traps her in the underworld—yeah, I read the SparkNotes on it. But first of all, *that's illegal.* Second, that's never gonna happen. Damon is talking to some girl he met at Olympia Con, and I don't think Fleur is interested in anyone—even though I could've sworn she was—"

"Wait, wait—I'm sorry, what? *Who* is Damon talking to?" HJ sputtered through a whisper, clinging on to the banister.

Amber filled her in on the few details Fleur had told her as they caught up with the others just as they approached the foyer. They were taking the biggest steps they could to catch up, and luckily, by the time Heath turned around to address Amber, they were right behind them.

"So, Amber … should I even ask about your coffer?" The words were heavy with regret, and Amber knew he was asking out of concern, as opposed to nosiness.

She let out a sigh and suddenly had everyone's attention. "They found it. Kronos has it. I'm not allowed to open it yet."

"What? Why didn't you tell me?" Kai sputtered, little bits of saliva flying in frustration.

"I didn't tell anyone," she reminded him. "It's kinda … broken."

Alexia's expression twisted up in confusion. "Broken how?"

"It's all banged up, and one corner was burned," she told them. The heaviness of it seemed to hit her all over again. She was revisited with that hollowed-out, sinking-gut feeling she had gotten when the Titans explained the battle they'd gone through to get it back.

"You said *yet*," Alexia encouraged. "As in you will get to open it at some point. Maybe they just have to fix it somehow."

Amber nodded. "They all assured me they'd do everything they could to get it back to normal, but they didn't want my powers to be affected if I opened it in the state it was in right now. So, I guess I'm just waiting." She shrugged, and Kai pulled her in for a hug.

It was sweet and exactly what Amber wanted, but it was still weird. They hadn't been affectionate in front of the others up until that moment.

Clearly, it didn't seem to bother any of them because Hanna June went right in to hug them over Kai's shoulders, and Alexia came on top of hers with Heath's massive arms coming in to enclose everyone.

God, I love them. I feel so loved, was all she kept thinking as the group hug seemed to supply magical abilities of its own. Tears rolled down Amber's face as she clung tighter to their embrace.

Chapter 48

ALEXIA

THEY TIPTOED INTO THE KITCHEN in a cluster, and the panel slid open without making a sound. However, the squeaking she had heard day and night grew closer.

"You have it, Amber?"

"Right here." The New World Demeter held out her hand, palm up. Five tarnished coins lay in her hand, ready to be exchanged for a ride to … well, if this led to where Alexia was thinking, Gunner would owe her two hundred push-ups.

"Go ahead," Heath urged her, and she stepped forward.

The trinket dish in the center of the platform danced expectedly at her approach, almost as if it knew *this* was it—that it was really going to get what it wanted this time.

From where she stood in the terribly lit room, Alexia could see Amber's hand shaking as she dropped the coins in, one by one. They each clattered into the bowl, and once it held all five, the noises stopped—the squeaking, the shaking, all of it. The room fell silent.

Until the coin tray tilted on its side, and out slid four of the pieces.

Their focus ricocheted from the dish, down to the floor where the rejected silver lay, and back up to the platform, where the one remaining coin flipped over and rattled still.

Amber stared at the group in awed silence before peering to her right. Alexia watched as she cocked her head, then jumped back at the same time the bowl slid to the far corner.

Four sets of feet ran the short distance across the kitchen floor.

"Look." Amber pointed at where their ancient ATM had relocated itself.

"We saw," Heath breathed.

"No, look inside. At the coin," Amber said.

Straining through the darkness to get a glimpse at what Amber had seen first, Alexia slowly made out an intricate design of a bundle of wheat.

"Wasn't there an owl?" Hanna June questioned next to her.

"There *was*. It changed to that," Amber told them, her eyes still wide.

Standing up straight, Kai said, "It wants you."

Alexia really disliked agreeing with him—call it an impulse—but she was thinking the same thing. "It's inviting you first."

As she squeezed her way out past Heath and bent down to pick up one of the dejected coins, she added, "Maybe it's going to do the same for us, one at a time."

The others copied her actions, plucking a coin from the floor.

"I don't really want to go by myself," Amber confessed, scratching at her forearm.

"You won't," Hanna June assured her. "We'll be right behind you. Promise."

Glancing at the floating platform inside the wall one last time, Amber let out a breath, clutched at her stomach, then gave the group one last look. "Okay … do I just … climb on?"

"I think so." Heath chuckled lightly. "We haven't done this part yet."

Amber gave him a look, and as she turned to give Alexia a sideways hug, Kai pulled her in and kissed her forehead.

Hanna June squeezed her hand. "We'll be right behind you," she repeated.

As she hoisted herself onto the platform, Alexia curled her fingers into a ball and dug her nails into her palm. *Don't let her fall, don't let her fall, don't let her—*

The second she settled into a crisscross position, the thing took off, not making a sound. The four Olympians left gazed up into the darkness and watched the wooden rectangle shrink in size … until, of course, the noise started again. This time though, it came from below them.

Another dumbwaiter was on the way, just like Alexia had hoped.

This time, Heath dropped his coin in. The inscription of Athena lay on the top when it landed, and after flipping itself over, the owl changed to a hammer and anvil—Hephaestus's symbols.

As he climbed up and was carried away, Alexia decided to try hers next. However, the streak of the platform inviting the god who had deposited the coin ended. After dropping hers in, she watched as it turned itself over to reveal a trident.

"Kai," was all she said, and he practically skipped past her, happily shoving his drachma into her hand.

She and Hanna June stood side by side, glaring at him as he was pulled upward, but not before he managed to call out, "Race ya."

"God, this is like dodgeball in gym class all over again," she mumbled into the near-empty room, waiting for the fourth dumbwaiter to stop at the opening.

"What do you think is up there?" Hanna June whispered, her voice shaking gently, and turned to look at Alexia.

Alexia stared back, hoping the next dumbwaiter would arrive before she had to answer. But Hanna June was staring at her intently.

"If I say Mount Olympus, would you think I'm crazy?" Part of her hoped she hadn't actually asked it—she knew how ludicrous it sounded.

Hanna June shook her head, and Alexia felt her face release the tension it'd been holding.

"Not at all."

"Sounds pretty stupid—saying it out loud, I mean." Her words came out with a forced laugh.

Hanna June shrugged. "It does. But it also might be true."

"The same thing you think is scribbled really tiny on the whiteboard."

Alexia stared back at her. "It sounds ridiculous to say there's a whole kingdom waiting at the top." Her words came out with a forced laugh.

Hanna June shrugged. "It does. But it also might be true."

A rattling sound emitted from the wall, and Alexia didn't get a chance to ask her friend if she was scared; she looked like she was. "You're going to be next."

The New World Hera looked at her. "You think so?"

She nodded. "Definitely."

And she was right. The girls watched her owl-sided coin flip over to show Athena in her original form and back over to now show a peacock, its wings spread gloriously.

The smile Hanna June gave her was small, tight-lipped, just before she climbed aboard. "I'll see you up there."

And then she was gone.

Waiting for her vessel to arrive, Alexia suddenly felt cold. She checked her watch, noting it was almost eleven, and decided they needed to be back in time for the sunrise. That would give them a few hours, which seemed like plenty of time … until she realized she had no idea what they were supposed to do when they reached their destination.

What if it took them just as long to get to wherever it was they were going? What if they got lost? What if they needed more drachma when they got there? Or to get back?

She realized she had not thought this through as extensively as she should have. On the other hand, she didn't have much of a choice now. The others were gone. And there was a wobbling wooden board inside the kitchen wall, urging her to make her exchange—payment for a ride.

Copying the movements of the others, she deposited her coin, and when her owl remained an owl she pulled herself up. The pulley began shifting immediately, and she rose into the darkness. The small coin dish next to her foot stayed in its place, her drachma rattling around inside it every few seconds. The platform glided smoothly through the vertical tunnel, and Alexia swore that she could see the bottom of Hanna June's platform above her in the dark.

A minute or so passed, though it felt much longer, and Alexia checked her watch. A half hour had gone by.

Then the darkness seemed to lighten; blackest black turned to a charcoal, which turned to a cloudy gray. She looked up and saw Hanna June's ride had stopped moving, and she was heading straight toward it—with no way to stop. As it filled the entirety of the space, there was no way around it—she was about to smack her head into it at full force.

Just as she was about to duck her head down and cover it, the strangest thing happened. Okay, well, maybe not the strangest thing because she *was* on a floating piece of wood inside a wall, heading to what she hoped was a magical land … but still.

The platform above her suddenly folded up on its side and melted into the wall. With it gone, Alexia was able to glide right up to the landing spot, where the other four Olympians were waiting for her.

"I win," Kai teased from where he stood.

Heath greeted her with a butchered version of a Twilight quote, asking where she'd been and calling her crazy, and an unsure smile stretched across his face as he held out a hand. "HJ told me to say that—I have no idea what it's from."

The girls burst into a fit of giggles as Alexia stumbled to her feet to meet a view she hadn't considered—the gates.

They appeared to stretch for miles, with no end in sight, and stood higher than most skyscrapers she'd seen. Bright gold, shiny and polished, with two tiny figures racing toward one other in front of them. As she watched them jousting atop clouds, she knew exactly who they were.

"Is this what I think it is?" Amber asked as the five of them gaped up at their surroundings.

"That depends," Alexia told her. "If you're thinking this is Mount Olympus, then I'm pretty sure you're right." And she stepped forward to lead the group toward the gods' kingdom.

Chapter 49

HEATH

THEY'D ONLY TAKEN A FEW steps toward the never-ending golden gates when Heath swung around to check on their ride back to earth, but the dumbwaiter was still waiting, right in the cloud-covered alcove it had pulled up into and deposited each of them.

There was nothing else around them. The clouds extended for miles in every direction. They seemed to get darker, the farther away they stretched, as if convincing visitors they shouldn't go any way other than to the entrance of Olympus.

"Oi!"

The voice came from the gates, and Heath had to run to catch up with the others, who had almost reached where it seemed to come from.

There were two boys—okay, they were both likely the same age as him—scrambling to get off the ground as their group approached them. They were completely identical, and Heath got the feeling that every time they returned here—because he figured there'd be plenty more visits in the future—he would have trouble telling them apart.

The one on the right stood up straighter and surveyed the five of them. "You came from the mortal world?"

"Yes, we came up from the dumbwaiter in the—" Alexia started, but his hand flew up, cutting her off.

"A'right, a'right. Now, what's behind 'ese gates is only for celestial bein's. How do we know you didn't just sneak on up 'ere?" The other one's eyes narrowed, passing over each of them.

"Sneak on up?" Kai sputtered. "We've been trying to get up here for months now! If there was a way to sneak up, we would've figured it out a long time ago!"

"We're supposed to be here—I mean, we're pretty sure we are," Amber offered.

The one on the left gestured between him and his twin. "Yeah, and we *know* we're s'posed to be here. We guard these gates to keep anyone from gettin' in who shouldn't."

His British accent is slightly thicker than the other's—that's his identifying feature.

Alexia pointed at the guards. "You're Alexiares and Anicetus, aren't you?"

"How'd you know that?" they questioned her at the same time.

"She reads a lot," Heath answered, not giving them a chance to cut him off. "Listen, for a long time, we've been trying really hard to get up here. We can't have come all this way to be turned around. We're supposed to get into those gates," he explained.

The two looked at Heath, then at each other, took in the other four, and then turned back to him.

The twin on the left asked, "Who are you?"

Before any of them could respond, Hanna June pushed her way to the front. "*I* am Hera, queen goddess of marriage, and, I swear on Hades, if you don't open the gates to our kingdom this instant, I will curse you both. No one'll *ever* fall in love with you for the rest of your immortal existence. You'll be forced to live out your lonely, pathetic lives right *here* for eternity. Understand?"

The moment she'd said her New World name, the twins' eyes had tripled in size. They didn't dare interrupt her though, and Heath could see their spears shaking in their white-knuckled grips.

The second she finished, they were scrambling to get past each other. The two took turns ping-ponging formalities toward HJ as they ran back to their posts.

"Yes, ma'am—Your Majesty. Yes, Your Majesty."

"Right away, Your Majesty."

"Deepest apologies, Your Majesty."

Heath saw Amber nudge HJ in the ribs as he tossed her a sly grin. That was the first time she'd ever said aloud her parallel identity, and he wasn't the only one thinking it—Alexia turned to him slightly and gave him a shocked look.

As the twins reported to their adjacent gates, they seemed to tap simultaneously on the sides, and with a loud, deep, and satisfying sound, both of the skyscraper-height golden gates began to open inward. The high wall of clouds that sat behind them turned to a flight of stone steps as they inched toward them.

"Thank you," Hanna June addressed them, as she started toward them.

They both bowed from their stations. "Yes, ma'am—er, Your Majesty."

Alexiares spoke up. "And, please, Your Majesty, call us Jack—"

"And Jordan, Your Majesty." Anicetus bowed his head as the group passed by.

Hanna June nodded once at each of them. "Jack, Jordan, have the gates ready upon our departure."

"Yes, Your Majesty," they said again, saluting them this time. Heath thought he saw a bead of sweat slide down Jack's forehead as he passed.

The steps were as wide as the gates, and, in Heath's opinion, unnecessarily deep. As they began their ascent, Alexia leaned toward HJ.

"What was all that?"

She let out a huff, and her accent returned. "They really weren't gonna let us in! After months of tryin', we were just gonna be turned away by two idiots simply 'cause they don't recognize us?! *Everyone* knows us—"

Her rambling turned quickly into angry murmurs that Heath only caught parts of. His focus quickly shifted to the sudden pins-and-needles feeling that settled in his earlobes, hands, and knees.

No, no, no. This is the worst possible time. Not now ...

He pushed on, taking his time before stepping up onto each new stair.

Maybe no one will notice ... if I just keep going, just push through it ...

"Alexia, who were those guys?" Amber asked over HJ's head.

"Alexiares and Anicetus," she clarified, likely glad for the change in subject. "The Horae are typically associated with guarding the gates of Olympus, but sometimes, it's those two," she explained.

Then, without warning, her arms flew out to the sides, and she stopped. "Guys, wait."

"What?!" Kai whined. "We're almost there!"

It was true; they were *so close*.

Heath would have protested, too, if he wasn't so miserably uncomfortable. *Why didn't I think to bring my meds?*

Alexia pulled up her right arm, pointing at her watch face. "It's just past a quarter after. We *need* to be back before sunrise. I suggest we plan to head back down these steps by five—at *the latest*. Agreed?"

But in natural Poseidon and Athena fashion, an argument ensued.

"You can't *suggest* something and then be like, *M'kay, we're all just gonna do what I say, right?*"

"I didn't say that!"

"You're right; I used less words 'cause, God, you talk a lot."

"I suggested a plan and wanted to see if everyone was okay with that!"

"You didn't give anyone else a chance to fuckin' talk! That's not how it works, Lex!"

"That's not my name!"

The disagreement would've just gotten louder, as they were both yelling over HJ's and Amber's attempts to get them to stop, had it not been for the voice above them that broke it up.

"Correct."

They all jumped and stared from where it had come from. Up on the top step stood three women. They seemed to glow from a light behind them just on the other side of the stone staircase they stood on. They looked down at the five of them, each with a curious smile on their face.

"Your name is really Athena," said the one in the middle. She wore a crown of pink flowers that Heath recognized from back home. "But we will call you whatever you like."

Heath could see out of the corner of his eye that Alexia was already assessing them. A faint smile ghosted over where her Kai-focused scowl had just been.

"*You're* the Horae."

Their grins stretched, and they curtseyed.

"Yes, Your Majesty."

Oh, please, not this again.

Alexia nodded a few times—more so to herself, he thought—and then took the next step up. Heath was right behind her.

"And I prefer Alexia," she added.

All five of them reached the top step at the same time, which meant they all froze in their stances at the same time too.

It was beautiful. It was expansive. It was all theirs.

Chapter 50

KAI

HE WAS IN A VIDEO game. He had to be. There was no other explanation for the view in front of him.

The stone under their feet rolled out for miles, in every direction, reaching to courtyards and buildings that looked like the crumbling structure in their backyard, except these were massive and in immaculate condition. Waterfalls poured from over balconies into streams that wound along the walkways and under footbridges and into an expansive central pool. An ornate fountain stood in the center of it, showering the residents who lived in the water below—and, *oh*, how Kai wanted to run into it.

"Welcome," said the girl on his right as they crossed the threshold and began down the stairs, heading toward the city they'd found above the clouds. The city for *them*.

He thanked her and felt Amber's hand wind around his biceps. Her perfect, freckle-speckled face was beaming up at him.

"Hey," he said.

"Hi." She smiled back, then bit down on her lip.

She was doing it out of excitement, and he knew that, but, *ugh*, he wanted to kiss her.

"This is real." She laughed. "This is really our life. We're here; it's really happening."

He tucked a loose strand of hair back behind her ear before she could incessantly twist her finger in it, like he knew she would.

"And we're together."

Her lips parted, and she pushed up on his forearm. Their noses were millimeters from touching, and he could smell the sweet traces of ambrosia on her breath.

"And we're together," she repeated, top teeth sinking into her bottom lip.

"No one I'd rather be in heaven with."

He laced his fingers through hers, knowing that this moment—*this* one right here—had just established itself as the most important of his core memories. He was going to remember this for the rest of his immortal existence, and he never wanted to forget the way her hair glowed like a warm fire in the light that surrounded them; or how her skirt hadn't stopped rustling since they'd gotten up the dumbwaiter, like there was a constant meadow breeze around her; or how he waited for each new smile of hers and how that number had definitely increased since they'd started making out like high schoolers. But this fifteen minutes they'd spent above the rest of the world left every other minute in the dust.

Kai was positive that, powers or none, cameras or not, she had always been a goddess to him. And he wouldn't tell her at this moment because he didn't want to ruin it, but he was certain with every fiber of his divine being that he was deeply in love with her.

A scaly tail flipped out of the fountain as they neared it, splashing Kai as they walked past. He gripped Amber's hand harder as they followed Hanna June down the winding stone path. It was impossible to know how high they were, and maybe it was the altitude change, but Kai felt better than he ever had before, even with the help of illegal substances.

He had just started imagining what it might be like if he consumed his body weight in nectar when there was a shrill scream. Amber clung to him, and Alexia froze in her tracks, jutting an arm out. They all stared ahead at the towering mountain-top palace. The clouds encircling the highest towers stirred as they darkened to a shade of gray. Within seconds, a small figure came bolting over the bridge that connected the entrance to the walkway the five of them stood on.

Splitting up, they opened a path for the distressed god to be able to run past them—except she didn't.

Is she wearing a cape? No, nobody wears capes anymore … oh no. She's wearing a cape.

As she sprinted nearer to them, her destination became clear—them. Her manic gaze jumped between all of them, jet-black hair swaying frantically in her face, unable to keep up with her jerky, crazed movements.

Unfortunately for him, he was the closest.

She grabbed his shoulders and shook. "Where is he?!" She sounded desperate as she sank her nails into his skin.

He would've answered her had it not been for the fact that he had no idea what she was talking about.

And to make things just a little more complicated, with how aggressively she was attempting to shake an answer out of him, he couldn't tell her if he wanted to.

"Who?" Hanna June demanded.

The girl stopped and turned to look at her, whacking him in the face with her long hair. "Your brother, Your Majesty!"

HJ's shoulders sank. "Which one?"

She sounded annoyed, and Kai knew what she was thinking—going from a single child to suddenly having half a dozen siblings hadn't exactly been on her bingo card. He had the two half-brothers, but never considered them family—until they were all forced to recognize it, of course.

The girl shouted, "Hades!"

Everyone else looked too put off by the girl to answer. But Kai was still being held hostage by her talons, so he answered, "He's back at the house."

This time, when she faced him, he could see her eye was twitching slightly.

"The house?"

He nodded, gesturing to the top of the massive stone steps. "Yeah, we took the dumbwaiter in the kitchen up here, and—"

She was gone, off and sprinting toward the gates, cape flying out behind her.

They all stared at her shrinking figure as she quickly approached where the three women still stood.

"Who *was* that?" Heath asked.

"Hecate," said a voice behind them.

This girl looked fairly normal, aside from the center of her hair being rainbow-colored. It reminded him of something Astrid would do.

She bowed and greeted them all. "She told us to call her by the name Jade, but to us, she is Hecate. Just as, to us, you are Hera." She bowed her head in HJ's direction. "But we will call you Hanna June, if you wish."

HJ tilted her head curiously and smiled at the girl. "Whichever you prefer—I'll answer to both. And you are?"

"I am your attendant, Iris. You may also call me Makena—I'll answer to both." She smiled back.

"Who's my attendant?" Kai asked. If she got a personal assistant, he wanted one too.

Makena's eyes lit up as she turned to him, glancing at Amber before she answered, "Your wife, King Poseidon."

An uncomfortable heaviness started to lace its way through his and Amber's fingers.

Alexia spoke up—even though no one was speaking to her

"Amphitrite? Is she here? Are there others?" She reached in her pocket and pulled out that annoyingly small notebook she wrote everything about them in.

As Makena began to explain to them that there were some others awaiting their arrival in one of the temples, Amber leaned against his arm.

"You okay?" she asked, peering up at him.

Well aware that the others were now following this girl to one of the miniature Acropolis buildings in the opposite direction, he looked down at her. A few birds pleasantly chirped in the distance, and the gentle sound of the fountain spray was the only other thing he could clearly hear.

The thought mulled around in his brain as he debated with himself if he should actually say it or not. It seemed to jump off the tip of his tongue and pry his lips open as he asked her, "You know we don't have to do every single thing they did, right?"

Her nod was tiny, against his biceps. "I know."

"You do?"

"Yeah."

Should I explain? Do I say, And by that, I mean that I don't necessarily have to marry whoever the Amphirinity girl is they're talking about? *Does she get that?*

"Alexia said it herself—that we don't have to follow *exactly* in their footsteps," he added.

"I know."

Does she though?

"And she's the smartest one."

"I know, Kai." Amber gave him a soft smile. "We should go before we lose them. C'mon." And she pushed off of him and tugged at his arm.

He felt drunk, following her lead, as the sunshine warmed him. Her hair flowed out behind her, and he decided that when they got back to earth, he'd hold her if she wanted to sleep. He knew he'd be too awake and excited to rest though. Whenever she woke up, he'd go with her as she meandered through the greenhouse, like they had fallen into the routine of doing since they'd returned from their trip to Los Angeles. And when they got back to the spot where they had finally fallen into sync, he'd tell her he loved her. He couldn't hold it in anymore, but he knew it needed to be special—as special as it could be for someone as extraordinary as she was.

Chapter 51

IN ONE OF THE TEMPLES, Makena introduces the group to the handful of gods who have been living in Mount Olympus. After she guides Hanna June over to a small gathering of girls, the others begin to review Alexia's notes.

Alexia: Okay, let me just make sure I have this all correct. Cassidy, you're the New World Cassandra, right? 'Kay, well, that's easy enough to remember.

Amber: And Cassandra was the [*leans in closer to Alexia and lowers her voice*] the compulsive liar?

Alexia: No, no. She was cursed by Apollo to share prophecies that *were* true, but to never be believed.

Amber: Huh …

Cassidy stays quiet, watching Hanna June as she's being introduced to three other girls by Makena.

Amber: [*points at them*] And those are more of the Muses?

Alexia: [*nods*] Three of them, which means we only need to find five more, since we already have Elliana.

Kai: [*directs his attention to the two young men talking*] And you're *sure* those two aren't Hermes and Dionysus?

Amber: They're who the last two files were on, so wouldn't it make sense that they're them?

Alexia: [*shakes her head*] The taller one is Jason, which makes sense why Kronos possibly had him confused for Hermes—he's his great-grandson. And the other is definitely Perseus—I just know it.

Heath: But Perseus wasn't a god?

Alexia: [*nods*] Correct—he was a mortal. However, some of the more legendary heroes were deified, like Heracles and Perseus.

Kai: [*zones out as he mulls over Alexia's words*] Wait … Perseus … why is that so familiar?

Amber: Well, there was that book series you thought—

Kai: No, no, not that. I … I remember something.

Alexia: [*crosses her arms to glare at him*] Oh, do you?

Kai: Yeah. [*his gaze locks on to hers*] And I think it … it involves you … somehow?

Alexia: [*waits for him to elaborate, but he doesn't, and she shakes her head at him*] You're despicable.

Kai: What is that supposed to mean?

Alexia: [*goes back to her notebook as she nears Hanna June and Makena*] I'll give you a hint—it's not good.

Kai: [*grumbles*] I assumed that.

Alexia: I'll let you figure it out, Poseidon. [*walks away*]

Amber: Well, even without the last two Olympians, we still found more people like us. And that has to be good, right?

Heath: [*smirks*] Kronos is gonna flip.

Kai: We're gonna have to find a way to tell him without pissing him off.

Heath: [*taken aback*] You think he's gonna be mad?

Kai: [*shrugs*] Notice how none of the Titans have ever spoken about the dumbwaiter before, no matter how many times we brought it up? Kronos definitely told them to just pretend it doesn't exist.

Amber: I mean, maybe?

Kai: No, I think if he'd wanted us to come up here, he would've helped.

Chapter 52

AMBER

AMBER WANTED TO LIVE HERE. Consciously pushing the thought of her father and sister to the back of her mind, she wandered between the temples in the square.

The stones were somehow both worn and untouched, telling stories of their past centuries, but silently begging her to tell her own.

Makena had told them they all had their own palace, but seeing as all of the Olympians had to be present in order to gain access to them, they weren't able to explore those. Amber was fine with that— there was plenty to see right here.

As the rest of the group was still exploring the city below it, Amber realized she was not only happy, but she was perfectly calm. Her whole life, she'd felt as though she'd been floating about an inch or so above her body. And now, she had finally settled in, and despite being a different version of the person she had been most of her life, she felt at home with her soul.

But, she thought, staring up at the towering, cloud-lined mountain above, *I might not be comfortable enough to trek up there on my own.*

The sandstone-colored streets below her had linen canopies and wooden carts staggered along the walkways. They were crowded with ambrosia clusters and oleander and short strings of beads, and nobody exchanged any currency. Everyone who walked by greeted her—they all knew who she was; they'd been expecting her and the rest of the Olympians. Feet above their kingdom, she watched as Alexia ran around like a child in a candy store, approaching everyone she could to interview them and identify their New World persona before Makena told her. Their pantheon was growing, with the few dozen deities ambling around Mount Olympus, living their day-to-day life.

What Amber found odd was that nobody she met could tell her how long they'd been there. *I guess if I lived here, I wouldn't keep track of the days either.*

"Miss Demeter!" a voice called from behind her.

Traven took the steps two at a time, catching up to her in seconds. As she turned around to tell him *again* that she really didn't need a bodyguard, she caught Kai's scowl. Traven was quite possibly the largest thing here, and Kai had had no problem vocalizing his feelings.

"We don't need your help, ya fridge," Kai said, attempting to shove his way past him.

"Traven, please, my name is Amber," she said gently.

She knew he was just Demeter's attendant and had likely been awaiting her arrival more than that of any of the other Olympians, but being called by her New World name hadn't quite sunk in yet.

"Yes, Your Majesty." He bowed. "Did you need any spices to bring back to the mortal world with you? Athena said you'd be departing shortly."

"No, thank you." She smiled at him.

He handed her tiny sachets of seeds anyway and excused himself.

"I don't like him," Kai said, louder than he needed to.

Amber just smiled back at him and showed him the large gray seeds in her palm. "Will you help me plant these when we get back?"

Kai's smile stretched across his face at the same time his blue eyes lit up, somehow more magnificently than normal. "Of course," he answered.

A chime sounded from across the little town, up near the gates. Alexia was waiting, standing between the Horae, waving to them.

Must be time to go.

As she and Kai walked hand in hand back across the sandstone-colored ground, they waved goodbye to the citizens of their newfound kingdom. There were nearly thirty others, standing outside the unmarked temples and fishing off the footbridges.

"I can't wait to come back," she sighed and leaned her head against his shoulder.

A baker ran up to them and stuffed a massive pastry into each of their hands. "Take it for the road!"

But Amber took a bite right away. When she lifted it up, strawberries and cream hit her nose. It seemed to melt away in her mouth without having to chew, and she just felt warm. It was like a hug. A hug from her mom.

It had taken the majority of their first two months in the house, but once Amber had actually sat down with herself and fully accepted that she was the New World Demeter—Greek Olympian goddess of agriculture and the harvest—she'd been able to *feel* things more. Emotion had never been one of her strong suits, and she knew that. Amber much preferred to shut off that part of her brain—and her heart—and think about things logically, without the messiness of *feelings* tangling the web even more. But now, everything was different. Now, she was able to think clearer, to feel more confident about her choices and less inclined to do something simply because everyone else was doing it. She was able to think about her mother without feeling the overwhelming urge to bawl her eyes out until her face hurt and her chest ached. She had loosened the reins on her father and was tentatively working on doing the same with Fleur.

I also haven't smoked or drunk in months. That might have had something to do with it.

As they climbed the last of the steps up to the Horae, Amber gave one last look back over her shoulder.

A pointed chin rested on her shoulder as Hanna June mumbled, "It's real."

"Yeah." Amber nodded.

"It's right here. And it's ours," her friend added.

Amber could sense that she might be trying to speak over a lump forming in her throat.

"All ours."

HJ sniffled, and then the added weight was gone and she heard HJ usher her back down to the gates.

"So," Heath started, "when do we tell Kronos?"

Alexia was intently writing in her notebook when she answered, "I've been thinking about that, and I honestly don't think we should—well, not yet."

"You wanna keep a secret from him?" Kai questioned her.

"I don't *want* to. I just think it's best that we do until we either have bigger, better news to deliver, like—I don't know—say … the discovery of another Olympian? Or maybe the location of a coffer?"

"I don't know. I kinda think we should tell him right away," HJ countered.

"What about the rest of the Olympians? Should we tell them?" Heath asked another good question—and the one Amber had been tossing around in her own head.

"I think Fleur is gonna know," she suggested, immediately adding, "Not that she'd tell anyone! I just think it would be best if none of us had to keep any secrets."

Hanna June let out a groan much too ugly for a girl that pretty. "Ugh, but what if they ruin it?"

"Say what you're really feeling, HJ," Kai tempted her.

I wish he wouldn't.

"What if Astrid ruins it?" HJ corrected her previous sentence, adding volume this time.

With the twins having followed their queen's orders, likely out of fear, the gates began to open inward as they got closer. They stood at attention and didn't make eye contact with her as she glided past silently. Amber went up to each of them and thanked them individually before joining the other four at the dumbwaiter platform.

Alexia pointed down at the drachma waiting before resuming her furious scribbles. "It looks like we're going back in the opposite order." Amber leaned closer, seeing that the standstill coin in the dish displayed an owl.

"So, I'll meet you all down there." Alexia ducked down and crossed her legs, giving them one final salute before being pulled down into the darkness.

Great. That means I'm last.

Kai turned to her the second Alexia was out of sight. "Are you gonna be okay, waiting by yourself?"

She snorted at his concern. "I don't have a choice. remember? We don't make the rules when it comes to any of this."

The second platform folded down from the invisible wall, and Hanna June said a momentary goodbye to them and climbed aboard.

He turned back to his girlfriend and rolled his eyes, but smiled. "I just … I don't know. I just want you to be okay."

"I *am* okay. In fact, I'm better than I've ever been," she told him.

His ride made itself known, giving a slight rattle, and Kai pulled her in for a kiss. A long, hard kiss. His hand went to the back of her head and held her there, close to him. Amber envisioned them as the halves of a yin-yang symbol, fitting perfectly against each other, like no one else ever could.

"You're gonna see her in, like, twenty minutes, dude." Heath's voice broke through the symphony that had started playing in Amber's imagination.

They all laughed, and he gave Kai a slight shove—the way guys did that Amber could never quite understand—as he made his way to the tunnel entrance. He turned back to say one last thing when his descent to the mortal world took him away.

"If I wake up and this whole thing was a dream, I wouldn't be surprised. I'd probably drop everything to write it down and make it a book, but I wouldn't be surprised," Heath repeated.

"Yeah, I know exactly how you feel." She half laughed. Catching sight of him grimacing, she asked, "Heath, are you okay?"

"Huh? Oh, yeah, no, I'm fine," he lied.

"You've been acting funny since we got through the gates. Is it … oh, wait. Is it your MS?"

Heath swallowed. "Yeah."

She nodded back. "I was really hopeful the whole immortal thing would kind of stop all that for you," she told him.

"Yeah, I was too."

Then it was his turn, and out of the goodness of his heart—which he seemed to have a lot of—he reminded her that they'd all be waiting at the bottom, in the plantation house kitchen, for her.

And then she was alone. Seven and a half grueling seconds passed, and although she had been reassured she was definitely immortal now, she was very aware of her heartbeat.

The last of the floating vessels folded down from its side, her tarnished coin with a bundle of wheat sitting undisturbed in the trinket dish. Amber gathered her skirt around her and stepped up to where the dumbwaiter lay in line with the solid clouds.

She gave one last look at the gleaming golden gates, promised herself that she would be back soon, and climbed on.

No light had found its way into the tunnel below her when she heard the arguing. In fact, she could identify every voice that spoke as she traveled downward for what felt like another several minutes before the faintest glow reached around the dumbwaiter.

"Where do you get off, thinkin' you can just go and-and-and fuckin' travel to a different universe?!"

That was definitely Gunner.

"Don't act like this is somethin' you ever even thought was a real thing!" HJ's twang carried up to Amber. "You know *damn well* that if any of us had asked you to come, you woulda laughed in our faces!"

True. Very true.

"You didn't ask *any* of us though, and I find that a little suspicious. It's like you only wanted certain people's help."

That was Astrid, and … that was also true.

"If you're implyin' that I didn't want you to come, then, yeah, you're right."

Why do they have to keep arguing? They're like Kai and Alexia, and it pisses me off.

"Okay, listen, LISTEN. NONE of you had any right—"

Rhianne's voice was the loudest she'd ever heard it, but the second Amber landed right at the opening in the kitchen wall, she stopped.

Everyone turned to look at her—*everyone.* All ten of the Titans they'd been able to locate, the rest of the Olympians, Damon and Fleur, and Zoey. And to Amber's surprise, there was also the girl who might go by Hecate but also might go by Jade, who had run out of Mount Olympus, in dire search of Damon, hiding beside him.

Did she take the dumbwaiter down?

And of course, there were half a dozen cameras, all pointed right at her.

"No one speaks!" Kronos bellowed, pushing himself past Gunner and Kai, making his way toward Amber. "Miss Hargrove,

I'm going to ask you a few questions, and I need you to answer them promptly. What was the plan when the five of you realized you could get in?"

Uhh …

"Um, we each had a coin, a-a drachma?"

"Mmhmm, yes, go on." He nodded, oblivious to the massive audience.

God, I hope this isn't live.

"And we figured it would take us up one at a time, which it did," she said.

"And who did you go with, Miss Hargrove?"

No sense in lying. He knows the answer. If you look at any of them, he'll think you're conspiring something. Just tell the truth. "Alexia, HJ, Kai, and Heath," she said carefully.

"Mmhmm, mmhmm. Anyone else?" Kronos pressed.

"No, sir."

Standing up to his full height, Kronos swallowed, but remained with his back facing the rest of the room. Amber saw Rhianne tug on Damon's elbow and murmur something to her sister, and then the four of them left the crowded kitchen, Jade's cape flowing out behind her.

Kronos nodded once, cleared his throat, and continued his verbal investigation. "And once you all got there?"

"Um, then they … they opened the gates for us." She altered the truth, deciding no one really needed to know that all five foot two of Hanna June had put the fear of the gods into the twin gatekeepers. "And then Alexia decided that we should leave at a certain time in order to be back before anyone … knew we were … gone " Her words drifted off as she looked around at the room full of people, aiming to avoid contact with the cameras. "Guess that didn't happen."

"How long were you gone for, Miss Hargrove?" Kronos asked her, leaning in closer. She felt as though he was watching her for any signs of a lie, signaling for her to give the right answer.

But Amber didn't know what he wanted her to say, so she told the truth. "About four and a half hours."

A collective groan filled the room. Cameras began to pan around, zooming in on her and Kronos and then catching her costars' reactions—the exasperation of those who hadn't been invited on the otherworldly journey and the defeat from those who had. Dayo was talking to HJ, her hands moving about wildly while Keaton lectured Kai and Heath. Alexia had whipped out her notebook and was walking Lucy and Pierce through her scribbles. Zoey pushed her way to Amber and shoved a mug in her direction.

Phoebe's hands went up, and the room fell silent. Amber could see veins pulsing in her forehead and neck as she moved forward, tapping her cane in front of her.

"You've all been gone for nearly five days."

Part IV

The
Eleventh
Olympian

Cult TV Show ... or Just an Actual Cult?

By Samara Connors

My job is to deliver news. Of course, I make it fun. There's a reason Columns has grown as much as it has in the past year, and it's not because of the content—because literally everyone is talking about the New World gods. It's because of *how* I share the news. So, you're welcome.

Anyway, my news is typically intriguing, maybe even positive. However, I have a touchy topic we're going to put out into the world today before the exciting part of the headlining story—the worldwide question of faith many people are going through.

As someone who didn't go to church once I left for college, I didn't have a very hard time picking up the idea that the Olympians—these newfound celebrities—were suddenly gods. Meaning they're in total control of *something*, whether that's the weather or a romantic connection between two people or how well the crops grow. I didn't have my belief system tied up in a neat little basket. Which, in turn, meant that gathering my eggs and placing them somewhere new wasn't too stressful. I guess I'm lucky, in that way.

The people all over the world who *did* have their eggs in one basket are ... well, to say it simply, they're going through it right now.

Everything they believed in has been uprooted and left out to dry. We all love the Olympians, but, according to their fearless leader, Dwayne Kronos, they can't actually *do* anything. Imagine someone praying for a speedy recovery from surgery, who do they pray to?

There are a lot of questions right now, and if you're like me, you likely aren't dealing with the crisis of faith that much of the world is. Please let this article serve as a formal reminder to be gentle to everyone you encounter.

For more resources, including spiritual therapists and prayer groups organized by location, please visit the tab on the Columns homepage.

Onto the fun stuff—don't worry; I'll keep it brief.

Europe and Asia Olympia Cons just wrapped up, and we've gotten a few new pantheon members, which is always exciting.

Most exciting though is that we have met our twins! While they're not old enough to actually join The Olympians yet, they've been seen at the plantation house a dozen times over the past few weeks. Our New World Apollo and Artemis go by the names of Luca and Camille Arturo, respectively. They're Olympia natives, just like Dawn—anyone else really miss her?—so I predict they'll be around often.

On a related note, anyone who's ever visited our former sleepy little town has made a stop at Bev's Taproom. It's right near campus, and they make the best gourmet tater tots you've ever had. Oh, and did I mention their mom *is* Bev? The downside to this is that since they just started their senior year of high school, it looks like we'll have to wait for them to make an appearance on the show. I, for one, cannot wait to see what species of chaos they bring.

As for upcoming events, the South America dates for Olympia Con just went up on the Parthenon website, and the Olympians will be heading there early 2016. If you haven't had a chance to attend yet, I highly suggest you try to get a ticket. It'll be the best weekend of your life.

In other news, this is the new topic that's being expanded on even more in our world of pop culture. Books are being written—the fan fiction I've read is *chef's kiss*; movies are in the works; and Julian Spencer released a new song last week, inspired by the very real possibility of going through the motions of your everyday life and waking up the next day to find out you're actually a god.

As if we aren't fully saturated in every version of this fantasy storyline come true, *The Olympians* goes back on the air next week.

Thank gods.

Chapter 53

Gunner: [*gestures to his phone, where the Columns article is pulled up*] Who is this Samara Connors chick anyway?

Kai: She goes to OC. She's, like, a journalism student, I think.

Alexia: I mean, that's a *bit* obvious.

Heath: She started out as a fan of the show last year and just posted about it on her social media and the blog she had about college life here. She'd been on the school paper, and when they found out how much traction she had gained from writing about the show and going downtown with you guys, they decided to give her a dedicated monthly article in each edition.

Gunner: That doesn't give her the fuckin' liberty to talk about us.

Astrid: Kronos said, and I quote, "I wouldn't talk bad about her if I were you," and then chuckled.

Amber: [*looks up*] He chuckled?

Astrid: [*nods*] He *chuckled.*

Amber: Oh, he totally knows something. Remember when Dawn visited last month and she realized that Zoey had been the barista at Ground Floor? Kronos *chuckled!* He acted like she had just solved a puzzle!

Alexia: [*mutters*] Can't believe I didn't recognize her first. It'd been months … saw her every day …

Hanna June: I don't know … just 'cause he laughed? Sounds like a stretch.

Kai: Where are the Titans anyway?

Hanna June: Half of 'em are lookin' for Gunner's coffer; half are lookin' for Alexia's.

Alexia: Rhianne suggested both coffers could be together, but I doubt it. They were given to mortals who worshipped them— different cults all around Europe, as it was expanding. Based on several passages from *Preserving Hellenism for Future Centuries*, the gods took a human form and then physically handed the coffers to the leader of a chosen group of theirs. At some point, most of the groups moved elsewhere, and seeing as they carried on their worship of a specific deity, it was highly likely that they wouldn't have crossed paths with another group, worshipping a different god.

Astrid: Did they give any hints as to where they were going?

Alexia: Well, I suggested any links to Alexander the Great would be a smart place to start [*gestures to Gunner*] for either of us. Macedonia, Egypt, or—oh! The site of the Battle of Gaugamela! Of course, I *did* consider the Colosseum, or—

Kai: So, you haven't thought much about it?

Alexia: [*ignores him*] I gave Kronos a copy of my list.

Gunner: [*shakes his head*] Pisses me off that we can't go with them.

Amber: [*groans in agreement, clearly still annoyed she couldn't go get hers*]

Zach: Yeah, I've talked to the Titans about that. I don't think that's very fair. I mean, we'd all be set on the same goal, maybe even more motivated than them … and the least it would do is just get us the hell outside. We've been cramped up inside these gates for too long.

Astrid: [*snorts*] If you said that to them, Kronos would argue that we just went to Shanghai, Seoul, Tokyo, *and* Singapore.

Amber: We saw them through windows.

Astrid: And *then* they'd remind you that you *did* get to go outside when we traveled around Europe the week before that! [*smirks*] For all of an hour.

Alexia: [*rifles through the books in her bag*] Ugh, I just want to go for a run.

Hanna June: Was I seein' things in Paris, or did they have someone run, like, ten steps behind you when you went out the first mornin' there?

Alexia: [*nods*] His name was Sergei, and he gave me his family's blini recipe. I'm going to make it as soon as we can actually taste real food again.

Amber: That should be soon, right? Cookie Dude will deliver here—I already checked.

Zach: Rhianne said another week or so.

Heath: At least we're *here* for the foreseeable future. Not that I particularly love this house, but I'm so sick of living out of suitcases.

Kai: No, no. *Here* is not good. *Here* means we start school soon.

Astrid: This will be a different kind of school though.

Kai: [*scoffs*] Not really. Not without powers. I mean, [*scoffs*] what are the rest of us gonna do? Sit and watch Heath blow himself up? *Fun.*

Alexia: Okay, okay, we all need to focus. Reel it in. Let's review why we're actually up here.

Everyone settles into their seats around the library on the top floor. It's a little cramped, but after they played nice in front of fans for the last two weeks at the Europe and Asia Olympia Con tours, it's no longer completely uncomfortable for them all to be in such close quarters with each other.

Zach: How do you keep track of everything? All *this* and a full load at OC? [*scoffs*] I can't imagine why anyone would do that.

Alexia: [*shrugs*] I like knowing things. Anyway, let's review what we know—that being that we've had nearly two dozen members of the pantheon added since we last met, not including those already in Olympus. And yet we still have the impending question with no answer: Who are the last two Olympians?

Zach: I haven't found anyone.

Astrid: Me neither.

Amber: I thought I'd found a girl, but the two we're missing are both guys, so I was wrong.

Alexia: Not necessarily! They might be switched—you never know. Can you give me whatever information you have?

Amber: [*nods*]

Alexia: Moving on then. We have almost all of the Muses, so that's exciting! And, Heath, I know you don't want to hear it, but I really think your girlfriend plays a role, so if I could just talk—

Heath: No.

Alexia: [*groans*] Ugh!

Hanna June: Can we talk about the newest three people—the ones Kronos just introduced to us?

Alexia: Let's.

HJ: So … none of 'em are gods, right?

Alexia: Correct.

Hanna June: And they're not any of those deified heroes you mentioned before?

Alexia: Well, she wasn't a hero, but Helen of Troy was supposedly made immortal by Zeus.

Amber: But the other two … Pat and …

Heath: Bailey.

Amber: Yeah. They're not?

Gunner: Well, Pat is Patroclus. A bit obvious with the name, but whatever. He was a human—uh, mortal. And even though he was a war hero, no, he wasn't made immortal after his gruesome death.

Zach: Wow. Didn't know you knew that much.

Kai: I didn't know you knew how to read.

Gunner: Man, shut up. I like the stuff about the heroes and shit. The rest of it is a little overboard.

Astrid: Okay, and what about that girl? The storage facility heir or whatever it was that she called herself.

Kai: She's a klepto, is what she is.

Alexia: Bailey Pappalardi, the reincarnated Pandora. Not deified, and I do agree with Newport—watch your things around her.

Zach: And Pandora opened the box … and what?

Alexia: She unleashed every form of evil into the world—disease, greed, hatred, despair, et cetera. Only hope was left inside.

Zach: So, she's the reason the world sucks?

Alexia: [*smirks*] You could sort of look at it like that.

Amber: Back to Helen for a second, please.

Hanna June: Mara? I liked her.

Heath: Yeah, but wasn't Helen of Troy the reason the Trojan War happened?

Gunner: [*scoffs*] She didn't do shit. The girl was just pretty, and everyone wanted her. She was married off to some rich guy 'cause that's what benefited her daddy. 'Cept she was in love with another guy, and she left the husband she didn't love to be with *that* guy. So, her husband went to basically go steal her back, and that's how it started. I'm right—look it up.

Alexia: [*smirks and slow claps*] Proud of you, Captain McHugh.

Heath: So, this chick isn't someone we have to watch out for?

Alexia: No, I don't think so.

Hanna June: So, since she's a human who was *made* immortal, do you think she'd be able to come up with us?

Amber: *If* we can get up again.

Hanna June: Oh, we're gettin' up there again. I dunno when, but we will.

Zach: We're gonna need to seriously plan it out. The Titans will have to be gone. But they'll have to have *just* left. Like, we couldn't go now 'cause they could come back any day. I don't think it's a coincidence they jam-packed our filming schedule while they're gone

Kai: You guys are each gonna need drachma to get up there.

Amber: I think Fleur went and got some more.

Heath: Can she come up?

Zach: [*looks at Alexia and shrugs*] I don't see why not. I read that book you gave me, Alexia—uh, *Thirty Names from Ancient Greece to Know*—and Persephone is called an "honorable Olympian" a bunch of times.

Heath: So, Damon and Dawn should be able to go up too?

Alexia: I would imagine so. Jade was waiting for Damon; it was like she expected him to be with us.

Kai: Speaking of, where is she?

Hanna June: [*shrugs*] I haven't seen her since I was tossed out of the dumbwaiter and had cameras shoved in my face.

Astrid: She was here yesterday.

Everyone turns to look at her.

Alexia: What do you mean, she was here yesterday'?

Astrid: Well, we were in my room the whole time. She was just there when we got back from the airport.

Amber: She was just in your room?

Astrid: Mmhmm. She had drawn me a bubble bath, so obviously, we went in that. Then I pierced her daith, and she taught me how to make affirmation sigils.

Kai: Wait, wait, wait. Back up to the part where you said you guys went in the bubble bath. You mean, like, together, right?

Amber: [*gives him a look*]

Alexia: Okay, [*claps her hands together, tries to refocus*] so going back to our fact review. We also know that—

Gunner: Were there a lot of bubbles? Or could you see the water?

Kai: Was the bubble bath scented?

Alexia: [*sighs*]

Chapter 54

His fingers intertwined with Hanna June's. "So … you knew about the files?"

"Mmhmm," she hummed back, still zoned out at the door to his closet.

"I don't even remember telling you that." *What else do I not remember? What else does she know about that she hasn't told me?*

Silence passed in long-drawn-out beats, stifled only by the whirring of the ceiling fan.

"How did Damon know about them?" he finally asked.

Her shoulder shrugged against his chest. "He said Rhianne had told him. The Titans recruited him to help them find them back in December, and I guess she had to explain what they were looking for."

"So it's true then? That his uncle is, like, a hit man?" He dropped their hands down so they crossed over her chest, keeping her close.

They hadn't lain together like this in a year or so. Definitely before they had come to Olympia. It was nice.

"I guess so," she murmured.

She probably doesn't know. It's not like any sane person would walk around and tell people their family member was a contract killer.

"I still don't trust that guy," he threw in, immediately feeling her bare, bony shoulder shift against him.

"He's your brother."

"Half-brother, and that doesn't mean I have to believe everything he says or does," he argued. In his opinion, Damon Montclaire reeked of ulterior motives.

"Well, he's been really helpful with a lot of stuff," HJ said.

"Yeah?" He didn't really care, but he knew she had to feel like he did. "Must be that private New York City education he was set up with."

She hummed back, but otherwise didn't acknowledge she had even heard him. This had become normal for her—she'd zone out after they had sex, ever since the five of them had been caught coming back from Olympus. He knew how guilty she felt for not telling him, and they'd even been able to talk about it a few times since then. But when she got like this, it started to worry him again. It reminded him of her breakdown in LA, and that opened up the rabbit hole of him wondering what else was happening in her head. What other things was she worried about? How many ideas did she have that she hadn't bothered to let him in on?

Luckily, he knew of a few ways to pull her back in. "We need to make sure our kids get an education like that," he said, and just like clockwork, her little head turned up to look at him, a perfect smile stretching across her face.

"Yeah?"

"Mmhmm, I want them to be Athena smart," he went on.

"But not a boarding school. I wanna see my kids." She curled up against him, their noses touching.

He tucked her hair behind her ear. "You're gonna be such a great mother."

"And we're going to make them up there," she told him, crawling over him.

Her naked body loomed over his as she told him how they were going to go up together and be fawned over like the immortal royalty they were and not spend a minute of their post-honeymoon trip in the heavens apart.

"Good. That's what I want."

But her smile back didn't convince him that she fully understood how he meant it.

"I'm serious, Hanna June. We've been in lockdown for most of the last seven months, and we've barely spent a moment with just the two of us. I need more time with you. We can't really go out for date nights yet, but we basically live across the hall, and we never see each other."

She sank down, settling on the top of his thighs. Her lips pursed as her fingers spread across his chest. "I've been with you basically since we got back from Olympus. I think I've slept in my bed once since August."

"I know, I know, and I've been loving it, baby," he said, his tone softening. "I just want us to keep doing that—I think it's good for us. Our lives are … insane, to say the least, and I think we need to make sure that we carve out plenty of time to spend together."

Even though she nodded back like she was on the same page as him, her gaze dropped and he could tell she was clamming up again.

Propping himself up on one of his elbows, he grabbed her face in his other hand. "I cannot wait to marry you, Hanna June. I think this whole thing is just going to keep getting bigger, and even though you'll be mine forever—like, on paper—I'm still gonna have to share you with the rest of the world. Forever. And I just want to make sure we don't lose this *thing* we have, ya know?"

HJ nodded back, but Zach still didn't feel like she really understood it. How left out he had felt, seeing her spill out of the tunnel in the kitchen wall with the others. She'd been missing for days and the state of panic he had fallen into was nearly unforgivable.

And the way she was acting now, as if they were spending too much time together?

He would have to remind her that, before all of this, she had really only had him. Her parents didn't count because, well, they were parents. There were parts of yourself you could never be fully open about in the same way you could with your friends. And her real friends, the ones from back home, were only her friends because she was linked to him and he was the biggest thing to have come across DC in the past twenty years. She was on the show because *he* was on the show. She was as big as she was because of her relationship with *him*.

He was just going to have to keep reminding her of that.

Chapter 55

ASTRID

JADE'S PERFECTLY WINGED EYELINER MADE her stare even more intense. "Come *on*, Astrid! Try it again! You did it last time. I know you can do it again," she urged, leaning over the back of the chair opposite her training target.

Sweat slicked down the side of her forehead. "I'm trying!"

"Not hard enough!"

Her chest heaved, and for the first time in months, she craved water. Knowing there wasn't any in the house, simply because it wasn't regularly needed, made her mouth even drier.

"I need a break," she panted and flopped onto the couch.

Astrid was sure the others heard the groan of excessive frustration come from Jade, and she kept her eyes glued on the door. The last thing she needed was any of them coming in here to check on her. With the way they questioned Amber if she'd been allowed to open her coffer yet, Astrid figured they'd be just as eager, if not more, for updates on her nonexistent progress with retrieving her own memories. At least Amber had been lucky enough to have her instructor for the special lessons Kronos deemed she needed—with her coffer being in such a horrendous state—switched from Kronos to Lucy. Despite not actually being able to *do* anything yet, she didn't leave her lessons crying anymore.

Jade was usually a good teacher, but for whatever reason, she had become more intense in the past week, and Astrid didn't think it was a coincidence that Kronos had been even more irritable.

Still, she didn't need an audience. It was bad enough that Hanna June knew, even if she hadn't let on that she was aware of the sessions Astrid now attended several times a week. If she had known her Past Partition classes would be as grueling as the goddess of magic and witchcraft was making them, she would've stayed in school, like Alexia and Heath.

It would be different if she could actually *do* it—if she could effortlessly perform a deep dive into her memory and just extract those pieces of key information that was needed to obtain the remaining coffers.

"It's like you don't *want* your powers," Jade grumbled as she crossed the room.

"Of course I want them!"

She whipped around, her jet-black hair swaying behind her. "Prove it! Try harder!"

Astrid glared at her. "You know, there's this thing called positive reinforcement," she said, propping herself up on her elbows. "I'm not saying I need to hear *good girl* repeatedly, but it would be a nice change."

Smirks passed between the girls, and Jade simply said back, "I used those all on you yesterday," before she left Astrid's room, slamming the door behind her.

Well, fuck.

That usually works on Gunner. Now what?

Alexia's handwriting was awful, truly. Hanna June had started rewriting the notes, but she'd taken a break in the middle of a word, and now Astrid didn't know if she was reading *cousin* or *couple*. Seeing as the Greek gods were rather known for inbreeding, either one made sense.

Facing the board blocking the window, she began to review the list of coffer location possibilities her costars had brainstormed.

The theory circulating around hers was that it was in Paris—they'd all seemed to cling to that suggestion when HJ brought it up last month.

They'd been on campus last month at a highly secured student event with no less than fourteen security guards around them at all times. During one of the panels, someone—who Astrid recognized from one of the few classes she'd started—asked if they were aware a fountain was being constructed in Paris in honor of the New World Aphrodite. Of course they weren't, as their access to world news had become even more limited. The second they were backstage, Hanna June brought up the idea that her coffer might be there. Naturally, she didn't address her when she said it, even if she was the subject of the matter, but still, she had thought about it, and that notion had been jostling around in Astrid's head since then.

Maybe she doesn't hate me ... or maybe she needs something else to focus on because if her coffer is ever found and she doesn't get any distinguished powers ...

Plus, she's probably trying to distract herself from wedding planning. I would be.

Refusing to let herself plunge into the spiral of thoughts she knew she'd get sucked up in, she sank onto one of the musty poufs and dropped her head into her hands.

Okay, focus, Astrid. Come on. You did it before. You can do it again, especially since no one is yelling at you now. No pressure here—it's just you. No timed trance sessions. You got this.

Whether it was the absence of an audience or the slight smell of vanilla floating into the room, she wasn't sure. All she was focused on was the darkness—the void her mind had become. Was she falling forward in her seated position, or did it just feel like that because her eyes were closed?

Light came at her through a tunnel, and she fell, fell, fell into it.

This must be what Alice went through.

And then she was in one of her many childhood bedrooms.

When she had been between the ages of four and sixteen, her father had made them move every year. This seemed to be the Pacific Palisades property they'd stayed in for a whopping seven months. It was also Astrid's favorite of her past homes. Her bedroom had a massive window seat that overlooked the ocean, and she used to fall asleep in it more often than in her bed.

The room was empty, but she could hear voices. They weren't far away, and if her memory served her correctly—it usually did—she thought she heard Miss Patsy's harsh Southern accent headed right toward her.

Nearly coming off its hinges, the door burst open, and a nine-year-old Astrid ran in. Although Jade had assured her she wouldn't be seen in the memories, she still felt like she should hide. Even though it was her own memory, she had hidden it away in the deepest trenches of her mind. It felt like she was barging in on her own private moment. Part of her very much wanted to keep this moment right where it belonged—in the back of her mind with over a decade's worth of dust on it.

Unfortunately, the other part of her knew that she needed to revisit it and that there was no point in hiding under her typically unslept-in bed.

Little Astrid ran *through* her, stepping up onto the cushioned bay window seat and settling down while rubbing her hands over her arms.

"You cold, baby?" Miss Patsy asked, tilting her head at her curiously.

She didn't look at her as she answered, but instead stayed focused on the waves crashing over the sand. "Just a little chilly."

Miss Patsy smiled and told her to take her shoes off. As past Astrid began to unlace her dirty Converse, she looked up at her nanny.

"Tell me a story, Miss Patsy," she asked.

It was like coming home. Astrid felt silly, tearing up at the memory that hit her hard and soft in the gut, and reminded herself that no one could see her. She didn't even have a reflection in the mirror on the other side of the room.

"All right." Miss Patsy obliged, even though it was obvious that she *wanted* to tell the tale she indulged Astrid with. "Do you remember the story I told you last time I was with you?"

Her fourth-grade self nodded, eyes wide and eager while she made the knot in her laces even more tangled. "About Queen Hera," she said.

"Well, her coffer was guarded rather heavily for a long time—so long, in fact, that it was rumored to no longer exist. Ya see, the followers of Hera took their job to protect her only lasting existence on our planet *very* seriously. When others would ask about it, they wouldn't answer. They'd just change the subject! This led the other humans to think that maybe it had been stolen at some point and her guards were too embarrassed to admit it."

It wasn't though, Astrid thought, knowing this conversation didn't end in devastation.

"It was stolen?" little Astrid asked, her mouth agape. Watching herself, she wasn't sure she had blinked since Miss Patsy had started talking.

She leaned in toward the little girl, a sly smile creeping across her face. The rest of the conversation was slowly coming back to Astrid, as she watched Miss Patsy tell her, "That's what they wanted ev'ryone to think."

Her miniature paused, then exclaimed, "They tricked them!"

"They did!" Her nanny laughed. "They did, and it worked!"

I knew it.

"Well, what happened to it?"

"It's been safe this whole time, o' course."

And it can be found … where?

A deafening silence went around, as both versions of Astrid waited to hear of its location, but Miss Patsy didn't share.

"Well, where is it?" Astrid asked at the same time her past self did.

The anticipation had stretched up inside her, the full length of her body and twice as heavy. Miss Patsy looked around, almost as if to make sure no one else was listening. And even though Jade had assured her that no one would be able to see her—"You're entering a memory, not time-traveling,"—Astrid was positive the nanny saw her. She felt that *click* as they made eye contact, locking in on one another, just before she turned back to the little girl she had been years earlier.

And then the worst possible thing happened.

As Miss Patsy opened her mouth, her little earrings gave a dangle as her head shook, just before Astrid fell forward.

Crumpling onto the floor, she began to push herself up, blinking an obnoxious amount of times. First, out of shock from her head hitting the floor … and then in a furious attempt to change the setting around her.

She wasn't there anymore. The memory was gone. She was no longer watching herself slouching on her old window seat, the Pacific painted behind her. Her nine-year-old self was gone, her nanny vanished. She was lying on one of the ornate rugs in the third-floor study of the Athanasios Plantation home on the East Coast in present day.

Footsteps thundered, coming up the stairs, and she pulled herself back up onto the worn-out cushion. Hanna June appeared in the doorway, out of breath and frantically looking around. As her gaze settled on Astrid, her breathing began to slow down from her run upstairs, and her shoulders dropped.

"Oh," she breathed, dropping her weight against the doorframe. "It's just you."

"Yep." Astrid swallowed. "Just me." *Breathe through your nose. Calm the fuck down, my God.*

Hanna June stood in the doorway, carefully watching her, to-go coffee cup in hand.

She must have sent Zoey to get her something. She'd never sneak out.

"It sounded like somethin' fell down," she said slowly, giving her venti contents a swirl.

Astrid stood up and sauntered over to study the boards. "I fell," she told her, keeping her back to her visitor.

In the reflection of the plastic, she watched Hanna June's head tilt, which was enough. She didn't say anything though, and Astrid knew she was still being watched.

Why isn't she leaving?

Looking up at Alexia's scribbles about the Labors of Heracles, she heard Hanna June swish the melted ice in her drink before she said flatly, "You're not wearin' a wig."

Goose bumps prickled up her neck as the realization settled in. She had been forced to wear the same blue bob for over a month upon their sudden shut-in. But ever since their previous living arrangements had been packed up by Kronos's henchmen and brought to the plantation house, Astrid had made sure to change her look every day.

But when she had woken up alone this morning, the desire to fully put herself together had been nowhere to be found.

"Gunner's not here." She bit back the words the second they left her mouth, hating herself for admitting it, especially to Hanna June.

Her head cocked the other way as she crossed one ankle over the other, seemingly making herself more comfortable in the doorway.

Why is she still here?

"You wear 'em for him?"

"No, I wear them for *me*. My scalp just wanted a day to breathe." She picked up a marker and scribbled down one word—*Netherworld.*

"Huh," was the only response Hanna June made.

Astrid hit her limit. But she also knew better than to push the little blonde—structural damage here would be severely more detrimental than what they'd caused at the Student Center.

"Did you need something, Hanna June?" Her back was still to her as she stared down at the word.

She heard her take a step into the cramped room.

How are we all gonna fit in here when there are twelve of us?

"So why did you fall?"

Well, now Astrid turned around, and the two of them stared at each other. A pointed look of determination buzzed around Hanna June, and Astrid knew that she knew. Seeing as she wasn't a liar, even when the truth was heavy and ugly and hurtful, it didn't make much sense to start now, so she told her.

"I was projecting, like Jade's been teaching me," she said, her voice hushed. None of the bedrooms on the top floor were inhabited yet, but she didn't know if Hanna June had brought up others to eavesdrop. "I was in a memory, and ... I don't know what happened, but I fell out of it—literally."

And, again, Hanna June replied with, "Huh."

"Yeah, so that sucks," she said and turned back around. *End of discussion. Maybe she'll leave.*

"You were in a memory about the coffers?"

"Yeah."

She took another step into the room and shook the ice bits. "Whose was it?"

Turning back around, Astrid stared at her. Hanna June knew what she was about to be told—she could see it on her face. She just needed the confirmation.

"Yours."

Everything froze—the curtains stopped fluttering in the October breeze, the birds stopped chirping outside, the dust floating in the streams of sunlight pouring in through the windows halted their journey.

Well, she's not gonna leave now. Nice going, As. "Yeah, it exists."

The curtain shimmied, and time seemed to restart.

"I know."

"Do you? 'Cause you act like you're the only one of us who won't be getting one."

Astrid might as well have slapped her, judging by the face Hanna June gave her.

"Of course I know I have one. Hera was the queen of the gods—why would she not have one?"

And of course, Astrid threw her back the same expression. "I don't know why! You yourself have said multiple times that *if* you even have one, there's nothing for you inside it. And I want you to know that's bullshit."

Three fast steps toward her, and she was within arm's length, finger pointed right in her face. "You don't know that." Her words were pushed out between clenched teeth, almost in a whisper. "You can't prove it." Hanna June's finger began to shake, and in the half second Astrid glanced down at it, big, fat tears filled up her eyes. Hanna June's finger wiggled inadvertently. "You have *nothing* to worry about. You'll be able to make people fall in love."

Aunt Joanne used to point her finger in Astrid's face when she was "demanding attention" as a child. She hated it—it was such an obnoxious taunt, if you asked her. So, as much as Astrid wanted to push Hanna June's perfect manicure out of her face, she didn't.

Instead, she lowered her voice to match the shaky, hushed volume it had just dropped to.

"Phoebe told me she thinks that ability will belong to Eros."

Hanna June's face twisted in confusion. She blinked, and her tears spilled over. "Who?"

Astrid ignored it—it was how she would want her blonde nemesis to react if their roles were switched. "Cupid."

"Oh."

"Yeah. So, I don't really know what else I would be getting. Maybe nothing."

Hanna June blinked at her through the tears settling into their streak patterns on her face, a stream of salt water making their mark through her flawless full face of makeup.

"Maybe we'll both get nothing."

Chapter 56

Heath: I've been thinking about something.

Kai: Me too

Alexia: Heath, what were you thinking about?

Kai: Why does he get to go first?

Alexia: Because he brought it up first.

Damon: Why do you have to argue?

Kai: You just don't like me

Alexia: Also true, but I think my original reasoning is completely valid.

HJ: Heath just go

Heath: We thought that whoever ransacked K's office and stole everything was also the same person who let out the secret... but K accidentally told the secret... so who stole the files?

HJ: Oh shit

Amber: wait...

Alexia: Shit.

Kai: **WHOA LEX CURSED**

Alexia: I'm allowed to curse, Kai.

Alexia: How did I not think about this?

Heath: None of us did.

Damon: I did.

HJ: You did?

Damon: Of course.

HJ: Wtf why didn't you bring it up earlier

Damon: I've been busy.

HJ: Doin what

Damon: Why do you have to argue?

HJ: Bc we're supposed to be A TEAM

Alexia: I second that.

Heath: Ok, ok, can we brainstorm this instead of fighting?

Alexia: Can we all be upstairs in ten?

Kai: No

Amber: I can

Kai: Nvm I'll be there

Alexia: Wait, wait.

Alexia : Kai, what were you thinking about?

Kai: I just wanted to know if different species of whale speak the same language

HJ: Omg

Alexia: I don't have an answer for you, but I'm pretty sure you'll find out at some point.

Chapter 57

ALEXIA

A FIERY ORANGE ARC ILLUMINATED out in the distance. Which would've been a nice sight if Alexia had made any significant headway. She dropped her body onto the worn sofa in the corner and stared at the whiteboard as the sunrise crept up the walls.

She'd been up there since three that morning. After not sleeping even a little bit, she grabbed a few extra pens and sticky notes and headed up to the top floor. Saying she felt insane, looking at the abundance of notes she'd added over the last few hours, was an understatement—she felt wholly overwhelmed.

Still, a year ago, she had felt like she was wasting her time with community college classes, knowing she was destined for bigger things. *This* wasn't exactly what she'd had in mind though.

Leaning forward, she balanced her elbows on the tops of her thighs and stared at the other topic she had been stumped on for too many weeks to count. It was abbreviated and had the letters written in the opposite order so no one else would be able to decipher what it was. They'd all given up on asking her anyway, unable to decipher her chicken scratch and seeming to want her to prompt them with an idea to center around.

The only person who had figured it out was Fleur, who'd become a frequent visitor of the third-floor study room. She often came by herself too, which was helpful because she was the only other person Alexia could bounce ideas off of when it came to the puzzle in the top-left corner of the board—who had Zach cheated on Hanna June with *on the property*? Mortals couldn't cross the property lines; it had become a widely known fact.

For a while, everyone, Olympians and humans alike, had assumed it was to either keep them in or to keep the fans out, and the tales of the injuries when the house had last been opened to the public entered their way back into social media circulation. Rumors of those who had successfully scaled the gated riverfront property turned into something between folklore and horror stories.

Of course, the Olympians knew they were all true—from the college student who had fallen unconscious the second he landed on the manicured lawn and woken up two days later with an absent memory of even approaching the property, to a long time resident of the city uncontrollably vomiting, to the teenager who'd managed to make it all the way to the greenhouse when she noticed a rash had broken out on her arms. In the handful of seconds it took for Gunner to yell at the girl, the rest of them had all pressed their faces against the window or stepped out onto the balcony. She wasn't covered in itchy red bumps anymore—golf ball-sized welts had overtaken every inch of skin, and some had started to ooze. Her eyes swelled up, and she fell to the ground just as security reached her.

No one else had tried to get inside the gates since.

Which meant that the girl Zach had snuck into one of the cottages was *like them*. And it had to be someone they knew. Zach would give anything for a moment to prove himself worthy, and keeping a member of their fast-growing pantheon a secret wasn't like him.

What about either of the girls from the breakfast in LA? No, no, this was before Olympia Con …

Or … wait. Ugh, God, how did I not think of it?! Something has to be wrong with me. Maybe I'm getting sick? Do gods get sick?

Fleur didn't say the person with Zach was a girl. She just said "person." Nearly all the gods had bisexual tendencies, Zeus included. It easily could've been a male.

Well … would Zach do that? I don't know him well enough to make that call, but … there was that guy Kronos and Rhianne introduced to us all that he and Hanna June knew from high school. They seemed pretty close actually. The New World Icarus—Cash? Was that his name? I wonder if—

BRRRRNG.

Her alarm sounded violently from where her phone had slipped under a pillow. She stabbed a finger at the screen to silence it, plucked open a marker, and wrote a *C* in the opposite corner of the board. She would have to revisit it later.

This has to be why. My handwriting sucks because I've been copying down notes as fast as I possibly can for a decade now, terrified the teacher will move on before I'm done and I'll have missed something important and miss a test question because of it.

The lecture hall echoed the sounds of keys furiously tapping away. Next to her, Heath was already done with the slide Professor Conroy had momentarily stopped on.

When he'd brought up needing another gen ed course and was considering the Intro to Political Science course, Alexia had jumped on the idea. Her original plan had been to save it until toward the end of her undergraduate degree, piling it in with the heavier parts of her mandated educational requirements. But she had come to enjoy Heath's company over the past few months. Not to mention, she liked the idea of having a built-in study buddy, especially since they were the only two Olympians who had opted to stay in school.

"All right … moving on," Professor Conroy announced. His finger tapped his laptop keyboard, the screen changed, and the doors to the room flew open.

"Alexia! Miss Chang! Can we get a picture?"

"Is it true you were made aware of your magic abilities being restored and *still* chose to attend your eight a.m.?"

"Do you believe there will be destructive repercussions upon opening your box—er, your coffer?"

Kronos shoved his way past the paparazzi crowded in the doorway with ease, pushing his way to Alexia. Jabbing a finger in the direction of her instructor, he yelled, "Empty the room, Chiron!"

Chiron? He must have meant Conroy. Unless … is Professor Conroy actually Chiron, the teacher of heroes?

Wait, they brought my coffer here?! Of course … anything for a staged publicity shot.

I haven't had enough coffee to deal with this.

Questions buzzed around her headspace as she mentally connected dots and jotted down notes on the corner of her open notebook page. He dismissed class, having to threaten the students who were refusing to leave with failing grades. Once the room emptied out, Alexia drowned out the fanfare coming from the hallway and realized they were all here—both Olympians and Titans had all come to campus this morning to witness the restoration of her powers.

Rhianne stepped forward, securely holding a wooden chest against her torso. She could see carvings of olive trees stretching up the face of it, spreading their abundant branches over the lid of the box. On the front, right in the center, was a key hole.

"There's a key?" she asked.

Rhianne's proud smile twitched. "Apparently. We weren't aware of a lock on any of them. Leave it to Athena." She attempted a laugh. Alexia blinked twice, and Rhianne added, "We're going to keep looking though."

"Where was it?"

Grenada leaned forward. "The site of the Library of Alexandria."

Alexia groaned. "Of course! That should've been the first place I thought of! I can't believe I didn't think—"

"Athena would not allow that kind of talk, Miss Alexia," Phoebe piped up.

Humbly nodding, she reached out to accept her coffer and placed it on her desk, shoving her thoughts away.

It was gorgeous—like it had just been carved and finished and painted. Light shades of gray covered its surface with notes of deep brown, olive green, and navy-blue accenting. She ran her hands over the lock and felt it hum against her touch. It was waiting.

With one sweeping glance at her roommates, her costars, her family, she landed on Heath. The delicate smile was still on her face when she felt her fingers begin to lift the top of her coffer.

It was a buzzy, comforting feeling, similar to the few times she'd had a little too much to drink—Athena used to let loose, so why shouldn't she? Her body was warm inside, like she'd been bathed in nectar. And then, as soon as she peeked inside, there was a zap. A stinging jolt went right through her fingertips that held the lid, rushing through to her chest and then splitting in half, both diving down toward the tips of her toes, and rushing up to seep into her brain.

And then it was over.

She blinked another few times, steadying herself, and looked back up. Hanna June had taken several steps closer and was intently watching.

"How d'ya feel?" she asked, eyes wide and unblinking.

How do I feel? I don't know. Unchanged? No, no. I need to try to make something happen.

"I feel the same." She nodded, giving her verbal self-assessment more so to the Titans watching. "I think I should try to actually *do* something though. But maybe not here." She looked around the dated lecture hall.

"Agreed." Phoebe nodded, her knuckles white as she leaned on her cane.

I wonder if she's ever seen a coffer or if she's always been blind …

Kai stepped forward. *Of course he has something to say.* "But Athena is the smartest. So, like, shouldn't Lex just, like, *know* everything now?"

"Not necessarily," Kronos began to explain. "The ways in which the world considers someone to be smart now aren't the same as they were when we first ruled."

The Olympians shifted their weight and tried not to look bored as he went into comparing how the wheel had been invented versus how computer programming had gotten its start.

Alexia, however, caught sight of the books sitting in her unzipped backpack near her feet. Ground Floor had only just opened when she reached downtown this morning, and she'd ended up with some extra time before class. Much preferring the library in the early hours, she'd headed into Aarden and checked out a handful of books on other types of mythology.

Pulling out the one dedicated to Yoruba—the topic she knew the least about—she felt nearly everyone else's eyes on her as Kronos continued talking.

Holding it between both hands, she pressed her palms into the sides of the hardcover, took a deep breath, and closed her eyes.

Her vision was clouded over by words she'd never heard of before, dashing by in bright neon colors, stretching toward her, as if being pulled into her head. Terms she wasn't familiar with were suddenly in her vocabulary, and she understood Oku wasn't entirely comparable to how Greek mythology viewed death and the afterlife. She suddenly knew that Obatalá had been given the duty of developing the earth. She could list every deity of the Orisha alphabetically and tell anyone who asked what they ruled over. She knew exactly how to worship the goddess Oshun. She knew everything.

"I'm a sponge," she stated, interrupting Kronos, who firmly cut off and turned to look at her. "An information sponge."

"Is that so, Miss Chang?"

"It is." And she shared her newfound knowledge and how it had all seeped into her brain. "I have never read about the West African religion, but … I know everything. Here, quiz me!"

The Titans chuckled.

"That won't be necessary, Miss Alexia—we believe you," Pierce assured her.

"Wait, wait, wait," Gunner said, his arms crossed. "You're tellin' me that all she has to do is touch a book and she just suddenly *knows* everything it says inside?"

A tapping against the floor was heard, and the attention turned again to Phoebe. "She might not even need to touch the books, you know. Perhaps, just try looking at it, Alexia. Focus solely on the title in front of you."

"She just has to *look* at it?!" Gunner sputtered.

"What the hell?" Kai joined in. "That's bullshit!"

At the same time, Gunner continued with, "That's sick."

"What?" Kai faced him, an array of emotions on his face.

"Do you realize how fucking helpful that is? That she can just absorb anything—real or made up—that any book in front of her says? She's easily the smartest one out of us, and she's made sense of most of all *this*. You realize how much time she'll be able to save now?"

That is true.

"She's our best shot at not losing control over the world again, at having the world exist in peace for once, and you know it. I mean, that's what this is all gonna come back to, right? Proving that we can rule better this time—that our future will be some Golden Age of prosperity that we bring the world back to and rule over for eternity, right?"

Eight Olympians, ten Titans, and Professor Conroy—*who's also most likely a centaur*—stared at the former Ranger.

Maybe he wasn't the dim-witted, self-absorbed buzz cut with anger issues everyone thought he was.

Chapter 58

As Hanna June and Amber run into the ballroom, a high-pitched scream comes from both of them. Dawn sees them coming, and Kai, who she was talking to, steps out of the way just in time. Both girls reach her at the same moment, and the three of them hug and excitedly talk over each other.

Dawn: I missed you guys *so much*!

Amber: How was Kansas? I haven't been there in so long.

Dawn: It was great! The investors out there took my team and me out to this great restaurant next to where the site is. You have to come visit!

Hanna June: You're really doin' it. It's crazy, Dawnie.

Heath joins in the conversation as he walks into the room.

Heath: I heard your reformation establishments on the West Coast have, like … just *ended* homelessness? Please tell me that's true because it just doesn't sound right.

Kai: Of course it's right! This is Dawn Sutherland we're talking about!

Dawn: [*huge smile on her face*] Thank you, guys. Thank you so much! The people in those facilities—you guys are all they talk about.

Zach: [*sarcastically*] Yeah, well, we're kind of famous.

Damon: Unfortunately.

Keaton pokes his head in the doorway.

Keaton: Are you all here?

Amber: No, we're just waiting on—

Astrid: Us? [*she and Gunner stroll into the room, clothes disheveled and Astrid's pink wig askew*] We're here!

Keaton: [*yells behind him*] They're ready!

A second later, the Titans all walk into the room, cameras swarming in around them, singing "Happy Birthday." In front of them, Zoey carries a cake bigger than her, candles lit all over. They approach the group, and she sets it on the table. As they finish their serenade, the mishmash group of Olympians look at them curiously.

Alexia: But … whose birthday is it?

Rhianne: Well, most recently, Fleur's.

Zach: But … we can't eat that.

Kronos: [*smirks*] Actually, Mr. Alexander, as of [*checks his pocket watch*] forty-seven seconds ago, you can.

Astrid: Wait, what?

Kronos: You are officially fully immortal now.

Hanna June passes a look between Rhianne and Natasha, but neither meets her gaze.

Kronos: The inner workings of your bodies have been rewired so delicately that you can return to feasting on mortal foods.

Heath: So, no more ambrosia and nectar?

Phoebe: Oh, no, you'll need to consume that periodically—just not in such aggressive portions.

Heath: [*smiles*] Okay, 'cause that stuff is really good.

Rhianne: This [*gestures to the cake*] is both a combined celebration for the most recent birthdays—being Dawn, Alexia, and Fleur—*and* as a sort of celebratory bridge back into mortal food!

Cake is cut, cameras pan around the room, and everyone begins to relax. The Olympians all make obnoxious sounds at their first bites, relishing in the creamy sweetness of the frosting and the sugary crunch of the sprinkles.

Gunner: So, how long can we go without having the ambrosia and stuff?

Rhianne: Well, we aren't sure of an exact time frame. Actually, [*approaches Amber*], dear, do you remember?

Amber: [*confused*] Remember what?

Rhianne: How long you lasted for before it kicked in?

Amber: Before—I'm sorry, what?

Phoebe: They still don't remember, Rhea.

Rhianne: [*sighs*] When Demeter was searching the earth for Persephone, she neglected to eat or drink, and her immortality faded.

Alexia: That's how the season of winter was established— according to Greek mythology, of course. So, it should be at least a few months?

Kronos: That's what we're thinking as well. However, we don't have a specific number, and we really don't care to find out. [*gives a tight smile to the Olympians*]

Chapter 59

ASTRID

YOU HAVE TO DO IT. She's not going to—at least not anytime soon. It's going to be better for all of us if you just put the offer out there.

You're not admitting anything because she's not gonna ask—she doesn't want that confirmation. This isn't you taking blame for anything; it's just you creating a more peaceful environment to work and live in.

You're a professional.

Astrid's fist gently rapped on the closed door.

The, "Who is it?" that followed was muffled, and after she simply replied, "It's me," there was a long pause.

Then the door creaked open, and Hanna June's makeup-free face was squeezed in the opening. "What?"

Just like you practiced. "I want to talk to you."

"Okay," she replied, still motionless.

"In private," Astrid clarified.

Hanna June glanced down the hall in both directions. "I don't see anyone else around," she said, her voice stoic, unwavering in her decision to not let Astrid in.

Pursing her lips in annoyance momentarily before lowering her voice, she attempted to reason. "You *know* there're two cameras pointed at us right now, Hanna June. Can you please let me in so we can talk? Like mature adults?" She made sure the pointed emphasis on the last question was direct but not rude—exactly as she'd rehearsed.

Hanna June glanced in the direction of both cameras without moving her head, and letting out a *huff*, she pulled open the door enough for Astrid to shimmy her way in.

Astrid had glanced inside Hanna June's room a handful of times, on her way to visit Amber or to head out to the balcony at the end of the hall. However, this was her first time inside. She had definitely taken her task with decorating as she saw fit seriously.

Astrid had chosen pieces from all different shops and companies, and her room had ended up being a conglomeration of styles and designs—which was exactly how she liked it.

Hanna June had taken her time curating the perfect components for her domain. Pastel colors were everywhere with gold accents and scalloped edges and pale pink gingham. A canopy hung over the bed that easily could've fit nine people, with sheer curtains pulled to the side, and a small peacock stuffed animal sat right in the center. Astrid recognized it—a fan at the Berlin convention tour had given it to her.

"What do you want?" Hanna June asked, dropping onto the love seat near her closet.

To Astrid, the thing looked horribly rigid. She much preferred squishy surfaces to sink into.

She took a breath and forced her shoulders down. "I want to call a truce."

Hold your stance. Calm demeanor, calm demeanor. She's going to laugh. Just hold it.

Astrid waited, but Hanna June didn't break into hysterics like she had anticipated. In fact, it looked like she had frozen.

As Astrid leaned forward—just slightly, only to confirm if she was still breathing or not—Hanna June spoke. "You're serious?"

She nodded. *You know your lines. Keep going.* "I think, not only would it make for a less hostile living environment, but in the long run, it'll make for better TV if we were to at least *try* to tolerate each other."

A smile slowly crept up Hanna June's face. "I actually think we make bigger headlines when we don't," she challenged.

She was right, of course. But Astrid had prepared with the counterargument.

"Oh, we definitely do." She nodded. "But ultimately … how does that end? Neither of us is going anywhere, and it's not like we can actually do any damage to the other, so what are we really doing it for? More importantly, *why?*"

Hanna June's smile dropped in defeated staggers—she knew why, but she couldn't say it. Admitting that she had been wrongly taking out her heated feelings of hurt and betrayal on Astrid instead of her fiancé would admit that he had cheated on her. It was one thing to assume something or to even believe it. But once you spoke it out loud, you put it out into the universe, and you shared your fear with everyone around you. Astrid had picked up on a lot of things about Hanna June Pruitt over their months of getting to know each other from their belligerent standpoints, but one thing she had picked up on was that it was far easier for her to show her anger than it was to display her fear.

"What do you suggest?" she asked, her fingers trailing over the upholstery on the couch.

"I say we hold the eye rolls and the whispers about each other when the other is talking. Maybe I stop avoiding going somewhere if I see you there first, and vice versa?"

Hanna June was nodding slowly as Astrid added her final suggestion. "We could also try to be … friends?"

The blonde's faint eyebrows rose, but she didn't argue, so Astrid continued cautiously, "We both know things that could help in untangling … whatever *this* all is. And I think we could work really well together, if we both stopped disliking the other simply for existing in the same space."

Hanna June smirked. "You just described different things though. You started off sayin' we should be better costars, better coworkers, right? Then you said we could be friends … but now you're talkin' 'bout us bein' detectives together. So, what do you want, Astrid?"

Well, she had her there. It would be really easy to point a finger and accuse her of not being on board with the idea, knowing she would never agree to it and saying that she just wanted to make Astrid feel like an idiot.

But she couldn't. The progress was obvious enough, with Astrid being—reluctantly—invited into her room and neither of them raising their voice or getting in the other's face. This had all been a step, and it was highly plausible that the question Hanna June had posed was a test. One that Astrid knew she could pass.

Costars ... friends ... sleuthing partners. What do you want, Astrid?

"I want to be friends."

Her pointed little chin rose, and she stared at Astrid. "Tell me a secret."

It was on the tip of her tongue to say, *You go first,* but she caught herself. That wasn't how this worked.

Astrid's mind started diving deep for something to share. It had to be a good one, nothing too obvious and nothing that could potentially be used against her. She was going off script now, and that made her nervous. She had never been very good at improvising.

"Um, okay, like what?"

"Like ... have you ever been in love?"

Ha, no. "I ... I don't think so."

A pause hung around them until Hanna June asked, "So ... you don't love Gunner?"

What? Love Gu—no. No. "Um, no," she forced out with a horrible fake-sounding laugh. Even she didn't believe it.

" 'Cause I think you do," she shared, raising her eyebrows—a silent beg for Astrid to argue with her.

She didn't.

Instead, she gave a tiny shrug. "Maybe."

As Hanna June nodded, silently taking in her response, Astrid prompted, "Your turn."

Hanna June's smile dropped, but her gaze hung on Astrid. An audible breath pushed out of her closed mouth before it reopened. "I cheated on Zach once."

Astrid was vaguely aware she had a volume problem—she was almost always too loud. But, thanks to the vocal paralyzation she seemed to have at the severity of what her colleague had just shared, she didn't give off her normal reaction.

"What?" she asked at a normal level.

"Remember that guy y'all met? Cash? He went to high school with me and Zach."

Astrid nodded as Hanna June pulled her knees up to her chest and hugged them. "It was a *long* time ago, at a party my best friend from back home, Kim, was havin'," she told her, averting her eyes from Astrid's now.

"I had just caught Zach for the first time—he didn't know, and I never told him I knew. I was drunk—I mean, ev'ryone was." The half laugh that came out was tangled up with sadness. Regret. Shame. "Cash practically worshipped me, and I was shit-faced and pissed off and … yeah. Not a good reason, I know. But that's why."

As she let the news sink in, Hanna June picked up her head, and not bothering to wipe away the tears that were forming, she forced another smile. "No one knows that. Not Kim or Amber—no one. So, if the news suddenly gets out, I'll know it was you." She wiggled her eyebrows at her in a teasing sort of way.

Now. Do it now. Astrid reached into her pocket and ran her fingers along one of the smooth edges. "So, um, this was in my room."

She pulled the stones out and showed them to her. Hanna June's expression tensed up immediately, then softened as she looked up at Astrid.

"There was a note to give you one."

She took one from her and turned it over in her hand. "Do you know who left them?"

Astrid shook her head. "No idea. It didn't look like Kronos's or Rhianne's handwriting though."

Hanna June held it up in front of her face.

"I don't really know what it's for," Astrid admitted.

The glance Hanna June gave her told her that she knew exactly what this thing was.

Don't ask. You'll ruin it.

"Breathe on it," she instructed.

Astrid did. The side facing her lit up a golden inscription. "This is a lexi-stone."

"It's a messaging device," Hanna June said and went on to explain how to use it.

Astrid kept reminding herself that, if she was going to trust her—to actually, *really* call her a friend—she couldn't ask too many questions yet. Hanna June wasn't stupid—she wasn't going to come right out and spell out how she knew how to work the tablet.

At the end of her lesson, Astrid felt as though she'd succeeded in her task. Sure, she had needed to improvise a few times, but it'd all worked out.

As she stood up and got ready to leave, lexi-stone in hand, she said, "Thanks, Hanna June."

"You can call me HJ," she replied from her seated position.

"Actually … I heard a fan at the Rome convention call you a name I like better for you."

Her head tilted. "What's that?"

"Thumbs." She smiled.

Hanna June smiled back, a bit crooked. "I haven't texted in a long time." She chuckled.

"You can message me now," Astrid suggested, holding up her lexi-stone. "You're still the fastest I've ever seen. And I'm from LA."

Hanna June laughed—a real laugh—and nodded. "Okay, yeah, you can call me that."

Chapter 60

AMBER

"YES, DEAR, YOUR FATHER LOVED the pie," Lucy reassured her for the third time.

"And you're sure? I know he prefers blueberries, but they're not in season, and the blackberries just looked so good," she babbled off, tugging at one end of the afghan on her love seat, and then the other.

"I'm sure." The Titan goddess nodded.

I give up. The damn thing must not be sewed straight. Which is my fault.

"Luce"—she turned to face her—"will I get to see him soon? I haven't seen his new house ..."

A smile sprang up on her face. She was arguably the youngest of the Titan gods, and the way she could rock a colorful sweatsuit was something none of the others had even tried to compete with.

"Don't tell the others, but I think it'll be very soon," she told Amber in a hushed voice.

They shared a childlike giggle before Lucy left, leaving Amber alone with her crooked blanket.

But only for a minute, as Fleur burst through the door.

"Okay, we need to talk." She leaned against the wood, closing it behind her. "You change the subject or just ignore it altogether literally every time anyone brings it up, so you kinda leave me no choice other than to corner you like a wild animal."

"Fleur, what are you talking about?"

Her little sister wrung her hands together and paced the length of the room as she spoke. "You know—you *know*—this is gonna happen. Everyone knows it, so don't even try to play dumb because it's embarrassing for *me* when you do. And the thing is, what I *want* to talk to you about—well, it doesn't actually have anything to do with that, but I need to bring it up because I've got this other thing going on and one thing kind of leads to the other—"

Amber cut off her sister. She had to; she could feel herself getting worked up, just watching her. "What are you talking about?" she repeated.

"Me and Damon."

Time froze. Not in the *Kronos stopped the clocks* way, but in the way that Amber's eye twitched once, and then her hands started shaking. Her mind was an endless, dark canvas, stretching into the void, and she had nothing to say.

She scrambled for something—*anything else*—to cling onto, instead of having this conversation, but she came up empty.

At the same time, her brain space was overflowing with horrible things. Slurs and trigger words that both Fleur and Damon would be linked to the second the worldview on them changed to anything other than the tagalong sister and bodyguard roles they'd been placed in since Olympia Con.

And now her little sister braced herself in a power stance, refusing to back down from what she had to know would be an uncomfortable conversation.

A conversation that, if you asked Amber, could wait a bit longer.

When the facade faded and the rose-colored glasses came off, that was when Amber really couldn't play dumb anymore.

But that could be years! By that time, Fleur might be off doing her own thing, and this would all be a distant memory, one that we'd never have to revisit.

She was well aware of the so-called fate the two of them shared. But that didn't mean it was *going* to happen, right? Kai and she were so incredibly happy together—the happiest they'd both been in a long time. The world was happy with them, and everyone who'd bothered to do their Greek mythology homework knew that Demeter and Poseidon weren't end game.

And this wasn't ancient Greece. This was 2015, and there were several billion people in the world, with running water and electricity and four seasons established. Damon didn't have to take Fleur away to some underground, undead kingdom he ruled before she was old enough to vote.

There was absolutely nothing notable signifying that Fleur Hargrove and Damon Montclaire were supposed to end up together. *Nothing.*

The fact that Fleur had said she wasn't even here to talk about that left Amber's mind—she didn't care what her intention was anymore.

The girls had barely spent much time together in the past weeks, especially since Fleur had started school again, and *this* was the conversation she felt like she had no other option but to bring up?

Pressing her shoulders down, Amber reminded herself that regardless of how she felt, she needed to try her damnedest to remain level headed. She was the voice of reason in her household, and ever since Dawn had left the Olympians, she'd tried to fill those shoes too.

"Fleur" —she took a deep breath— "listen to me. Just because the history books say *this is the way it happened last time* does not, in any way, mean that it has to happen again."

The sixteen-year-old rolled her eyes. "Tell that to Zach and Hanna June."

Amber paused. "Okay, yes—*some* things are the same, but lots of things are different—"

"Right, yes!" Fleur interrupted, her voice picking up with anticipation. "Which is what I wanted to *really* talk to you about. So, there's this—"

"Fleur, this conversation is over."

"But I haven't even said what I'm trying to tell you."

Calm voice, calm voice, calm voice. "And that's because we're not talking about this anymore," Amber said softly, clutching the back of the couch. Her fingertips dug into each other through the knitted blanket.

"But, Am, this is important! History *does* repeat itself sometimes—"

"But not all the time."

A quick nod from Fleur, paired with pursed lips, and she tossed back, "And how do you know you and Kai are endgame? You don't."

Stunned, Amber blinked at her. "Excuse me?"

"You don't know what's going to happen this time around—nobody does! There are gods on the earth for the first time since its creation, and you honestly think I'm worried about a guy? I can't believe that's your mindset!"

Fleur hadn't finished crossing her arms when Amber lost it.

"You don't speak to me for *weeks*. Weeks! And now—*now*—when there are cameras every ten feet and I have half-assed powers I'm not even allowed to figure out how to use, how to *help* people with, and now that I'm *happy*, you bring up this sick love story that—"

"For the hundredth time, that's not why I'm here!"

The Hargrove girls yelled over one another for a minute until Amber took a breath and Fleur saw her opening. "Look, I came here to see if you could get me interview time—*that's all!*"

Amber scoffed. "You think you're entitled to being in front of the camera now? You think you're somehow entitled to that because of who *I* am?"

"Holy fuck, are you kidding me right now?"

Maybe it was that Amber had always seen Fleur as the six-year-old they'd adopted. Maybe it was that Amber had seen herself as her guardian ever since her mom had passed because her dad wasn't really a functioning parent past that point. Or maybe it was the conversation bubbling up to this point—Fleur insisting that she had some ulterior motive and bursting into Amber's room and forcing the conversation upon her. Whatever the reason, hearing her curse was the breaking point.

Fleur's mouth kept moving, but Amber heard nothing. She watched the small brunette with a feeling that was newly directed at her—envy.

Fleur was free.

She didn't belong to the show or to a goddess. She didn't even really belong to a family. She could go wherever she wanted, do whatever she pleased, *be* whoever she dreamed of. Even if she was the reincarnated Persephone, she wasn't attached to anything that defined who she might be in this new life. She was allowed to write a new book on who the goddess of spring could be.

Amber wasn't.

And that thought grabbed on to all the other horrible thoughts Amber had cycled through in the past few minutes, and even though she could feel ichor burning and bubbling in her veins, laced with anger and furious disappointment, she couldn't stop it.

"Fleur, *stop*! God, you are so selfish! There is absolutely nothing signifying you're her, or that you have a place on the show or in any part of this world, okay? And involving me? Seriously? I have enough going on! I can't afford to think about your stupid little issues, Fleur. *Dammit!* Why—why did you have to bring this shit up? I have enough going on! Fuck."

Fleur stared back, with a look on her face that made Amber question if she had even heard her.

Finally, she took a breath in and lifted her chin. "Your bloodline always was good at ignoring the real issues you have going on."

As she turned to leave, Amber's nails pushed so deep into her palm, and there was a fleeting moment where she wondered if she'd broken skin.

"Get out."

Fleur froze, her hand on the brassy doorknob. "What?"

"Leave. I want you out of this house, off the property. Empty your cottage. Go back to Dad's. And stay there, whether he is or not—I don't care."

Fleur whipped around, her dark brown hair lashing against her face. Her face that in no way resembled Amber, Rose, or Shawn. "You're kicking me out?"

Amber's teeth clenched together as she jutted her chin out. "You're the one who wants to be dramatic—I'm *exiling* you. Stay away from the Athanasios Plantation."

A laugh barked out from Fleur's mouth. "Are you kidding me?"

"You don't get to talk about my family—about my *bloodline*"— she spit the word back— "and get to waltz around here like you belong. You *don't*. Leave."

The tension between them glitched and fizzed, like hot, irritated static filling up an old television set. Amber thought she was going to have to repeat herself. She could feel the word clawing its way back up her throat for a second round when Fleur grabbed the handle again and left.

Chapter 61

Alexia: Crius and Iapetus.

Kai: No clue what language ur speakin

Heath: I think they're gods

Alexia: Not just any gods. They're the two missing Titan gods.

HJ: Knew they sounded familiar

Heath: Breakdown pls

Alexia: Crius was the Titan god of constellations. At the end of the Titanomachy, he was imprisoned in Tartarus.

Damon: And where are you thinking he is now?

Alexia: Well, I don't know, and neither do they.

Alexia: Along with Iapetus, Titan god of mortal life and sometimes seen as the original god of death. What's interesting about him is that he had four sons, each of whom were said to have passed on a certain detrimental quality to humans.

Heath: Those being?

Alexia: Brash courage, scheming, stupidity, and violence.

Kai: Ok ok so ur telling me that if it wasn't for those four guys, we wouldn't be such a fucked up civilization?

Alexia: Ignoring your comment now, but open to discussing it later.

HJ: K but why'd you bring them up?

Alexia: I think one of them, possibly both, may be responsible for the files.

Heath: Oh shoot

Damon: That seems plausible. Especially if none of the Titans know where they are.

Heath: And they seem to have a bad streak

Alexia: I suggest, after filming tomorrow, we take an hour to brainstorm.

Kai: You mean where you tell us things and we either agree or disagree based on what sounds best to us with no background knowledge?

Alexia: Open a book, would you?

Kai: Why? You don't

Kai: OH WAIT

Kai: THATS CAUSE YOU DONT HAVE TO ANYMORE

Kai: I suggest we redirect our brainpower to where our superpowers might be

Kai: Speaking of, do you think Dawn has used her dragon breath yet?

HJ: Course not

Heath: I don't think she'll ever use that, she wouldn't need to

Kai: Never know. I bet when her investors are considering if they should really dump all the money they won't miss into one of her sites, instead of buying a golf course or whatever, she just kinda shoots out a little bit, just to scare em, ya know?

Kai: Like when it's cold outside and you wanna see that air cloud come out of your mouth? I bet she does that and it's like a mini fireball threat

Kai: God it must be so cool

Damon: Do you realize you're basically having a conversation with yourself?

HJ: I'm changing the subject. Heath, have you gone to see your niece?

Heath: HJ, I still don't know her name

HJ: Srsly? I thought it just wasn't public info

Heath: Well, it's not like he actually sees me as family...

HJ: He's definitely been better in the last week or so. Maybe he'll come around.

Heath: I hope so.

Alexia: Has anyone spoken to Amber since dinner?

Damon: I asked her if she was all right, but she ignored me.

HJ: I hung out with her for a bit, but she told me she was tired and wanted to go to sleep

Kai: Yeah, she told me she was turning in early tonite too

Alexia: Hmm. All right, well, let's just keep an eye on her. I thought I saw Fleur leave earlier.

Damon: She did.

HJ: Wait, Fleur left?

Kai: How do you know?

Damon: Because since you wanted to be a complete idiot months ago, before all this happened, I get to play her personal security guard. And part of that means that she has to tell me where she is when I'm not there.

HJ: Where'd she go??

Damon: I don't know.

Heath: She told you she left, but not where she went, even though you just said that she's supposed to tell you where she is?

Damon: I didn't say she always did as she was supposed to.

Kai: Omg did you lose her?

Damon: I didn't lose her, Kai.

Kai: But you don't know where she is

Damon: Okay, listen. Don't worry about Fleur. She's fine, I promise. You should be worrying about your girlfriend, Newport.

Kai: Dude don't tell me what to do

Heath: BUT out of curiosity, why do you say that?

Damon: Were none of you paying attention at dinner?

HJ: There was an oyster bake AND bbq Damon

Damon: And?

HJ: And we haven't had real food like this since MARCH. So if they wanna roll out huge meals for us, we're gonna spend as much time indulging in it as we can

Heath: I'm with HJ

Damon: Okay, well since none of you guys put two and two together, remember the massive cookie spread?

Kai: Of course

Damon: Amber didn't have even a bite of one.

Heath: So?

Kai: Oh shit

HJ: Wait... omg

Alexia: I don't get it.

Heath: Me neither.

HJ: They were from Cookie Dude

Heath: And...

HJ: Amber's like their patron saint

Heath: Oh... so that's bad

HJ: It's VERY bad. Something must be really really wrong

Alexia: Wait a second...

Alexia: Damon, how'd you know all that?

Damon: You think I'm not above watching the live feed inside the dining room?

HJ: THERE'S A LIVE FEED???

Chapter 62

GUNNER AND ASTRID ARE THE last to arrive in Kronos's office. The rest of the Olympians are gathered there, with Hanna June, Kai, and Alexia huddled around Amber, who looks like she hasn't slept in days.

The Titans are there as well, and they murmur among one another while they watch the next generation with one eye.

Kronos: Let me start off by telling you that, yes, the cameras are on you; however, they are not live. This is set to air Thursday, at the normal viewing time.

Gunner: Okay ... why is that any different from what we've been doin' the last few weeks?

Kronos: Because, Mr. McHugh, what I'm about to tell you is going to change how things operate around here. But before I share that, I want to first inform you that your request to have a Halloween party next week has been approved.

The Olympians all smile and begin to excitedly exclaim when Kronos continues.

Kronos: [*gestures to the Titans*] We will all be gone for a few days, to give you some privacy. However, this gathering will be quite important, as this will be the first time you will meet with many of the New World deities, heroes, and even mortals we have located.

You will all be expected to show them a good time, invite them in, and be hospitable. Please.

Alexia: Yes, sir.

Kronos: Now onto the bigger, more relative-to-the-moment news. We are allowing you to leave the property.

Hanna June: Wait … what?

Kai: [*chokes out a laugh*] Are you serious?

Kronos: You will abide by a curfew, and you will have an escort [*gestures to the Titans*] who *will* be with you at all times. Any objection to these rules or the failure to follow them will result in these off-property leisure being taken away—from everyone, not just those who break it. Understood?

The Olympians nod, and Kronos reminds them that the cameras can follow them at random and to always be ready for them before he assigns them to a designated Titan.

Zach and Hanna June talk for a moment and then Zach tells her he'll only be a few minutes away, at the Zeta Upsilon Sigma house, if she needs him. She smiles and thanks him. He kisses her goodbye and leaves with Pierce. A cameraman tails them out past Kronos's office, down the front walk, and gets in a car with them.

Kai and Amber talk among themselves, before they ask Don and Lucy if it's possible to go to Corolla for a few days to visit Kai's mom. Don and Lucy love the idea, so they all go to pack bags while Rhianne organizes to have the jet take them to a private airport in the Outer Banks.

Gunner tells Phoebe he wants to go to a gun range in Columbia a half hour away, but she asks him to wait for a moment. She pulls Heath to the side and asks to invite Emma over for dinner that night. Heath doesn't like the idea but he knows better than to argue with any of the Titans—especially Phoebe. He agrees, not bothering to question if it will be safe for her to come inside the gates. Many of the others suspect she may be a part of the pantheon, and although he has asked them multiple times to leave her out of all this chaos, he knows it would be a lie to say that he hadn't considered the possibility.

Astrid first asks to go up to Olympus, thinking her chances of being allowed up might be better if a Titan went with her. She is wrong. She then asks for a lesson with Jade and tells Dayo that she will be going downtown with her later that night.

Alexia begins to discuss with Grenada about going to city library when Heath overhears them and asks to join. He and his guard, Keaton, venture to campus with them.

The room empties out, and only Hanna June and Natasha are left, facing Kronos and Rhianne.

Kronos: Not taking advantage of your reestablished freedom, Miss Pruitt?

Hanna June: [*stands firmly, her face unreadable*] I want to speak to the person in charge.

Kronos: [*confused*] You are, Miss Pruitt.

Hanna June: [*shakes her head*] You know what I mean, Kronos.

He sighs, turning to Rhianne, who just nods.

Chapter 63

HANNA JUNE

IF HANNA JUNE HADN'T BEEN living in the same house the past few months, with countless days to map out the expansiveness of the floor plans, she probably wouldn't have been able to find her way back to her room. Everything, everywhere, had been spinning since Dr. Lockett had opened her mouth.

Should've put the pieces together myself. Could've figured that out. How was I so stupid?

Her back thudded against the wall, and she slid down to the floor as the scene with her new physicians replayed in her head on a loop.

The husband of the doctor duo, Vladimir, left the room, and Nina asked Hanna June what was on her mind.

"I'm sorry, Hanna June." She shook her head sadly. "Your immortal conversion is processed. Your body isn't functioning in the same ways it did when you were human. Well, it is in some ways, but not that way."

Her voice was so kind, so soft. Hanna June wished the news she had delivered had been just as gentle as her words.

She blinked back at the woman. Hanna June thought she looked like Fleur, just twenty years older. "What?"

The corners of Dr. Lockett's mouth twitched. Whether it was meant to be a sad smile or a grimace, HJ wasn't sure. "Your period isn't late, dear. It's not coming anymore."

HJ made several attempts to form a sentence before she worked out, "But what about when I want to have kids?"

The doctor leaned back and sat up straighter. She knew what was coming— she knew how this conversation would end, and she wasn't ready to accept it.

Swallowing over the sympathetic lump in her throat, she replied, "You can't have children, Hanna June."

Everything went dark after that. She hadn't passed out, but her mind had left the conversation. It was like when she drank too much and could only remember ten-second time spans here and there. Except this hadn't been brought on by vodka. This was shock.

And now she sat on her bedroom floor, not feeling anything. Her mouth was agape, and she was vaguely aware she hadn't blinked in an ungodly amount of time. She stared at her massive bed in the center of her gorgeous room, fit for a queen.

She was a queen. The queen of the heavens, and the goddess of marriage and family. *Family.*

How? How did this happen? More importantly, why? Why would Kronos and Rhianne and Zoey make sure I became fully immortal if they knew it would prevent me from bein' a mom someday? That's the only thing I'm supposed to be. I've known it my whole life, even before all this.

What if they don't know it did this? Last time, the gods came into the world as gods. We came in as humans this time, so maybe they don't know this happens with the conversion thing. Maybe they have no idea.

No, no, they have to know. Right?

There has to be a way to undo it. What if I just stop eatin' the ambrosia? Stop drinkin' the nectar? Demeter lost her immortality once, and it was restored fully after. What if I just stop takin' it when I want to have a baby and then go back to it after? Yeah, that'll work. I mean, why wouldn't it? Right?

Will they let me stop takin' it?

They fuckin' held me down … forced me to do it. They made me turn into this. They did this. And there's no way they'll let me lose it.

It was at that moment that she began to cry. She'd expected to in the doctor's office or when she locked her door to ensure her misery be observed only by her, but the tears hadn't come.

Now, the floodgates had opened, and she intended to keep the barrier uninterrupted.

She cried about her relationship with a boy who definitely loved her, but not always in the right ways. She cried about her engagement to him and her tug-of-war feelings about it. She cried about loving him more than she could ever really love herself, painfully aware he didn't deserve her.

She cried about her newly established friendship with Astrid and how overdue it was. She cried over why they had spent so long hating each other.

She cried at the time lost and realized that by hiding in her room and being sad about things she had no control over, she was losing even more time. That made her cry harder.

She thought back to the conversation she had had months ago, the deal she'd made with the voice in the curio cabinet.

The only difference was that now, the future she'd been destined for, the thing she felt like she had been made for, had been taken away from her. Now, the tears were subsiding, and the anger was settling in.

Now, she would make sure everyone knew what happened when you took away a goddess's ruling domain.

Chapter 64

HANNA JUNE, ALEXIA, AMBER, AND Astrid all stand together in one corner of the ballroom, as they sip on their drinks and talk.

Amber: I really think that girl Bailey is changing her costume. She looks different every time I see her.

Hanna June: That's the wine, babe.

They all laugh as their glasses shake in their hands and droplets of their drinks splash on the floor.

Alexia: Who are those three siblings supposed to be?

Hanna June: Okay, I asked 'em before. Get this: they're the three stages of Britney!

Astrid: Oh, I get it! They're, like, "Toxic" era. She's the breakdown—

Amber: Oh, yeah, with the umbrella.

Astrid: And then Circus era!

Alexia: Interesting. And who are they to *us?*

Hanna June: [*nods, gulping down her drink*] They're Helios, Selene, and Eos—the sun, the moon, and the dawn.

Amber: And they're actually siblings, right?

Hanna June: Mmhmm.

Amber: Wait, Helios—

Alexia: AKA Sonny—

Amber: [*turns to Hanna June*] Isn't that—

Hanna June: The stand-in interviewer from last season when Kronos wasn't there? Yep.

Amber: I knew they seemed familiar.

Astrid: And who's the black-swan girl over there?

Alexia: She's the muse of dance, Terpsichore. We know her as Odette.

Astrid: That's fitting …

Hanna June: [*smirks and nods to a spot on the opposite side of the ballroom*] Over there, Damon actually looks engaged in a conversation—don't all look at once!

Alexia: Well, it's with Jade. And Hecate was one of the few who lived in the underworld, so that makes sense.

Amber: Speaking of other worlds … HJ, you're *sure* you don't want to come with us?

Hanna June: [*sighs*] It's not that I don't want to go. I just need to get into his office without him here.

Alexia: And you really don't want any of us to come with you? Play lookout?

Hanna June: [*shakes her head*] No, I need to do this myself. Plus, I'll prob'ly be way quicker than y'all. Maybe I'll come up after.

Amber: [*pouts*] Well, we're gonna look really ridiculous, just Blossom and Buttercup, going up with Betty Boop over here.

Astrid: I can be a stand-in!

Amber: Oh, yeah? What powers do you have?

Astrid: Strangulation via garter!

They all laugh together.

Heath: [*leans close to Zach*] The girls are talking about going up tonight. It's the perfect time.

Zach: [*nearly drops his drink*] Wait, are you serious?

Heath: [*nods behind his drink*]

Zach: Shit, ugh.

Heath: What?

Zach: I can't go.

Heath: [*expression screws up somewhere between offended and stunned*] Are you kidding? You've been asking me for months when we're gonna go again, and now you can't go?!

Zach: I know, I know. It's just—I'm trying to sneak out tonight. I have to go pick up something for HJ.

Heath: [*narrows his eyes at him*] What is it?

Zach: [*groans, looks around the room, lands on her on the other side of the room*] I can't tell you. But, it's—it's gonna make her happy. Happier.

Heath: You're not gonna be able to sneak out. You'd be stupid to try.

Zach: [*smirks half-heartedly*] I'm not stupid, but I'm pretty close to desperate. Besides, what's *really* gonna happen if they find out we broke curfew and wandered around without a babysitter?

Heath: I don't know, but I don't want to find out.

Zach: Well, I have to. You guys won't even notice I'm gone.

Heath: Maybe not, [*glances at the cameras in the corners*] but I'm pretty sure someone will.

Luca: I don't get why you wouldn't believe it though.

Gunner: [*glares at him*] Because it's not real life.

Luca: [*smiles big at him*] Except it *is*.

Gunner: Well, yeah, but before it was … confirmed, it wasn't. It wasn't possible. It was like waking up in a fuckin' fairy tale. Like some fantasy book.

Camille: I doubt you've ever read a fantasy book.

Gunner: I know that this *thing* that's happening here isn't normal—and, yeah, I've accepted it. But that doesn't make it any less unbelievable.

Luca: [*shakes his head and smiles*] I would've gone right along with it if I were you.

Camille: You *did* go right along with it.

Luca: And if you had watched the show with me, you would have too.

Camille: Doubt it.

Luca: [*sighs dreamily*] And now we get to live it.

Gunner: [*looks at them skeptically*] You guys *really* want to immerse yourselves in this world?

Luca: [*nods eagerly*]

Camille: [*looks at him curiously*] What do you mean?

Gunner: [*glances around*] How much time do you guys get here?

Luca: Mom said we can stay the whole weekend, and Rhianne was fine with that. She thinks the more time we spend with y'all, the better.

Gunner: [*nods*] 'Kay. So, [*leans in closer and lowers his voice*] the Olympians and I are gonna go on a little adventure in a bit, after the rest of 'em leave. I think you guys should come.

Luca: Really?

Camille: Where to?

Gunner: [*smirks*]

Jade: Sorry, who did you say that was?

Damon: Which one?

Jade: The guy leaning against the buffet table.

Damon: Name's Lyle—Hypnos.

Jade: Oh, *that's* why he's barely awake.

Damon: [*disinterested*] Mmhmm.

Jade: And how did you find him?

Damon: He was just there.

Jade: Just where?

Damon: At Washboards.

Jade: [*eyes him skeptically*] Okay … what about those two, with the blondes?

Damon: [*glances over to where Zach and Hanna June are talking to some of the newer additions*] Hugo and Mara?

Jade: Yeah, sure. How'd they come into all of this?

Damon: The Titans located them—

Jade: At whose suggestion?

Damon: [*glares at her*] Why didn't you ask about Pat? He's talking to them too.

Jade: [*waves her hand*] I know how he came into this mess. I want to know about our new Odysseus and Helen of Troy.

Damon: [*stares at her in silence for a minute before lifting his glass to his lips*] I was tipped off about Mara, and I tracked down Hugo.

Jade: [*nods smugly and looks away from him*] I knew it.

Damon: You take that to the underworld with you—understand?

Jade: Aye, aye, captain. Okay, so what about the girl with Hephaestus?

Damon: *Heath,* and she's his girlfriend—Emma. Our new Aglaea.

Jade: Mmhmm, how'd they get together?

Damon: [*shrugs*] I don't know.

Jade: [*a crazed look in her eyes*] Sure you do.

Damon: Jade …

Jade: Tell me, tell me, tell me—

Damon: You cannot come with me if this is how you're going to be.

Jade: [*mockingly*] And I can't help you if you won't be honest with me.

Damon: [*rolls his eyes*]

Jade: So … tell me, tell me, tell—

Chapter 65

HANNA JUNE

THE MOONLIGHT STRETCHED ACROSS THE dark office as she silently shut the double doors behind her and tiptoed into the room. *Looks like a floor model in a furniture store. Everything is cleaned up and displayed like it's ready for the first customers who walk in the next morning.*

The massive wardrobe-like thing stood where it had since the day it had appeared, unbothered. Hanna June thought it hummed, similar to how the dumbwaiter did … as if it was waiting for her … but, no, she couldn't get distracted; she had something to do.

The instruments on the shelves had doubled in quantity and appeared untouched. Shadows cast over them as she reached the center of the room, where the curio cabinet was waiting. It had been placed on the wall since her last visit, and being just over five feet, she had to stretch up to center her face in the case.

Leaning her forearms against the edges of the shelves to keep anything from falling out, she shoved the tarnished little trinkets aside. She would put everything back before she left, purposely in the wrong places. She wanted it to be obvious to Kronos that she had taken matters into her own hands.

She spoke as loud as she could without feeling like anyone down the hall could hear her, even though most of their visitors had ventured out to the grounds or gone back to their cottages by now. "Hello?"

She waited.

"Hello?" She spoke louder this time, but still nothing.

"It's me; it's Hanna June—uh, Hera."

She called who she was hoping was listening by name, but it made no difference. "It's just me. I'm here by myself."

She waited for a minute or so, simmering in silent frustration. She had been told that if she ever needed anything—"Anything at all"—to just let them know. Their metaphorical door was always open. Of course, every time she asked to contact them, no matter which Titan she confronted, she was immediately shot down. No one wanted to hear her reasoning. They didn't care what her purpose for reaching out was. The answer was no.

"I know you can hear me!" She was yelling now.

She didn't care; if anyone heard her, she'd just claim she was losing her mind. Which, in her defense, would make sense, given how her life had been turned upside down in the past year.

"I know you're listening! I know you can hear me!" she repeated herself, gripping the shelf inside the cabinet. "I know he's scared of you, but I'm not. I'm not afraid of you. I want your help. I need your help," she pleaded. "You said you would help me."

Hanna June stood in front of the cabinet for another ten minutes. She pulled her pigtails out and took off the belt from her costume. She paced the length of the room, stalking through the moonlight that poured into the office. She strode over to the window and looked at the stars and wondered who out there in the universe was really going to have jurisdiction over those tiny balls of gas billions of miles away someday.

She tried one more time with the portal inside the curio cabinet before slamming the doors shut, and then she began to help herself to everything in Kronos's office he had demanded nobody touch.

The Olympia College campus looked the same as she had last seen it.

That was, if you put scaffolding around half the buildings. It looked like it was in the process of getting a major makeover, whether it was the outdated buildings being restored, or the landscaping team suddenly having an additional ten gardeners, or all the construction walls that listed the names of chain restaurants, along with *Coming soon!* At the front of Olympia Park was a directory, letting students and visitors know about the goings-on on the property. The one at the top assured readers that the Student Center was still open during its renovation and would soon be renamed the Dwayne Kronos Student Center.

Hanna June sat on the edge of the fountain, right at the center of campus. Small groups of students stumbled by on their way back to their dorms from the bars and clubs downtown. No one paid her any mind.

She didn't know how long she'd been sitting there—she'd purposely left her phone on her bed in the mansion—when she heard the footsteps. Joining her in silence, Natasha sat down next to her. She glanced over her shoulder to where HJ's toes touched the edge of the water.

"Is it cold?"

Hanna June rested her chin on top of her knees as she hugged them. "A little."

Natasha reached back and placed a finger in the fountain water. Three seconds later, it was a much more comfortable, lukewarm temperature.

Hanna June dropped her knees gently and let her legs fall in. "Thanks."

"You know you're not supposed to leave the house without me."

She knew, of course. The problem was that she didn't remember leaving.

She remembered storming over to the giant closet and pulling the doors open. She remembered walking inside it and staring at the buttons on the wall, thinking it resembled an elevator. She remembered worrying that, if it took her somewhere, time could move differently, as it did on Olympus, and she could end up getting into even more trouble than they had the first time. More trouble than she'd already set herself up for.

She remembered walking back out into the office and approaching the tables. Two birds with blue feathers and long red beaks had sat inside a cage. She'd looked at them curiously, and they'd stared back at her. She remembered the jars, bugs, flying around inside. She remembered that familiar humming sound as she had lifted the jar. As she peered inside, she could feel it vibrating in her hand, sending the buzzing sensation right through her fingertips. It had begged her to open it. She remembered putting it back down.

She remembered the giant egg that sat encased in a heated dome. On one of the corners of the enclosure, someone had scrawled *Ladon*.

She remembered everything up until that. Then, it was a gap, a big blank space of missing time.

And now she was here.

She couldn't explain any of that to Natasha though, and it didn't really matter.

So, she simply replied, "I know."

A minute passed, then two, and Hanna June wondered when she would tell her they had to go back. But after a while, Natasha still hadn't said anything, so Hanna June turned to face her.

"Am I in trouble?"

Natasha looked at her, and instead of answering her question, she asked, "How are you, Hanna June?"

HJ squinted at her in the glow of the streetlights. "I'm fine. Why?"

"Because it's my job to make sure you're okay," she replied.

'Kay, we're havin' two different conversations. "Yeah, from, like, crazy fans or conspiracy theorists who think we're out to take over the world or somethin'."

Natasha shook her head gently. "Not necessarily. I'm here to protect you from anything I can."

Hanna June stared back at her.

She leaned in to add, "Even yourself."

Their gazes stayed threaded together for another second before HJ tore away. She watched the water bubble out of the top of the fountain and pour down the tiers, ending in a pool around her calves. She tried to find a droplet at the top and follow it all the way down, but she kept losing track of it. It was a game she played over and over despite knowing she'd never win.

When she was ready, she said, "I don't feel anythin'."

Natasha leaned back and placed her whole hand in the water.

No change came to HJ, and she was about to ask what she had just done, when the Titan goddess replied back, "You don't feel anger?"

"For a little bit." Hanna June shrugged back. "It leaves faster than it used to, and it's not … as strong."

"What about sadness?"

She kicked her feet and watched a wave push forward and crash into the fixture. "I think I've been sad for so long that it doesn't actually register as a real feelin' anymore. Kinda like my body just got used to it and the novelty of bein' sad has worn off, but I can't feel anythin' else really, so I'm just left as this … shell."

"And happiness?"

"I don't feel happy."

"Ever?"

"Never."

"When was the last time you *were* truly happy?" Natasha asked at the same time the fountain kicked up a bit. Hard bubbles of water poured over and plopped their way down the tiers, and Hanna June decided not to answer her.

Chapter 66

ASTRID

Since the first five had trekked up the dumbwaiter, Astrid had been fascinated. Angry? Definitely in the beginning. But it had morphed quickly into a feverish need to go herself.

She'd made Amber share every detail with her about the dark ascent to the top—the cloud-covered landscape that sat high above the world, the shining gates guarded by the twins from across the pond, who took their jobs very seriously … and everything that sat on the other side of the football-field-wide stone steps.

Then, she'd made Alexia give her every detail she'd spare, and most recently, she'd gotten to hear HJ's version of Mount Olympus Their descriptions had all been slightly different golden-tinged versions of the same heavenly oasis that sat, waiting for them.

She could picture it perfectly, but nothing was going to beat the real thing.

The only thing that would make it better is if we were all going.

HJ had regretfully excused herself, and Astrid really hoped she would come up after. Zach had left the Halloween party early, saying he had business to take care of.

Apparently, that was more important than reaching a kingdom above the earth we'd all been eagerly waiting to get to since the summer.

But everyone else was going, even the twins. Luca and Camille rounded out their group perfectly, and the whole world—well, most of the world—had immediately fallen in love with them.

It was interesting—at least to Astrid—that Luca seemed to fit the whole Apollo persona to a T, but Camille wasn't much like Artemis at all.

Now, she walked next to Astrid, bubbly and bouncing on her heels, happily answering Alexia's questions as she mentally scanned her—Astrid could tell. She was trying to read her, place her, figure out how on earth this high school senior—captain of her color guard team and part of the homecoming court, was supposed to be the New World goddess of the moon, the hunt, and wild animals. Astrid—was wondering the same thing.

They arrived in the kitchen and let the coin in the trinket dish choose its first rider. Amber went first, and then Kai, followed by the twins. Camille was first, with her drachma flipping itself over to reveal a bow and arrow, and Luca's became a lyre. It was enthralling to watch—the simple way the coin, thousands of years old, changed. These ancient—annoying—devices invited only these certain members of the pantheon to enjoy the empyrean that lay just above the mortal world.

Seconds after the squeaking of Luca's platform completely drifted away, a new one replaced it.

Leaning against the countertop, Gunner spoke. "Last ones added, last ones to go."

The two of them stood facing Alexia and Heath, drachma at the ready.

The next dumbwaiter arrived, and in dropped four tarnished coins. Three spit out onto the floor, and the one left, waiting for its traveler, now had a swan on it.

"That's you," Heath mumbled, his eyes on Astrid.

Hanging on to his gaze longer than she probably should have, she murmured back, "Thanks," which wasn't exactly the most sensical answer, but it was all she could come up with at the moment.

It's happening. I'm going …

She climbed up, and it took off.

This is nothing like what they said, was all she kept thinking.

The gates were unguarded. As they walked toward them, yelling for Jack and Jordan but with no success, they unlocked with a horribly loud clanging echo and opened themselves. The steps were dusty, and no one was waiting at the top for them.

"I don't get it. Where *is* everyone?" Amber asked.

The city still held its ethereal glow … but it was abandoned. Not a soul in sight, even though Alexia continued her unconvincing reassurance. "Any second now, Traven will show up for you, Amber. Or maybe Makena! She's probably been waiting for HJ to come back!"

But no one did. They wandered around the stone streets, weaving their way through the closest of the empty temples. Astrid yearned to go into the palaces.

Alexia looked around frantically. "We're going to have to get going soon."

"We just got here!" Gunner argued.

"Right." She nodded. "And if my calculations are correct, about four hours have already passed on earth."

Luca sighed, "Well, if there's no one here and we can't really *do* anything anyway—"

"Wait!" Kai was running to the massive fountain in the center of the square.

He threw himself over the ledge and was leaning close to the water when the rest of them caught up. Astrid wrapped her hand around Amber's elbow, craning her neck to see who he was talking to when she was hit with a splash of water.

"Oh, are these the others you told us about? Hello!"

There was a girl in the water. Her fingers wrapped around the edge of the fountain where Kai was kneeling, a sparkly glow coming from where her forearm was pressed against the wall. Astrid had a wig the same color of her teal-green hair.

"Hey, Sila," Heath greeted her. "Where is everyone?"

A scaly pink tail flipped out of the water behind her as she gestured to Kai. "I was just telling King Poseidon, they are in the Temple of Hermes." She smiled and pointed toward the cluster of three temples far back at the other end of the little town, near the base of the mountain.

"Hermes?" Camille asked. "I thought you hadn't found him yet."

Astrid met Gunner's gaze. "We haven't."

Alexia took off running, with everyone else just a step behind, toward the pristine Acropolis on the other side of the lake.

Camille was by far the fastest of them, even in her little kitten heels. The rest of them thundered to a halt behind her as they stopped in front of the steps.

Gunner swung his arm out. "Wait, wait, wait. What's the plan?"

"Plan? What are you talking about—a plan?" Kai rattled off. "We just storm in and demand to know how this person got up here and how they know they're Hermes. We don't need a plan!"

Alexia wandered around in small circles, her hands on her hips. "Gunner is right; we need a plan."

Letting out a groan, Kai slumped against a column.

However, before any real brainstorming began, they heard footsteps running toward them from inside. Regaining their composure, the eight of them reassembled themselves as the massive doors opened to reveal … Makena.

"Olympians! Hello!" She floated down the steps and greeted each of them as if she'd been waiting for their return, even though she hadn't met Astrid, Gunner, or the twins yet. She looked them in the eye and gave Astrid the best hug she'd ever gotten from a complete stranger. It felt like coming home.

"Makena, we were told Hermes was here," Alexia said once introductions subsided.

"Yes"—she nodded—"that is correct, Miss Athena—Alexia." She smiled as she corrected herself, proud of remembering Alexia's preferred name.

"Can we speak with him?" she asked.

"Of course! Right this way," she said as she ushered them up the steps and into the stone temple.

"That was easy," Heath mumbled.

They entered a massive courtyard. Lush greenery, sporadic fountains, and what seemed—to Astrid—like an unnecessary amount of topiaries decorated the space. They followed HJ's attendant down a pathway and toward the back, and there he was.

Stretched out across a chaise lounge, he couldn't have been older than any of them. His dark hair looked greasy, and his clothes were dirty and rumpled.

There were three girls fawning over him, and Astrid saw Alexia turn back quickly to face the others and mouthed, *Muses*.

As they got closer, the girls calmed their giggles and stood up straight.

Makena greeted the stranger. "Master Hermes, several Olympians wish to speak with you," she told him, gesturing to the group behind her.

Alexia started to take a step up when Kai pushed past her.

"Who the hell are you, and how did you get in here?"

The girls looked terribly offended and one even stepped toward him. Heath pulled Kai back by the shoulder at the same time the supposed New World Hermes dismissed his entourage.

The Muses of love poetry, tragedy, and astronomy left, along with Makena, and Alexia and Gunner stepped forward, shoulder to shoulder.

The boy pushed himself up, squared his shoulders, and leaned in close. His words came out in a rushed whisper.

"Look, I don't know what's going on or how I got here, so don't ask. I've been trying to remember for days. I don't even know how long I've been here—a week maybe? All I remember is, I was in a holding cell in Toronto one second, and then I closed my eyes—and I *know* I didn't fall asleep—and when I opened them, I was here. Except I don't even know where *here* is. And before you judge me, yes, I'm going along with it because I hadn't eaten in days before I got here. But the weirdest part is … they all seem to think I'm a god."

He was a stranger, not only to Astrid, but to them all, and yet he was one of them—she could feel it. Astrid looked around at the others—even Luca and Camille, who'd spent minimal time with the rest of them—and she could tell by the way they all seemed to be studying him, they were all thinking that he belonged in their chaos. Astrid had a feeling that, if she hugged him, it would feel like coming home too.

She looked at Amber, who passed a look to Kai, who turned to Heath, and around went a silent exchange of, *How are we going to tell him this?*

And to everyone's surprise, Gunner stepped up. "What's your name?"

"Max."

"Max, you should sit back down. Hey, Makena? Let's get this guy something to eat, huh? And us too actually. We're about to have a long talk."

Epilogue

DAMON

Before today, Damon had never received one of the dreaded *we need to talk* texts. But seeing as his first had come from Fleur, he wasn't too worried about it. What would they have to talk about anyway?

His assumption was that there must have been a development in the feud between her and Amber. His mind began compulsively listing the possibilities as he cleaned in the few minutes he had before her expected arrival. How she had managed to figure out where he lived, he still wasn't sure. She was definitely clever, more resourceful than any of the Olympians took her for.

Fleur: Here

After she pushed her way inside, he did a sweep of the parking lot to ensure she hadn't been followed—paparazzi still hadn't located him, thank God—before locking the door and facing the anxious sixteen-year-old.

Now, ten minutes later, Fleur had finally stopped her pacing and frantic talking with her hands and sat cross-legged on his couch, waiting for an answer.

Damon couldn't seem to find one though—not because he hadn't anticipated her proposal, but because he had planned to suggest the same thing.

"Would it make you feel better if I said this wasn't up for discussion?" she asked, a tired smile gracing her face.

Damon smirked at her. He wouldn't have let her argue with him about it either. "I agree with you."

Her features twisted as she sat up straighter. "You do?"

Damon nodded. "I was going to ask you the same thing, back in June."

Fleur dropped her posture. The corners of her mouth turned up into the grin Damon was so familiar with. "June?" She laughed. "You've been thinking about this *that* long? Why didn't you say anything?"

"Didn't want to hurt your feelings." He shrugged.

"Please," she scoffed, "I don't find you as big and scary as you try to be."

They sank into opposite ends of his couch and chuckled at each other. *We're good,* he thought as their gazes settled on each other.

In the same way Kronos clapped his hands together, as if attempting to gather all his thoughts into one condensed space, Fleur brought her palms together, demanding they review the timeline of her detailed plan once more.

"And you're *sure* you're okay with this?" she asked again as she stood up to leave.

"I promise."

"Because … well, you know, we're *gods*." She wiggled her eyebrows in a taunting manner.

But something in her words pulled Damon out of the bubble he'd fallen into minutes earlier. The comfort in her thought process being on the same track as his, the reassurance she'd offered—it all vanished.

It dawned on Damon that she was about to leave and he wouldn't see her again for a long time. He quickly realized that, once the door closed behind her, he had no friends left. Dawn was busy saving the world, Hanna June had been closed off to everyone the past few weeks, and now Fleur was about to embark on her own mission, one that could take years.

Silent moments of settled-in sadness filled the space between them until Fleur stepped in for a quick hug. Her arms wrapped around his torso for a fleeting second, and then she turned and bolted out the door.

Gravity pulled the door closed gently, and while Damon considered opening it to give her one last wave, whether she saw it or not, he didn't.

Instead, he locked the door and told himself that, in the grand scheme of things, a few years was really a few seconds when you were immortal.

Acknowledgments

This book almost didn't happen. Well, it probably would've happened eventually … like, in the next decade.

I had a beast of a time forming words and completing full sentences that made sense, and to make matters worse, I wasn't selling any copies of the book that had come before this—in its original form. But that was because I wasn't marketing it. Well, why wasn't I marketing it? Good question. Probably because my overworked little brain concocted an obnoxiously complicated storyline that didn't fit into a nice little box, like fantasy, romance, or mystery.

Some cynical part of my brain decided it was easier to just try to forget about it. So, I dropped the book and left it there. And in doing so, I delayed being able to write this one. I prevented myself from moving forward with this epic series that played out in my head like a movie.

What exactly was it that rewired my brain and made me look at it differently? I can't say. I don't remember. I wish I did.

Anyway, a little over a year later, here we are. I have the second book in my debut series almost done, and it would not have come to life without a handful of incredibly talented people, dedicated to their craft.

Jovana, we went a long time without talking, and when I did reach out again, it was chaos—no surprise. You've been so patient with all the unnecessary technical issues I encountered along the way, and I'm so grateful you made time to work with me again. Thank you for your keen eye for detail and your willingness to hear me out, even when I'm all over the place—which is, like, all the time.

Juniper … I'm confidently writing this without even seeing the cover because that's how much faith I have in you and your creative mind. I will never not tell anyone who will listen to me talk about the art you concocted, how you worked your magic with essentially no direction other than, "I like the column." I can't wait to see the next three you design for me … hee-hee, no, really.

Vanna, God, I'm so glad you exist. More so that you exist in the same time and space as me. I know we hit, like, the ultimate rough patch for quite a while. And all I thought during those years we didn't have each other was *I miss her so much, more than any of the other friends I've lost*—and it's true—that feeling never wavered. The hug I got from you at our last meeting felt like coming home. And the ways you've helped me with my crazy little story, I am immensely grateful for you. I miss you tons, and I can't wait until we can sit on the floor of Walmart together and smell candles again.

And to all my cheerleaders on the Gram. Thank you for rooting me on, for giving me the much-needed support as I powered through this story. I hope I can meet you all in person someday.

About the Author

Hallie Parker gets bored easily and likes to experience new things, which is why all her characters are so different. She is most definitely living vicariously through them.

When she's not writing, she likes to rewatch shows she's seen dozens of times; spend time with her dog, Harley Rae Skywalker; and listen to music that she relates to too much.

Hallie is a graduate of East Carolina University and currently lives in New York.

The Ambrosia Project is her debut series.

Follow her for updates, playlists, and chaos on social media.

Instagram: @hallieparkerwrites

TikTok: @hallieparkerwrites

Pinterest: @hallieparkerwrites

Spotify: @hallieparker

MORE BOOKS BY HALLIE

The Clandestine Dawning of the Gods
(The Ambrosia Project, Book 1)—available now.

Every Wish Come True—a small-town holiday romance novel,
releasing late 2025.

www.ingramcontent.com/pod-product-compliance
Lightning Source LLC
Chambersburg PA
CBHW020232010826
48973CB00006B/1481